ACCL
HARRISON
The Third Illusion

================================

"A terrific tale."—T. J. MacGregor

"Vivid and suspenseful, *The Third Illusion* will keep
the reader's mind turning with the pages.
One not to be missed."—John Lutz, author of
Single White Female and *Spark*

"Once again, Harrison Arnston delivers the goods."
—George C. Chesbro, author of *Bone* and
The Language of Cannibal

"A fascinating detective story with complex characters
and plot. Don't miss this one."—Sandra Scoppettone,
author of *Everything You Have Is Mine*

"A bang-up mystery that will keep readers
spellbound."—*The Tampa Tribune*

"Fast-paced."—*Publishers Weekly*

"Everything you want in a solid thriller: colorful
characters, a blow-your-mind plot, hard-edged
suspense that builds to a spectacular climax, a hero—
smart, funny, wise—you're eager to join on his next
adventure."—Erika Holzer, author of
Eye For An Eye

ALSO BY HARRISON ARNSTON

*The Third Illusion**

*Trade-off**

*Act of Passion**

The Big One

Death Shock

Baxter's Choice

The Warning

*Published by HarperPaperbacks

ATTENTION: ORGANIZATIONS AND CORPORATIONS

Most HarperPaperbacks are available at special quantity discounts for bulk purchases for sales promotions, premiums, or fund-raising. For information, please call or write:
Special Markets Department, HarperCollins Publishers,
10 East 53rd Street, New York, N.Y. 10022.
Telephone: (212) 207-7528. Fax: (212) 207-7222.

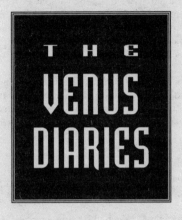

THE VENUS DIARIES

Harrison Arnston

HarperPaperbacks
A Division of HarperCollinsPublishers

This is a work of fiction. The characters, incidents, and dialogues are products of the author's imagination and are not to be construed as real. Any resemblance to actual events or persons, living or dead, is entirely coincidental.

HarperPaperbacks   *A Division of* HarperCollins*Publishers*
10 East 53rd Street, New York, N.Y. 10022

Cover photograph by Herman Estevez

First printing: January 1994

Printed in the United States of America

HarperPaperbacks and colophon are trademarks of HarperCollins*Publishers*

❖ 10 9 8 7 6 5 4 3 2 1

For Papa Joe and that
bright sunny day on the
promenade when the idea
first formed. And for
Terry, who wouldn't let
the idea die.

JOEY:
THE KID FROM BROOKLYN

Part One

1

_He_ was dying. He could see it happening, his own eyes witness to the horror of it, watching helplessly as the blood trickled from his shattered ankle, out of reach, his very lifeblood draining away. For the first time, he regretted the impetuous, youthful impulse that had brought him here.

He wasn't Joseph DiPaolo then, that ferocious September of 1940, when the world's eyes were focused on a paltry few hundred square miles of the earth's surface—and above it. He was simply Joey, a brash American kid who'd joined the Royal Air Force seeking glamour and excitement. A big, passionate kid from Brooklyn, with black, curly hair, dark, expressive eyes, and a penchant for talking too much.

To him, it wasn't a war. It was a game, an exciting, dangerous test of brain rather than brawn, the ultimate contest, where the grand prize was life itself. He'd seen many of his friends disappear forever, though he'd not seen their shattered bodies. That and his youth served to insulate him from the grim realities of death. Death was intangible, nonexistent.

To his mostly English fellow pilots, he was an enigma. He seemed more a creation of Hollywood than a real person; the stereotypical loudmouthed American, strutting through life at a terrific pace, turning up his nose at tea and warm beer. A neophyte, with the uninformed arrogance to instruct a people who'd endured for thousands of years on all they were missing.

He was a man with but a single mood—obnoxious effusion. When he wasn't sounding off about some sports team named the Dodgers or bragging about the superiority of New York delis to anything found in England—English food was dog food, he would say to anyone within earshot—he was trying to convert them to American sports, like basketball and baseball.

"Football?" he'd bellow, his face reflecting his scorn, when the ground crew boys would mark off the grass, choose sides and take a break from the war. "That's not football. That's soccer! In football, you don't just kick the goddamn ball, you throw forward passes. Aaayyy. Don't you guys know anything?"

Most suffered him as gently as possible, because it was the war, and pilots, especially good pilots, were in critically short supply. Joey was a very good pilot. They gave him that much. Besides, the English pilots, drawn mostly from the upper classes in the early stages of the war, prided themselves on being gentlemen of breeding, and English gentlemen were innately courteous to their visitors from other Allied countries. Much later, most of the English, regardless of class, would find the Americans a giant pain in the ass.

Even so, there were some who chose to teach Joey

some much-needed manners in a way that men have sought to teach such things through the ages—with their fists. To their dismay, they quickly learned that Joey was not a gentleman in any sense of the word. To him, a street fight was a street fight, even if it was taking place in the middle of a meadow, or behind the officer's mess, or anywhere outside a ring. In Brooklyn, you fought to win, period. A finger in the eye, a knee to the crotch—whatever it took.

He was mystified by those who clung to the belief that there were "rules" in man-to-man battle. How could there be rules when the object of the exercise was to knock each other unconscious? To Joey, it made no sense.

"Listen, pal," he'd say to another unfortunate nursing a very sore jaw after receiving a thunderous left hook. "You wanted a fight, you got a fight. Aaayyy. You guys wanna put the gloves on, then we got rules. Out here, there aren't any rules. Keep that in mind."

It never occurred to them to gang up on him. It just wasn't done. Frustrated, a few of them built a makeshift ring in one of the hangars. One by one, they would put on the gloves, step into the ring, nod to the referee and wait for the whistle to blow. No matter. Rules or no rules, the kid still had a devastating left hook. To almost everyone's satisfaction, the CO finally ruled that all of their energies should be saved for the struggle in the sky, and the ring was taken down, never to be seen again.

The relationship between Joey and his newfound brothers in arms was love-hate. They hated his lack of manners, his braggadocio, his swagger, his know-it-all attitude and especially his Americanism. The United States was a country of enormous wealth and resources choosing to sit on the sidelines while the most evil bastard the world had ever known tried to enslave them all. The English resented America's decision not to get directly involved.

At the same time, they loved this big Yank who had chosen not to watch. They loved his almost unflappable good humor, even if they didn't understand it. They loved his positive attitude, his willingness to fight—especially his willingness to fight. He was here, after all, for whatever reason, taking his turn with the rest of them as they tried to ward off the strutting paperhanger with the maniacal eyes and the idiot's mustache.

As a pilot, Joey wore the Spitfire like a second skin. He'd already become an ace, with six kills to his credit, the only ace in the squadron, in fact. More importantly, he'd managed to save the lives of many of his mates by exposing himself sacrificially, flying like a fool and forcing German fighters to turn away from damaged RAF planes, sure targets, and attack him instead.

He seemed to have eyes in the back of his head and an almost precognitive sense as to where everyone was at any given moment. He was as close to a natural as they came, even with less than forty hours under his belt. Of course, forty hours in the midst of the Battle of Britain was an achievement in itself. Almost awe-inspiring.

So some hated him, others loved him, and most were ambivalent; but they all respected him—this tall, muscular, boisterous, handsome, nineteen-year-old Yank.

At the very height of the Battle of Britain, they were based at a place called Brickston. Less than a year ago, it had been a flat piece of grazing land. Now, it buzzed with round-the-clock activity. By day, sortie after sortie. At night, the riggers and fitters worked to repair their wounded birds, pushing themselves at a frenzied pace, for they knew the price of failure. England was on the ropes, hanging by a very thin thread.

The war had scarcely begun in earnest, and already

fully half of Joey's squadron had been killed or were listed as missing. Those that remained alive went through their never-ending sorties either feeling immortal or accepting death as inevitable. In some, that fatalistic attitude created a somberness of mood that was temporarily vanquished by nightly parties in the officers' mess. Not Joey. He would be off somewhere, getting laid, as he so crudely expressed it, returning to the base with a big smile on his face and lipstick on his collar. He was immortal, or so they began to think. Until, on this warm September day, the odds caught up with him.

He was sitting with the others in the ready shack located at the east end of the base. Already, the squadron had been up twice—two sorties—as wave upon wave of Goering's best continued their quest to make Hitler a prophet. Between sorties, most of the pilots read magazines without really seeing the words. Others played darts, trying to force their muscles to relax before the next unavoidable call. Still others, perhaps those who had accepted the inevitable, managed to sleep.

They were all instantly alert as the phone jangled. A corporal reached through the open window, grabbed the cord attached to the brass bell, and set the bell clanging. Another scramble.

The pilots raced toward their Spitfires, machines now blanketed with thick, blue smoke as the powerful V-12 Merlins roared into life. Throughout the day, one of the riggers or fitters would sit in each cockpit ready to fire the engine at the sound of the scramble bell. A few precious seconds saved here could make a big difference.

Joey was hastily strapped into his seat, and within seconds, the Spit was bouncing across the grass, gaining speed until, like some ancient pterodactyl, the wings grabbed the air and the airplane broke its contact with the earth.

As Joey snapped his mask into place, his nostrils were assailed by familiar smells. Cordite, glycol, oil, stale sweat, even the pungent smell of the dope used to repair small bullet holes in the fuselage. As the wheels came up, he heard the voice of the air controller in his headset.

"Hello Red Leader. We have bandits approaching, one hundred plus at angels twenty, sector five. Range twenty-five miles."

Over a hundred of them. Still over the Channel. Jesus! Another familiar sensation, the rush of adrenaline priming his nervous system. Joey heard his squadron leader acknowledge the call in that cool, blasé voice of his, once again belying the anxiety they all felt at such moments.

"Roger Blue Fox, this is Red Leader. Message understood. Attention Red Squadron, follow me."

Twelve Spitfires, down from sixteen just this morning, clawing their way into the sky without time to get above the raiders. They'd have to approach head-on. With that many German planes in the air, other squadrons would have already been dispatched to intercept. Brickston was usually held in reserve. Not today. Everything that could fly was in the air. This raid was only one of several expected. The sky was filled with airplanes.

They were at sixteen thousand feet when they saw the Germans, a large group of Junkers bombers accompanied by what looked like a hundred Me 109s. Already, other defending Spitfires and Hurricanes were fully engaged. The sounds of battle filled Joey's ears.

"Roger Bix, the bastard's on your tail. Turn right."

"Blue Leader, three of them behind you."

"Green Leader, this is G for George. I've been hit. Bailing out."

"Bloody hell!"

"Reggie! Turn left now!"

"God's teeth! Forget the bloody bastard. It's the bombers we're after!"

The squadron was still climbing when the first short bursts from Joey's Brownings shook his airplane. Then the squadron flew through the enemy formation amid a hail of gunfire coming from the noses of the Junkers. In seconds, they were above the formation, fighting for position, watching for the fighters as they came at them from all directions.

The target of this particular raid was the Southampton docks, the very docks that had marked Joey's first steps on foreign soil. As he banked to the right, he could see, in the distance, bombs hitting their target some twenty thousand feet below. On this almost cloudless day, the German bombers were having a field day, inflicting heavy damage.

Bombs gone, the German formation turned for home, and the battle swung back over the Channel. Having been dogged throughout most of their flight, the Me 109s were getting short on fuel and breaking off the fight. To his surprise, Joey heard his leader's voice in his earphones. "Let's give them a bit of their own, lads. After them!"

Spitfires and Hurricanes chased the winged armada back across the Channel, trying to shoot down as many of them as possible before they made landfall.

Joey got off three good bursts at one of the bombers, but wasn't able to see if he'd done any terminal damage. There were too many German fighters in the area to allow anything but the most cursory glance at the bombers, now no threat at all. It was the fighters—

There was one to his left, almost level with him, headed home. Bastard! He cranked the stick toward his belly as he pushed the left rudder pedal. The Spitfire responded instantly. Now he was above and behind, in perfect position. He pushed the stick forward just a touch and pushed the button imbedded within the circular handle that sat atop the stick. The Spitfire shuddered as a two-second burst raked the German fighter.

The air was filled with bits and pieces of the Me 109 as it began to disintegrate. A great billowing of smoke and steam, the thick, acrid blackness of burning oil. He could smell it. The bastard was finished.

"M for Mary, this is Red Leader. You have three on your tail. Break left."

He cursed his momentary lapse of concentration as he heard the warning, instinctively smashed his left foot on the rudder pedal and jerked the stick of the Spitfire at the same time. He felt his body being pushed into the seat as the nimble fighter plane banked sharply to the left.

Then he was spinning madly, trying to avoid the shells from a trio of Me 109s that were trying to shoot him out of the sky. Where had they come from?

With a start, Joey realized the squadron had been goaded to precisely the action they'd been warned against. He remembered the words of the air commodore as he fought to lose the three fighter planes—part of an enemy group fresh with fuel sent to intercept this ill-conceived chase, born of frustration and counter to existing standing orders.

"You are not to pursue the enemy over the Channel," they'd been told. "You are needed for the defense of the islands. This is vital. The Germans will attempt to engage you in activities closer to their home bases, but you are to resist at all costs!" Today, the orders had been ignored.

His airplane shuddered as some of the enemy shells found their mark. Quickly, he scanned the instruments jiggling in front of him. At first glance, everything seemed to be in order. The Rolls-Royce Merlin roared unabated as he pulled back on the stick, trying to gain some altitude.

He cursed himself. Normally, he looked in his rearview mirror a minimum of every five seconds. For some reason, he'd become obsessed with this stupid—

He could see them in his mirror, two of the bastards. He pushed the stick forward, then pulled it back sharply. Again, he was thrust back into his seat as the G-forces grabbed him. Then, another shudder, a horrible ripping sound, and the engine began to cough.

Numbness spread through the area of his right ankle and foot. At the same time, thick black oil began to splatter against the windscreen. At first, it was a series of large globules, spreading slowly. Then it became a torrent. Finally, he couldn't see a thing. He knew he was in serious trouble, with the engine starting to die and the plane vibrating badly.

Suddenly, he saw flames to his right, just outside the canopy. The Spit was on fire. He held the stick between his knees. Reaching up with his left hand he pulled back the canopy while his right unhooked his seat harness. He jerked the stick to the left. To his relief, the Spit rolled over. He felt himself exit the upside-down airplane, falling, tumbling through space, the sounds of engines and guns receding in the distance.

The wind tearing at his face was bitterly cold. He was over three miles above the earth. The numbness in his foot turned to pain with an intensity that was almost unbearable. The pain raged as he continued to free-fall through space. At about twelve thousand feet, well below the fighting going on above him, he reached for the parachute handle and found it, then gave it a sharp tug.

His body was slammed hard by the straps as the chute filled with air. He looked around at the battle still raging above him, then at the ground below.

His heart started to pound as he realized he was

over enemy territory. Then, when he saw the source of his pain, the fear came crashing into his consciousness with the suddenness of a bullet.

His right shoe was entirely blown away. The black sock was torn, revealing a blood-covered right foot and ankle that was horribly shattered. He could see bits of bone sticking out through the flesh. Worst of all, he could see the blood, a small but steady stream of it emanating from the wound and dripping off into space.

A scream escaped his lips as the reality of what was happening struck home. He was bleeding to death. Almost immediately, he felt himself drifting into unconsciousness.

He fought the deepening shock. His hands pulled at the white scarf still, by some miracle, wrapped around his neck. By sheer force of will, he lifted his throbbing leg and wrapped the scarf around it, just above the knee. It was as far down as he could reach. Then, using every ounce of his ebbing strength, he pulled the scarf tight and tied it in a knot. The effort drained him of what little energy remained in his body.

He hung limply, suspended in air, terrified. It wouldn't be enough, he thought. Not nearly. He felt his heart pounding against his rib cage, the force of it adding fuel to his panic. Even with the added adrenaline coursing through his veins, he was fading. I'm going to die, he thought.

As the dimness behind his eyes grew, enveloping him in a dark, wraithlike cloud, he began to mumble.

"Hail Mary, full of grace . . ."

2

$\mathcal{H}\varepsilon$ was lucky, this young Yank. He'd drifted to the ground just outside the town of Abbeville, not far from the Channel. A few minutes more or less of flight would have meant a difference of miles. Abbeville was a town filled with German soldiers and airmen—and a hospital.

Even in war, the airmen had a rapport, an ancient, unwritten code. It was the airmen who rushed him to the hospital and transfused him with blood, and barely in time. French blood. German blood. Rh-positive A, according to the dog tags around his neck.

Deep in shock, the body of Joey DiPaolo prepared to shut down. First one, then a score, then thousands and finally millions of neuro-switches began to click off. The blood-pressure readings kept dropping, and his skin took on a deathly pallor. The doctor in attendance was convinced he was done for.

Clinging tenuously to the last wisps of the here-and-now, the body of Joey DiPaolo rallied unconsciously, fighting, clawing, clinging to life, exhibiting a tenacious will to live that surprised them all.

After some twenty hours, they declared him fit enough to withstand the shock of amputation. To delay would entail further risk. They amputated his foot.

When Joey finally awoke for good, after two days of drifting in and out of consciousness, he was disoriented. For two days and nights, his mind had been a jumble of confused images and hallucinations. Now awake, he still wasn't sure he was alive. It couldn't be heaven and it couldn't be hell. There were no angels, no fires. Purgatory? he wondered. Where were those who would remind him of his sins?

Finally he realized he was alive. He could see a ceiling, the yellowed paint peeling off in small sheets, and light bulbs. And flies. And he could smell the ether in the air. He was in a hospital. The sense of relief was, at first, overwhelming.

He could feel the hot tears in his eyes. His lips moved as he offered prayers of thanksgiving. His joy was soon tempered by the furious pain that throbbed in his lower leg and by the belated realization that he was in a hospital located somewhere in France. And when he moved his head and saw the Luftwaffe colonel talking to the nurse at the doorway leading into the ward, his heart sank to new depths.

He slammed his fist against the mattress in a gesture of futility. The colonel noticed the movement and came over to the side of the bed. He smiled as he said, in passable English, "Well, Flying Officer DiPaolo, I see you have finally decided to join us. Welcome to France."

The colonel was a tall man, with closely cropped blond hair and bright blue eyes mounted in a face that seemed to have been chiseled from granite. The perfect example of Aryan superiority—except for the missing arm.

Joey looked around, then back at the colonel and finally at the foot of the bed. It looked as though some sort of device had been placed over his feet, because the sheets took the form of a mound before reaching the end of the bed.

"Ah, yes," the colonel said, making a clucking sound with his tongue. "Your foot. Unfortunately, they had to take the right one off. That is why I am here. To let you know that life goes on, even after one loses a limb."

He said it so coldly, so matter-of-factly, that for a moment the words didn't sink in. When they did, Joey thought it was some cruel joke. A way to soften him up for the questions that were sure to come.

As though reading his mind, the colonel's eyes warmed slightly. "I'm afraid it's true, Flying Officer DiPaolo. The foot was removed just above the ankle. However, you will be a guest of the Fatherland until the war is over and we determine your usefulness. You will have plenty of time to adjust, as I have had to. It is not so difficult. Not like the loss of sight, or the hearing, as some of my friends have experienced. Or, for that matter, your life. You are still alive and that is, after all, the best news."

He extended his good hand. "My name is Colonel Gerhardt."

Joey ignored the extended hand. Instead, he tried to marshal his senses. The man had to be lying. He could feel his foot. It was there, throbbing like hell.

Again, the man seemed to read his mind. He reached for the covers and pulled them back. Almost against his will, Joey looked down to the bottom of the bed.

The man wasn't lying. The foot was gone. Joey drew the pillow over his head, so no one would see him weeping.

▪ ▪ ▪

For several days, he remained in the hospital, cared for by a trio of nurses working in shifts, all but one of whom spoke no English. They refused to allow him to feel sorry for himself. There were other patients, mostly German pilots, some of whom were grotesquely burned, others who had lost limbs.

The nurses seemed strangely unmoved by the carnage. Instead, they insisted on berating him for his self-pity. He didn't understand the words, but he felt the tone. To Joey, it seemed heartless. The only saving grace was that he didn't know what they were saying.

In a matter of days, he'd changed. He was no longer a kid. No longer immortal. No longer the grinning, joking, bellicose American from Brooklyn. He was as vulnerable as any other mere mortal. The quips were gone.

He could imagine little children pointing at him. "Hey! Look at the crip!" they would say. As a kid, he'd uttered those very words more than once.

He thought of Sophia, back in Brooklyn, awaiting his return from a war she'd regarded as a rival for her affections. What would she think? She was beautiful, animated, intelligent, constantly pursued by an army of panting *amorosi*. Healthy, virile men. What would she do?

He knew the answer. At least, he thought he did. She'd drop him like a hot rock.

He sighed as he sank deeper into the morass of despair. No more football. No more boxing. No more dancing. No . . . What woman would want to make love to a man without a foot? Didn't the nurses know that? Of course they did. They just didn't give a shit.

The one nurse who spoke English was an especially unpleasant woman named Yvonne Dijon, who seemed to go out of her way to be cruel. Not only was she unsympathetic, she insisted he get out of bed on his second full day of wakefulness. She brought him crutches and showed him how to use them. Then, brusquely, she hauled him out of bed and got him moving.

Standing up made him dizzy, but she insisted. "You lost a lot of blood, but it was replaced. There is no need for you to lie in bed. The sooner you get moving, the sooner you can get out of here. The bed is needed for others."

She chided him for fighting in a war that had nothing to do with America. "France is better off," she said, in halting English. "Where there was disorder, there will be order. That is all to the good."

He looked at her as though she were mad.

"Your country is not at war," she continued. "You have no business being here. You should have stayed at home."

Joey hated her instantly.

For three days, the nurses helped him as he learned to walk, all scornful. The Dijon woman, especially. She was a woman who could truly be called ugly, with small, beady eyes and a thin hook nose. With the thin lips and the scrawny frame, she looked every inch a witch.

After four days, his stump was fitted with a protective device fashioned from leather and wood. He was told that he would be leaving the hospital that evening.

"Where am I going?" he asked the witch.

"A prisoner of war camp. What did you think?"

That night, Colonel Gerhardt entered the room, flanked by two soldiers armed with rifles. With his good hand, the colonel clutched a hanger, on which hung Joey's uniform.

"You are being moved, Flying Officer DiPaolo. You are to get dressed."

"Where am I going?"

The colonel simply smiled.

While the soldiers watched, Joey struggled into his uniform. The right pant leg had been cleaned but he could still see the bloodstains. The single sock they gave him was new. They'd kept his sheepskin jacket, but returned his watch.

"Where's my other stuff?"

"You won't need that. Come."

Joey reached down and picked up his crutches. The foursome made their way out of the ward and down the stairs.

He was helped into the back of a small truck. Gerhardt stood outside and said, "Goodbye, Flying Officer DiPaolo. I hope we meet again someday. Until then, good luck."

Joey said nothing.

The truck, its headlights heavily taped, made its way from the hospital to the narrow highway leading from the town. A driver, Joey, and two guards. Joey looked out the back of the machine, took a quick fix on the stars, and determined that he was moving south. He strained to see some signs that might indicate where he was, but it was too dark. All he knew was that they were headed south. Away from England. As if anticipating what was to come, the leg was throbbing again.

They had traveled for about ten minutes when the vehicle came to a sudden halt on the highway. Joey looked out the small slit in the wooden barrier between the driver and the back of the truck. He could see through the front window. The highway was blocked by a horse-drawn wagon loaded with hay. The wagon had lost a wheel and was tilted at an odd angle. Half the load had fallen to the ground. An old farmer sat by the side of the road, flapping his arms in the air as though that would solve the problem.

One of the guards got out and started screaming at the farmer in German. The farmer shrugged, then started kicking the wagon. The German soldier screamed louder.

Suddenly, the night was filled with the sound of gunfire. The soldier sitting beside Joey started to move. He was immediately slammed back against the sidewall of the truck as bullets smashed into his body. At the same time, the driver slumped forward over the wheel, and the guard who'd been yelling at the farmer fell to the ground.

Stunned, Joey turned and stared into the eyes of a man standing just outside the rear of the truck, a machine gun in his hands. "English! Move! Vite!"

The man was joined by two others. They reached inside the truck. Joey felt strong arms pulling him out of the truck and almost dragging him around the broken wagon. On the other side of the wagon was a small car, its motor running, the back door open. Joey was shoved into the car, the crutches were tossed in after him, then the door slammed shut. The man with the machine gun leaped into the passenger's seat. Instantly, the car jerked into motion and began hurtling down the highway.

It had taken seconds.

The man in the passenger's seat turned around and threw Joey a toothless smile. The wrinkled face was twisted into a big grin and a hand was extended over the seat.

"Welcome, Comrade DiPaolo."

Joey, breathless, stared at the man. "Who are you people?"

The grin grew wider. In somewhat fractured English, he said, "We are small. A . . . how you say . . . cell . . . who have vowed never to submit to the Germans. De Gaulle has implored Frenchmen everywhere to fight on, to form a resistance movement that will create . . . what you say . . . problems . . . for the Germans. All of France! We are small, but we get bigger."

"How did you know who I was?"

"We have friends everywhere."

"Where are we?"

"Abbeville," the man answered. "We are taking you to a place where you will hide. Then we take you to England."

"England. How?"

"Ahhh! You will see. You will see. You will be safe now."

Joey sat back in the seat and sighed. "You called me 'Comrade.' Are you a Communist?"

"Oui. Certainement!"

"I thought that the Communists and the Germans were pals."

"Non. The Russians and the Boche are friends. I am Frenchman first, eh? Then Communist. Plus grand difference."

Yes, indeed, thought Joey, as the car bumped along the dark highway.

They drove for half an hour until, finally, they came to a small farmhouse with several makeshift wood and wire chicken coops in the rear yard. A woman greeted the trio from the front door of the old house and beckoned to them. The two Frenchmen hurriedly carried Joey into the house, sat him on the worn blue sofa, laid the crutches beside him and bid goodbye. Quickly, they were out of the house and on their way back to wherever they had come from. Still slightly bewildered, the airman sat on the sofa and wondered what would happen next.

The woman who had first greeted them entered the small living room carrying a tray bearing a pot and two teacups. She placed the tray on the table beside the sofa and said, in very good English, "I'm sure you would like some tea. I'm sorry it is not a better quality, but the war . . ."

She was an attractive woman in her mid-twenties, with light hair and blue eyes. She was of medium height, but the shapeless dress she wore prevented any assessment of her figure. Joey took the proffered cup and said, a note of surprise in his voice, "You speak English very well."

"That is one of the reasons I have been chosen to be your hostess for a while."

"I appreciate your kindness. My name is Joseph DiPaolo, what's yours?"

"Denise Dijon."

Dijon. The name rang a distant bell somewhere. Where had he heard that name before? He searched his memory, but nothing came through. Then the woman said, "Yvonne is my cousin. She is a nurse at the hospital."

Of course. The bitch who looked like a witch.

Joey's jaw dropped. "She's your cousin? She's part of this movement of yours?"

"Yes. That's how you were taken from them. Yvonne pretends to be a collaborator with the Nazis. That way they aren't so careful about what they say. They think she is one of them. She learned that you were to be taken to a place where you would be beaten. They like to question the wounded before they are shipped off to the prison camps. Wounded soldiers are sometimes more ready to talk. So she alerted me. I contacted my other cousins and they waited until you were to be moved. They've been waiting for over a day, watching the hospital from a nearby house. Some others were in position to move the wagon when they got a radio signal. It was almost to be called off, it took so long."

"You took a hell of a chance. You still are, for that matter."

"It must be done. We have to show the Germans that they do not rule France. Later, when this war is over, there will be time for a new kind of France. A country that is run by the people. We will always fight for that."

Joey sipped the tea. It was quite weak, but at least it was hot. He would almost have killed for a cup of his mother's special coffee. He asked, "Are you a Communist too?"

"Of course. I'm sure you don't understand, but someday you will. We shall talk about that later. Right now, I'm afraid I will have to hide you in a sort of a prison for a few days. The Germans will be checking on everyone at the hospital and searching everywhere. Anyone working at the hospital will be looked upon with suspicion. Even Yvonne. The Germans will be very upset at the death of some of their men right under their noses.

"Within days, perhaps hours, they will search this place. We have prepared a special hiding place for you and others to follow. It is uncomfortable, but it will not be discovered. It has been put to the test twice already. Come, I will show you."

Joey, using his crutches, carefully, and very slowly, followed her down some stairs to a musty, cluttered basement that was floored with brick. In one of the corners, a hole had been dug, eight feet long, three feet wide and four feet deep. The walls had been shored with lumber, as had the floor. Beside the hole, stacks of bricks sat beside a pile of sand.

Inside the hole were several loosely corked wine bottles, loaves of black bread, fruit, a few candles and a low cot, upon which sat some blankets and a pillow. It looked like a well-equipped grave.

His face must have expressed a certain amount of concern, for she said, "I realize that this will be uncomfortable, but it is the only way. Once you are in there, I will place some wooden planks over the hole, replace the bricks and fill them in with sand. You will be in there for two or three days at the most. You'll have to stay until the Germans have searched the house and the barn and are sure you are not here.

"There are some basins under the cot for your . . . use. You must be very careful about noise. The wine bottles contain water, but I can give you wine if you prefer."

Joey shook his head. "No, this calls for a steady mind. The water will be fine."

She continued, "Your air will come from a pipe through the wall. We use candles to light the basement, but make sure you snuff yours if you hear the Germans. I will come down and talk to you from time to time, but the Germans might come at any time, so we must be on guard."

She looked at him, the concern clearly etched on her face. "Now, it is time. Will you be all right?"

"We're about to find out, aren't we?"

For the first time in his life, he wondered if he was claustrophobic. He prayed he wasn't.

"I'm sorry," she said, "but—"

"Hey, it's great. I'll be fine. It beats having the crap knocked out of me. Don't you worry. Just try and talk to me whenever you get the chance."

"I will."

He crawled into the hole, moving carefully, managing to make it without banging his bad leg. He lay on the cot and lit one of the candles. The crutches were placed beside him.

He felt strange as he watched her put the wooden boards in position. They were thick and heavy, but she seemed to handle them without difficulty. And then he couldn't see what she was doing, just hear it. The bricks first and then the sand. Finally, he could hear her sweeping the floor with a broom.

"Can you hear me?" she asked.

The voice was muffled, but understandable. "Yes," he said. "I can hear you just fine. I think I'll get some sleep now."

"Sleep well, Flying Officer DiPaolo."

"You too, pretty lady."

Then she was gone, and Joey was left alone with his thoughts. For a fleeting moment, he wondered if perhaps she was part of the Gestapo and this whole elaborate scheme was simply to extract information from him. If so, he mused, it would be successful. A few days of this and he'd be ready to tell the bloody world whatever it was he knew, which wasn't all that much.

Quickly, he dismissed the thought. The Gestapo didn't need this kind of guile. All they needed to do was take a hammer to his bad leg.

The leg. God, how it throbbed!

It seemed he'd just fallen asleep when he was awakened by the sound of voices. German voices. He had no idea how long he'd been asleep, for he was in total darkness. The first of his candles had gone out on its own, so he assumed it had been some hours.

There were three voices—two men and Denise Dijon. He could hear the boots scraping against the sand and bricks as they conducted a search of the cellar, poking through the boxes and crates. One of the Germans spoke some French and seemed to be asking many questions which Denise answered in a controlled voice.

For a moment it was quiet. Then, he heard the boots against the bricks directly above him. The German voices rose. Small grains of sand peppered his face. He was sure they'd found his hiding place, but held his breath.

The scraping continued. And then he heard Denise talking again, her voice calm and casual. His imagination was working overtime. He could visualize the Germans lifting the bricks, removing the boards and standing there, looking down at him—but it never happened.

The voices were receding now, and he could hear

some boxes being thrown to the floor. And then they were gone. The house was completely silent.

He waited for half an hour, listening to the pounding of his heart, and wondered if he should light a candle. As he fumbled for the matches, he heard someone approach.

"Flying Officer DiPaolo? Are you all right?"

"Yes."

"The Germans have been here and searched the house and the sheds," she said. "I must not let you out yet. They will probably be back. They are doing a quick search now, but once you are not found, they will want to search again. These Germans are very . . . how you say . . . diligent."

"I understand. I'll be fine. I thought they'd found me for a moment. What happened?"

"One of the soldiers noticed the difference in the color of the sand. I told him I had repaired some broken bricks and invited him to remove the floor if he so desired. He kicked it with his boot, then looked elsewhere. I told you it would work."

"Yes, you did."

"I must go upstairs now, in case they are watching the house. I'll come back later."

"Okay."

He was alone again. He fumbled in the dark, found the matches, lit a candle and broke off a piece of the black bread. That and a couple of apples washed down with some water constituted his dinner. He still didn't know what time it was, or even what day it was, but it really didn't make much difference. The pain in his leg was easing. That, at least, was good. He was still free, in a manner of speaking.

Denise came by two or three times during the next day and chatted with him for a half hour or so. And then, just as she had predicted, the Germans were back, this time in force.

He could hear the sounds of the search as they poked

and prodded. He was sure he would be discovered. There seemed to be so many of them. But, for whatever reason, after some more bashing of boxes, they moved back upstairs and Joey started to breathe again.

If he hadn't been claustrophobic when first placed in this hole, he was fast becoming so. The darkness seemed to be an enemy, hiding all sorts of vile things. His breath kept coming in shallow gulps and his heart beat wildly. Despite the coolness, he could feel the sweat seeping from his skin, soaking his clothes. For a moment he wanted to scream, but he fought the impulse with every ounce of his energy.

For an hour he lay there, trying desperately to regain control of his emotions, fearing he was losing his mind, and then he heard her. At last. Picking at the bricks and telling him that he was to be freed from this dungeon. It was not a moment too soon.

She was smiling as she lifted the last boards and helped him stand up. Instantly, waves of dizziness shook him. He sat on the edge of the hole until they passed. Then he tried it again. This time, it seemed to be all right. Denise reached down, picked up the crutches and placed them under his armpits.

"Can you walk?"

"I think so."

Every bone in his body ached, and it took some time for his eyes to adjust to the light, but he managed to make it up the stairs. Denise escorted him into her bedroom. An old, cast-iron tub sat near one wall—a tub filled with hot, steaming water. The very sight of it almost made him cry out in joy.

"I'll leave you to your bath," she said. "Make sure you keep the stump dry. I'll come and change your dressing once you've had your bath. Try not to take too long. We are still taking a chance."

"I'll hurry," he said.

When she left the room, he turned down the gas lamp for a moment and carefully pulled back a corner of the blackout curtains for a look around. It was dark outside. Nothing seemed to be moving.

He turned the lamp back up and took off his clothes. He looked in the round mirror that stood above the bureau. To his horror, he discovered that he was covered in large, red, angry-looking sores on his body. It figured. He hadn't been out of his clothes for three days and nights.

Despite the pain, the bath felt great. As quickly as he could, he soaped his body, then toweled off and stood in front of the mirror. The face that looked back at him seemed like that of a thirty-year-old.

A razor had been put out, and he used the soap and the razor to give himself a shave. By the time he was finished, Denise was at the door.

"Are you done?"

"Yes, but I'm not dressed yet."

"Wrap yourself in the towel."

She came in the room armed with two bottles of liquid and some bandages.

"Sit on the bed," she commanded.

Quickly, efficiently, she removed the old dressing, washed the wound with first one liquid, which stung a little, and then the other, which was a thick oil of some type. It felt very soothing. Then she wrapped the leg in new bandages.

"You do that like a nurse would," Joey said. "Are you a nurse, like your cousin?"

"No. Yvonne told me what we must do. I have looked after wounds before, although never one like this."

Joey winced. "Pretty awful, isn't it."

She looked at him sharply. "The wound is healing well. At least you are alive. Stay here. I will get something for those sores."

It was then, for the first time, that he noticed the wedding ring on her finger. "Is your husband . . . ?"

She looked at the floor. "He's dead. As are my two

brothers. They were killed when the Germans attacked France in May."

"I'm sorry."

Slowly, she raised her head and looked at him. "No matter. Just be thankful you are alive."

He could see the tears in her eyes.

The nurses at the hospital had chastised him for feeling sorry for himself. Now, this woman was doing the same thing, for very good reason.

They were right. What was a foot? At least he could still breathe, and talk, and see, and hear.

She left him alone for a moment, and then returned with another ointment, which she spread on the sores.

"I can't thank you enough for your help," he said. "Risking your life for me like this is . . . well, I don't know what to say."

She finished and stood up. With a new firmness to her voice, she said, "Say nothing, except this—when you get back to England, tell them what we are doing. Tell them that there are hundreds, no, thousands of us, who will never stop fighting. Tell them to help us with weapons and radios and money and other things. Tell them to contact us. We will do what we can from here to fight the Germans."

"I'll do it. How can they contact you?"

"You have seen my cousin Jean-Luc. The one without teeth?"

"Yes."

"He is at the post office at Abbeville almost every day at noon. He is the leader of our group. There are others starting up, and Jean-Luc is trying to find out who they are so he can band them together. We have asked before and heard nothing."

"You get me back to England and I'll make sure Jean-Luc is contacted. I'm very sorry about your husband and your brothers."

"It's the war. Perhaps . . ." For a moment she

looked wistful, then she seemed to force herself to smile. "Come. I will give you some decent food and then you must rest."

"I don't need any more rest. I need some activity. I've been flat on my back for days."

She laughed. "I can imagine how you must feel, but rest is what you need until you are safely back in England. In the morning, they are coming to get you."

"Who?"

"My cousins. They are taking you to the Demarcation Line and then across. You will be put on a train to Marseilles and from there you will take a ship to Gibraltar. Once there, you will be in the hands of the British. We have done it before."

Joey shook his head. "You people are amazing. You've really got this organized."

"I'm glad you are convinced. See if you can convince the stupid British once you get back."

She handed him some clean underwear. "These will be small, but they are clean."

He started to ask who they had once belonged to and thought better of it. Denise left the room and closed the door behind her. Joey dressed and hobbled into the kitchen. The table was set for two. In the middle was a small vase filled with freshly cut flowers.

The meal was simple, but delicious. Boiled chicken and potatoes. As they ate, they talked about their lives, their countries and the war. He learned that she'd lost almost everything and refused to quit. It made him feel ashamed.

"Do you live here all alone?" he asked.

"I do now. We . . . I raise chickens and have some milk cows. The Germans keep taking things and I don't know how long I'll have anything. Once it's all gone I guess I'll join my cousins and just fight. Are you married?"

"No, I'm not. I had a girlfriend back in the States, but that's all over."

"She found someone else?"

"Not exactly. It's just that . . ." He let the words trail off.

"I'm sorry. Do you still love her?"

"Yes."

"But she doesn't love you?"

"It doesn't matter," he said.

"It doesn't matter? Of course it matters. She must be one of the spoiled ones. I read about them. Their lovers go to war and they become bored. Such children."

"It wasn't like that."

For a moment, she said nothing. Then, suddenly, she grinned. "Are you a virgin, Joseph?"

He turned beet red. Quickly, he said, "No."

"Certainement. You know about women, eh?"

"I didn't say that."

She let out a deep-throated laugh. "I think I can guess what the problem is."

He couldn't meet her gaze. "Look, it's all right. It doesn't matter."

"It doesn't matter? But you love her."

"So what?"

"But you presume to think for her?"

"I don't understand what you're talking about."

She smiled at him and placed her hand on top of his. Her eyes were filled with compassion, unlike the nurses at the hospital. "You think that because you have lost a foot, she will find you unattractive. Is that not so?"

"This is none of your business."

"Perhaps you're right," she said, her expression one of bemused interest. "But I am curious. I have never before met an American. You are different than the English. You think you are no longer desirable, is that not so?"

He was almost as uncomfortable as when he'd been hidden away. "Can we talk about something else?"

She was enjoying his discomfort. "When a woman loves a man," she said, "she loves him no matter what. If this woman loves you, the fact that you have been wounded will make no difference. Do you think that the loss of a foot makes you less of a man?"

He shifted in the chair. "No. Not exactly."

She smiled and pressed his hand. "Come, I will teach you something about women."

She stood up and took his hand and then threw his arm over her shoulder. Then, with Joey hopping on one leg, she guided him back into the small bedroom and placed him on the bed.

Joey looked at her in surprise and said, "You don't need to—"

She put her fingers to his mouth, then started to unbutton his tunic. "Be quiet. I want to teach you something. You don't need two feet to make love."

He grabbed her hands and held them tight. "I don't need your sympathy."

"You are not the only one with needs, my American friend. I am surrounded by cousins. I am a widow, therefore I must be chaste. Do you not think I have yearnings? My God! I am a young woman. I need love as much as you.

"We can help each other, Joseph. Do not be put off by my aggression. Life is short. There is not time for romance."

His hands fell away and she continued to work at undressing him. Finished, she pushed him back on the bed and began to remove her own clothes. He felt embarrassed. His manhood lay limp and withered. But when Denise lay naked beside him, revealing a surprisingly voluptuous body, he felt old, familiar longings.

She smelled of flowers. He was touched that this

woman would use some of what must be a small treasure hidden away for the rare special occasion in these terrible times. Suddenly, he found himself filled with desire. He wanted very much to make love to Denise Dijon.

She was risking her life for him. He understood that she was filling her own need. At the same time, she was performing some sort of psychiatric magic, making him realize that he was still desirable, no matter the injury. That a woman would care this much for a stranger . . .

He found himself caressing her gently, kneading her breasts, then licking the nipples, now hard and erect. As he did so, he heard her let out a gasp.

They made love for a half hour. In that time, Denise climaxed three times, each time more fiercely than the last, her body stiffening, then releasing, a fine film of perspiration covering her skin.

His shyness and the pain in his foot had delayed his own fulfillment. Now, the shyness was gone, and the pain forgotten. He could wait no longer. He thrust himself deep inside her and let the sensations build until he was drifting in that exquisite moment between incredible sexual tension and ultimate release. He drew her to his body as if to crush the very life out of her, his animal desire blocking out a confusing array of emotions he barely understood.

They lay side by side for a moment, both gasping for air. Finally, Denise said, "I was wrong. You were not a virgin after all. You're still a man, Joseph. Very much a man. You must always remember that."

He kissed her on the lips and held her close. "I will," he said. "I'll never forget it—or you."

In the morning, Jean-Luc arrived. He carried a bundle of clothes, which he threw at Joey. "Put these on," he said.

They were small and dirty. Joey's uniform was to be burned. Jean-Luc pulled out a pair of scissors and cut Joey's hair short, then placed a black beret on his head. "Now," he said. "You look big for Frenchman, eh? We have papers for you that say you are mute. You know? Idiot. Sometimes idiots are quite tall, n'est-ce pas?"

"I don't know."

"Well, it best we can do. No matter what happen, you say nothing. Just . . . how you say . . . grunt. Eh? You understand?"

"Yes."

"We take chickens to Beaune. We have relatives there. When we get to Beaune, we take you through Demarcation Line to Mâcon. That will be bad part. We travel at night, on foot, over fifty kilometers. From there, you take train to Marseilles. Vichy." He spat on the ground. "Vichy. They are worse than the Hun. Traitors! You must be on guard. You will not be safe until you reach Gibraltar."

He pointed to the leg and said, "We will carry you."

Joey stared at him. "You're going to a hell of a lot of trouble to get me back to England. I don't know what to say or how to thank you."

Jean-Luc glanced at Denise. "You told him?"

She nodded. Jean-Luc turned his gaze on Joey. This time there was no smile. The eyes were cold and hard. "You want to thank us, there is only one way. Make the British help us. We need guns and money. Twice before, we help pilots to England and almost every day I stand at post office waiting. Nothing.

"We don't do this for . . . how you say . . . fun. We have a plan. We make plus grands problems for Germans. But we need help. You tell the British what we doing here. Understand?"

"I'll make sure they know."

The little Frenchman pulled out a box camera and motioned to Joey. "Come outside now. Stand beside Denise. I want picture of all of those we return. For my memoirs." As he said it he laughed heartily.

They all went outside. Joey stood by Denise. The camera recorded the moment for posterity. Then Jean-Luc put the camera away and said, "Come, we go now."

Joey looked at Denise and pulled her into his arms. "Thank you, Denise. For everything."

She kissed him on the cheek. "It was, as the British say, my pleasure. Now, go. God be with you."

And then he was sitting in a small flatbed truck loaded with crates of cackling chickens, their feathers flying in the air as the truck fired up and started down the road.

It was October 6, 1940. . . .

3

Joey DiPaolo limped up the short walk to the front door of his Brooklyn home. At the door, he hesitated. He hadn't announced his arrival ahead of time, wanting no greeting party, no fanfare, no celebration. He opened the front door and stepped inside.

His mother and father were in the front room, sitting by the radio, sipping espresso while they listened to the late news. His mother saw him first, and dropped the small cup in her hand. She leaped from her chair, screamed, then ran into his arms, her face flooded with tears.

His father came forward and wrapped his arms around the two of them. "Why didn't you tell us?" he said angrily.

Joey kissed them both and said, "I wasn't sure just when I'd be here."

Together, the three made their way to the sofa and sat down. As the pant leg rose up, the brace holding the prosthesis to the leg came into view. Joey's mother noticed it immediately. Her face went ashen as she clutched both hands to her chest, squeezing her eyes shut. Then a wail of agony, not unlike the one she'd uttered the day he'd first left Brooklyn, escaped her lips.

Vincent DiPaolo wrapped his arms around his wife and tried to comfort her. To Joey, he said, "She'll be all right. It's just that seeing it . . . makes it real."

"I know," Joey said, wrapping his big arms around his mother. "Mama! I'm fine. Losing a foot is nothing compared to what might have been. I'm alive! I can walk and talk. Be thankful for that."

His father looked at him closely. "You've lost a lot of weight."

"Yes. Mama, please. Stop this crying. I'm home. I'm safe. I'm alive. Be happy for that, please."

The three of them sat huddled on the sofa, hugging. Finally, Joseph's mother wiped her eyes and stood up. "You need to eat," she said. "You're skin and bones. I'll make something."

"Okay, Mama."

He turned to his father and said, "I want to go upstairs and change. Then, I'd like to take a walk. Just you and me, Papa."

His father looked at him suspiciously. "Yes. That's fine. We'll walk."

Joey changed into the clothes still hanging in the closet of his bedroom. He was momentarily frightened by the way they hung on him lifelessly. He had indeed lost a lot of weight. He put on a thick sweater and then grabbed the old leather windbreaker.

By the time he got downstairs, his father was waiting, dressed in his overcoat and fedora. Already, the familiar smell of food frying in olive oil had begun to permeate the living room.

The two men stepped out into the cool, crisp air of a November night in Brooklyn. They walked down the narrow street for a while without speaking. Then Joey stopped and faced his father.

"Papa," he said. "I'm afraid."

His father's eyebrows shot up. "Afraid? What is this afraid? Afraid of what?"

Joseph hung his head and said, "Sophia. I don't know what to say to her."

Vincent DiPaolo laughed. "You fly a plane in combat. You become an ace. The papers have been full of news about you. You're a hero, my son. Sophia? She calls every day. 'Have you heard anything? When will he be here?' What are you afraid of?"

Joey looked at the sky and shook his head. "She didn't want me to go in the first place."

"Neither did your mother. Neither did I. You think we don't love you anymore?"

"No, of course not. But, it's different with you."

"Yes. We're required to love you."

Joey threw his hands in the air in frustration. "Papa!"

Vincent DiPaolo placed a hand on his son's arm and said, "Listen to me. You're still a young man. I'm sure Sophia will not be affected by your injury. If she is, then she isn't the woman for you. You're too young to get married anyway, so what are you worried about?"

Their eyes met for a moment as both stood on the sidewalk silently. Then Vincent asked, "What are your plans?"

"I'm going back. I'm going to fly again."

For a moment, it looked as though the older man might explode. He stared at his son, his mouth twitching in anger, his hands forming into fists and then unclenching. Finally, he said, "We begged you not to go, but you turned your back on us. What is this thing we've done to make you hate us so?"

"I don't hate you."

"No? Then why do you punish us?"

"We already had this discussion."

"Yes, and you showed what respect you have for your mother by refusing to listen. For almost a year, she has lived in mortal fear that she would never see you again. Now, thanks to God, you are back. You have lost a foot. That's not enough? You want your mother to spend the rest of her life on her knees?"

"It has nothing to do with you and Mama."

"No? What, then? You have to prove something? To whom? Who is it that makes you feel you need to do this? Tell me, and I'll rip out his heart with my bare hands."

"Papa!"

"What, Papa? How can you fly without a foot? This is nonsense. The British are so weakened they make the wounded fly the planes?"

Joey turned and walked away.

He arrived in Washington just before noon. At Grand Central, his mother had cried when he left, but the tears were not the tears of agony she'd displayed on other occasions. These were tears of relief.

He hadn't spoken of his plans. His father had said scarcely another word to him. As the two men hugged each other, Joey could feel the stiffness in both of their bodies, neither of them willing to yield. He was, after all, his father's son. His only son.

Dressed in civilian clothes, Joey took a cab to the Senate Office Building and looked for the office of Senator Walter Rice, for whom Sophia worked. The senator was a friend of Sophia's family back in California. In fact, it was through the senator that Joey and Sophia had met in the first place.

In the summer of 1939, Vincent DiPaolo was representing two Brooklyn interests at some political meetings and had suggested that Joey come along and see Washington. After the meetings, there'd been a short cocktail party. Joey and Sophia, both teenagers, and at least twenty years younger than anyone else in the room, had naturally gravitated toward one another.

"Hello. My name is Joey DiPaolo," he'd said, as he stuck out one of his big hands.

She'd taken it and looked at him with twinkling eyes. "You're Italian!"

"That's right."

"So am I. My name is Sophia Rizzo. What are you doing here?"

He'd told her about his father, and she'd told him about the senator and the summer job. "I was planning on going back to California to attend college, but I think I'll stay here instead. At least for a year or so."

"You like Washington?" he asked.

"Yes! It's so exciting. You know they keep saying there's going to be a war in Europe. Can you imagine?"

It was probably the excitement in her voice that had caused him, two short months later, to take a freighter to England and join the RAF. He thought it would impress her. And, in fact, it had.

Now, the memory of that first meeting scratched at his brain. It seemed so very long ago.

When he opened the door to Senator Rice's office, he could see a small desk in the anteroom and doors leading to two separate offices behind it. An older woman, her gray hair piled in a bun atop her head, looked at him from above her thick glasses and said, "May I help you?"

"I hope so. I'm looking for . . ."

Before he could finish, he could hear a single word, more a scream, as it came rolling out of one of the offices.

"Joey!"

And then she was running into his arms, hugging him, kissing him, oblivious to the startled look in the receptionist's eyes. Sophia's hands patted his face as though trying to make sure he was real, not an apparition.

"Oh God, it's so good to see you. I was so worried. When I first heard . . . God! You're skinny! Are you all right?"

He smiled and looked over her shoulder at the receptionist. Sophia took the hint and whirled around. "Tell the senator that I've taken the rest of the day off. Tell him Joey just got back. He'll understand."

Then she grabbed his arm and said, "Come, I'll take you home. You need a good meal and then . . ." The expression on her face was positively lascivious.

Joey hesitated. "There's something I have to tell you."

She squeezed his arm and then kissed him. Placing her lips by his ear, she whispered, "The foot? I know all about it. Do you still have . . . all of your other parts?"

Joey stared at her in shock. "What?"

"You heard me. Do you?"

"Of course!"

"Good. Then let's not keep the lady waiting."

Joey stood there, his mouth open, his heart pounding, not believing what he was hearing. He tried to say something, but the words wouldn't come.

Sophia, the long, black hair framing her beautiful face, the dark eyes twinkling with merriment, the red lips parted slightly, the perfect white teeth gleaming, whispered, "Joey, if you don't come with me this very moment, I'll . . ."

They left the building arm in arm.

▪ ▪ ▪

Later, lying in Sophia's soft bed, the hot embers of passion momentarily banked, she turned to him and said, "I want to marry you, Joseph. And I want to do it now."

He was stunned. "You want to marry me?"

"Of course. I love you, silly. Don't you love me?"

"Very much," he said.

"Well?"

He looked into her eyes and then turned away. "We can't," he said.

"Why not?"

"Because I'm going back."

She sat bolt upright. "What? You can't! You've done your share. My God! You could have been killed. Besides, you can't . . ."

He looked at her sharply. "Go ahead. Say it!"

Her face was flushed. "It's just that . . ."

"That I can't fly?"

"No!"

"Yes! That's what you meant. Admit it!"

She clenched her hands into fists and stared at the ceiling. "Well, why would you want to? There are others."

"There's a pilot flying now with two artificial legs. His name is Bader. Douglas Bader. He's got seventeen kills to his credit, last I heard. If he can do it, I can do it. I'm going back, Sophia. We'll get married after the war."

She took his head in her hands and pulled it toward her. "You're such a stubborn man. Can you tell me why you have to do this?"

He thought for a moment, then said, "At first, it was the adventure. I read where guys my age were fighting the Germans, flying powerful airplanes. It sounded so exciting.

"The reality is even more exciting. It's impossible to describe, being up there. But it's not just that. It's different now. I see what's going on. The bombing's stopped for now, but that's just because the weather's lousy. They'll be back soon enough, stronger than ever.

"With America out of the war, they need every man they can get, don't you see? I can't just sit and let it pass me by. We went through this the last time."

"You hadn't been wounded."

"Nothing's changed. I can still fly."

She sighed. "I know better than to try and talk you out of anything. If you insist on going back, the least you can do is marry me. If I am to stay here and worry, let me do it as your wife. It's only fair. I love you!"

"You really do, don't you?"

"Did you think I was making it up?"

He held her close and told her he loved her too.

Two days later, he was still in Washington, staying at Sophia's apartment. As Sophia readied herself for work, there was a knock at the door. Joey, dressed in pajamas, opened it, and stared into the eyes of an RAF group captain.

"Good morning, DiPaolo. Group Captain George Baldwin. May I come in?"

Joey held the door open. "Of course, sir. How did you know where to find me?"

Baldwin entered the room and said, "Your father. I talked to him less than an hour ago. How are you getting along?"

"Fine, sir."

"I have your orders."

"My orders? I thought I was going back to Brickston after leave."

"I'm afraid not. You're being assigned as a liaison officer. The lend-lease program, actually. You'll be right here in Washington. I should think you'd be delighted. After all . . ." His gaze swept the room.

Joey was anything but delighted. "Sir, I want to fly, not shuffle goddam papers."

Baldwin stiffened. "There's more to war than flying, Flight Lieutenant DiPaolo."

"Flying Officer," Joey corrected.

"Flight Lieutenant," Baldwin insisted. "Your promotion is effective immediately. They've also added a bar to your DFC."

Joey was momentarily surprised. Then he said, "Sir, while I appreciate the promotion and the rest, I joined the RAF to fly. That's what I want to do. The foot—"

"The foot has nothing to do with this. The fact is, we desperately need a man who can hobnob with these American politicians. Who better than yourself? You're a bit of a hero here, whether you realize it or not. For another, you're an American, so you'll certainly be listened to. As an American, and a member of His Majesty's Royal Air Force, you can be of tremendous help. I'll grant that you're a little bit young for this work, but your CO claims you have the audacity of a man ten years older.

"That's exactly what we need, DiPaolo. We British have an aversion to rudeness that is often mistaken for weakness. You're just the ticket."

"Sir, I'm not a politician."

"I realize that, but you'll do as you're bloody well told. Unless, of course, you wish to be released. That can be arranged."

For a few moments, the two men glared at each other. Joey, somewhat chagrined, asked, "What does a liaison officer do, anyway?"

A month later, Joey and Sophia were married in Saint Patrick's Cathedral in New York City. There were two hundred invited guests in attendance as well as a number of reporters.

He was, after all, an ace.

DENISE DIJON

Part Two

4

Jean-Luc Dijon arrived at the Abbeville post office a few minutes before noon, as he did most every day, with steadily decreasing enthusiasm.

It had been some six weeks since the American RAF pilot had been sent on his long, dangerous journey back to England. Reports coming back to Jean-Luc indicated that the American had been placed on the ship at Gibraltar exactly as planned. Still, there had been no contact from the British.

It was frustrating. Jean-Luc and his group had risked their lives to establish themselves as viable contacts for the British, and it seemed as though all of their efforts were for nothing. The risks were enormous. Yet the stubborn British, for whatever reason, didn't see fit to even attempt to contact this small group of men and women, dedicated to fighting the Germans at every step of the way. He couldn't understand it.

He lit a cigarette, went inside the post office and asked if there was any mail. There wasn't.

He went back outside, waited a few more minutes and then started to walk toward the old car parked some fifty meters from the post office. He stopped for a moment to watch as a German truck convoy hurtled through the streets with no concern for people or animals that might be in the way.

Like the other convoys that had gone through the town during the last several weeks, this one was headed south, away from the coast. It was clear that the planned invasion of Britain had been shelved. Was that the reason for the British lack of interest? If so, they would surely regret such an arrogant attitude.

As Jean-Luc reached for the door handle of the car, he felt a hand on his arm. He turned and looked into the eyes of a man dressed much like himself, with dirty trousers and an unmatched jacket, a well-worn shirt open at the neck with several buttons missing, a small beret on his head, and mud-caked boots. The man was in his mid-thirties and wore about two days' growth of beard.

His brown eyes were steady as he looked into those of Jean-Luc and said, "Jean-Luc Dijon?"

The French was good, but the accent seemed to be from the southern provinces. Jean-Luc answered hesitantly. "What do you want?"

"We can talk in the car."

Jean-Luc felt a twinge of fear go through his body. The man could be German! They might have been discovered!

"Talk here," Jean-Luc said, his hands moving slowly toward the knife tucked in the back of his pants.

"I'm a friend. I was sent here at your request. Please, let's get out of the street."

Jean-Luc stood firm. "What friend? I don't know what you're talking about."

The man looked around the street. Then he said, "An American with a foot missing. You arranged for his passage back to England."

For a moment, Jean-Luc's heart leapt. Then caution took hold. He eyed the man suspiciously. "American? I know of no American. You have made a mistake."

"I'm not from the Gestapo, Jean-Luc. You arranged for this man to be transported through the Demarcation Line. You took him to Beaune with a shipment of live chickens. Then, your cousins took him by stretcher across to Mâcon, by train to Marseilles, and by ship to Gibraltar. His name was DiPaolo and he was most insistent that we contact you. I'm with British Intelligence, you idiot. Now, can we go?"

Jean-Luc's face lit up. The man had to be telling the truth. If he was Gestapo and knew all of that, Jean-Luc would already be dead. He slapped the man on the shoulder and hurriedly got into the car. The man slowly walked around, folded himself into the left-hand seat and closed the door.

"Don't drive fast. This place is crawling with Germans."

Jean-Luc, his heart pounding with excitement, started the car and drove slowly through the town. He headed for the farm of Denise Dijon.

As he drove, the man in the other seat told him that his name was Ronald Higgins and that he had been sent to assess the needs of Jean-Luc's organization as well as to coordinate their activities with other resistance groups in the area. He concluded by saying, "I can tell you that we're bloody well impressed with what you have done. The three pilots you've returned safely are most grateful. So is the British government. We want to help you in every possible way."

Jean-Luc swelled with pride. He'd almost given up

hope that he'd ever be contacted, and now, here in his car, a British agent had been sent to help. For the first time in weeks, he felt vindicated.

"I thought you'd never come."

Higgins eyed him carefully. "There were others before me. Hasn't anyone managed to contact you before this?"

Jean-Luc shook his head violently. "Non! No one! You are the first!"

"And you've heard nothing of their whereabouts?"

"Non! I had no knowledge. None of us did. We simply thought you were ignoring us."

They pulled up in front of the farmhouse and went inside.

Jean-Luc introduced Higgins to Denise. The Englishman smiled at her and said, "I have a message for you."

"Yes?"

"It's from Flight Lieutenant DiPaolo. He wanted you to know that he's back in the States, safe and sound. He asked me to thank you personally for all that you did."

Denise's hand went involuntarily to her throat. "How is he?"

"Fine."

"The war is over for him?"

"No. He's doing some liaison work in Washington, but he wants to fly again. I'm sure he will. I think the Ministry will be hard-pressed to keep him out of an aeroplane. The man is quite stubborn. Is there any message I can give DiPaolo from you?"

Denise thought about it for a moment and then said, "No. Just tell him I'm well." Then, wiping her hands on an apron, she said, "You must be hungry. I'll prepare something."

They sat around the table and ate what little food was available, a small piece of chicken and an egg.

Jean-Luc told Higgins what he needed, and

Higgins made him repeat it several times so he could commit it to memory. Then they began to discuss some other groups and the possibility of having a meeting with them. As they talked, Denise looked more and more ill at ease. Finally, she left the table and walked quickly to her bedroom, closing the door behind her. The two men could hear her retching.

Jean-Luc got up and walked to the door. "Denise," he called, "Are you all right?"

A weak voice answered him. "I'll be fine. Just give me a few moments."

"Do you want me to fetch the doctor?"

There was no answer. Then, the door opened and Denise, her face pale and covered with perspiration, leaned against the frame, running a shaking hand through her hair. In a voice that was almost a whisper, she said, "A doctor cannot help me, Jean-Luc. Only God can help me."

"What are you talking about?"

Tears began to stream down her cheeks. Her lips trembling, she turned away. Jean-Luc started to reach for her, but his hand stopped in midair. For a few seconds, he stood stock-still, thinking. Then, his arm dropped to his side.

"Stay in your room," he said harshly. "I will talk with you later."

He turned and left, closing the bedroom door behind him. He returned to the table, noticed the curious look on Higgins's face and said, "It is nothing. She is suffering from the curse. It always takes her like this."

The two men talked for a while longer and then went outside to look at the chicken coops. When they returned, Higgins said, "All right. You can put a radio in one of the sheds. Do you know Morse code?"

Jean-Luc shook his head.

"All right," Higgins said. "I'll give you a practice

key and a sheet straight away. You must learn how to transmit and receive Morse code if we're to keep in contact. First, you will learn to use the key. Once you have mastered that, we can talk about other things."

"I understand. I will learn. I have other skills. I am a good photographer. It is a hobby of mine. I develop my own negatives and make my own prints. I have a collection of photos that I have taken of the Germans. I have several of the nearby bomber base. Would you like to see them?"

Higgins's eyes danced with excitement. "Yes, indeed."

Jean-Luc grinned a toothless smile. "When we are finished here, I will take you to my place."

Denise lay on the bed, sobbing quietly. She could hear the two men talking about radios and codes and other things until, finally, they left the house. She had seen the look of venom in Jean-Luc's eyes and dreaded his return. She could well imagine what he'd do.

It was her third day of illness. She'd begun to suspect the truth when her period was a week late. A week later, her suspicions grew significantly. Now, there were no more suspicions, only truth—and the terrible consequences.

A double disgrace.

The first went back to the roots of the Dijon family. Strangely, though the Communists eschewed religious faith of any kind, Jean-Luc's Catholic upbringing went deep, and many of the old ways persisted. All of Jean-Luc's people attended Mass on Sunday and continued to practice their religion openly, without rebuke from their supervisors. All of them would look upon her with shame once they knew of her condition. She would be an outcast in every respect.

She'd conceived a child out of wedlock, which in

itself was a terrible sin, but not the worst. Soon, she would be useless to the cell that Jean-Luc had forged. That was the second, more important disgrace. The unforgivable sin.

In their system, women were considered equal to men in many respects. They were expected to kill and bomb and do all the things the men did. It was one of the reasons she had embraced the ideology in the first place. She'd rebelled against the traditional idea that women were mere chattel. The Communists viewed women as more than just bearers of children, cleaners of clothes, and cookers of food. In return, women were expected to refrain from sexual activity.

She lay there for over an hour, besotted in misery. Then, she reached in the dresser drawer and removed a small red diary. She opened it and removed a photograph. It was the one Jean-Luc had taken the day the American had left for his journey back to England.

She stared at the photograph. The image of Joseph DiPaolo stared back at her, his arm around her, the grin on his handsome face warm and friendly. The father of her child. A man she was unlikely to see again.

She turned the pages of the book until she came to an unused page. She began to write. To her diary, she expressed her innermost thoughts, the unbearable pain she felt in her heart, and the hope that the Holy Mother would somehow look after her in the months ahead. She put the photograph back into the book, closed it and placed it back in the dresser drawer, left the bedroom and began to tend to the laundry.

An hour later, Jean-Luc was back. He flung open the door of the small house and stormed inside, his face contorted with anger. Denise retreated to the bedroom, but he was right behind her.

"You," he said, his finger pointed at her stomach. "You're pregnant."

She did not answer.

"How could you? Pierre is still warm in his grave!"

She leaned against the wall, her entire body trembling. Jean-Luc grabbed her by the arm, spun her around and slapped her across the face. She reeled back and fell heavily onto the bed.

He took a step forward. "The American, yes?"

Denise nodded.

Jean-Luc swore. Then, he backhanded her across the face. "Your husband is dead fighting for France and you do this! You bring disgrace to us all! You're nothing but a common whore! The first in the Dijon family!"

Her cheek burned from the blow. The shock had stirred her anger. Her eyes filled with defiance, she screamed, "What do you know of whores? I made love to a man at a time when we were both in need of some affection. Yes, Pierre is dead and will never return. Am I to die as well? Is that what you want?"

She stood up. "Then do it. Kill me now and speak no more to me of whores!"

Jean-Luc raised his hand as though to strike her again, then slowly lowered it. He sighed. For almost a minute, he paced the floor.

"You will have to go away," he said, finally. "I have a cousin in Paris. No one will notice you there. You can have the child and give it to the Sisters. They will find a home for it."

Denise had expected nothing less. She knew she would be sent away. It was useless to argue. When the time came to have the child, she would decide then what to do. Who knew? With the war raging throughout Europe, anything could happen.

She smoothed the bedcover. To Jean-Luc, she said, "I will do as you wish. You can take care of the farm?"

The anger remained in his eyes. "Yes, I will look after the farm."

▪ ▪ ▪

The next day, Denise sat in the truck with a single suitcase containing her most precious possessions, and watched her world disappear behind her. She wondered if she would ever see it again.

She'd been born in Abbeville, had grown up there and had married not long after the death of her parents. First one and then the other. Her father had died under the wheels of a tractor gone berserk and her mother had died of grief. At least, that's what the doctor had said. He could find no other reason, he'd said.

When Pierre Dijon had come calling on her, she had welcomed his friendship. The friendship had flowered into romance, and soon the terrible sense of loss seemed to slip away. They had married in a small church in Abbeville a week before Hitler invaded Poland.

Pierre and Denise's two brothers had been called up to serve in the army immediately. She'd watched the three of them leave together. As the bus taking them to the call-up center receded in the distance, she was once again consumed by that terrible sense of loss. The days had not been so bad because there was plenty of work to do. But the nights ...

After months of inactivity, which some had called the "phony war," the Germans had struck France in full force. In the very first attack, Pierre, her brothers, and half of the young men from Abbeville had been killed. A slaughter.

Everyone she'd ever loved was dead. For two months, she was so despondent, she was barely able to move. It had been Jean-Luc who had encouraged her to join his group to shake her from her lethargy.

Shortly afterward, he'd brought the first RAF pilot to her farmhouse. Together, the three had dug the hole in the basement floor. Denise had hidden the flyer while the Germans looked in vain. Jean-Luc had traveled to Saint-Quentin to meet with some other cousins and set up some sort of escape route.

The escape route had worked flawlessly. And then another pilot had floated down from the sky in a silken parachute, been snatched from the clutches of the Germans, and hidden away in the same fashion. He, too, had been spirited back to England under the very noses of the Germans.

Then the American had been brought to the house after an attack that was both daring and foolish.

A mere child, he'd been so frightened, more of losing his lover than his life. He'd seemed so . . . devastated. Was it any wonder that she'd found herself yearning to be touched by this man? She'd wanted to bring him to her breast and make him feel comfortable, and so she had. Their pleasure had lasted just a few minutes, but her agony was to last a lifetime.

She was being punished again. She sat silently beside Jean-Luc as the truck bounced down the road and wondered, for the hundredth time, what horrible deeds had been done to have God place such a curse on her head.

5

$Henri$ Cousteau was a man in his fifties who maintained a small barber shop in the town of Maisons-Alfort, located south of Paris, not far from the River Seine. He lived alone in a small apartment above the barber shop and, for the most part, kept to himself.

A lifelong bachelor, he seemed to Jean-Luc to be the perfect man for the job of keeping Denise out of sight until the baby was born and placed with the Sisters for adoption. For one thing, he was a quiet man. For another, he was not in a position to protest. Jean-Luc knew of Henri's homosexuality, information that, if given to the Germans, would mean immediate death for Henri.

Standing in the living room of the apartment, Henri listened as Jean-Luc explained why Denise had been brought to his home and what was expected of him. He sighed wearily and said he would take care of her. To Denise, he said, "I expect you to earn your keep. You must do the cooking and the cleaning and clean the shop as well. I have a mattress that you can sleep on in the front room. That will have to suffice."

Denise nodded without speaking.

"When is the child due?"

Jean-Luc looked at Denise, then counted on his fingers. "The first week of July."

"This is November! You ask much of me, Jean-Luc."

"I know. Someday, I will repay the favor." He pulled some papers from his pocket and handed them to Henri. "These are her papers. I have taken the liberty of having a marriage certificate prepared that shows you as husband and wife. The Germans may ask questions, but I don't think so. The wedding is shown to have taken place in the northern provinces. I doubt that they'll be that concerned. If they are, there is nothing to worry about, for we have altered the church records just in case."

"Why was I not consulted about these things?"

"Because there was no time. Besides, this makes it look better for you. I would not complain."

Henri looked very much as if he wanted to complain. His attention turned from Jean-Luc to Denise and back to Jean-Luc again. The anger was evident on his face but he said nothing. Jean-Luc said his good-byes. With scarcely another glance at Denise, he turned and went down the stairs, stepped into the car and drove away.

Henri sighed. "He is a cruel man, your cousin."

"No. It's the war. It changes people. Perhaps forever."

"Well, enough of this. You can begin by doing my laundry. It's in a wicker basket beside the bed. I don't like starch, so you'll not find any. The rest you'll find under the sink—the washboard and the soap. There is a clothesline that runs from the bedroom window. I have to get back to work. I have customers waiting."

Denise watched the man go down the stairs, placed her suitcase in the corner and sat cross-legged on the barren wood floor. She looked around the small apartment, the walls unadorned with paintings, the furnishings sparse and worn. For the first time in her life, she thought seriously about taking her own life.

It would solve two problems. She knew it was a sin, but she was being punished unmercifully for sins both real and imagined already. God had forsaken her. And yet, she had heard the warnings. An eternity of utter agony awaited those who committed such a sin as suicide.

Perhaps she could will herself to die. Would that be considered suicide? No one had ever asked the priests that question.

Then, the face of the American seemed to hover in front of her, as though trying to reach out and give her the strength to go on. The young face, the eyes expressing worldliness and innocence, first one and then the other, as if the mind behind them was in a state of perpetual upheaval, not knowing which direction to take.

She reached out and tried to touch the ethereal vision, but of course it was just an illusion. Then she felt a pressure in her abdomen which she took to be the vision's way of communicating, saying to her that she must not kill this child of the American—that somehow there was a future for both her and the child.

When Jean-Luc Dijon returned from Paris, he placed one of his nephews in Denise's house to look after the place. Under the tutelage of the British agent, he began to study Morse code. Within three days, he'd all but mastered the key.

That accomplished, Higgins turned to the cryptographic codes, codes that were changed daily. Jean-Luc was taught how to read, write, and choose codes. He was also taught how to turn documents into microdots using his own photographic equipment, augmented by a new lens for his enlarger.

The training proceeded to the art of manufacturing explosives from various chemicals and disguising them as everyday objects—time bombs disguised as cans of food, incendiary devices that looked like loaves of bread, all sorts of seemingly innocuous objects that would kill or maim.

As yet, Higgins had not introduced Jean-Luc to any other groups that were operating in the area. The British agent was away for days at a time, and Jean-Luc assumed that Higgins was building a network of spies and saboteurs. As for the network that Jean-Luc had set up to rescue the three pilots, it was kept intact. Higgins had said that there was no way they could improve on that system.

During the next six months, through winter and spring, Jean-Luc and his group successfully destroyed three locomotives, miles of train tracks, one railway bridge, and at least a hundred German troops. In addition, six more pilots followed the same path to England that Joey DiPaolo had.

The British supplied increasing amounts of material and money to keep the group going, and Higgins had shown up twice in person to exchange information.

And then it all came crashing to an end.

It was June 15, 1941, a week before Hitler was to attack Russia. One of Jean-Luc's men, a man named Leduc, got drunk one evening. As he staggered home, he was interrupted by a trio of German soldiers.

He was asked for his papers, and instead of meekly handing them over as he had been taught to do, he started shouting obscenities at the soldiers in French. Worse, he bragged that they would soon see death as others had.

One of the Germans removed the rifle slung over his shoulder and raised it above his head, preparatory to bringing it crashing down on Leduc's skull. Another held up his hand and said, "Wait!" Then, he turned to Leduc and asked, in very precise French, "What do you mean, 'as others have died'?"

The startled Leduc quickly realized the error of assuming German soldiers couldn't speak French. His voice said nothing, but his eyes spoke volumes. The soldier realized that the terror reflected in the face of Leduc was more than simple fear of being killed. He smiled at Leduc and said, "Come, my French friend. Come with me."

Leduc was taken to a military camp not far from Amiens. He was brought into a small, green, windowless room and told to take off his clothes. With pounding heart, he did so. Then he was told to sit in the only chair in the room. Again, he did as he was told. For nearly an hour, he was questioned quietly. Then, the Germans went about it in earnest.

Electric probes were attached, one clipped to Leduc's penis and another to his testicles. Leduc looked in sheer terror at the questioner, an SS major.

The major smiled as he crouched down and placed his hand on a small dial sitting atop a small black box that had been plugged into an electrical outlet.

"Now, Mr. Leduc, if you ever wish to have children again, I would suggest you tell me everything you know about the underground."

Leduc shook his head. "I told you! I know nothing. I was drunk! I didn't know what I was saying. I am a poor farmer, that's all."

The major turned the dial to midrange and

returned it immediately. A short bolt of electric current surged through Leduc's privates and he screamed in pain. His body arched, then sagged, the perspiration seeping from every pore in his body.

"I say again, Mr. Leduc. Tell us what we want to know and you will end this. I will let you go free. That is a promise. But you must understand, I cannot allow you to go free if you do not cooperate with me. You are a simple farmer. I am a simple soldier. We both must find our way in this life. Is that not true?"

"For the love of God, Major. I beg you. I know nothing."

Again the dial was turned, this time more slowly.

Leduc's eyes almost bulged out of his head.

Within ten minutes, he told them everything he knew. When he was finished, the major ordered him untied and told Leduc to put his clothes back on.

"You see?" he said. "That wasn't so bad, now was it?"

Leduc, consumed with guilt, could hardly move. He looked blankly at the major and then lowered his head in shame. He never saw the Luger as it came up, never felt the bullet as it smashed into his brain.

Jean-Luc Dijon was preparing to make his daily report. For months, he had used Denise Dijon's farm as his secret place for making radio transmissions, thinking that if, by some chance, the Germans searched his own place, they would find nothing. There was nothing to find. Even his photographic equipment had been moved to Denise's former home.

He crouched down in the chicken coop and waited. The report would be made at three minutes after one in the morning, ten minutes from now. He had transposed the message into code and had attached the batteries to the radio to warm up the tubes.

Suddenly, he heard the sound of motorcycles and

trucks as what seemed like a small army roared into the front yard.

Quickly, he doused the candle and feverishly worked to remove the crystal from the radio. He reached it, flung it to the ground and crushed it with his boot. Then, he returned the radio and batteries to their hiding place. Chickens clucked with dissatisfaction as he worked in the dark to restore some semblance of order. Then, as calmly as he could, he left the chicken coop and walked slowly toward the house.

"Halt!"

It was the voice of a German soldier, his rifle aimed at Jean-Luc. Another soldier aimed a flashlight in his direction.

Jean-Luc stopped and put a hand to his eyes to ward off the bright light.

"What do you want?" he asked.

As he spoke, he saw several soldiers dragging his nephew, still in pajamas, from the house and throwing him on the ground. A major in a black uniform with the dreaded symbol of the SS on the lapels strutted over to Jean-Luc and said, in excellent French, "Your papers, please."

Jean-Luc pulled them from a jacket pocket and handed them to him. The major walked over to the soldier with the flashlight and looked at the papers for a moment, then put them in his own pocket. He said something in German to a group of soldiers, who rushed into the chicken coop and started tearing it apart.

In German, the major said, "Be careful. Don't let those chickens loose. They will be appreciated."

Jean-Luc stood helplessly in the dark as he waited for the inevitable. A few moments later, one of the soldiers brought out the radio and the code book and showed it to the major, who smiled in satisfaction. He turned to Jean-Luc and said, "Come, we will look in the house. Together."

They walked into the house and the major turned up some lamps. "Now," he said. "Show me where you hid the English pilots."

Jean-Luc felt his heart leap to his throat. They knew! But how? Who had talked?

His fear turned to anger as he realized that death was moments away. He lunged for the major and tried to get his hands around the man's throat, hoping he'd be shot in the process. Instead, a rifle butt crashed against his skull and he fell to the floor, unconscious.

When he awoke, he found himself inside the very hole that had served as a hideaway for the pilots. The major was crouched down on his haunches, leaning over the opening.

"Most ingenious, Dijon. Now, tell me everything I want to know and do it quickly."

Jean-Luc's head pounded with pain. He tried to move a hand to rub the spot but they were bound, as were his feet. The major picked up a brick and dropped it on Jean-Luc's stomach. "First," he said, "who is your contact in England?"

"I have no contact."

"Really?"

The major picked up another brick and held it above Jean-Luc's face. Slowly, he stood up and let the brick fall. It landed on the Frenchman's nose and blood began to pour from the shattered flesh and bone. A tortured scream escaped Jean-Luc's lips.

He closed his eyes to block out the horror of what was happening to him. For a moment, there was silence. Then, he heard, "Open your eyes."

Standing at the side of the hole was his nephew, held by two soldiers. The major had a Luger placed at the ear of the young man. "Tell me who your contact is. Tell me everything, now! Or this young man will stop breathing."

Jean-Luc groaned in agony. "He knows nothing. He just looks after the farm."

"Tell me!"

"I can't."

The room was filled with the sound of the Luger as it fired, the sound bouncing off the walls and crashing against Jean-Luc's ears in waves. To his absolute horror, he saw his nephew's head jerk to the side and the body fall to the ground.

"You bastard!" he screamed. "You're an animal. As sick and stupid as your crazy master! You can—" He was silenced by another smash from a rifle butt.

When he awoke, he was in a small green room, totally nude, tied to a chair. Wires had been attached to his penis and his testicles. Something was very wrong in his head. The room spun violently, and Jean-Luc immediately vomited all over himself. The vomit mixed with old and fresh blood that covered much of his chest.

He felt a sudden surge of electricity attack his genitals. His body jerked back against the chair involuntarily. He was semiconscious, but could still hear the voice of the major.

"You will know pain like no other you have ever experienced, Dijon. I am losing patience with you. Now, for the last time, tell me what I want to know."

Jean-Luc tried to open his eyes, but couldn't. He began to mumble prayers.

Again, a surge of electricity smashed him against the chair. The pain was excruciating. This time it seemed to be centered in the middle of his chest, radiating out and down his left shoulder. He tried to breath but couldn't. Something was blocking his throat. He tried to move his hands so that he could reach whatever it was that was stopping him from breathing, but they were tied fast.

The pain intensified. Then it receded quickly and left altogether. Jean-Luc felt at peace.

The major put a hand by the dead Frenchman's throat, feeling for the carotid artery. After a moment he cursed.

"He's dead. Take him back to his own farm, throw him in the house and burn everything to the ground. Then burn the farm of the woman. I want them all to know what happens to those who work with these people."

"Yes, Major."

"And bring me the next one. We will see what he knows. Let's hope his heart is stronger than this one's."

"Yes, Major."

The major watched as they dragged the body of Jean-Luc Dijon out of the room. In a moment, another man was brought in. The major held up his hand and said, "Not yet. Get someone in here and clean this place up. The smell alone is enough to make me sick. These people are like pigs. They die without dignity."

The soldiers pulled the terrified man back out of the room. The major followed them. He stood in the hallway and removed a package of American cigarettes from his pocket, pulled one out and lit it. The Americans, he thought, did so many things well. Especially cigarettes. Their cigarettes were excellent.

6

The labor pains had started over an hour ago, signaling the imminent birth of her child. Denise Dijon was paralyzed by fear, not of the birth itself, but of the aftermath. It might be the death of her, but she would defy Jean-Luc.

The war had changed everything. Tens of thousands of children were now homeless. Some wandered the streets wide-eyed, their tiny hands thrust out in the traditional pose of the beggar. Others were kept in large halls, the tags around their dirty necks the only means of identification. The lucky ones ended up in orphanages run by the stoic nuns or their compatriots. There they would stay until the war was over—or worse. Placing them was almost impossible.

Denise wanted to comfort her child when it cried, hold it close, sing the old songs, protect it as best she could from the cruelties of a world gone insane.

Beneath that maternal instinct lay another, perhaps even stronger—Denise's overwhelming need to be loved.

Her parents were dead. Her husband and brothers were dead. As far as she knew, her cousin Jean-Luc was alive, but she hadn't heard from him in months. No matter, for he was a cunning man. The Germans would never get Jean-Luc.

To return to the farm with a small child in her arms would be viewed as an arrogant admission of sin, akin to thumbing her nose at tradition and decency. She would be considered a slut, an outcast, a women attended only by those who'd turned their backs on the church.

What did it matter? There was no one left to love her. With her immediate family gone, the party had become her family, but to the party, she was simply another worker. They simply wanted to use her, Jean-Luc included.

Denise would fill the needs of her child, and the child would respond with love.

Denise would protect her child, as only a mother could, from the harshness of life, until it too would have to face the inevitable realities. Even those realities would be easier to accept with a background of love and affection.

She stared out the window of the small front room, idly watching the locals as they walked or bicycled, automobiles being a rarity in these times of severely rationed petrol. She gritted her teeth as another contraction almost doubled her up. They were coming closer together now. Yes. She would have the child and keep it, no matter what.

She heard the sound of footsteps. Two men. She muffled a groan.

Henri had been kind during her long sojourn with him. He was a fastidious man and somewhat demanding, but he'd provided food and lodging, and on rare occasions, conversation. He'd accepted her without assessing guilt, perhaps because of his own conflict with the church, a conflict that had turned him into an agnostic Communist.

He was, however, a homosexual, and there were times when he needed some privacy. When he brought a man to the flat, Denise was required to wander the streets for a few hours, or, if it was past curfew, sit in the closed barbershop. She read books or made entries in her diary.

She would always receive a haunted stare from the visitor as he came down the stairs and made a dash for home, perhaps wondering if she would reveal his secret.

Now, as the two men entered the front room, she struggled to her feet. She felt weak, but knew she had to make it downstairs, away from them. It was fortunate that Henri had found a new lover at this particular moment. It gave her the opportunity to go to the closed barbershop, to be alone. With any luck, her labor would be short and the baby would come before Henri could drag her off to the Sisters. A dangerous, terrifying choice, but the only one. There was no alternative.

"Denise?"

"Yes, Henri. I'm going now."

"No. It is something else. May I introduce Claude Beauport? He is an associate of your cousin Jean-Luc. He has . . . news."

"News? I haven't had a letter for months. Why has he not written?"

From the look on the stranger's face, it was clear the news he brought was not good.

"Mam'selle Dijon," Claude said, "I have very bad news. The Germans . . . they. . . ."

Denise's hand flew toward her mouth in anticipation of what she sensed was coming next.

"The Germans found them. Jean-Luc and the rest . . . were killed."

Denise felt faint. She had always thought that somehow they would prevail. Jean-Luc was so shrewd, always thinking ahead. It was impossible.

"All of them?"

Claude nodded. "The farms were destroyed. Burned to the ground. Both of them, yours and Jean-Luc's. The Germans took the chickens and now there is nothing but scorched earth."

She felt a stab of pain in her heart. There was nothing to return to! The last of her family and that of her husband, even the cousins, had been wiped out. She was totally and irrevocably alone.

Her lips trembling, she asked, "The ones in the south? Are they all right?"

"Yes. Jean-Luc and the others never spoke of them. They endured . . . terrible things, but they never spoke."

"They must know about me!" she wailed. "They'll be after me as well."

"No! They know of you, but they don't know where you are. If they had, you and Henri would be dead by now. Jean-Luc must have perished before they found out where he had taken you."

"What will I do?"

"I have another group that is centered in Saint-Quentin. You can come there after the baby is born. There are sixteen of us. Thirteen men and three women. We could use your help."

Denise shuddered. There was something about his eyes that chilled a heart already caked with the ice of terrible news. He was about her age, twenty-six, a small man, with a large nose and eyes that seemed too close together. His hair was thick and curly and his face was angular, almost coming to a point at the chin.

She looked into his eyes. Dark, brooding eyes, with no white surrounding the smoldering shadows. Evil eyes that frightened her.

"And you?" she said. "How is it that they never found out about you?"

"Because of the precautions taken by the British. They made sure that all the group leaders met under assumed names. We were never allowed to know anything about another group's operation. That way, if a member of one group was caught, the others would not be betrayed to the Germans."

"But you are here. You know about me, about the ones in the south . . . everything!"

"I was told by the Englishman Higgins. He says you've met."

"Yes."

"He was the one who told me what happened to Jean-Luc and his group. It was a warning to be careful. Jean-Luc told him where you were, and Higgins told me. He asked that I contact you. He felt that you should be made aware of what had happened. He also said you were a valuable member of Jean-Luc's group and should be encouraged to join mine. Of course, neither he nor I knew about your . . . situation. But, no matter."

It made sense. Denise's immediate fears were subdued.

"We want you with us," Claude said. "It's up to you. Perhaps you'd rather stay in Paris."

Henri shook his head. "No. She cannot stay here. There have been too many questions already. With Jean-Luc dead, the Germans will continue to investigate. Sooner or later they will trace her movements. I can't take that chance."

Claude looked at her again and asked, "You look like you are very close to your time. When do you go to the Sisters?"

"I'm not going."

"What?" Claude croaked.

"I'm not giving up my child. I'm going to have this baby and keep it. I'm going to bring it up and pray that this war is over by the time—"

Henri screamed at her. "You can't do that!"

"I can! And I . . ."

Perhaps it was the shock of learning of the death of her cousins, the destruction of her farm, the end of her former life. Perhaps it was just time. For whatever reason, at that moment, she slumped to the floor in agony. The pains of labor began anew, with increased intensity.

Henri Cousteau grew pale. "I'll go for a doctor."

"No!" Denise screamed.

She crawled to the rolled-up mattress in the corner of the room. With shaking hands, she unrolled it and then lay on it. "No!" she repeated, breathlessly. "There will be too many questions. I will deliver the baby here, by myself if necessary. If you cannot help, then just leave me be."

Claude turned to Henri. "Get some towels and heat some water. This may take some time."

The barber stared at the man and remained immobile. A look of pure terror filled his eyes. "She can't have the baby here. It's impossible!"

"Whether you like it or not, she is giving birth. We have to help her. Now go!"

As a badly shaken Henri scurried away, Claude leaned over Denise and said, "You can bring the baby back to Saint-Quentin. It will make things a little more cheerful around there. Do not worry."

His words failed to comfort her.

Four hours later, she gave birth to a baby girl, who announced, after the solid slap on her bottom administered by Claude, her entry into a strange new world with a hearty howl. Denise was sure she could see resemblances to the father, as the baby's hair and skin were darker than her own.

Claude, despite his sinister appearance, had proved to be an excellent midwife. Now, he cut and tied the umbilical cord, cleaned the baby, and wrapped her in a white towel. He handed her to

Denise. "What will you name her?" he asked.

"Josephine," she said.

"Why would you honor Napoleon's first wife?"

"I don't. I honor someone else."

He stood up. "Well, you have your child. I must go for a few days. When I get back, I'll take you to Saint-Quentin. Unless you have a better idea."

"I can keep the child?"

"I said so, didn't I?"

"Then I will go to Saint-Quentin."

"I'll have to register the birth. Your papers say your name is Cousteau. That is the name we'll use."

Denise nodded. It made no difference. Whatever worked.

The Germans, with their cold efficiency, put much stock in papers. Without papers, a person was nothing. Without papers, a person was taken away and placed in some dark prison, or worse. Papers were everything. With the right papers, there was food, access to doctors, freedom of travel. Without them, nothing. Papers had replaced humanity.

Claude, after talking with Henri for a moment, made his departure. Henri took a nervous look at the baby, patted Denise on the forehead and returned to his bedroom. Denise was left alone with her child.

She smiled as a thought entered her mind. It was July 4, 1941, the American Independence Day. Her child, half American, had been born on a most appropriate day. Denise hoped it was a portent of better days to come.

Then, she began to weep. She was alone, penniless, wanted by the Germans, headed for another cell of resistance fighters run by a man who frightened her. There were no options. As she wept, Josephine began to cry, the wails from the tiny mouth mixing with the sound of her own sobs.

Denise placed the baby at her swollen breast. Josephine began to suckle immediately. After the feeding, Denise burped her, then together, mother and daughter lay on the mattress. From the suitcase, Denise withdrew her diary and a small pencil. She opened the diary to a fresh page. As she had every day for the last three years, she began to make her entry.

She stopped, reached into the suitcase again, and retrieved a small pair of scissors. Carefully, she cut a lock of the child's hair and pressed it between the pages of the diary. She again removed the treasured photograph, now worn at the edges from the constant inspections, gazed at it and slipped it back in the diary. Then she resumed her narrative.

Five days later, Claude returned. He loaded Denise, Josephine, and the suitcase into the rear of a battered old car that looked even worse than the one Jean-Luc had owned.

Saint-Quentin was almost 150 kilometers from Paris. With the incessant German road blocks, the trip took ten hours. It was dark by the time they finally reached the farmhouse on the outskirts of the town.

Claude parked the car in front of the house, got out, and looked around for a few moments. He waved at a man staring out of the window of the house, then beckoned Denise to follow him to the barn. As she walked along the dirt path leading to the barn, she could see the cattle as they lay in the warm summer night air, the moonlight casting a strange glow over their brown hides.

Once inside the barn, Claude took a pitchfork and rapped on one of the main columns holding up the roof. He rapped three times, paused, and then rapped three more times. Almost immediately, a wooden plank rose from the floor and a man with a pistol in his hand peeked out. He smiled and opened the plank fully, so they could both climb down the wooden ladder to a rather large room that had been created beneath the barn.

The room was a subterranean home for Claude's group of resistance fighters. The walls were shored with lumber, and small oil lamps hung from two of the thick wooden poles that acted as supports for the floor above.

A large group of people sat around two tables, drinking wine and listening to a small radio receiver. One of the men was taking notes. No one spoke until the radio was turned off. Then, their attention was given to Claude.

"Welcome back," one of the men said. "I see you found her."

Claude introduced Denise to the group, whose names were just a jumble. The three women immediately gathered around Denise and the baby. Josephine, asleep, never moved.

Claude turned to one of the men. "What was the message?"

"I haven't decoded it yet. A minute."

Claude took Denise's hand and led her to the far wall, where the homemade bunks stood. He threw her suitcase on one of the straw-filled mattresses and said, "This will be yours and the baby's. I'll give you a couple of days to get used to things and then we'll put you to work."

Denise lay on the bed and felt Josephine begin to stir. It was time for a feeding. As she placed the child to her breast, the three women gathered around again, asking questions and marveling at the child. No one asked who the father was, an indication that they knew the circumstances.

Denise talked with them until Josephine had had her fill, then placed the child over her shoulder and patted it gently on the back. After a few burps, Denise wiped the child's face, then replaced the soiled diaper with the one remaining fresh one she had left in her suitcase.

"Where can I wash these out?" she asked.

The one named Marie brought a galvanized pail with some water and placed it by the bed. "This is all we have," she said, a note of sadness in her voice. "Here, we are called the underground. It is not without good reason."

Denise washed the diapers as best she could and hung them on the side of her bunk to dry. Then she lay back on the bed and fell asleep.

True to his word, Claude put her to work in two days. It wasn't what she expected, but rather the same thing she'd been doing for Henri, only this time it was for seventeen people plus a child. Cleaning, preparing meals, all in the fetid confines of the underground room beneath the barn.

Each day, the waste was taken in pails upstairs and buried behind the barn. Fresh water was drawn from the well and placed in wine bottles. What little soap there was had to be rationed. All meals were cold, as the ventilation in the room was poor and it was feared that a cookstove would consume too much oxygen. Fresh vegetables taken from farmer's fields, eggs, eaten raw, milk and bread formed the basic diet.

They were living like animals.

They took turns leaving the room and going outside to perform the chores needed to keep the farm in operation. The farm belonged to Claude, and he had forty-five milk cows at the moment, but that figure could go down any time. Once, he'd had over a hundred cows in his herd, but the Germans took what they needed whenever they felt like it, and there was little he could do about it.

After two weeks, Denise was relieved of her stint

as the maid, and allowed to join the group for their nocturnal acts of sabotage. For Denise, it was a welcome change, and after she'd handed the baby over to Marie, she practically flew up the ladder. For months, she had been forced to react. Now, finally, she could act again, as she had when Jean-Luc was alive.

Tonight's mission was an exciting one. One of the men in the group had learned through French railway workers that a German troop train would be moving at night to avoid the probing eyes of pilots in British reconnaissance planes. The train would pass over a small bridge that crossed a river near the village of Bohain-en-Vermandois, some twenty-two kilometers from Saint-Quentin. The plan was to blow up the bridge as the train crossed it, hopefully taking a lot of German troops to their deaths. Claude would lead the raid, along with three men, Denise, and one other woman. The two women would act as lookouts while the charges were set.

The plan called for the truck to be parked on a road some distance from the bridge. Explosives would be placed along the entire length of the bridge. A long wire would connect the explosives to a plunger located about halfway between the bridge and the truck. Once the explosives were detonated, Claude would race to the back of the truck, and they would make their escape.

The driver of the truck knew all of the roads in the area like the back of his hand, and could drive them at moderate speed without any light whatsoever. The moon was bright on this cloudless night and the opportunity was golden. Whatever trepidations Denise might have felt were squelched by the sheer joy of being able to strike back at those who had killed her last remaining relatives and burned her farm to the ground. While the fear was there, it was subjugated by the tremendous sense of release, almost orgasmic, that she felt at being able to act.

They arrived without incident at the spot chosen earlier. Claude took a heavy burlap sack from the back of the truck and, accompanied by two men, disappeared into the darkness. The driver remained behind the wheel of the truck, which had been turned around and now faced the opposite direction.

Denise and the other woman crouched in the back of the truck, machine guns at the ready. The guns were not to be used unless absolutely necessary, as their muzzle flashes would signal their position.

The night sky was filled with a million stars, but Denise had to concentrate on the ground. Her eyes scanned the countryside while her ears strained to hear the slightest sound. She could feel the adrenaline coursing through her veins.

It seemed to take forever, but within half an hour, the men who'd been with Claude returned, gasping for breath. Claude remained with the plunger.

They waited quietly on the back of the truck for another hour. Then, at last, they could hear the distant sound of a train as it puffed its way toward their position. As the sound grew louder, the tension mounted. Now they could see the small slit of a light at the front of the locomotive, hear the wheels screeching as the train rounded a curve and the clatter as the wheels made contact with the rails on the bridge.

The locomotive had almost crossed the bridge before Claude pushed the plunger. The bridge exploded in a blizzard of broken wooden timbers. Three of the cars, along with the coal carrier, fell into the river, dragging the puffing locomotive down with them.

Denise could hear the screams of those trapped inside the cars. Almost immediately, the sound of rifle and machine gun fire came from some of the cars that had fallen beside the track. But it was indiscriminate fire, more a reflex reaction than anything else, and as Claude jumped onto the back of the truck, the burlap sack in his hand, some additional explosions were heard, meant to cover the sound of the truck as it made good its escape.

They were at least a kilometer away from the wreck before Denise could breathe normally. The truck was hurtling through the night, bouncing on the dirt road, traveling without lights of any kind. They all kept quiet, saving the celebration for the moment when they were safely underground again.

The truck pulled up to the farmhouse and the raiders leaped off and ran toward the barn. Claude picked up the pitchfork and rapped on the wooden support column the way he had before. The floor opened up and they were all safely inside, except for Claude, who would sleep in the house with three others, in readiness for the German inspection expected within hours.

Marie handed Denise the baby and slapped her on the shoulder. "Nice work, Denise. Now you're really one of us. I think your baby needs to feed."

Josephine was crying. Denise went to her bunk and placed the baby to her breast. She was still panting from the excitement, and it took some time before the milk began to flow. She leaned back and felt the comfort wash over her like a warm bath.

The Germans never did come to the farm. After three days, the members of the group began to relax. That night they were visited by the British agent assigned to coordinate their activities, Ronald Higgins.

He noticed Denise immediately, and when he saw the child, his eyes widened.

"So," he said, "that explains it."

"Explains what?"

"Don't be coy, Miss Dijon. Your cousin said you were a very important member of his group. Yet when you went away, he appeared not to be upset. I couldn't understand his thinking, especially when he asked that I find you, should anything . . . I'm sorry about what happened."

"My name is now Cousteau," Denise said.

"Of course. Do I know the father of your child?"

"No," she said. She wanted to tell him the truth. She wanted to say that it had been the American in the RAF uniform. Higgins would know where to find him, if he was still alive.

Joseph. Perhaps he was married now. If he learned of the birth of his daughter, it would ruin everything for him. It was bad enough that Denise's life was in tatters, there was no need to destroy another.

Higgins looked at the baby and smiled. "A beautiful child. Boy or girl?"

"A girl."

"What's her name?"

"Josephine," she answered.

"That's a lovely—"

He stopped and stared at her. It seemed to Denise that he was counting off the months in his mind, because a strange expression came over his face. Then he looked at the baby again and back at her, this time with a new awareness.

"Josephine. I was going to say that's a lovely name. And indeed it is."

He paused for a moment as he continued to watch her. "I'm arranging a supply drop for Claude. Is there anything I can get you? These are harsh conditions for a child. It wouldn't be difficult to include some things."

Denise could feel the blush coming to her cheeks. The way Higgins looked at her, she knew that he knew. The name told it all. Josephine. The timing. It had to be more than a coincidence and he knew it.

"Yes," she said. "There is something. A little cornstarch. The child has a rash."

"I'll see that you get it. Anything else?"

She hesitated for a moment. Then, she said, "Yes, there is one other thing."

"What's that?"

"The American. You know the one."

"Yes. What about him?" There was a look of triumph in his eyes.

"If the question ever comes up, I want you to tell him that I was killed with my cousin when the Germans discovered our group."

"Why in God's name would you want to do that?"

"Now it is you who is being coy, Mr. Higgins. I want you to do it because I have asked you to do it. You know the services I have performed. I have helped rescue your pilots. Jean-Luc probably rescued others after I left. You owe us something. This is not too much to ask, and I do ask."

"Denise, this is wrong. You should let him know. At the very least—"

She placed a hand over his mouth. "No. I have the child's birth certificate. There is no way you can change anything. Just do what I ask. Please!"

"It's not right."

"And what is right in these times? I'm not asking you to contact him. I'm only asking that if he ever asks after me, that you tell him I'm dead."

Higgins stood up and brushed off his pants. "He's already asked after you. Several times, in fact."

"He has?"

"Yes."

A little voice inside her warned against further questions, but she shrugged it off. "How is he?"

"He's fine, as far as I know. He's back in the States right now, doing liaison work. Some day the Americans may enter this war."

"You must not tell him," she said.

Higgins stared at her for a moment. "As you wish," he said, finally. "I'll take care of the cornstarch."

"Thank you."

Higgins turned and walked away.

Ten days later, the supply drop was made. Included with the explosives, detonators, and other necessities was a small carton containing cornstarch and a host of other baby things ranging from diapers to little rattle toys—and a coded note.

When decoded, it read, "To Denise: I'll keep your secret. Your friend is married. I'm sorry." The note was signed, "Higgins."

1

Claude Beauport and his group of Communist resistance fighters were a constant thorn in the side of the Third Reich. From their base of operations in Saint-Quentin, they ranged as far away as fifty kilometers, blowing up trains, bridges, and roads. Their efforts, along with those of the many other groups working throughout occupied France, were instrumental in making the average German soldier extremely nervous as he went about his duties.

A German soldier never knew when the road ahead might erupt in flame, or a tree crash down on his head, or a truck explode the moment he pushed the starter button.

Denise Dijon, now known as Denise Cousteau, became an increasingly important member of Claude's group. Anxious to please and wanting to put her own troubles aside, she threw herself into a frenzy of work. When she wasn't helping blow up bridges and trains, she was cleaning the quarters she shared with the others, hoping that in some way it would make the place more suitable for Josephine.

After two months in the underground sanctuary, Denise had become concerned that Josephine would suffer irreparable harm by being denied the benefits of sunshine. She approached Claude and told him of her feelings.

"She's just a child, Claude. You always have people in the house keeping watch and looking after the farm. Why not allow me and the child to stay in the house? I can even cook hot meals for you and the rest. It would be a better diet than the one you have now."

"It couldn't work," he said. "I am listed as the owner of the farm and three of my comrades as hired field hands. The Germans have that on their list. If you were seen, there would be a lot of explaining to do. It's too risky."

"But couldn't you say that I was a simple woman who had lost a husband and you took me in?"

"No. There would be too many questions. The Germans would want to see your papers. They might contact Henri. They are thorough, these Germans, especially since we have been causing them so many problems. No. We must keep things as they are. We have been lucky so far. Let's not try to change something when it's working. I can't afford to take the chance."

"You could make new papers. You've done it before. Please, for the sake of the baby."

The eyes she feared so much grew harsh. In a voice that was barely controlled, he said, "Your selfishness offends me. My decision to allow you to join us was an act of kindness. Do not make me regret it. We have more important concerns than the life of a small child that is of no use to anyone. I have given you my answer. Let me hear no more of this."

Denise went back to her bunk and lay down. He was a strange man, this Claude Beauport. More a machine than a man. A killing machine. He smiled only during or after the act of killing. Strange.

When he'd first brought her to this secret hiding place, he'd made her sign an oath that included a pledge of celibacy. There were three women besides herself in this hole in the ground. Neither Claude nor any of the others had made a sexual advance of any kind to any of the women. It seemed unnatural. Oaths aside, Denise wondered why, and decided to ask Marie Benoit, who had become her closest friend since her arrival. They were huddled in a corner of the room when Denise put the question to her.

Marie smiled wistfully and said, "When we formed this cell, Claude laid down certain rules. One of them forbade sexual activity. Did you not sign the oath?"

Denise nodded.

Marie smiled and said, "But you thought it was not serious. Is that not so?"

Again, Denise nodded.

"Claude must always be taken seriously," Marie said, a touch of melancholy in her voice. "Did you know that Jean-Pierre and Mathilde are husband and wife?"

Denise's jaw dropped in astonishment. "No! They are husband and wife?"

Marie nodded. "Yes. You see, Claude believes that any romantic encounters within our cell will create jealousies that will tear the cell apart. Think of it! There are thirteen men and four women. If four men are to be allowed to enjoy female companionship, what of the others? We are all facing the same perils. We four women would become whores for the men. Except we wouldn't get paid."

She laughed at her little joke and continued. "Claude believes it is one of the sacrifices we must make. Although he no longer belongs to the church, he regards us the same way as priests and nuns, who also give up their sexuality for a cause.

"To Claude, the cause is everything. No sacrifice is too great. To be frank, I agree with him. Anything else would be chaos and would tear us all apart. So, by living with the oath we took when we joined his group, we sacrifice, but at least one of the problems is eliminated."

Denise felt a shiver go down her spine. "Don't they ever get . . . feelings?"

Marie smiled and said, "I'm sure they do, but we're never alone here. They believe in the cause. For them, it is worth it."

"And you?"

"Me?"

"Yes. Don't you ever . . . yearn for a man?"

The look in her eyes was almost answer enough. "From time to time," she said. "But I shut it out. I have to. So must you."

Lowering her voice to a whisper, Marie said, "When I first saw Claude, I found him . . . frightening. He has a look about him that makes me uneasy. I've never been able to get over it. And yet there is something about him that attracts me. I can't explain it. If you think I'm crazy, you're probably right."

She leaned back against the wall and brought her knees up to her chin. "You see, Claude enjoys killing Germans. He enjoys it more than eating or breathing. The Germans killed his mother and father in front of his very eyes not long ago. At the time, Claude was not even involved in the movement, but twelve German soldiers had been killed by a land mine placed in the road. The Germans just went into houses and pulled out twelve people and shot them in the street as a warning. Claude's parents were living in town and he came upon the scene as they were lined up against the wall. He saw the bullets strike them down. There was nothing he could do.

"At that time, something snapped inside his head. He made discreet inquiries and finally was able to contact British Intelligence. Then he was invited to set up this group, and he did so. All of us are, like you, dedicated Communists who have lost relatives to the Germans."

She paused for a moment and then continued. "Killing is something we must do. It is, after all, a war. Besides, we all have revenge in our hearts for what the Germans have done. But Claude is different. For him, I think it is almost a sexual act. The moment he sees the life go out of the eyes of a German, he looks different, as though he were in a state of grace. He can never get enough."

Marie stood up. "But," she said, "he's a brilliant man. We've achieved much in a very short time. He keeps us fed, and safe, and away from each other's throats. He makes us like a machine as well. You have to admire that."

Denise looked at the woman carefully. "Yes," she said, slowly, "you must admire that."

As Marie moved away, Denise lay down beside the sleeping Josephine and gently stroked her hair. She gazed at the peaceful face and wondered what was to become of them. All of them. Especially Josephine. Someday, this war would end, as all wars ended. If the Germans were victorious, would that mean that this underground war would continue forever?

The Englishman Churchill had said that the British would never surrender. Claude Beauport was no less dedicated.

Was this the meaning of her life? Was this the reason for Josephine's conception? Was she to grow up and become another part of the machine? Killing and killing with no end?

As Denise looked at her sleeping child, blissfully unaware of the world around her, she realized she'd made a terrible mistake. Jean-Luc and the others had been right. She should have given up the child. This bleak life guaranteed that the child would never have a chance for any sort of happiness.

As it had on other occasions, another flicker of hope in the soul of Denise Dijon began to dim. Like a wick in an oil lamp. Shrinking smaller and smaller.

8

With America's entry into the war, Denise's lingering melancholy was temporarily replaced by the fresh breeze of new hope. Surely, she thought, with America on the side of the Allies, the Germans would be turned back in their attempt to plunge Europe into a new era of darkness.

Even the morose and ruthless Claude appeared affected, for he relented, rescinded his mandate that Denise and the child stay underground. He allowed Denise to take Josephine for long walks in the countryside by themselves, where they were both able to get some much-needed sunshine.

Claude exhibited a new sense of confidence. A system had been set up with lookouts posted at various strategic spots throughout Saint-Quentin, all equipped with small radio transmitters. Whenever the lookouts noticed suspicious activity, signals were transmitted that warned the rest of the group in plenty of time. For Denise, a bell was placed beside the house, to be rung if she was required to return.

For three and a half perilous years, Claude's resistance group operated undetected, widening their sphere of influence to include six other organized groups. Now, in 1944, Claude commanded a total of 357 men and women.

Besides creating havoc for the Germans, they had set up three different escape routes for the ever-increasing number of British and American airmen fortunate enough to parachute to earth within their grasp.

Josephine was growing fast and seemed to revel in all of the attention that came her way. Still, there were times when her eyes took on the haunted look of the refugees that still wandered through the countryside. Not yet three, she appeared older.

She had developed a habit of clinging tightly to her mother's leg whenever they were together. She needed constant reassurance for her fears. She seemed to be terrified that her mother might be killed.

Though Denise provided as much attention and affection as time would permit, it was clear that the child was not developing normally. This only served to intensify the guilt that weighed heavily on the heart of Denise Cousteau.

Rumors were growing stronger every day that soon there would be an invasion. As they had once before, German troops and panzer divisions began moving toward the coastal regions, particularly Calais.

Four years earlier, members of this same army had moved along these very roads, singing and laughing, fully anticipating a quick jump across the Channel. Now, the troops moved to prepare a defense for an invasion. This time, the soldiers were filled with concern and fear.

The Germans had suffered terribly on the eastern front. Now, they faced another onslaught from across the narrow waterway. Although they had been told they would push the Allies back into the Channel, they weren't so sure, and it showed in the way they marched.

On a late May night, Claude, his immediate group, and the leaders of the others under his command were visited by Ronald Higgins, who confirmed that the invasion was not far off. Instead of talking with Claude alone, as he usually did, he stood before the entire group and made what amounted to a speech.

"All of you," he said, "have worked with tremendous ability and diligence for the defeat of Germany. I simply can't tell you how important your role has been. Now, the long-awaited deliverance is almost at hand. As I speak to you, final plans are being drawn up by General Eisenhower and his staff that will result in the ultimate defeat of Hitler's Germany. The part you will play in these plans is no less important than the part you have played in the past. If anything, it is more important.

"The task that confronts us is formidable. During the next few weeks, your duties will be clearly defined. Each and every action will be coordinated as part of the master plan. It is important that you adhere to these missions exclusively. By that I mean there is to be no indiscriminate, independent action of any kind."

He stopped and looked each member of the group directly in the eye. "In the past," he continued, "we were quite content to see you killing Germans however you saw fit, but this effort requires that we use all of our resources to maximum effectiveness. We can't take a chance on losing a single one of you. You're an important part of this invasion plan and frankly, much of the success of the entire invasion will depend on how well you carry out your assigned tasks.

"General Eisenhower has asked me to personally offer his deepest appreciation for the sacrifices you have made. He needs your continued cooperation.

"As you know, all of our radio transmissions have been carried out in Morse. That will continue, but I have brought with me today another radio that will bring in the BBC. Each night, the BBC will broadcast additional messages by voice. The messages will be in French and coded.

"You will be advised what to listen for. When you hear it, you will know that the deliverance of France has begun."

A loud, long cheer went up.

"I will be sitting down with Claude and giving him the plans for the next few weeks," Higgins continued. "I wish all of you the very best of luck and hope that the next time we meet, it will be in the presence of Allied troops, here in Saint-Quentin."

Another cheer.

Claude and Higgins moved from the underground headquarters to the house for a private talk. Claude opened a bottle of wine, took two glasses from the small cabinet and placed the three items on the old, chipped table. He pulled up a chair and sat down, filling the glasses.

Higgins cleared his throat and said, "Claude, I meant what I said down there. There is to be no independent action."

Claude took a drink of wine and ran a hand across his lips. "My friend," he said calmly, "there will be none, but once France becomes ours again, we will reap the rewards that we have sacrificed so much to gain."

Higgins looked at the man cautiously, "Such as?"

"That is none of your concern."

"Look, I know that you and the others have some plans of your own, but you must understand that we can't have you fighting among yourselves. We aren't about to risk the necks of millions of Allied troops so that bloody civil war can begin inside France. You're going to have to work within the system."

Claude's eyes narrowed. "The system? What system is that? The one that allowed the Germans to destroy France in the space of six weeks? You call that a system?"

"Claude—"

"No. You listen to me. There must be a new system, one that restores France to the people. It is the people who have suffered during this horrible time. It is the people who have stayed and fought the Germans at every step. It is the people who will be responsible for the liberation of France from the Germans. It is the people who must now step forward and take what is rightfully theirs."

Higgins felt very uncomfortable. He needed this man and his group of resistance fighters. He needed all of them badly, but there had already been discussions regarding the future of France after the war. The Communists were not about to be handed the country on a silver platter. Yet that was really what they'd been fighting for. To completely discourage them now ...

"There are other resistance groups," Higgins said, "who have also fought long and hard, and they are not Communist. Are they to be denied their rightful place in the government?"

"Of course not, but there is no place for those who have collaborated with the Germans. There is no place for those who have run away. There is only a place for those who have stayed and fought. Vichy must be eliminated and all of the scum who cooperated with them. The leaders of France are here, now, ready to take their place. Representatives of the people. The Allies must understand that. We will not be denied. We have earned our place and we intend to take it."

"Just what do you plan to do?"

"As I have said, my friend, that is not your concern."

"The hell it isn't! If you aren't going to work with us in the future, then we might as well part company right now. This country will be in chaos. It will need leaders, no question, but leaders who are willing to work with us to ensure that the people are taken care of properly. Food, clothing, shelter . . . all of it. There will be tremendous logistical problems. We're counting on you to help. If your plan is to seize control of certain areas, you'll be left outside. You'll receive no support from us whatsoever."

"This is our reward?"

"No! Your reward will come once a proper system of government has been set up. You'll be included. That's a promise. But, we can't simply step aside and let you take over. You're going to have to share power with others."

"So, Frenchmen will be ruled by the British and the Americans instead of the Germans. Is that it?"

"Not at all. For the immediate future, there will be some control exerted by the Allies, but only until the war is at an end. Then, elections will take place and you'll have the same opportunities as everyone else.

"I'm sure that the average Frenchman will be well aware of the contributions made by your organizations, as well as your comrades on the eastern front."

Claude took another sip of wine and leaned back in the chair. "Ah . . . elections," he said. "Tell me, Mr. Higgins, how will they know who to vote for? Are you going to tell them? Where will the British and American money be going? Will it go to Claude Beauport and the others who have lived like animals for five years, or will it go to the rich bureaucrats who got us into this mess in the first place? Answer me that!"

Higgins glared at the Frenchman and then cleared

his throat. "I told you you'll be included. That's a promise."

Claude stood up and finished his wine. "Of course. And as an officer and a gentleman, you are to be trusted, no?"

"Don't you think you can trust me, Claude? After all of this time?"

Claude turned and started to walk toward the door. Over his shoulder, he said, "I trust you, Mr. Higgins. The British and the Americans? That is another matter. We shall see."

Then he walked out of the house.

For the next few weeks, the pace of activity slowed. They were waiting for that special moment when they, and hundreds of other groups near the Channel, would spring into action.

The entire coastal area was being pounded day and night by British and American bombers, softening up the area ahead of the actual invasion, some of the sorties reaching as far south as Saint-Quentin.

Then, on the night of June 5, the group gathered around the radio, listening to the BBC broadcast, as they had done for weeks. The messages were meaningless to the casual listener, each one specifically designed for a specific group.

Claude, almost asleep, snapped upright when he heard the words, "La femme a plus de pommes que de poires." The woman has more apples than pears. A silly little phrase, their special code. The invasion was on. Their mission, the most important one in their history, was to commence immediately.

Claude turned to the group and said, "This is it. We go to Abbeville for a special job. All of us. Denise, we need you because you know the area personally. You can leave the child with Marie."

Denise nodded, hugged Josephine, then handed

the child over to Marie. She felt her heart pounding.
For some reason, she was overcome with a feeling
unlike any she'd ever had, a feeling magnified by the
odd look in Josephine's eyes—a look of resignation.

Quickly, Denise opened her suitcase and extracted
the diary. To Marie, she said, "If I should not return,
make sure that Josephine receives this diary. I know
she can't read yet, but some day she will. It is the
only thing I have of any value."

Marie took the diary and grabbed Denise's hand.
"Don't be afraid," she said. "You've been doing this
for years. Nothing will happen now, not at this late
date."

"Promise me you'll do as I ask."

"Yes, of course. But . . ."

Denise pulled away and raced up the ladder to
catch up with the others.

The mission was to lay a new type of land mine
along two of the main roadways that ran parallel to
the coast. The land mines had been previously
dropped by parachute and secreted in, of all places,
the ruins of the former farmhouse of Denise Dijon.
A total of eight hundred mines had been supplied,
and were to be placed on the roads on either side of
Abbeville. They were to remain in position, unex-
ploded, until the signal was given. Then, they would
be activated by a signal transmitted by a radio supplied with the mines.

By the time the group reached the farmhouse in a
convoy of battered vehicles, avoiding German posi-
tions along the way, it was almost daybreak. Two
other groups had already come and gone, taking their
deadly cargo with them.

As Claude's group loaded the remaining 250 mines
into the vehicles, they could hear the steady rumble
of bombs being dropped all over the coastal regions
by British and American bombers. It was a cloudy,
rainy night and Denise wondered how they could

possibly see what they were bombing.

The group split into two sections. Claude took half the team and Denise the other. She knew exactly where the mines were to be placed and directed the driver through the farmlands to the point without incident, which was a minor miracle in itself. The weight of the mines plus the passengers, now forced to stand on the outside of the cars, was enough to flatten the springs completely. Each bump was more like a small earthquake. They fully expected the entire convoy to blow up at any minute.

They stopped beside the roadway and began taking the mines out of the three cars and hauling them, one by one, into position. Quickly they dug holes in the roadway, placed the mines, and covered the holes, leaving only a short, thin piece of wire exposed. The wire would act as an antenna. Their movements were fluid, honed over the years to a practiced precision.

Denise carried with her a small radio receiver. Lookouts with walkie-talkies had been placed two hundred meters on either side of their position. They had placed over sixty of the mines when the radio squawked, "German truck convoy heading east."

Denise whistled and motioned her people to take cover. Quickly, they scooted off the road and hid in the ditches on either side of it, machine guns at the ready, waiting for the truck convoy to pass.

She could hear the trucks now as they approached at high speed. There were several of them, rushing to some unknown destination.

She crouched down as the first truck came into view, its headlights covered with tape so only a slit of light could be seen. Then, a tremendous explosion as one of the mines exploded prematurely. The truck flew into the air, rolled over and crashed in flames.

Instantly, the other trucks screeched to a halt. The soldiers leapt into action, fanning out into the fields, quickly surrounding Denise's position. She could scarcely believe it. A faulty mine had botched the mission. There'd been no time to flee, no place to hide.

The countryside was alive with German soldiers. Denise clutched the machine gun tightly and listened to her heart pound as the soldiers came closer and closer. She heard a machine gun open up on the other side of the road and the answering fire of ten German machine guns. In front of her were at least fifteen German soldiers, closing rapidly.

She lifted the gun to her waist and squeezed the trigger, letting a spray of bullets find their mark. Instantly, the ground around her seemed to come alive as bullets from the German guns kicked up little piles of dirt and grass. She dove to the ground and flattened herself against the earth.

She could hear them coming closer, cursing in German, barking orders. She lifted her head. They were almost on top of her. She sat up and fired off a short burst, then ducked as the answering fire grew more intense.

She could hear the whine of the slugs as they ripped through the air on either side of her. And then, her body was filled with pain as some of the German bullets smashed into it, the impact forcing her onto her back. The machine gun slipped from her hand.

Her thoughts turned to the little child she'd left behind.

Claude Beauport and his group had met a better fate. They'd destroyed both roads on the west side of Abbeville, then returned to the burned-out remains of the Dijon farm. The invasion was now in full swing and any attempt to make it back to Saint-Quentin under these conditions would be foolhardy.

They parked the cars under some trees and covered them with brush. Then the six men and two women went down into the ruins of the basement and covered themselves with broken and burned bits and pieces of the house. Their mission had gone off like clockwork.

The noise of exploding bombs continued. Though they didn't know it at the time, the actual invasion was taking place in Normandy, not Calais as everyone had expected. The British and Americans continued to pound the Calais area, trying to keep the Germans guessing. At this moment, the first Allied troops were wading ashore on the target beaches farther to the southwest.

Claude looked at his watch. Denise and her group were overdue. Considerably overdue. The others in the group looked at Claude and then each other, but no one said a word. Finally, Claude got up and said, "Something must have happened. I will go and see."

He set off on foot to the spot where Denise's arm of his group was to have positioned the mines, some five kilometers from the farm. It took him a good hour to reach the spot. When he did so, he was aghast.

The road was unscathed, except for a large crater that had been quickly repaired. No Germans were in sight, but the bodies of his people were lying by the road, stripped of their clothes, left to rot or be eaten by wild animals. The roadway was pocked with marks that indicated the mines had been discovered and dug up. By the side of the road, a German truck lay on its side, burned and bent.

It was clear what had happened. Somehow, they had mistakenly blown up one of the trucks. Probably one of the mines had been activated by accident. It had happened before. Claude had complained bitterly on many occasions about the terrible equipment being provided.

They were all there. Denise, Jean-Pierre and his wife, the others—all dead. Even the lookouts on either side had been discovered. They too had been stripped and lynched from the very trees they'd used to hide. Now, their lifeless bodies hung swinging in the wind.

There was no time to do anything. He would have liked to bury the bodies, but that would be a sentimental waste of time and needless risk. He headed back to the farm.

Later that day, back in Saint-Quentin, Claude told Marie, in whispered tones, what had happened. Marie turned and looked at the sleeping Josephine and began to weep. Through her tears, she said, "She knew, Claude. Before she left, she knew she wasn't coming back. Who will take the child?"

Claude looked at her with a strange expression in his eyes. "The child belongs to me. For the moment, you will look after her, but the child belongs to me."

Marie said nothing. Once again, she looked at the child, almost three and beautiful beyond description. What, she wondered, did Claude want with a three-year-old child?

JOSEPHINE: THE SEEDS OF HATE

Part Three

9

In August of 1944, American, Canadian, and British troops poured through the town of Saint-Quentin, the Allied offensive forcing the German troops into ferocious and truculent retreat.

For the French, it was a period of unequivocal chaos, their supreme joy tempered by the lingering fear that it all might be just a fantasy, that the fortunes of war would see the Germans return, stronger than ever, their mission one of violent retribution.

The change created a vacuum in civil leadership, which surrendered control of town to the military. Claude Beauport saw the moment as an opportunity to seize political control. For three days, he and his group, now roaming freely throughout the area, rounded up German collaborators, summarily executing the most despised on the spot. His capricious form of justice was being duplicated all over northern

France, as embittered Frenchmen and women sought revenge for the humiliation and deprivation suffered at the hands of the hated Germans.

Some women, those who had been accused of consorting with German soldiers during the occupation, were brought to the center of the town and forced to sit on platforms high enough for everyone to see. Their clothes were stripped from their bodies, their heads shaved, and swastikas painted on their foreheads. They were paraded through the town, screamed at, spat at, and urinated on by a people engaged in an orgy of retribution.

For those hapless German soldiers left behind, there was another gauntlet to run. Men and women held sticks or rakes or shovels, and brought them crashing down on the heads and shoulders of the terrified prisoners as they were dragged screaming to the wall. Sometimes, the collaborators and German soldiers would endure hours of abuse until a volley of shots mercifully ended their lives.

Claude proclaimed himself mayor of the town. He and his men occupied city hall—for all of one day.

The group was visited by an American colonel named Scott who stormed into Claude's office with twelve armed American soldiers and ordered Claude to vacate the premises forthwith.

Claude stood up and stared at the man in total disbelief.

"Colonel," he said, "I am the mayor of this town. It is you who must vacate the premises."

Colonel Scott would have none of it. "Look, Beaufort, or whatever the hell your name is, this town is under military control. I happen to be in charge of this sector and I haven't got time to argue with some asshole farmer. Now, get your ass the hell out of here before I throw it out."

Claude cursed in French. "You don't understand, Colonel. I am the leader of the resistance in this entire area. I have been working for British Intelligence for years. Without us, you would not be here today. I am French. Saint-Quentin is French. You are American. I am the one who can best put this town on its feet again. You have no rights here."

"Look, I don't give a tinker's damn who the hell you worked for. If you've got a beef, talk to British Intelligence. My orders are to take control of this town and arrange for food and medical supplies, and I'm damn well going to carry out my orders. From what I've seen, you're killing a lot of people without proper legal authorization, and that has to stop. I want you and your people to lay down your weapons and go back to whatever the hell you were doing before the war."

He took off his helmet and lit a cigar. Then he continued, the anger in his voice subsiding somewhat. "Look, pal," he said, "I'm sure you are who you say you are, and that's fine. But what you've got here is anarchy, not government. Right now, I'm in charge and that's the way it has to be. You have no authority here. For you, this war is over. Now, for the last time, get the hell out of this building."

"You can't do this," Claude protested. "I have—"

The colonel, his patience exhausted, turned to the soldiers and said, "Get this nut out of my sight."

The soldiers moved toward Claude, grabbed his arms and took him out into the street, a street filled with men who had been under the command of Claude Beauport for years. Now, disarmed by the American troops, they stood around, baffled and angry. They grumbled for a while, then formed a circle to listen to the words of their leader.

"We will meet at the farm tonight," Claude ordered. "Seven o'clock."

Claude returned to the farm, bewildered and upset. With hardly a word to Marie, who was now keeping house for him, he pulled out the radio and tried to contact British Intelligence. Time after time, he tapped out his code signal on the key, but there was no response. Mindful of the fact that he was broadcasting outside of his normal time period, he finally switched off the radio and poured himself some wine, then stared out the window.

"What is it, Claude?" asked Marie. "You seem so upset."

"The Americans. They've disarmed us. I've been told to stay away from city hall and to have nothing to do in this town. It's incredible!"

He turned around and faced her, his face contorted with frustration. "For years, we have worked to lay the groundwork for this day, and now it is like we are nothing. They even ordered us to stop killing collaborators. For four years, it was just fine, but today it is no longer allowed. For four years we risked our lives and now we are nonpersons."

He glared at Marie, as though it was somehow her fault. "We have been used. Our lives meant nothing to them. We were simply another weapon to be used against the Germans and then discarded. My worst fears have been fulfilled!"

Josephine wandered into the room from the kitchen and ran toward Claude. "Uncle Claude," she said. "The Germans are gone from the town. When is mama coming home?"

Claude looked down at the child and shook his head. "I told you, chérie, she has gone on a long trip. She won't be back for some time. I'll let you know."

The beautiful face of the child fell and the smile turned into a pout. "It's been so long."

Claude stroked her hair and said, "I know. She was on a very dangerous mission. She'll be back soon. Now, go to the kitchen. I have to talk to your aunt."

Josephine turned and shuffled back to the kitchen.

Marie wrung the towel in her hands and said, in a low voice, "You really can't do this, Claude. You must tell her soon."

He glared at her. "I'll tell her at the proper time. Right now, there are more important things. I have a meeting tonight. Prepare some food. There should be about twenty or thirty."

"What are you going to do?"

"I don't know. We'll decide tonight."

Marie went back to the kitchen. Josephine was sitting at the table, looking forlorn. Marie sat down beside her. It was so strange, she thought. Here they were, a man, a woman, and a child, living in the same house, but not related in any way. Claude was a bachelor and Marie had never married. Though she'd been in love with Claude for years, Marie had never made her feelings known to him in any overt way, hoping instead that he would understand how she felt from the way she looked at him or the tone of her voice.

Now, with the Germans gone and their subterranean hiding place vacated forever, she saw no need for the continued oath of celibacy. Yet for Claude, nothing had changed, and he continued to ignore whatever subtle signals she sent in his direction.

What was to become of them now? she wondered. Would it always be like this? The Americans were running the town, but that wouldn't last. In due time, they would turn it over to the French. It was what Claude and all of them had fought for—a chance to be in the driver's seat for a change.

What would become of Josephine? She clung only to her doll. Kisses went unreturned. Soft caresses on her forehead made no impression. It was as if the child was sleepwalking through life.

That night, Claude met with his men. Barely under way, the meeting was interrupted by the appearance of Ronald Higgins. For the first time, the Englishman was dressed in the uniform of a British Army colonel. He was accompanied by six soldiers who brought with them two cases of champagne. Higgins was all smiles.

"You've done it, Claude!" he said, exuberantly. "France has been liberated!"

The soldiers opened the cases of champagne and passed the bottles among the group. Claude was not impressed.

"Higgins! What is to become of us?"

"Whatever you want to happen. France is now free. You've achieved what you were fighting for. The Germans are back in Germany and soon, they will lose that as well."

"That's all well and good. But you know what I mean."

"General Charles de Gaulle, the leader of all the resistance organizations, your own leader, has been installed as the head of the provisional government in Paris. He has a list of all resistance leaders. Your name is on that list. All you have to do is contact the government, identify yourself, and you'll be assigned your tasks for the future."

"De Gaulle?"

"Yes. Believe me, the general feels that the leaders of the resistance are to be among the leaders of the country."

"But we're Communists."

"So what? You're Frenchmen first and Communists second. Isn't that true?"

"Yes."

"Then that's all that counts."

Claude stared at Higgins for a moment. Then, his face broke into a grin. He held the champagne aloft and shouted, *"Vive la France!"*

The group answered in kind.

"Vive de Gaulle!"

Again, they answered the toast.

Claude went to Paris the very next day. He never did get to meet with General de Gaulle, but he did manage to arrange a meeting with one of the general's lesser lights, a major named Chapelle. Major Chapelle looked at the file and nodded approvingly at the man standing in front of his desk with fire in his eyes.

"Ah, yes. Here it is. Claude Beauport. You've served your country well, Beauport. We are eternally grateful."

Some of the anger went out of Claude's eyes. "I wish you would tell that to the Americans," he said.

The major grinned. "Yes, I know what you mean. At the moment, they are flushed with the excitement of victory. You'd think they were the only ones in the war. Do not be concerned. We have plans for you."

"What plans?"

The major lit a cigarette and leaned back in his chair. "Well," he said, "General de Gaulle has set up tribunals to deal with the collaborators and manage the towns. Later, once the war is over, elections will be held and you will be invited to run for office. In the meantime, you will serve on a tribunal with six other men, four of them with the army and two from the civilian ranks. The army people are already on their way to Saint-Quentin. The two civilians are a man named Robitail, a lawyer, and another named Pouliot, a doctor. Both are from Saint-Quentin. You know them?"

Claude shook his head. "No. The doctor I have heard of, but we never met. Neither of these men was involved in the resistance. What are they doing on the tribunal?"

The major rubbed his chin and said, "General de Gaulle feels that the tribunals should be made up of men from all walks of life. You represent the resistance. The other two represent those noncombatants in the town. Of course, for a while, the army is in charge of things."

"The army will have four votes on the tribunal and we will have three. This is nothing but a charade!"

"No. You are wrong. If we were not going to involve you in the process, we would not bother to have tribunals at all. As soon as possible, the army will withdraw their people completely, but as long as we are still at war, they must be in control. Besides, there has been too much indiscriminate killing. I feel as you do, that there is no place for collaborators in the future of France, but we cannot be made to look like bloodthirsty savages in the eyes of the world. That makes us no better than the Germans. There must be some level of justice to these affairs."

Claude Beauport looked at the major and shook his head. "I think, Major, that I can see what is really happening here. My usefulness is at an end, now that France is free. My men and I risked their lives for over four years to see this day. But General de Gaulle, who watched the war from the relative safety of England, has been installed by the British and the Americans to do their bidding.

"You can get someone else for this so-called tribunal. Nothing will change. France will go back to sleep, just as it was before the Germans. The workers will do the work and the rich will enjoy the fruits of their sweat. I won't be a party to this."

"I think you should reconsider, Beauport. Give it a chance. France has been free of the Germans for a matter of days. It will take time to sort things out."

Claude spat on the floor. "It's already been sorted out," he said. Then he turned on his heel and left.

When he returned to Saint-Quentin, Claude Beauport had a final meeting with his people and told them what had happened in Paris. The men and women who had worked so hard for so many years sensed in Claude a defeated man. A man no longer willing to fight for what he believed in. No longer wanting to become embroiled in the battle for political power.

They perceived him as a man who had lost his will. Even his soul. Quietly, without humiliating the man, they talked among themselves and decided that Claude had outlived his usefulness to the party in general and the cell in particular.

They appointed another man as their leader and wished Claude well in his return to a more sedate life.

He raised no protest.

10

By the summer of 1948, bitterness and hate had transformed Claude Beauport from a cunning and vengeful soldier to a withdrawn, brooding, and neurotic cyborg.

During the war, he was able to vent his anger through the savage killing of German soldiers. Now, in peace, there was no such outlet for his malice, a hatred that included the British, the Americans, and even his own people. He was a simple farmer, performing the same mindless drudgery as before and during the war, raising cows and selling the milk to the dairy in Saint-Quentin. The dangerous and exciting life of a resistance fighter was over, and still he missed its passion. It was the only time in his life when he'd felt truly alive.

To Marie and Josephine, he offered no smiles or conversation. When he did speak, it was simply a repeat performance, another vitriolic tirade against those who'd failed to keep their promises, real and perceived. The rest of the time, he ate, worked, and slept in silence, the expression on his face as fixed as that on a marble statue.

Marie had continued to live and work on the farm, but her motivation had changed. Before, she'd stayed close to Claude in the hope he would acknowledge the affection she once felt for him. It had never happened, and her unrequited love had slowly dwindled to nothing. Then, irrevocably, the emotional scale had tipped in the opposite direction. Now she loathed him with a passion almost as intense as her previous illogical love for him. Her interests were focused on Josephine, a child of seven, who was clearly troubled.

When the war in Europe finally and mercifully ended, Marie told Josephine about the death of her mother. Josephine cried for two straight days, seemingly inconsolable. Then, like a gritty little soldier, she unaccountably stopped her wailing, threw her shoulders back, wiped away the tears, and attacked her chores with renewed vigor.

Marie marked that terrible moment as the turning point. In the three years since, the child had emulated Claude, smiling only once, and that when a loose wooden beam in the barn came loose and banged Claude on the head, rendering him momentarily unconscious. Aside from that one incident, Josephine was quiet, obedient, and chillingly remote.

For Marie, life had become empty and intolerable. More importantly, she feared for Josephine. It wasn't normal for a child of seven to be so unresponsive, so joyless, so lacking in youthful exuberance. Living in the shadow of man filled with hate was slowly killing them both. Something had to be done, and soon.

So Marie wrote to her cousin Yvette, who lived in Lille with her husband and four children. Marie explained the situation, and begged for help. In three weeks, Yvette wrote back, telling Marie that she and Josephine were welcome to come to live with them whenever she wanted to.

The day the letter arrived, Marie made her decision. After dinner, she sent Josephine off to milk the cows, then sat down with a cup of tea in her hands, and looked deeply into Claude's eyes.

"Claude," she said, "I must talk to you."

"What is it?"

Marie toyed with her teacup and began the speech she had practiced for many days. "Claude," she said, "I'll soon be thirty-five. I'm almost past the child-bearing time. I've never been married and it isn't because I haven't wanted to. In fact, for some time, I hoped that you and I—"

"What silliness is this? Married. I have no intention of getting married."

"I know that. But . . . haven't you seen the love that I feel for you?"

"Love? Are you mad? There is no place for love in my life. Love is for silly children who have nothing better to do with their lives. It is not for people who have to work to keep the bread on the table. It is not love you feel, but gratitude for the fact that I have taken care of you all these years. Speak to me no more of this."

Marie cleared her throat and said, "Claude, I'm trying to tell you that I'm leaving. I want to try and find a husband, get married, have children, all of those things that I—"

Claude's face twisted into a mask of anger. "Leave?" he screamed. "You want to leave?"

"Yes."

"You're like the rest. You don't need Claude anymore. His usefulness has come to an end. Because he doesn't act like an animal and mount you whenever the spirit moves him, he is to be discarded like a worn coat. You're all the same. All of you."

"It's not that."

"No? Don't you think I know what goes on in the minds of the women in the town? They gather and talk and all they ever think about is filth!"

"Claude—"

"Shut up. I don't need you anymore. The child is old enough now. She can cook and clean and tend to the chores. You want to leave? Then leave!"

"I'm taking Josephine with me."

It was the first time he'd smiled since the war. "Josephine stays here. She belongs to me."

"No, she doesn't. You have no claim to her. She is an orphan! Denise asked that I take care of the child, not you. It was her last word."

"Denise is dead. She speaks no more. The child is mine." His voice was filled with glee. "I arranged for it. That asinine tribunal de Gaulle set up so many years ago. At least they were good for something!"

Marie gasped. "You couldn't have!"

Claude slammed a hand on the table. "You can check it yourself. The records are there for all to see. You say you want to leave? You do it now. This very minute. Go! The girl stays here with me. I am her legal guardian."

"I won't leave without her!"

"Yes, you will," he said, as he grabbed her by the arm and pulled her toward the door. He grabbed the handle, opened the door and threw Marie out into the sunshine. Then he yelled, "Don't move. I'll get your things."

Josephine, having heard the commotion, came running out of the barn, and stood by the fallen Marie. The child's face was a study in coldness.

"Get back to your duties," Claude snapped.

Josephine stood her ground. Claude whirled and went into Marie's bedroom, gathered up some of her things in his arms, threw them into a suitcase, and sent it flying out the door. Marie was sitting on the ground with her arms around the child, trying to explain what was happening.

Claude stomped down the front steps, ripped Josephine from Marie's arms, and slapped the child across the face. Then, he dragged her up the steps and threw her inside the house.

Marie uttered a scream and ran toward the house. Claude met her on the steps and punched her hard in the face, sending her flying to the ground. He moved quickly, bending over so that his face was directly above Marie's. "If you come back here," he said, his eyes no more than slits, "I'll kill you. Do you understand that? You stay away from here. You stay away from the child. I'll warn you no more."

He stood up, spat on the ground and went inside.

Marie, her heart pounding with fear and anger, her jaw screaming with pain, stood up, brushed herself off, picked up the suitcase, and started running toward the road. It was six miles to the town. She had to get help from someone. Perhaps the gendarmes. Anyone. She couldn't leave the child in the hands of such a madman.

The police captain looked at the woman sitting in the chair, her clothes dirty and torn, her hair a tousled mess, her eyes red from crying, and shook his head.

"Madame," he said, "I have told you, there is nothing I can do. There is nothing anyone can do. The girl was declared a refugee in 1944 and the proper papers were obtained by Claude Beauport. He's a man with a good record and the assignment was approved by the monseigneur himself. Yours is the first complaint we've had and frankly, it is not enough."

Marie wrung her hands in her lap. "But he beats her," she said, her voice filled with anguish.

The policeman shrugged and stretched his arms

out, the palms facing upward, an expression of helplessness. "So you say, but you provide no evidence. Your statement claims that he provides for the child, sees that she is at school, and, in your own words, has never caused you trouble.

"You lived there of your own free will and the man let you leave. Of course, he was angry and that may explain why he lost his temper, but with what you have told me, there is nothing indicated to cause me to investigate further."

He let his hands fall to the desk and a smile reached his lips. "Is it not more a case of a woman who had hoped to become a wife being disappointed and perhaps, just a little vindictive?"

Marie was horrified. "You don't understand," she said, her voice almost choking. "Something has happened to that man. He's become insane."

The captain stood up and placed a hand on her arm. "I'm afraid it is you who does not understand, Madame. There is nothing I can do. No crime has been committed. Now, I have other matters to attend to. You'll have to leave."

It was incredible. He'd listened to her story with studied patience, heard her explain how somber Josephine had become, let her pour her heart out about the embittered and obdurate Claude, to no avail. The papers were in order, and that was all that mattered.

Marie left the police department and walked dejectedly to the train station. There were a thousand thoughts swimming through her head as she waited for the train that would take her to her cousin's place just outside Lille. She shuddered as she thought about the little seven-year-old living alone in the house with a crazy man.

She opened her suitcase to see if Claude had left her with a sweater she could use to cover her filthy dress on the train ride. As she rummaged through the mess, her hand fell upon a book. She recognized it immediately. It was Denise's diary, a journal Marie had promised to keep safe for Josephine.

She sighed and put the diary back in the suitcase. Now was not the time, but there would come a day when Josephine would have it in her hands, able to read everything that had been written there. In the meantime, there were more important concerns. She had to find a way to help the child.

Claude Beauport sat Josephine down in a chair, patting the top of her head.

"That's better," he said.

The child sat rigidly at the table, fighting back the tears that had just recently stopped flowing.

"Marie doesn't like us anymore," he said. "I will take good care of you. I am your legal guardian now. Do you know what that means?"

"No."

"It means that I am like a father. Your father is dead, but what does it matter? You never knew him."

Josephine looked at him with her big, dark eyes and said, "Did you know my father?"

Claude shook his head.

"His name was Cousteau," she said. "How do you know that he is dead?"

Claude smiled at the child. "Your father's name was not Cousteau. That name was given to you when your mother gave birth to you during the war, at a time when the Germans were trying to kill us all. I know your real father is dead because your mother told me so, before she herself was killed."

Slowly, the tears started to come again. Claude took the child and held her close to him. "Don't cry. Many of us are alone. I have no parents, just like you, but we have each other you and I. We will make our own family."

"Why did Marie go away?"

"I told you. Because she doesn't like us anymore. You're too young to understand. There will come a time when I will explain it to you, but for now, I want you to forget about Marie. You go finish your chores. Then, we will eat."

Reluctantly, Josephine slipped down from the chair and went outside to do her chores. Claude watched her as she walked to the barn, and a smile came to his lips.

Yes, he thought, you will learn soon enough the ways of women who have only sex on their mind, harlots who throw their bodies at men, seeking only the pleasures of the flesh. That will never happen to you, little one. I will protect you from those evil thoughts. I will teach you what you must know.

Soon.

Leo Laurier had lost an arm in the war. He was a quiet man, subject to periods of depression, but the moods usually passed quickly. At other times, he was placid and industrious, refusing to allow his handicap to hinder him as he worked his farm, one much like Claude's.

His wife Yvette was a bubbling, corpulent woman, filled with energy and ideas. While not close to Marie Benoit, Yvette had maintained regular contact with her cousin over the years, feeling it important to maintain familial connections, however remote. When Marie had written and told her of her problems, along with making a plea that she and the child be allowed to come to work and live with them, Yvette had talked it over with Leo. At first, he had rebelled at the thought, but Yvette insisted.

"You keep talking about hiring some help," she said. "Well, Marie has experience, and she can do the work of any man. She's been doing it ever since the war. This isn't charity."

"Another child in the house? We're already overrun."

"So? You love the children. Four or five, what's the difference? You'll never notice. You always have your big nose buried in your books. The children walk on your head and you never feel a thing."

He smiled.

"Besides," Yvette continued, "Marie fought with the resistance all through the war. She's trying to raise the child of a woman who died in battle. Can you really turn your back on them?"

Leo relented. Yvette wrote Marie, hoping the letter would at least provide some comfort. She doubted her cousin would ever really leave the man. She'd met him once, an ugly man, with eyes like Rasputin's, and a personality not unlike that of Guetainne, the undertaker.

When Marie Benoit arrived in Lille without the child, both her hosts were astonished, not only at the fact that she'd left the child behind, but at how quickly events had transpired. When Marie described what had happened, Yvette was even more shocked.

"I don't know what to do," Marie exclaimed.

Yvette felt genuine compassion for this poor woman, so distraught and unhappy. She put her arm around Marie and said, "Look, you need to rest and not think about this for a while. After a few days, we'll talk about it and see what we can do."

"There's nothing you can do," Leo said. "She's already been to the police and they've said as much. The man has the child and until there is evidence that she has been mistreated, no one will lift a finger. Besides, she's not Marie's child in the first place. She's simply a waif orphaned in the war like thousands of others. I think Marie had better get used to the idea that the child is gone."

Yvette shot her husband a sharp look. "Let Marie get some rest. We'll talk about it later."

Leo looked away.

It was two days before they spoke about it again. This time, Yvette had a look of anguish on her face as she sat down beside Marie and spoke to her.

"I've talked to a lawyer I know in Lille, as well as the monseigneur. They both agree with Leo. They say that nothing can be done. The monseigneur suggested that you come and talk to him. He feels that you need some comfort. He's a fine man, Father Hebert. You'll like him. If you want, we could go in tomorrow."

"Is there nothing that can be done? Are you sure?"

Yvette looked at the floor and shook her head. "The problem is that Claude has done all the legal things. Unless you could get someone to testify to the fact that he is truly crazy, there is nothing one could say that would influence a court. You know how they are, the judges. They don't listen much to women in the first place.

"You have no family ties to the girl, or even the man, for that matter. If Claude were your husband, it would be still be difficult, since it was you who left, but he's not. He's nothing to you, nor is the child. From what you've said, the man keeps to himself so much that a witness would be hard to find. And even if you found one, what would they say?"

Yvette got up and moved toward the hand pump beside the sink. "Do you want some tea?"

Marie shook her head. Yvette pumped the well water into a pail and then poured some of the fresh water into a brass kettle. As she pulled down a cup from the cupboard, she said, "I think you'd be better off doing what Leo suggested, forgetting about this girl. She'll just cause much pain for you."

"I can't do that. I can't simply abandon the girl. Especially not with that man. I could never live with myself."

"Marie, I know this is difficult, but you're going to have to face the reality of the situation sooner or later. There's just nothing you can do."

Marie looked at her cousin with eyes that brimmed with tears. She understood the reality of the situation only too well. Facing it was another matter.

Less than a week after Marie's departure, Claude Beauport sexually assaulted his seven-year-old charge for the first time. He told the frightened and confused child several things. The first was that he was showing her what she must never do, that he was teaching her things on orders from God. The second, that she must never tell anyone about it, or God would kill her. Third, he told her that Marie Benoit was an agent of the devil, and to think of her was a mortal sin.

Finally, he told Josephine that her mother and father had died in the war because God knew of their iniquity. They hadn't died at the hands of the enemy, but had been crushed by the hand of God himself. He explained that God had made Claude her protector. Her only protector. The only person in the world who cared about her. To disobey would mean instant death, not from Claude, but from God Himself.

For the next month, he repeated the assault—and the inculcation—every night. And when the last flicker of doubt finally disappeared from the child's eyes, he seemed strangely at peace.

For the next few months, Marie Benoit worked on the farm and tried to put Josephine out of her mind, but it was impossible. She'd seen him strike the child only once, but there was something about Claude's demeanor that terrified her. Her imagination conjured up many images of what might happen to the girl, some of which made her physically ill. To write, she knew, would be pointless, as Claude would destroy any letter sent.

When summer waned and autumn arrived, Marie knew Josephine would be returning to school. As her guardian, Claude would not want to take a chance on trouble by keeping her out. Marie decided to take the train to Saint-Quentin and visit the child at school, to see how things were going.

The school was an old stone building about three blocks from the train station, run by the church, like most of the schools in the area. After being shown to the office of the headmistress, Marie told one of the assistants that she was a friend of Josephine Cousteau and wished to see her for a moment.

"Only family is allowed to see our students. I'm sorry."

"I knew her mother during the war. We were in the resistance together. Her mother was killed."

"Yes?"

"Yes, well, I promised her mother I would always look in on the child."

"I see. I'm sorry. You're not family, you see?"

"She has no family!"

"She has a guardian."

"Listen to me, please. After the war, I lived with Claude and Josephine. I was like her mother."

The nun's eyebrows arched.

"Really."

"We weren't lovers, just two people working on a farm together."

"Go on."

"Well, a few months ago, I was forced to leave. You see, Claude Beauport may have legally adopted the girl and become her guardian, but he's no father in any sense of the word. He's a very bitter man. The war affected him terribly. I think he expected to become a politician after the war. When the opportunity was denied him, he became hostile and unfeeling. He's been that way for years. It's bad for the child."

"So you left?"

"I had to. He forced me to go. I haven't seen Josephine since. My heart aches just to catch a glimpse of her. If I could talk to her for a moment, just to know she was all right, it would be so helpful."

The nun allowed a small smile to reach her lips. She bent her arm, beckoning Marie to follow, and together they walked down the hall to the room where Josephine had been assigned. After a short talk with the teacher, the sister brought Josephine out into the hallway to see Marie.

It was the worst day of Marie's life.

Josephine stood rigidly and stared at Marie with hatred in her eyes.

Marie held out her arms to the little girl and said, "Josephine, it's me, Marie. I've come to see how you are. It's been so long."

The little girl looked at the sister and said, "I don't wish to speak to this woman. She used to work for my uncle and then she left. She is a bad woman."

The sister raised her finger at the girl and said, "Josephine, what have we taught you about being polite? Your friend has come a long way just to say hello to you."

The girl stood rigidly. "Please talk to my uncle," she said. "He will tell you about this woman. She is an evil person and I have been told I must never speak to her again. My uncle warned me that she might come here. I don't want to talk to her."

Marie could feel her heart breaking anew as she looked at the beautiful Josephine, still cold and remote. Whatever affection the child once held for Marie had inexplicably disappeared. Now, Josephine harbored terrible thoughts, obviously drummed into her by Claude. She turned away as the sister took the girl back into the classroom.

As Marie and the nun walked down the hallway back to the office, Marie asked, "Would you do something for me? You can see for yourself that the child is cold, almost unfeeling. I fear that something is going on at that house. Claude has threatened to kill me if I ever show up there. Could you look in on the girl occasionally, just to see she's all right?"

The sister looked with genuine concern into Marie's eyes. "My dear woman," she said, "I'm sure that you are making more of this than is necessary. Obviously, you and the girl's guardian have had a falling out. Distressing as that is, these things happen."

Her fingers touched the cross on her chest as she spoke. "I am sure the girl will be fine. She did very well in school last year. While this term is just beginning, she appears very interested in her studies. We've learned that severely troubled children do poorly. I think your fears are groundless."

"You don't know—"

The nun held up a hand. "However, if she shows any sign of distress, I will talk to the monseigneur and see what can be done."

"Thank you," Marie said, realizing further protestations would achieve nothing. She reached into her handbag and withdrew a small package with Josephine's name on it. She handed it to the nun.

"This is the diary of Josephine's mother," she said. "I wish to leave it with you."

"Why?"

"Because I may never see the child again."

"I see."

"Her mother was a member of the resistance during the war. She was killed the morning of D day. Before her death, she asked me to make sure Josephine received this when she was old enough to read it. She is still too young to understand. Will you give it to her at the appropriate time?"

"I will give it to her guardian. He can make that decision."

"No!" It was almost a scream.

The sister looked at Marie in confused silence. Marie, fighting to control her emotions, said, "I know this sounds rather stupid, but I fear that he may simply throw it away without ever giving it to the child.

"I realize you think I am simply a hysterical woman, but I beg you. The diary is all her mother had to leave to the child. Perhaps you could read it. Then you'll understand my concern. Claude is not the child's father, only her guardian. He has no interest in history. This diary is the only connection Josephine will ever have with her real parents. It's a legacy. If you can't give it to Josephine without involving Claude, then I will take it back. I'm afraid they might move away. I would lose contact."

She was rambling, she knew, but he was filled with dread. She had to make this stupid woman understand.

"I beg you to read the diary. If you do, you'll understand what I'm trying to say. Can you not do this for a desperate woman?"

The sister appeared to mull it over and finally nodded. "All right. I'll see that it's kept for her. In two or three years, she should be able to understand it. I won't open the package if I have your word that what it contains is the diary of the mother."

"You have my word, but I want you to read it." Marie said.

"That won't be necessary."

"Please."

"No. I will do what you ask and give the diary to the child at the appropriate time. If that is unsatisfactory, then take it with you."

Twice, as Marie walked back to the train station, she turned and gazed back at the old stone building. Then she turned for the last time and ran down the road, saying a silent prayer that God would protect the little girl inside.

Six months later, the sisters at the school finally began to take notice of Josephine Cousteau. Her dark eyes were cold and expressionless, her motions devoid of exuberance. She kept to herself and spoke only when spoken to. She never smiled and had no friends. But her marks remained good. She never gave anyone any trouble and there was no real reason to be concerned.

Claude brought her to Mass every Sunday, where they both took communion. In addition, Claude went to confession regularly, and saw to it that the girl did as well. There was no cause for alarm. Josephine, although quiet and remote, was functioning well and wasn't that different from many of the other children who had suffered terribly because of the war.

Nevertheless, at the urging of the assistant headmistress, Josephine was brought to the headmistress's office and asked a series of questions. They were answered politely and completely.

It was enough. They were satisfied.

JOSEPH DIPAOLO: THE RELUCTANT POLITICIAN

Part Four

═══
II
═══

No one except Sophia called him Joey anymore. He was Joseph DiPaolo now, no longer a kid, but a well-respected lawyer working in his father's firm in Brooklyn. He was married to the mother of his two children, children who'd brought incalculable joy to Joseph's mother and father—and to Joseph.

Behind him lay a distinguished military career, first in the RAF and later in the American Army Air Corps, which he'd joined in the middle of 1942. He was one of a small group of men who'd become triple air aces, and one of a handful to do it in two different outfits. He'd returned a hero five years ago, his missing foot replaced by a prosthesis that left him with an almost unnoticeable limp. They'd paraded him down Fifth Avenue with the rest, but in Brooklyn they'd held a special parade on Flatbush Avenue for him alone.

Before him lay a bright future. He was finally doing something his father had always hoped he'd do—except his father wasn't there to see it. A year earlier, just a week after Joseph learned he'd passed the New York Bar examination with flying colors, as if waiting for that precious moment, Vincent DiPaolo had died quietly in his sleep.

Three days later, Vincent DiPaolo was buried in Saint John's Cemetery in Queens. The number of people who turned out was almost staggering. Many of them Joseph knew, but there were scores of them he didn't recognize. It was one of the biggest turnouts for a Brooklyn funeral in years, and it impressed Joseph immensely. He'd always known his father was well respected in the community, but this was *tributo*.

Halfway through the ceremony, Joseph was seized with a feeling of strangeness about it all. Ever since he'd been shot down over France, he'd been aware of his own mortality. This, he thought, was the way it was supposed to be. The parents died first, then the children. The normal order. Not like war, when the parents stayed home and waited as their children fought the battles.

The hero hated war.

Five months after Joseph had been sworn in as a member of the New York Bar, a year after the death of his father, Joseph was visited by Senator Walter Rice, Sophia's old boss during the war years. The senator brought with him two other men, men whose faces were vaguely familiar to Joseph. Senator Rice's eyes were sparkling as he introduced them.

"Joseph, shake hands with two friends of mine. Luigi Provetto and Frank Tuppio."

Joseph shook their hands, the senator's, then sat down, a curious look on his face. At the mention of the names had come belated recognition. Tuppio and Provetto were members of the low-profile New Brooklyn Political Club, a branch of Carmine De Sapio's resurgent Tammany Hall organization.

Once all-powerful, Tammany Hall—named after a person, not a place, and an American Indian at that—had firmly controlled New York city and county politics in the latter part of the last century and the early part of this one. Then, in the thirties, a reformer named Fiorello La Guardia had almost put them out of business. Almost. Now, Tammany Hall was back, and these two were as connected as it got. It didn't take a genius to determine that they wanted Joseph to run for something, and the presence of the senator was a clear indication that it was something more than local politics.

"Senator," Joseph said, "I'm surprised and delighted to see you in Brooklyn. Why didn't you let me know? Does Sophia know you're in town?"

"No, she doesn't. Under normal circumstances, I would have called first and we could have made an evening out of it, but this isn't a normal circumstance. I came here to see you. After our meeting, I'm heading right back to Washington."

"She'll be very disappointed."

"As am I. I wanted to see your newest. For some reason, I feel like a grandfather to your children. Another time. Soon, I hope."

Joseph eyed the two strangers. "You came to see me? What can I do for you gentlemen? Somebody needs to be sued, perhaps?"

Tuppio grinned, looked at the senator, then turned and faced Joseph. "It's what we can do for you, Mr. DiPaolo."

"Oh. Well, if it's what I think it is, you've come to the wrong man."

Senator Rice held up his hand and said. "Don't jump to conclusions. Hear these men out before you start making rash decisions."

Tuppio placed his hands on the desk, palms down, and spoke softly. "We've got a real problem here. In less than six months, we have an election coming up. We've just learned that Representative Romano is hangin' 'em up."

Joseph was shocked. Doubly shocked. Victor Romano had been in Washington a long time. The fact that he was retiring was shock enough, but these men were obviously here to discuss the resultant vacancy, an even bigger shock.

"Why?" Joseph asked. "Is he ill?"

Tuppio was a beefy pol with thick bushy hair and eyebrows that rivaled those of John L. Lewis, the labor leader. "We don't know why. He seems fine. He just advised us that he wants to retire and spend more time with his family, that's all. We've tried to talk him out of it, but his mind is made up."

His thoughts racing, Joseph said, "You can't seriously be thinking of me to replace him."

"We are," Tuppio said.

"You're outta your mind. I've been a real lawyer for less than a year. I'm twenty-nine years old. I have no experience in politics. The people around here wouldn't stand for it. You guys have slipped a cog somewhere."

The senator interjected, "You're wrong about that. You're a war veteran. An air ace. You have no idea how famous you are. So what if you're only twenty-nine? The people are looking for young, vital leadership. You fill that bill admirably. Besides, your father was a fixture in this city, respected and loved by a lot of people he helped along the way. He had a terrific reputation for decency and honesty. That, combined with your own achievements, makes you a winner in my book."

Joseph held up his hands. "Hold on. I'm just getting started here. Since Papa died, I've had to let one of his associates go. There's just me and one other person in the office. I don't have the time or the money to fool around with politics. Besides, I hate politics. I spent a lot of years in school to get to this point. If I get involved in politics, it'll have been a total waste. Any idiot can become a politician."

"Thanks very much," retorted the senator, looking deeply hurt. He wasn't. Joseph's views were no secret. Politics was something they'd talked about often.

"No offense, Senator," Joseph said. "Besides, I've got a wife and two kids to support and another on the way. I can't afford to maintain a place in Washington and I can't afford to commute. You guys better pick someone who has the money to take this on, not to mention the inclination."

Tuppio and Provetto looked a little disappointed. Senator Rice, not to be deterred, carried on.

"You listen to these men," the senator said, leaning forward. "Just listen for a few minutes. You don't have to decide this very minute. There's plenty of time. But before you make a very shortsighted decision, let them at least tell you a few things. Frank, tell him why you came to me."

Frank Tuppio pulled a large black cigar from his inner pocket, bit off the end, which he offhandedly spit into the wastebasket, then lit the cigar.

"I went to the senator because I knew your wife used to work for him. I figured you might not even let me in the door if I came alone."

"You were right," Joseph said.

"You shouldn't believe everything they print in the newspapers, Mr. DiPaolo. Mr. De Sapio is interested in getting the best man for the job, that's all. No strings. This ain't like the old days."

"Go on."

"We did a little poll. We put down the names of eight people and showed them to about five hundred people all over the district. We asked them which

one they'd like to see go to Congress. You came out
first hands down."

Joseph stood up. "You had no right."

"Sure we did," Provetto said, speaking for the first
time. He was short and thin, with a hawk nose and
dark eyes. Mr. intensity. "How do you think we find
out what people are thinking? We ask, that's how. If
people like you turn their backs on public service,
we're left with those who have selfish reasons for
seeking office. If there are crooks in office, it's people like you who make it possible. You think the senator is a thief?"

Joseph resumed his seat. "Of course not."

"Then what makes you think working with us is so
goddamned dirty? We provide the money, that's all.
It costs a goddamned fortune to get elected these
days, and we're the ones who raise the money.
Nothin' wrong with that."

"In return for what?"

"Nothing. Sure, we'll ask you to listen to people
from time to time. People who need something.
That's what politicians do, listen to people they represent. Nothin' wrong with that. But we won't be tellin'
you what to do. You make your own decisions."

"Really?"

The senator waved a hand, quieting the other two.
"Time to grow up, Joseph. There are people who get
things done and those who don't. If it weren't for
FDR, England would have lost the war. You know
that as well as I. And here in Brooklyn, you'd still be
taking the ferry back and forth to Manhattan.
There'd be no bridges, no tunnels, nothing. Politics is
the business of getting things done, pure and simple.
Things that benefit everyone."

"I'm sure you can find someone else," Joseph said.
"Someone who shares that philosophy."

"We already have," the senator said. "You know a
man named Fred Taranga?"

"Yeah. At least, I know who he is. I've never met him."

The senator turned to Tuppio. "Tell him," he said.

"Well," Tuppio said, "Taranga's name came in second after yours on the poll we did. You turn this down and he's it. In this district, the party's a shoo-in, so whoever we select is gonna be a congressman, no doubt about it. Taranga is the wrong man. It isn't that he won't win. That's not the problem. It's that he has some friends we're not too crazy about."

"Like who?"

"We're not sure, and we can't prove it, but we think he's tied to the organization."

"The mob?"

"The mob. You, on the other hand, are so squeaky clean you shine like a beacon. You're someone who can speak for the people here, someone who's already got a lot of respect. You're perfect for this."

"I'm flattered by your compliments, but it still doesn't change anything. There are lots of guys who fill that bill besides Taranga. I can think of six without even working up a sweat, all honest, forthright guys who'd probably be delighted to run for Congress. Guys you never had on your list, I'll bet."

Senator Rice got up and started pacing the floor. "There are other considerations."

Joseph leaned forward. "Other considerations?"

Senator Rice stopped pacing and leaned against the wall. "Yes. For example, your own future. I . . ." He stopped and turned to the two local men. "Why don't you leave us alone for a few minutes."

Provetto and Tuppio stood up and left the room. Senator Rice closed the door behind them, then said, "I know why you got into law. It was because of your father. You were afraid his heart problems were due to your own decision not to follow in his footsteps. You've never liked the law. You never wanted to be a lawyer."

"Did Sophia tell you that?"

"Yes."

"Wonderful."

"Don't be upset. I was like a second father to your wife when she worked for me. I've been a friend of her parents for years. You know that. There were lots of times when she needed someone to talk to and I was it. There's nothing wrong with her telling me what's on her mind—or yours."

"Go on."

"Okay, so you did what you did for good reason, but your father's gone now. Your mother has a trust that'll look after her needs for the rest of her life. There's no reason for you to continue with this charade."

"I have to eat."

"Come on. You'll eat just fine. Better than ever. Forget about yourself for a moment and think about Sophia."

Joseph's eyes narrowed. "Let's keep her out of this discussion."

"No can do. She's your wife, yes, but she's been a friend of mine since she was six years old. I know her better than you do. You know what I'm talking about. She loved working for me and she loved the Washington scene. Sure, right now she's happy being a wife and mother because she loves you very much and she's the kind of woman who makes the best of whatever situation. But sometime down the road, the kids will be all grown up, and you'll be looking fifty in the face. What then? Do you think she's really going to enjoy living in Brooklyn, being the wife of a small-time lawyer with a family practice? I don't think so."

"You're hitting below the belt."

"Big deal. You can take it. You got big balls, Joseph. Let me tell you something else. It's an honor to serve your country whether it be in the military or the public sector. It doesn't seem right to me that you turn your back on this without giving it your fullest consideration.

"Those two men came to me because they have a problem. The party is about to choose a man who has links to some pretty unsavory characters. Their hands are tied unless they can offer an alternative that the party would be hard-pressed to refuse. If you turn your back on them, you do your city a disservice. And that's all I have to say."

The senator was a wily reader of faces. He'd pushed pretty hard. It was time to back off.

"Senator Rice," Joseph said slowly, "with all due respect, I think the relationship between me and Sophia is none of your concern. I know how much she treasures your friendship and I have no quarrel with that, but she's my wife and the mother of my children. If she's got a problem she can come to me. So far, I haven't heard any complaints.

"As for service to my country, I don't appreciate those remarks either. I served my country long before a lot of others got off their asses. I went over and joined the RAF when most Americans were screaming that we should stay the hell out of the war. Sometimes, I think that the reason people make such a big fuss over my war record is because they feel a little guilty about that. In any case, I served my country and I don't need you or anyone else telling me what debt I might or might not have left.

"I've already told you I don't like politics. Your presence here is a perfect example of everything I despise about the business. You people will trade on anything to get what you want. Friendships, family— none of it means a damn. The party is what counts. Getting elected is what counts. None of the rest means shit."

Senator Rice stood up and shoved his face in front of Joseph's. "You weren't listening very well, my friend. The party could probably put up one of Hitler's old pals and the guy would get elected. It's not a case of getting someone elected. That's not the problem. The problem is that the party is stuck with a man who represents the worst in politics. He's the epitome of everything you hate about the business.

"It's all very well for you to sit there and say how much you hate this shit. Well, there are certain things I hate about it also, but when good people refuse to become involved, it means that guys like Taranga get the jobs, and the whole damn country pays the price. What we're trying to do here is get away from politics as usual and send someone to Washington who will make a difference.

"There are monumental problems ahead, not only in Brooklyn, but throughout the whole country. We've got a new enemy now, one that strikes me as more ruthless, in many ways, than even Hitler. Look at the Berlin airlift. What the hell was that all about? The Russians have the bomb now and that changes everything. And then there's the Chinese situation. Damn it, the commies are spending a fortune catching up to us, and the way they do business, they'll do it! Did you hear McCarthy last month?"

"What? About that list of two hundred people in the State Department who are supposed to be Communists? That's crazy."

"Maybe. Maybe not. Whatever, you know damn well it's just a matter of time before we're faced with some real serious situations that require men with cool heads and lots of brains. We can't get by anymore with political hacks who get the nomination because they've been loyal to the party for a certain number of years, or have succeeded in raising a lot of money for the party's candidates. And to send a man to Washington who's got connections with the underworld is just plain asinine!

"Now is the time for some real, honest-to-God

dedicated men to step forward. If you won't do it for me, the party, or Sophia, think of your kids. What kind of world do you want to see in ten or fifteen years? I'll tell you this: if you sit on your ass and let the others take care of things, you won't like it. Not one damn bit!"

The man was a formidable debater. "I'll have to talk it over with Sophia."

Senator Rice brightened. "Of course you do. That's all I ask, that you talk it over with Sophia or whomever else you want. These two men need an answer in a week. After that, it'll be too late. I'd take it as a personal favor if you would at least consider the situation for that length of time. Talk it over. Think it out. If you say no, I'll understand."

Joseph stood up and stuffed his hands in his pockets. "No, you won't. You guys don't understand anything. You're just a bunch of hucksters trying to sell something. All the time, you're selling things. And you still haven't answered my question. How the hell am I supposed to afford all of this?"

"That's the easy part. The party will raise the money for your campaign. Once you're elected, you can make speeches for which you get paid an honorarium. With your war record, you'll be in great demand. That will augment your income quite nicely. It'll take care of the costs of maintaining a home in Washington. As for this law office of yours, you'll have no trouble getting associates to work for almost nothing. Having the experience of being in the legal firm of a congressman is something every young lawyer wants on his résumé, not to mention the additional clients it will bring in. Believe me, you take this deal and money is the smallest problem you'll have."

"You really think of everything, don't you?"

Rice grinned and said, "If you mean I don't like to make a sales call totally unprepared, you're right."

"Again, no offense, but you're from California. What the hell do you care about Brooklyn? What are you really doing here, anyway?"

"Well, for one thing, Provetto and Tuppio came all the way down to Washington to talk to me about it because they wanted some sort of entrée to you. For another, I know Sophia pretty well and I think she'd love it. Then, though I know this sounds like bullshit, I really feel strongly about the needs of the country. I'm very concerned about the future.

"The biggest thing is you. It's tough getting the right people in government. Everybody knows that. You've got the qualities we need. I think you'd make a fine congressman, and after a few years, who knows? This situation in Brooklyn is rather unique. You've got an opportunity to step into a spot without having to bust your ass raising campaign money. The only problem will be selling the other party leaders, but Provetto and Tuppio think they can do it. I agree. I'd like to see it happen. I really would."

"Well," Joseph said, "I can't let you leave without seeing Sophia. If you want me to seriously consider this thing, you'll have to take the time and come see her. Otherwise, no deal. She'd be hurt if she knew you were in town and didn't come by for an hour at least."

The senator grinned. "Deal. I'll take a later flight back to Washington. See how easy it is?"

"What?"

"Politics is the art of compromise. You just made your first deal. You're a natural."

"Don't make me sick."

First, they fed the children and put them to bed. Then, over a dinner of chicken cacciatore, thick bread, and Italian tomatoes in olive oil, Senator Rice and Sophia got caught up. They talked and laughed and swapped stories. Not once did the senator mention the reason for his quick trip to Brooklyn, leaving that to Joseph. And when the senator bade them both goodnight, Joseph told her. She was immediately ecstatic.

"Oh, Joey," she gushed. "You should be so proud, so honored. A congressman! Imagine. It could be just the beginning. Some day you might be sitting with Walter in the Senate. Who knows where it could all lead?"

"Let's not get carried away," Joseph said solemnly. "If I crawl into bed with these guys, they expect me to vote their way on every bill that comes down."

"That's not the way it is," Sophia said.

"No? How can you say that?"

"Because I worked with that man for years. Sure, he does things for people. All politicians do. But he never voted against his conscience on any important bill. I know that for a fact. You're making far too much of this so-called Tammany Hall connection."

"Maybe things are different in the House."

"I doubt it. Besides, if you back away from this, Taranga gets elected. Is that what you want?"

"No."

"Then do something about it. These people have the power, Joey. How many times have you complained about those with power? About the waste of money, the back room deals, the pork-barrel politics? Do you really think you can change something from the outside?"

"No," he said, "but that doesn't mean I want to emulate those I despise."

"You despise Walter?"

"No. He's different."

"Then why can't you be the same? If you want to change things, you have to change them from within. I've seen Walter at his best and his worst. I've seen him vote for little things he didn't like, seen him make deals he would have rather walked away from, but they were inconsequential things. On the important issues, he voted from his heart. I've also seen him get things done that many thought impossible."

"Like?"

"Like, during the early stages of the war, when you were in England, there were many opposed to us giving so much aid to England. Walter was adamant about doing so, and so was FDR. All right, maybe some businessmen got rich because of deals that were made, but in the end, England got what they needed, and that's what really counts. That's the way things get done. You need something for your district, so you help a fellow representative get what he needs and when your turn comes, you've got the votes. It may not be perfect, but it works.

"You'll have a voice, Joey. More than that, you'll have political power. Not a lot in the beginning, but some. You can't imagine how much that power means, how much good you can do. You can fight for your district by—"

He held up a hand. "It doesn't bother you that De Sapio is behind this?"

"Not at all. Who do you think gets people elected these days? Groups like De Sapio's, that's who. It happens all over the country. You're either in or you're out, and you should thank your stars that you're being given the opportunity to be in. You can't say no to this, Joey. You just can't."

He looked into her blazing eyes. "You really mean that, don't you?"

"Let me put it this way," she said softly. "If you turn down this opportunity, I'll be more disappointed than you can possibly imagine."

"It's that important?"

"Yes. You're a leader, Joey. A natural. People like you can't sit on the sidelines and let others do what needs to be done. It's a waste. Besides," she said

grinning, "I love those parties. God! They have a zil-
lion parties in Washington. We met at one of those
parties, remember?"

"I remember."

"Well? That should be an omen, don't you think?"

Joseph looked into her eyes. Behind the glow,
there was something else, something stronger, more
intense. For a moment, he didn't understand, and
then, in a flash, it came to him.

"He called you, didn't he?"

"Who?"

"Senator Rice. You knew all about this before he
even talked to me, didn't you?"

She nodded. "I'm sorry."

"You should be."

She placed her hand on his cheek. "Tell me the
truth. Aren't you just the teeniest bit flattered?
Doesn't the idea of being a member of the United
States House of Representatives excite you just a little? Be honest, now."

He stood up, walked over to the ice box and
leaned against it. Then, he grinned.

Sophia flew into his arms.

12

On June 25, 1950, North Korean troops poured over the border into South Korea, triggering the commencement of yet another war. As the news flashed around the world, an oblivious Joseph DiPaolo sat beside a hospital bed and held his wife's hand. They congratulated each other on the birth of their third child, a seven-pound, three-ounce girl they named Mary.

Sophia, still a little groggy, smiled up at her husband and asked, "Have you seen her?"

"No, not yet. The nurse said they'd be bringing her in shortly. How're you feeling?"

"I'm fine. She's beautiful, Joseph. Really beautiful. She looks like you."

"That's a contradiction in terms," he said, laughing. "She's either beautiful or she looks like me. Now which is it?"

Sophia smiled and slapped him on the hand. "Oh, you."

The nurse entered the room with the baby in her arms. "Feeding time," she said cheerfully.

Joseph looked at his new daughter. Sophia was right. The child was beautiful. As Sophia prepared to nurse the baby, she turned and smiled at her husband. "I love you," she said softly.

Joseph leaned over and kissed her on the lips. Mary was busy already, her tiny little mouth clamping onto a nipple and drawing the milk greedily. Joseph took his finger and placed it within one of the tiny hands of the child. Mary gripped it tightly.

"She's strong," he said.

"All of our children are strong. Like their father."

"And their mother."

"We make a hell of a pair."

"We do indeed."

"I'll leave you two alone for a few minutes," he said. "I'll be back."

"Don't be long."

"I won't."

Joseph walked back to the waiting room, where Frank Tuppio had been waiting patiently. The veteran party functionary, now Joseph's campaign manager, looked up at Joseph's arrival and asked, "Well?"

"A girl," Joseph said. "Seven pounds, three ounces. As they say, both mother and daughter are doing fine."

The older man stood up, grinned and slapped Joseph on the shoulder. "That's great. Congrats." Then, he looked at his watch. "We've got four hours before you're supposed to make that speech to the dockworkers. You wanna cancel?"

"No, but I want to stay here until I have to leave. It's about a twenty-minute drive over there. Why don't you come back for me later?" He pulled a cigar from his pocket and handed it to Tuppio. "Here. Have a cigar."

"Thanks, boss." Tuppio stuck the cigar in his mouth and hustled down the hall of the hospital maternity ward.

Joseph sat down in the waiting room and lit a cigar of his own. He hardly ever smoked them, but he had, after all, just been blessed with another healthy child. It was time to celebrate. Still, he felt slightly uncomfortable. It was all happening so fast.

The legal office was being effectively managed by the associate and two new men who'd jumped at the opportunity just as Senator Rice said they would. Joseph was now officially a candidate for the congressional seat to be vacated by Representative Romano. His election was all but assured, such being the nature of Brooklyn politics in 1950. It was exciting and yet somewhat terrifying, for though he'd been assured he would be free to vote his conscience, he doubted the truth of that assurance. In his heart, he felt he'd made a Faustian bargain.

His thoughts were interrupted by the sudden reappearance of Tuppio, rushing toward him, a brown box in his hands.

"What's up?" Joseph asked.

"The goddamn North Koreans have invaded South Korea. Truman's havin' a fit. You can figure we'll be at war by tomorrow or the next day."

"What?"

Tuppio nodded. "I just got off the phone to downtown. They want you to change your speech. They got some people workin' on it right now."

"Forget it. I do my own speeches."

"I know, boss, but this is a special deal." He handed Joseph a small radio. "I grabbed this downstairs. Why don't you go listen to the radio for a while and get caught up. Then you'll know what's goin' on. You can't go down there and look like a jerk."

Joseph plugged in the radio and listened. The news reports had pushed normal programming off most frequencies. Reports were coming in from Kansas City, where President Truman had declared the North Korean move illegal, and from Lake Success, where United Nations Secretary General Trygve Lie had called for an emergency session of the Security Council.

Later, thirty minutes before he was to address a group of about three hundred dockworkers, Joseph read over the speech that had been prepared for him. Since it accurately reflected his own feelings, he had no qualms about reading it, but the nagging doubts he'd experienced earlier still draped him like a cloak. He kept wondering when the other shoe would drop.

The Korean War seemed, at first, destined to be a short one. By late October, United Nations forces, mostly Americans, had pushed all the way to the Chinese border under the leadership of General Douglas MacArthur. But in November, three days after Joseph DiPaolo was elected to the United States House of Representatives, the Chinese entered the war, and chaos ensued. With America again on a war footing a short five years after the end of World War II, most political eyes were focused on Korea, and it was probably for that reason that Joseph, a war hero, was assigned to the House Armed Services Committee. It was a plum assignment.

He immediately threw himself into his work and forgot about the reservations that had initially dimmed his enthusiasm for politics. In Brooklyn, the law firm was doing well. Within a week after his election to Congress, the firm had three new accounts on large retainers. If there was a connection between the new accounts and Tammany Hall, Joseph couldn't see it, nor did he worry much about it. The threat of a third world war was uppermost in everyone's mind, and that threat looked very real. Joseph set aside personal considerations.

For all of his first term, he worked extremely hard. He had several mentors who coached him on various procedures, all of whom also helped ingratiate him with those considered most important. It wasn't difficult. Joseph, a quick study, was a polished orator and witty raconteur. He treated everyone with respect and deference, exhibiting none of the arrogance so often displayed by new members of the House. He quickly gained respect from associates and staff alike. He spent most of his working days listening and learning, an almost invisible politician, further endearing himself to those carrying the ball.

He stayed in a small apartment in Washington during work weeks and on most weekends took the train back to New York. To his surprise, he found he was beginning to enjoy the work, especially the meetings with voters in his district. There, in a small office set up for the purpose, he received a steady stream of people who came to see him, most of whom were seeking favors. Usually, Joseph would get on the phone and talk to some of the local pols and solve the problem. At other times, he would simply say, "I'll see what I can do. No promises. I never promise what I can't deliver." The fact that he took the time to listen was often enough. The nefarious were quickly shown the door.

He was building a solid reputation, and during the summer of 1951, the reputation grew. Instead of spending his time at the law office—an office purring along quite well without him—Joseph opened up a larger storefront office on New Utrecht Avenue, where he spent the summer listening to anyone who wandered in the door. He was one of the most accessible politicians on the face of the earth.

In the fall, he returned to Washington for the new term, almost a full year of experience under his belt.

He was well into his regular routine when, in late October, his office received a call from the White House. The President wanted to talk to him—alone.

Within minutes of his arrival at the White House, he was escorted to the Oval Office, where he found himself staring down at the diminutive man from Missouri.

"I've been hearing a lot about you," the president said, pumping Joseph's hand enthusiastically.

"I hope some of it's good."

"It is. All of it. They say you're a fine young man."

"Thank you, sir."

"Are you wondering why I called you here?"

"Yes, sir."

Truman waved to a chair. "Well, have a seat and I'll tell you all about it."

Joseph took a seat in front of the president's desk. His hands shook slightly. He'd been in the presence of the president many times, but never alone, and never here in the Oval Office. It was an awe-inspiring experience.

"This has been a hell of a year, Joseph," the president said, pulling up a chair and sitting down beside him. "The Korean affair has been a nightmare. I'm being pilloried by the press for sacking MacArthur, for my entire Asian position, and just about everything you can think of. Of course, MacArthur keeps running all over the country, telling anyone who'll listen what a total incompetent I am. Did you know there are some in the party who want to replace me with that pompous rogue?"

"I've heard rumors."

"Well, they're welcome to him. Be the biggest mistake they ever made. I may not be the best man to ever sit in this office, but I'm a damn sight better than Douglas MacArthur. The man's ego is out of control. Could've started World War Three, the way he was heading."

"I agree with you," Joseph said.

"Then, I've had the railway workers and the miners to contend with. Everybody's in one great hurry to make up for lost time. They all want more and they want it now. Strikes. These people don't give a tinker's damn about the country, if you ask me. And now I've got the New York dockworkers to worry about. Asked Tom Dewey to help me out on that and he's just sitting on his hands. I think the man takes pleasure in seeing me have my feet in the fire. Poor loser."

"Yes, sir."

Truman stared directly into Joseph's eyes with a piercing look. "I understand you have some friends up there."

"Well, I . . . I know some of the people involved."

"I don't understand it," the president said, slapping his thigh. "I thought that contract was agreed upon. The thing was signed and sealed. Now, they say they want to tear it up and start all over again. Is this just a fight between locals or is there something else?"

"It's more complex than that, sir. Sure, there's some fighting between locals, but there's some cooperation as well. There's an underlying motivator."

"And what would that be?"

"The shipbuilders feel they're being cheated, Mr. President."

"How?"

"Too much naval shipbuilding is being moved to other ports. San Diego, for example. The New York shipbuilders don't think they're getting their fair share of the work. They're worried about their futures. The dockworkers' actions have been taken in sympathy."

"I see. You're saying that this strike business being about a new contract is all a smokescreen?"

"I think it is. They heard that the new carrier was going to be built in San Diego a day after they signed the contract. They feel that information was withheld from them deliberately."

"Do you think it was?"

"I have no idea, sir."

"Really. That's not what I was given to understand."

"Are you referring to my discussion with the naval undersecretary yesterday?"

"I am."

"I simply told him what the men told me. I didn't imply in any way that I agreed with such an assessment. If he says otherwise, he's lying."

The president removed his glasses, wiped them, then put them back on his nose. "So, where do we go from here?"

"I have no idea, sir. I wouldn't presume to suggest—"

"Cut the baloney, Joseph. I didn't ask you here for tea."

"Well, you have certain powers at your disposal."

"That's not what I'm asking."

Joseph hesitated, then asked, "Do you want the truth, sir?"

"Absolutely."

He took a deep breath, then said, "Very well. You've lost credibility with those men. As I say, they feel cheated. When men feel cheated, words mean very little. They're good men, hardworking, with families to be concerned about. Many are veterans. I think you need to take positive action."

"Such as?"

"Give them another ship."

"That's out of the question. For one, we can't afford it. We're already spending too much money on defense."

"Then you'll just have to order them back to work."

"What if I asked you to have a talk with them?"

"I'd be happy to talk to them, but what will I say?"

"You can tell them that we're in a war, that every

day they stay off the job, supplies—vitally needed supplies—pile up on the docks. We've got soldiers dying because those bastards are sitting on their asses."

Joseph stood his ground. "They know the supplies are needed, Mr. President. But if I walk into a room filled with dock workers, shipbuilders, pipe fitters, and a dozen other trades, and I give them a lot of drivel, I'll be thrown out on my ear. The fact is, sir, they are getting screwed. There's always a need for new ships. We build them all the time. You let me tell those men that the next big one will be built in Brooklyn, and I think this strike will be over real quick."

The president stiffened. "That would be tantamount to giving in to blackmail, Mr. DiPaolo. I don't like to be blackmailed. I won't be blackmailed."

"It's not blackmail, sir. It's simply correcting an oversight. Those who do the planning have their own agendas. For some reason, the New York shipbuilders are on the outs. They have a right to be upset."

The president stood up, signaling the end to the meeting. "I'll tell you what, Mr. DiPaolo. You find a way to get those men back to work and I'll see what I can do. First things first, you understand?"

Joseph was chilled by the quick change in the president's tone. "If I can't give them some sort of guarantee—"

"You can't. Hell, you tell 'em whatever you like, as long as it doesn't come from me. And I'll be paying close attention to exactly what you do say. Of that you can be sure."

Joseph stood up and shook the president's hand. "I'll see what I can do, sir."

"Thanks for coming by."

Joseph took the train to New York that very night. In the morning, he huddled with Frank Tuppio and three union leaders in a small diner less than a mile from the docks. There, he told them about his conversation with President Truman. Gene Conners, short, stout, and bald, business agent for one of the shipbuilders' locals involved, blew cigar smoke in Joseph's face. "That's what that little prick is doin' to you, DiPaolo. Blowin' smoke in your face."

Joseph had met this ingrate many times. He'd found the best way to deal with him was to keep his head. "Maybe," he said, "but I talked to three people before I left Washington last night. I can't tell you who they are, but I can tell you what they said."

"Which is?"

"You play ball and they'll play ball."

"Which means?"

"Do I have to draw you a picture?"

Conners laughed. "You buyin' all that shit? Listen to me, DiPaolo. You're still wet behind the ears. Those assholes in Washington are rubbin' your nose in it. Unless we got it in writing, we ain't about to take nobody's word for nuthin'."

"In that case, you're being a fool," Joseph said calmly. "These people aren't about to submit to guerilla tactics. The longer you stay off the job, the less chance you have of gaining anything. Truman is a man who holds a grudge. You make him look bad on this and he won't forget it.

"I've been told that the Pentagon has plans for a new aircraft carrier. It could be built right here. But I'll guarantee you it will be built somewhere else if you keep this up. Absolutely guarantee it."

"But there's nobody willing to say we'll get it if we go back in," Conners countered.

"True, but I have some cards I haven't played yet. I want you to know this—if I play them, I'll be in political debt for some time. Paying back a favor is never cheap. I'm sticking my neck out a mile by doing this. If you let me down, my career as a politician won't be worth much. I could well be finished."

"You're breaking my heart," Conners snapped.

DiPaolo stood up and signaled to Tuppio. "Have it your way, Mr. Conners. There's a time to play it tough and there's a time to play it right. The choice is yours. I've done what I can, but if you stay out, my hands are tied."

"Wait!"

"For what?"

"How sure are you this will amount to anything?"

"I'm not sure at all. I told you that."

"Why the hell should we trust you?"

Joseph smiled. "You have a better offer?"

Six months later, Joseph watched as the first heavy timbers—supports for the new aircraft carrier Morgan—were put in place. It had taken some doing, and he'd not been alone in his quest, but he'd been the ringleader, and everyone in the yard knew it. All day, they'd pounded him on the back and offered their hands. Now he was a different kind of hero.

There was a price to pay, he knew, but he was prepared. In his first term, he'd accomplished much more than he'd imagined possible. More important, he had learned to love it, this life of wheeling and dealing, cajoling and begging. One hand washing the other. He felt he was good at it.

Most of all, he'd seen the look in Sophia's eyes. She was bursting with pride. Wherever she went, men doffed their hats and women gave her a nod, all of them paying homage to her and her husband. She reveled in it, this recognition, this tribute, and she showered Joseph with more affection and praise than he felt he deserved. And he loved that, too.

He sighed contentedly. He seemed to have found his place in the world.

JOSEPHINE:
A CHILDHOOD
ENDED

Part Five

13

"*Sit* down, Josephine," the nun said.

The girl sat down, placed her hands in her lap, and stared vacantly at the assistant headmistress whose owlish, fat face was pinched and puffed out by a heavily starched white wimple. Josephine had often wondered how the nuns were able to speak with such restrictive head coverings.

"Josephine, you've done very well in your classes, and I commend you."

"Thank you, Sister Helena."

"Do you know much about your mother and father?"

The girl looked at her in surprise. For the first time, Sister Helena noticed the incredible beauty in the face of this ten-year-old. Her eyes, usually expressionless, were dazzling when touched by emotion of whatever kind. With her high cheekbones and flawless skin, she looked much older than her years.

It was remarkable. She could easily pass for someone three years older.

According to her teachers, Josephine was even more remote than when she'd started attending school. She was always courteous, never tardy, diligent and bright, though the latter was only evident when the child was asked a direct question. In or out of class, she never volunteered anything.

She had no friends or enemies that they knew of. She simply stood apart, refusing to bond with any of her contemporaries, unlike the other children. Neither did she attempt to draw their enmity. Her marks were excellent, and for that reason, she was simply considered a quiet child, one affected, like many at the school, by the loss of her family during the war.

"My mother and father?" the girl asked.

"Yes. What do you know of them?"

The girl seemed puzzled. For a moment she said nothing, then, "My mother and father were with the resistance in the war. They were both killed. I was born in sin, for which I must pay—"

Sister Helena interrupted her. "I didn't ask you because of that. I just wondered if you knew them."

"No. I know of them, but I have no memories of being with them. My father was killed before I was born. I was only three when my mother was killed."

The sister picked up a package and turned it over in her hands. "This," she said, "is the personal diary of your mother. It was left to you when your mother was killed, with instructions that you receive it at a time when you could read and understand it. I think that time has come."

Josephine's eyes widened in shock. "A diary? My mother kept a diary?"

"Yes."

"Where did you get it?"

"It was left here by Marie Benoit. Do you remember her?"

"Yes. She lived with my guardian for some time, but abandoned us. Have you read the diary?"

"No."

The child looked disappointed.

Sister Helena handed the package to Josephine. "I've thought often about the wisdom of giving this to you," she said. "However, since it was your mother's wish, I feel compelled to do so. While I don't know what is written here, it's highly probable that reading it will cause you pain, my child. If it does, I want you to come to me and we'll discuss it. Will you do that?"

"Of course, Sister."

"Good. Perhaps, you will derive some comfort from the diary. I've been told that your mother wanted you to have it very much. God be with you, my child."

"Thank you, Sister."

Josephine took the package back to class and placed it in her backpack. She wanted to read it now, but decided to wait. It would be an adventure and a treat, like a rare dessert after dinner, something to be savored. She'd read it after chores and dinner. No. Too soon. Claude would visit her room again, as he had every night for three years. He might catch her reading and ask questions. She would wait until he was done with her and sound asleep. The book would be her secret. She'd hide it in the barn, somewhere where Claude would never find it.

It was two in the morning when Josephine finally crept through the darkness and made her way to the barn. Carefully, quietly, she lit one of the oil lamps and retrieved the package from its hiding place. Some of the cows stirred at the unaccustomed interruption. She paid them no heed. She removed the wrapping from the package and held the diary in her hands. It was red, with a clasp that covered the edge and locked on the front. Stuck to the front with tape was a small key that fit the lock.

She unlocked the clasp, and opened the diary in the middle. As she quickly flipped through the pages, a small photograph fell onto the ground. Josephine picked it up and looked at it. It depicted a man and a woman, their arms around each other, smiling at the camera. The man was dressed in the uniform of an officer in the Royal Air Force. The woman looked much like herself. On the back was inscribed, F.O. Joseph DiPaolo and me, 6 October, 1940.

She'd never seen a photograph of her mother, though she remembered Marie describing her, a description that fit this woman. Her father was French, so she knew this man could not be her father. Still, she was curious, because of the date, nine months before her birth. Perhaps her father had been the one to take the picture.

Hurriedly, the girl turned the pages of the diary as she tried to find some reference to the picture. Stuck between two pages was a small lock of hair. She removed it and looked at it closely, wondering if it was her own. Carefully, she put the hair back in the book and continued her search.

Within fifteen minutes she found a passage that held her spellbound. As she read, her body trembled with excitement.

> . . . is so young. His name is Joseph but he calls himself Joey for some reason. An American with an Italian name who fights for the British. He pretends to be a man, and I must admit that anyone who flies in the face of death is indeed brave, but still he is not a man. In many ways, he is a child, afraid of both death and women. To be afraid of death is understandable, but to be afraid of a woman? I have never before met such a man.

When we made love, he was awkward and shy, not at all like I would have thought an American to be. I expected the same rough selfishness as Pierre, but Joseph, with his shyness and guilt, was a sensitive lover. His touch was gentle. I think he was actually afraid of hurting me, and when he finally spent himself, the expression on his face was one of surprise, like a child who had touched the flame by mistake. It was obvious to me at that moment that he was a virgin, a fact he later confessed.

He is on his way back to England. He says he wants to fly again, and perhaps he will. He has matured much these last few days. Jean-Luc has taken a picture of us together, and when it is developed, I will place it here as a souvenir.

Josephine rushed through the pages, looking for more. She found it.

Jean-Luc has discovered my secret. I am to go to Paris until the baby is born. The child is to be given to the Sisters. It will be the most terrible moment of my life.

With fumbling fingers, Josephine turned page after page until she came upon another telling paragraph.

I have named her Josephine, after her father. Everyone will be outraged that I am keeping her, but I'll die before I give her up. She is all I have in the world, the only one who will love me. I am to stay with Claude and his group. He is a strange man. His eyes frighten me. I must not think of that. I must think of the kindness he has extended in allowing me to keep my Josephine.

It took her breath away. Her father was the American! He might still be alive.

Eight pages later, there was this entry:

I have learned that Joseph is alive and back in America. He has married. The note sent by Higgins did not mention the bride's name, but I am sure it is the one he was worried about. I hope he lives a happy life. I will never let him know about his daughter, and I have received a pledge from Higgins and Marie that they will never tell him. Someday, when the time is right, I will tell Josephine the truth, but not until she pledges to keep the secret of her father's identity, for it can only cause pain.

Stunned, Josephine turned to the final entry in the diary.

It is almost upon us, her mother had written. Deliverance Day. The mission tonight will be the most dangerous we have ever undertaken, for the Germans are aroused and angry. They sense the war has turned against them. I have talked with Marie and begged her to look after Josephine if anything should happen. I know I'm wasting my breath. Marie will do her best, but if the Germans find us, we will all die, including Marie. Josephine's fate will be no better. The Germans have no heart or soul, only an obsession to destroy.

Josephine felt faint. She was breathing heavily, the interior of the barn spinning, beads of perspiration forming on her forehead and upper lip. She never heard the quiet footsteps of Claude as he walked up behind her.

"What are you doing?"

The sound of his voice made her leap in total shock. The diary slipped from her hands and fell to the straw-covered floor.

Claude's face was twisted with anger. He noticed the book on the ground, reached down and picked it up. "What is this?" he asked.

Josephine was still trying to catch her breath. "It's a diary," she gasped. "My mother wrote it during the war."

"Your mother?"

"Yes."

He leafed through the pages for a moment and then slammed the book shut. "You must not have this," he said. "Nothing but lies! Your mother was a liar, just like all the rest."

"Please, Uncle Claude," Josephine cried, as she reached for the book. Claude slapped her across the face and she fell back against the wall.

"You will do as I say. Now get back to the house. In less than an hour you'll have your chores to attend to."

"Give me the diary," she screamed.

His eyes widened in shock. "Do not use that tone of voice with me. Have you lost your senses?"

"It's mine. I want it back."

Again, he slapped her across the face, sending her reeling. "Enough!" he shouted. "I have told you that this is not for you. Now get back to your room!"

The anger and frustration had been building for a short lifetime. Suddenly, it bubbled to the surface of her consciousness, bursting forth in the form of blind, unthinking rage. The diary was her only contact with her mother, her only solace from a life that was dreary and frightening. This man . . . This monster . . . This revolting, cruel animal—her master—was going to take it away from her for no reason but grotesque vindictiveness.

Without a thought, her hands reached for the handle of a shovel leaning against the wall that was normally used to clear out the milking pens. She grabbed it with both hands, raised it above her head and swung it with all her strength at this man, the source of her agony, now raising his arms to take the shovel away from her.

His defense was too late. Perhaps because the anger was so intense, so pure, the adrenaline giving her a strength beyond her size, the shovel crashed against the powerful left arm of Claude Beauport, opened a gaping wound and created such extreme pain that he screamed and dropped to his knees.

He stared in shock at his profusely bleeding arm, unaware that Josephine had raised the shovel again. This time, she brought it down squarely on top of his head, edge first. Like a mammoth scalpel, the shovel split his skull, crashed into his brain and killed him instantly. He slipped to the ground in a bloody heap and never moved.

Josephine felt the shovel slip from her hands and fall to the ground. Gasping for air, she sank to her knees beside the fallen Claude. For a moment, she stared at the product of her anger, a head split wide, the brain exposed.

Her heart pounding unmercifully, she searched for and found the diary, picked it up clutched it to her chest. Still on her knees, she searched for the rest. She found the photograph, which had fallen from the book, but the hair was gone, as was the key.

She searched fruitlessly for five minutes, but it was hopeless. The straw and dirt were thick and she knew she'd never find them.

She stood up. Her legs were surprisingly steady. The anger and fear were gone, replaced by a strange calmness foreign to her. She breathed normally. A thin smile graced her lips.

She walked over to the oil lamp, looked at it for a moment, then removed it from the hook on the wall. She walked slowly toward the barn door, turned, and threw the lamp to the straw-strewn floor. Instantly, flames erupted from the broken lamp and started marching across the floor.

She grabbed a piece of oilskin, closed the barn door, and slipped the wooden bolt. Then, trance-like, she walked behind the house, dug a hole in the ground with her hands, wrapped the diary in the oilskin and buried it. Finally, she entered the house, washed her hands, and crawled into bed. As the first fingers of flame started to eat their way through the wooden beams of the barn, Josephine closed her eyes and fell fast asleep.

14

In the morning, Josephine was awakened by the sound of someone pounding on the front door. Still in her nightgown, she got up from her small bed and walked slowly to the front door. When she opened it, she saw two policemen, both wearing strange expressions on their faces.

"Josephine Cousteau?"

"Yes?"

The smell of smoke hung heavily in the air—and something else. Something terrible.

"Where have you been all night?"

She rubbed her eyes. "Asleep. Who are you? Where's my uncle?"

The two policemen didn't answer. Instead, they stepped inside.

"What's happened?" Josephine asked.

One of the policemen motioned to the couch. "Sit down, young lady."

She sat on the couch and placed her hands in her lap.

The policeman pulled up a chair and placed it so his big, moon-shaped face was close to her own. She could smell the tobacco on his breath. "Do you know what time it is?" he said.

"No."

"It's almost ten o'clock. This is the last day of school. You're usually there by eight. Why not today?"

"Uncle Claude always wakes me up. I have chores to do before school. Today he forgot." She looked around. "Where is he?" The question seemed innocent, but her eyes betrayed her, exhibiting a cold maturity beyond her years. The policeman had seen eyes like that before.

"I think you know," he said. "Why don't you tell us what happened?"

"I know nothing," she said impassively.

It was her absence of passion, the far-off look in her eye, that made him immediately suspicious. He told her to get dressed, and when she did, he escorted her to the police car that would take her to Saint-Quentin to be questioned.

As she got into the back seat of the car, she could see the barn had burned to the ground. The blackened skeletons of several cows were clearly visible, as were the men who sifted through the ruins, holding handkerchiefs to their noses as they picked up a small item here, another there.

The death of the cows bothered her a little. She recognized the terrible stench she had smelled as their charred remains. A pity. She liked cows.

At the police station, she was ushered into the office of a man who identified himself as Captain Deshanel. A large man with a florid face, he sat behind a battered desk and put the pipe he was smoking in an ashtray. Josephine was placed on a chair in front of the desk, where she sat quietly, her hands in her lap.

"What have we here?" the captain asked.

One of the policemen said, "Captain, we received a call from the school that Josephine Cousteau had not arrived. The nuns asked us to go to the farm and check things out. When we got there, we found the barn burned to the ground and the remains of a man. We believe him to her guardian, a man named Claude Beauport."

"So, he died in the fire?"

"Not exactly. The body was badly burned, but we discovered his skull had been split and his brains bashed in. We also found what was left of a shovel beside the body and a broken oil lamp on the ground that appears to have been the source of the fire."

Captain Deshanel stared at Josephine.

"The girl was still in bed when we arrived," the gendarme continued. "She made no statement and claimed to have slept in. We still have some men on the scene, but we thought you'd want to talk to the girl. It appears to us, at least—"

"Yes, yes."

The captain picked up the pipe and sucked on it for a moment while he stared at Josephine. "Claude Beauport, you say?"

"Yes," the policeman answered.

The captain racked his brain for a moment, then slapped his hand on the desk and leaned forward. He directed a question to Josephine. "Wasn't there a woman living with you . . . two, three years ago?"

Josephine nodded.

"What was her name?"

"Marie Benoit."

The captain sighed in satisfaction. "And when she left, wasn't there an argument of some sort? Between your uncle and her, I mean. Is that not so?"

Josephine was startled. "How . . . How did you know that?"

The captain smiled and turned to one of the policemen. "Somewhere in the files is a report on a woman named Marie Benoit. I remember it from some years ago. Find it and bring it to me."

One of the policemen left the room. He returned a few minutes later, clutching the file. The captain took it, read the contents carefully, then closed the file and looked at Josephine.

"Why don't you tell me what happened?"

"I don't know what happened," she said. "I was asleep."

The captain tapped a finger on the file on his desk and said, "He used to beat you, didn't he? And finally you got upset and hit him with the shovel."

"No."

He pointed to a bruise on her cheek. "Where did you get that bruise? He hit you, didn't he? In the barn. Then you hit him with the shovel and bashed his brains in. Then you threw the lamp on the floor and burned the barn to the ground. Isn't that what happened?"

"No!"

The captain turned to one of the policemen. "Get the prosecutor in here. And I want a doctor to examine this girl." He threw the file at the officer. "There's a report in here filed by Marie Benoit. She moved out of town to a place in Lille. I want her found and brought down here. Get moving!"

The men left the room and Josephine was alone with the captain. He sucked on the pipe for a few moments, then, in a soft voice, said, "Don't worry, little one. Maybe the bastard had it coming. We'll find out soon enough. There's no hurry. You just relax. Sooner or later you'll tell us everything."

He leaned forward and smiled at her. "If you tell me now, it will go a lot easier with you. Believe me, I know about these things. You're a young girl with your whole life ahead of you. Killing someone can result in a trip to the guillotine. We wouldn't want that pretty head of yours chopped off, now would we?"

Josephine said nothing.

The captain's smile widened as he said, "I'll make sure that won't happen to you, but you've got to trust me. You've got to tell me what happened. I'll listen to your story and talk to the prosecutor on your behalf. You probably won't even go to jail. But you've got to tell me now. If you wait until this thing goes before the judges . . ."

He extended his arms out from his body and his face took on an expression of concern. Then, very slowly, he brought one hand across his neck as though to slit his throat. Her face remained expressionless.

For the next ten minutes, the captain asked question after question. Some were answered yes, some no, but none were given more than a word or two. Then, there was a knock at the door. Before the captain could utter a word, Sister Helena swept into the room, her face contorted by anger. "Captain," she shouted, "I want this girl examined immediately. I'm going to take her to the hospital."

The captain stood up and said, "I've already made arrangements for a doctor, Sister."

"Not good enough."

"I'm sorry, Sister, but she must remain here. There's been a killing and—"

The nun wasn't listening. With fire in her eyes, she took Josephine by the hand and started to pull her out of the room.

"Sister," the captain protested, "you mustn't—"

The nun turned and glared at him. "Where can she run? Nowhere. You should be ashamed, Captain. Ashamed! She's just a child. You can see her after she's been to the hospital and I've found a lawyer to look after her interests. And I'll hear no more from you!" Then, pulling the girl by the hand, she left the room without another word.

The captain sighed and hung his head. To the two policemen who questioned him, he simply said, "Just keep an eye on her, that's all. And get that Benoit woman down here as fast as you can."

The policeman seemed confused. "The train to Lille isn't for another hour yet."

"The hell with the train," the captain bellowed. "Take the car. This is a murder case. How many murder cases do we have in this town? Now move!"

As the policemen hurried out the door, the captain resumed his seat behind the desk, put some fresh tobacco in his pipe, lit the pipe, and patted his ample stomach. She'd tell him soon enough, he thought.

He was wrong.

The doctor who examined Josephine was an unusually enlightened man. He'd taken a year of psychiatric training before deciding on a career as a surgeon, and prided himself on his perceived insights. He sensed that this terribly withdrawn child was a victim of some kind of abuse.

His physical examination confirmed it. The X rays revealed that several of Josephine's ribs had once been cracked. The physical examination confirmed that Josephine had engaged in both vaginal and anal intercourse.

His gentle questions regarding the sexual abuse were answered with nothing but a blank stare. When he became more specific, Josephine answered, "I don't know what you're talking about. No one has ever touched me."

"How did you crack your ribs?"

"I don't know."

"You must have felt pain. Cracked ribs hurt."

"I felt no pain."

"Ever?"

"Ever."

For two days, they all tried to get Josephine to talk about what had happened. The police captain, Sister

Helena, the lawyer Sister Helena had arranged for, all were treated in the same fashion. Josephine refused to budge. She insisted she was asleep the entire night and had heard and seen nothing.

When Marie Benoit arrived at police headquarters, she spent an hour with Captain Deshanel, then was taken directly to Josephine's cell. Marie was astonished at the change in the girl. Josephine had grown considerably and looked much older than her ten years. There were other, more ominous changes.

"Josephine," Marie pleaded, "you must speak of this. You simply must! It doesn't matter what you think of me or the others. In order for anyone to help you, you have to tell them what happened. If you don't, I fear for what might happen to you. It's not just what the police might do, although that is worry enough. It's what might happen to your mind. You can't keep this inside you. It's not right. You have to tell someone, if only in confidence. Otherwise, there's no telling what could happen. Don't you care what happens to you?"

Josephine stared at her vacantly. Then she said, "Do you remember the diary?"

Marie's heart skipped a beat. Perhaps she had managed to get through somehow. Quickly, she answered, "Your mother's diary? Yes, of course."

"You must promise not to tell anyone."

"Tell them what?"

"They gave it to me. At school. I hid it."

"I don't understand. They gave you the diary at school and you hid it. Why did you hide it?"

"You must promise me you won't tell."

"Did the diary have something to do with what happened to Claude?"

"No. I just hid it so he wouldn't see it. If I tell you, will you promise?"

"Yes. I promise."

"I hid the diary behind the house. I buried it in the

ground about six meters from the middle of the back wall. I want you to dig it up and keep it for me. I don't want the police to find it."

"Why not?"

"Because they'll take it away from me."

"Why would they do that?"

"I don't know. I just know they will. It's the only thing I have of my mother's and they don't want me to have it."

"Did you hide the diary after . . . Claude was killed? Did it have something to do with what happened?"

"No."

"Josephine, I love you. I've always loved you. You're the daughter of the dearest friend I ever had in the world. I wouldn't ever do anything to hurt you. You must know that."

There was no answer.

"I'll keep the diary for you if you wish, but if it has anything to do with the . . . what happened . . . please let me talk to the police about it. I'm only trying to help you. There's nothing in the diary that could hurt you. There's no reason they would want to keep it from you."

"You promised."

Marie held up her hands. "I know. And I'll keep my promise. I'm asking you to let me help you."

"I don't know anything. I didn't do anything. I was asleep. I've told everyone that. Why won't anyone believe me?"

The words were uttered in a flat monotone, through lips that hardly moved. Josephine gazed at Marie with eyes that lacked expression of any kind. Dead eyes, slightly sunken in their sockets.

Captain Deshanel appeared at the bars and leaned against them. "Your trial has been scheduled," he told Josephine. "Three weeks from today. I suggest you start talking to someone, child."

The day before her trial in juvenile court was to begin, Josephine had still not spoken to anyone about the events surrounding the death of Claude Beauport. Marie, desperately seeking some way to help the girl, broke her promise and took the diary to the defense lawyer who had been hired to handle the girl's case.

Pierre LaTour was tall and thin, with long brown hair combed to one side of his head. His voice was surprisingly deep for a man so thin.

"So you think this is the flint that sparked the violence?"

"Yes," Marie said. She patiently explained the diary's significance.

"It doesn't really matter," LaTour said.

"It doesn't matter? You haven't even read what's inside!"

"It's locked."

"I'll break the lock."

"Don't bother. I told you it doesn't matter."

"Of course it matters. Can't you see that the diary is what triggered whatever it was that made Josephine do what she did. If, in fact, it was Josephine?"

"You say the diary was her mother's. Perhaps Beauport did want to keep it from the child. Perhaps not. But even if her guardian was going to take it away from her, it doesn't excuse her from killing him. We're better off going with what we have."

"And what's that?"

"Not much. There is evidence that the girl is no longer a virgin, that there has been additional physical abuse, but nothing that proves her guardian was responsible."

"Who else could it be?"

"No one. I know that, but we have no proof. We're going to contend that the girl simply lost her temper in an argument and killed Claude Beauport in a fit of rage."

"That's all?"

"Without her direct testimony, it is all conjecture. She refuses to speak. A stupid position."

"She is only a child, and all of this has been terrifying for her. Can't they see that?"

The lawyer grimaced as he tried to explain. It was always like this with people unfamiliar with the law. They knew nothing of rules and procedures. "Of course they see it," he said. "That's the worst part of all."

"Stop talking in circles," Marie shouted.

LaTour sighed deeply and tried to explain. "I am left with two choices," he said. "One, she is convicted of manslaughter and is sentenced to a juvenile detention school until she's sixteen. Or two, she is declared mentally unfit and goes to an asylum where, despite the law, she'll most likely remain for the rest of her life. To me, the six years in school is the better choice. Don't you agree?"

"Isn't there anything else? Is there no chance she'll be found innocent?"

"Not in a million years. Her behavior is consistent with someone who has done something they know is wrong. I agree she's been shocked by the events, but I can't shake her. No one can. The evidence against her is too strong. Our only hope is that the judge will see fit to adjudicate the case on these surface merits. If he really digs into it, the girl will be sent away to the asylum for sure."

"But she's a victim," Marie cried. "She might well have been acting in self-defense. She won't speak because she's been prohibited from speaking for years. Claude was so strict with her. She might even be unable to talk about the case. Can't you see that? The man was sick! You admit she was badly beaten. What was she to do? Let him kill her?"

"I know how you feel," LaTour said softly. "I feel the same way. The doctor agrees. But without her statement, we have nothing. There are no witnesses. I agree with you that her mental condition is caused by the incident. Any fool can see that.

"The judge, however, will look at things as they are. He's not concerned how they got that way. Right now, the girl is disturbed. Seriously disturbed. It doesn't matter that her condition is the result of sexual and physical attacks. All that matters in the eyes of the judge is that she is disturbed. If that is what we show, she'll be sent to the asylum for treatment.

"I can tell you, she'll receive no treatment in that place, only a lifetime of madness. My only chance is to deal with this as a straightforward case of a young girl losing her temper. If I stay away from the abuse aspect and simply contend that she killed him in a blind rage, there is a very slim chance that the judge will put her in detention school for six years. As bad as that is, it's infinitely better than the asylum."

Marie was aghast. "But that's terrible," she said. "And so unjust! Can't the doctors testify that her silence is caused by the trauma of her abuse?"

The lawyer threw his pencil on the floor and put his hands in his pockets. "Mam'selle Benoit, I know it's unjust. So is murder. Judges, especially juvenile court judges, take a very dim view of children killing their parents or guardians, no matter the reason. I cannot allow the doctor to testify. The moment we start delving into the girl's head, we bring the entire matter of her sanity into question. That is precisely what I don't want to do.

"We French see too many American movies. Our laws are different, yet the average person doesn't know that. It will be all I can do to keep her out of the asylum, I assure you. I am not without experience in these matters."

The trial was a short one. The prosecutor presented his case without fanfare or theatrics. He showed the shovel, the broken lamp, called his experts, and read into the record the autopsy report proving Claude had died before the fire.

Three witnesses claimed that Claude Beauport was a responsible person who paid his bills on time and who came to church every Sunday with his ward. The prosecution rested.

LaTour presented his witnesses. Marie testified that she had known Josephine from birth, that the child was good-tempered and had never caused a moment's trouble. She was not asked about the incidents surrounding her leaving the home almost three years ago or her life with Claude. LaTour was afraid that her testimony would make Claude look like a saint.

The teachers at the school testified that Josephine was a quiet, somewhat withdrawn child, who managed to get consistently outstanding marks because of her voracious appetite for reading.

Josephine did not speak on her own behalf. The judge decided, as was his right under French law, to question her himself.

"Do you have any statement to make regarding the charges brought against you?" he asked.

"No, *Monsieur le Juge*," was the simple answer.

"Did you hit Claude Beauport with a shovel, as the prosecutor contends?"

"No, *Monsieur le Juge*."

"Are you in any way responsible for the death of Claude Beauport?"

Again, the answer was a quiet, "No, *Monsieur le Juge*."

"Is that your final word?"

"Yes, *Monsieur le Juge*."

The judge looked at the girl for a few moments. He noted the long dark hair that hung midway down her back, the dark, cold eyes, the perfect features. Such a beautiful child and so obviously disturbed. In a soft voice, filled with compassion, he said, "I'm sure you realize that we are concerned here for your welfare. It is a very serious thing to be accused of the crime of murder.

"The evidence that has been presented here is circumstantial. By that I mean that there were no witnesses to the actual crime. But there are compelling reasons to find you guilty of these charges. For one, you were found in the house after the crime at a time when you would normally be in school. Your statement to the police was that you simply slept in. I find that difficult to believe.

"When the barn burned down, there were a number of animals burned to death. The house is close enough to the barn for you to hear the sounds of those poor animals as they struggled to escape the fire. I doubt anyone could have slept through such a thing. Especially a young child."

He paused and stroked his chin for a moment. Then he said, "I am sure that something must have happened, events to which you were witness, or in fact, party to. By that, I mean, you either saw what happened or caused what happened. By remaining silent, you are not helping yourself in any way. What we seek here is simply the truth.

"If you did kill your guardian, there may be a good reason. Perhaps he beat you. Perhaps you were acting in self-defense. If that is the case, you have committed no crime. But you must tell us in your own words. We cannot guess. Were you acting in self-defense?"

"No, *Monsieur le Juge*."

"Did Claude Beauport threaten you?"

"No, *Monsieur le Juge*."

The judge sighed. "Perhaps he was cruel to you in other ways. There has been no evidence presented indicating that this was so, but your words would be listened to by the court. I urge you to tell me everything you know. It is the only way I can render a just decision in this matter."

Josephine remained silent.

"For the last time, do you have anything to say?"

The girl looked at the judge with clear, cold eyes. In a voice that was devoid of emotion, she said, "No, *Monsieur le Juge*."

The judge turned to the prosecutor.

"Has the child been examined by a doctor?"

The prosecutor noted that she had.

"Why did you not call him as a witness?"

LaTour mumbled something unintelligible.

"I want the doctor here as a witness," the judge said. "We'll recess until then."

A half hour later, court was reconvened with the doctor in the witness box. Attorney LaTour fidgeted nervously in his seat as the judge asked the doctor a series of questions. This was precisely what he'd been worried about. If the doctor testified that the girl was mentally disturbed, her life might well be over.

"You examined the girl?" the judge asked.

"Yes, *Monsieur le Juge*."

"What did you find?"

The doctor told him.

"She engaged in sexual intercourse as well as sodomy?"

"Yes."

"With whom?"

"We cannot know for sure. The body of Claude Beauport was so damaged, tests were impossible."

"Have you some medical explanation for the refusal of the accused to talk with the court?"

The doctor nodded. "I brought in another doctor for consultation, a psychiatrist. I have his report."

"Let me hear it."

In an American court, it would be considered hearsay and nonadmissible, but this was France in the year 1951. The doctor opened the file and began to read. "The report states that the girl has been traumatized by something that has shocked her significantly. She may or may not be aware of the events surrounding the death of Claude Beauport, but this cannot be fully determined at this time."

"I see. All right, Doctor. You are dismissed. Call Marie Benoit to the witness box."

Marie nervously took her place.

"Mam'selle Benoit," the judge began, "you testified that you had lived in the Beauport home for a number of years. What was your relationship with Claude Beauport?"

"I was simply a friend. At the time, Josephine was a young child and needed caring for. Claude asked me to help take care of the child and to assist him around the farm."

The judge peered over his reading glasses at Marie for a moment and then asked, "Were you in love with this man?"

Marie blushed, lowered her head and said, weakly. "I was, at first."

"At first?"

She looked at the judge and said, "That's all I want to say."

The judge frowned. "Mam'selle, you must realize that the duty of the court is to dispense justice. To do that, we must have all of the available facts. Now, I feel you are holding back something. You've testified that you loved this man. You testified earlier that you left him. Why did you leave?"

Marie brought a hand to her eyes and shook her head. "Please, I really—"

"You must answer!" thundered the judge.

Josephine's attorney had warned of the asylum, a frightening prospect. It was all Marie could think of as she said, "I cannot tell you. Do what you want with me, but I cannot place this girl's life in any more jeopardy. She has suffered long enough!"

The judge stared at her for a moment, then turned away. "I want to see the prosecutor, the defense attorney, and this witness in my chambers. Court is in recess."

Once the group had gathered in chambers, the judge, sans his official robes, took his position behind a large walnut desk. Clearly enraged, he snapped, "I want to know it all, and immediately. The doctor has testified that this girl has engaged in sexual relations, possibly at the hands of the deceased. If that is so, it would explain not only her actions but also the severe emotional strain that she exhibits today. I want to know why these facts were not brought out by both the prosecution and the defense. I don't appreciate having to conduct this trial in a vacuum. LaTour, you first. What's going on here?"

The defense attorney looked like a defeated man. "Sir, the confusion is my fault. In all candor, I feel that the girl has suffered terribly because of what happened to her over the years. My fear is that you will rule she should be sent to an asylum for treatment. With all due respect, I think that would be worse than the guillotine."

The judge glowered at the defense attorney. "So you presume to see into my head? To determine what I will rule? Such arrogance! You have no faith in French justice?"

LaTour was about to say yes, but wisely held his tongue. The judge then turned to Marie. "And you? What do you know about this?"

Marie looked terrified. "I know that for years, I tried to seduce Claude Beauport and he showed no interest. I know that for years he looked at Josephine quite strangely. I know he's a twisted man—was a twisted man—bitter because of what happened in the war."

The judge leaned forward. "I want to hear it all," he commanded.

Marie told him everything she knew, including the

part about the diary, which she handed to the judge. He looked at it and said, "It is locked. Where is the key?"

"I don't know," answered Marie.

The judge handed it back to her. "Did you ever witness the beating of the girl?"

"No."

"Did you ever see this man touch the child in a sexual way?"

"No."

"You're quite sure?"

"Yes."

"Very well," the judge said, a sigh escaping from his lips. "I think I can make a ruling." He glared at LaTour. "I understand your concern about the asylum, but you must realize that this child is deeply disturbed. Nevertheless, I am prepared to send her to the supervised school provided she receives psychiatric treatment on a regular basis.

"The doctor treating her will report to me. If, in his opinion, the child's mental state can be determined and effectively treated outside the asylum, I will allow it. If, however, the doctor feels restrictions are required, the child will be transferred to the asylum.

"I want a private practitioner on this. Who can pay the medical bills? Are there any relatives?"

"She has no relatives," Marie said. "But I have a little money and I will get more. I will take the responsibility."

"Very well. So noted. We'll go back into court and I'll make my judgment. As for you two attorneys, I'll see you after this is over."

The two attorneys looked at each other and cringed. They could almost imagine what was going to happen. It wouldn't be pleasant.

Back in court, the judge determined that the evidence showed that Josephine Cousteau was guilty of killing her guardian, that the reasons she did so were clouded in mystery, but there was a possibility that she was acting to protect herself. Since there was no clear ulterior motive, he sentenced her to be taken to the supervised public school for juvenile offenders until her sixteenth birthday, at which time a further determination would be made regarding her future.

She was to receive regular, private psychiatric care paid for by Marie Benoit. If, for any reason, the private treatment was ended, or if there was any deterioration in Josephine's mental condition, the girl was to be immediately transferred to the asylum.

Josephine said nothing.

Hours later, Marie, sitting on the train, the still-locked diary clutched in her hands, wept all the way back to Lille. She'd taken on a frightful responsibility without fully knowing whether she could do it or not. She'd have to leave the farm in Lille and take a job in Paris near the school where Josephine was to be ensconced.

They called it a school, but it was really a prison. And it would be Josephine's home for the next six years—if she was lucky.

15

Within hours after her trial, Josephine Cousteau left for Paris on a bus, accompanied by a woman from the juvenile department of the national correctional system. The child's face remained impassively stoic, but behind the exterior, a twisted mind was hard at work.

When the shovel had split his skull and killed Claude Beauport, Josephine had felt a sense of joy unlike anything in her experience. When she realized he was forever unable to scream at her with his crazy rantings, to press his smelly body onto hers, forcing her to perform those terrible, sinful acts, to threaten her with her very life—her soul was immediately permeated by an unfamiliar sensation; she was infused with pure tranquility for the first time in her life. She was rid of him forever. It mattered not what happened now—at first. Then, an innate cunning took hold.

She was wise enough to realize the impact of expressing her true feelings. She knew instinctively what would happen; she'd be placed in some awful insane asylum for the rest of her life. Everyone had heard about those terrible places. So she'd resolved to say nothing, to appear stunned and unaware, but polite. Always polite.

She'd gambled and won, and the thrill of victory, the triumph over the all-knowing adults in charge of her life, was almost as exhilarating as the killing of Claude. Now, as a result of her conquest, she faced six years of prison school, a much harsher environment than previously, but nothing compared to the asylum. Besides, she was tired of her school, weary of the nuns and their constant piety, bored with their incessant preachings. Their utterances were not much different from Claude's, and she knew what Claude was really like. Who was to say the nuns were any different?

She liked learning about new things and new places. It would help her meet her goal. She wanted to be somebody when she grew up, someone rich, who lived in a big house in the city and drove around in a flashy American car and wore jewelry and fine clothes. She knew learning was the key to success. She never wanted to see another farm animal as long as she lived. She never wanted to see her hands dirty and cut from the never-ending chores.

For most of her short life, she'd been told she was pretty, and she believed it. When she grew up, she wanted to be beautiful, like the women she'd seen in forbidden magazines. She wanted to be important. She wanted to be the one who gave the orders, not the one who always received them.

She'd keep a diary, as her mother had done. She'd keep a record of everything that happened to her from now on, the good and the bad. She'd be true to the diary, but no one else would ever know what went on in her mind. Her thoughts were dangerous and had to be kept secret. No one must ever read her diary. If they did, she would kill them.

When she arrived at the school, she was taken through initial indoctrination, given a uniform to wear and books to study. Classes would start the next day. She would be given chores to do, just like at the farm, but these chores were less of a hardship. She was showered and deloused and examined by a doctor. Then she was told the rules. There were plenty of them, and adherence or nonadherence would result in either merit or demerit points being recorded beside her name. Five demerits and she lost all privileges; five merits and she would receive special treatment, easier chores, and more free time to do as she pleased in the grounds, even though they were surrounded by high fencing. There were other rewards and punishments, such as increased or decreased visitation periods with relatives.

The lantern-jawed matron checking her in looked at her chart and scoffed. "It says here that you get to see a head doctor once a month. You crazy?"

Josephine shook her head. "No, Madame."

"No? Then how come the head doctor?"

"It was the judge's order. I refused to testify at my trial and they thought that was because I was scared by what happened."

The matron glanced at the chart again and said, "You killed a man with a shovel?"

"No, Madame. I was convicted, but I didn't do it."

"Really? You're just like the rest in here. Well, don't give me any trouble."

"I won't, Madame."

She was shown to a bunk in a room that was shared by seven other girls, ranging in age from eight to fifteen, then left alone. The oldest of the girls, Michelle, was eager to reestablish her position of power. She stuck out her chin and said, "I run this room, understand? Outside this room, the matrons run the place, but inside, you answer to me."

"I understand."

"Good. Don't give me any trouble."

"I won't."

"Well, you're a pretty little thing, aren't you? What'd you do?"

Josephine sat quietly on her bunk and said, "They said I killed my guardian."

The others, all wards of the state for lesser crimes, were instantly awed—and intensely curious. Even Michelle was wary. "You killed him? How?"

"I didn't. They say I bashed his brains out with a shovel. Split his skull right open. They're wrong. I did no such thing."

It was the way she said it that got their attention. Coolly, calmly, with a thin smile on her lips. The other girls stared at her, feeling an almost palpable sense of danger. To them, she looked about twelve or thirteen, and a little small for her age. She was pretty. Very pretty. But her eyes were more than just cold; they were forbidding.

These were not pretty girls. Some were thin, others were fat, but all bore that special look of deprivation. Most had scars on their faces or arms or hands, all were used to danger and abuse, and cruelty, and a host of other inhuman acts. But none had ever seen such pure malevolence in the eyes of a new internee in this school for juvenile offenders. This one looked like she would stick a knife in any of their backs and never bat an eye.

They left her alone as she put away her meager belongings and crawled into bed.

"Michelle?" Josephine asked.

"What?"

"Where can I get my hands on a diary? I want to keep a record of my experiences."

"You can ask the matron, but I warn you—they look at those things."

"They do?"

"You don't have any privacy in this place, kid. You're a prisoner here. If you keep a diary, they'll look at it every day."

Josephine lay back on the bed and put her arms under her head. That would never do, she thought. There were things she wanted to say in her diary that no one must ever see. She'd have to wait until she got out, it seemed.

The psychiatrist hired by Marie made his first visit to the supervised correctional school two weeks after Josephine arrived. Short and gaunt, Dr. Peter Vanias looked like an old man, with a beard and mustache and steel-rimmed glasses that made his eyes look bigger than they were. His real age was forty-six, but he was a man so enamored of Sigmund Freud that he made every effort to look as much as possible like his idol.

One of his fondest memories was of a visit to Dr. Freud in London in 1939, not long before Freud's death. The two talked for almost an hour, and when they parted, the feeble Freud had shaken Vanais's hand weakly. Even so, Vanais had felt electrified, as if some of the man's genius were flowing through his own body.

When Marie Benoit made an appointment to see him, he assumed it was for her own benefit, but when she arrived, she discussed instead the case of Josephine, showed him the court order requiring monthly treatments, and tearfully explained her personal financial difficulties. At first, Vanais refused to become involved, but the more Marie explained the facts surrounding the child's violent act, the more Vanais became interested.

Like Freud, Vanais was convinced that sexual impulses were the root cause of all neuroses. He perceived the Cousteau case as one to further prove such contentions. According to Marie, the child had killed Claude Beauport after years of sexual abuse, though this had not been proven in court. A doctor had testified, but the child had denied claims of any and all abuse.

Vanais decided to take the case, and even lowered his fee to a level that Marie, now working in a clothing factory, could afford.

The first meeting between the doctor and Josephine was held in the school's infirmary. The child was brought in by a matron and introduced to the doctor. He smiled warmly and told her to sit in a chair and try to relax as much as possible. The matron left and the doctor and his new patient were alone.

Josephine was wary. She knew this man could have a great influence on her future. His reports to the court would determine what happened to her six years hence. She resolved to tell this man what she thought he wanted to hear, but to do it carefully, slowly, never revealing her true feelings lest they be used against her. She displayed a cunning far beyond her chronological age.

Dr. Vanais began by asking her how she felt.

"How do I feel?"

"Yes. Right now. This very instant. Sitting here and being questioned by a strange man with a beard who wants to look inside your head. Do you feel comfortable, or do you feel that this is a cruel and unnecessary inquisition that you would much rather live without?"

"I don't know," she said. "I've never talked to a—"

"Psychiatrist?"

"Yes, a psychiatrist. I've never talked to one before."

"I understand. Does it make you nervous?"

"Yes. I think it does."

He nodded and clasped his hands across his stomach. "I imagine it would. Well, let me tell you a few things that might make you feel better. Though I am to answer to the court, you are my patient, and my first concern is you. I will never lie to you, I promise. I will be honest and fair, and I will listen carefully to what you have to say. I do not make judgments, Josephine. Do you know what I mean by that?"

"I'm not sure."

"I mean I will not scold you for anything. There are no wrongs and rights to be considered, only thoughts and events. I want to know what you think, feel, and do. I will never say that your thoughts and feelings are wrong, only explain your motivation, if I can."

"I understand."

"Good. Actually, there are several reasons I took your case. Of course, you are aware that the court requires you be visited by a competent psychiatrist on a monthly basis?"

"Yes."

"The judge in your case was a very enlightened man, you know. In years past, the sentence in your case would have been much harsher. But, during the last few years, some of the judges in juvenile court have attempted to employ new ideas to see if they are more beneficial to the accused . . . in certain cases.

"Your case fits the criteria. By that, I mean that the judge feels you could be helped by someone like me. Over the next few years, we'll work together and see what we can see. If it proves successful, others will be helped as well."

He paused and stroked his beard for a moment. "There are other reasons I took the case," he continued. "You have a friend, Marie Benoit, who is very concerned about you. She feels you have suffered terribly at the hands of your late guardian. She wants you to be happy. She wants to see you do well here and when you get out of this place, go on to a full and rich life. And then, there are my own reasons."

Josephine seemed puzzled. "Your own reasons?"

"Yes," he said. "You see, the science of psychiatry, if you can call it a science, is rather new. There are many people engaged in developing different theories as to what makes us behave the way we do as human beings. Each time I am presented with a case that fits my narrow field of practice, I learn things that help me gain confidence in my own views."

Josephine asked, "And what are those?"

The doctor smiled and said, "There's plenty of time for that. The important thing right now is for you to understand that I am here to help you. By helping you, I am also helping myself. Therefore, I have every reason to be honest with you. Do you see what I am trying to say?"

"I'm not sure."

He leaned forward and peered at her through the thick glasses, as if trying to hypnotize her. "Let me try to make it clear. I believe most people do things for selfish reasons, even when helping others. When we help others, we feel good, and that is the selfish motive. You see?"

"I think so."

"Good. I have something to gain by helping you understand yourself and your feelings. If I can successfully help you become a happier person, I will have proved certain of my own theories, and that will make me a more important person. Since everything we do together is aimed at helping each other, you have nothing to fear.

"If you feel better after we have worked together, I will be better off. If you don't feel better, I will be worse off. Therefore, it is in my own best interests to help you feel better. Which means you can trust me. Do you understand?"

"I think so."

He smiled. "I understand your reticence. Having examined your case, I think, if I were you, I would be very distrustful of anyone, including myself. I want you to know it's fine for you to feel that way, for the moment, at least. Hopefully, we'll work together and discover what lies at the root of those feelings and see if they can be . . . modified."

Josephine stared at him.

He leaned back in the chair and beamed. "Now, tell me, how do you feel about being in this place? About the trial? About your guardian's death? Tell me how you feel."

Josephine took a deep breath, then said, "Well, I like it here. I like learning things. The teachers are all right and my roommates are interesting. There is one thing, though . . ."

"Yes?"

"Well, I want to keep a diary. I think it might be fun to keep a record of my experiences here, but I've been told the matrons look at everything. There's no privacy. If you could arrange for me to keep a diary and be allowed to keep it completely to myself, I would appreciate it."

"I think a diary would be a very worthwhile thing," he said. "However, if it's privacy you want, this is hardly the place. I understand some of your roommates are very adept at picking locks."

"That's true," she said. "If you can make sure the matrons and the teachers can't look at it, I can handle the other girls."

The doctor looked at her carefully for a moment, then nodded. "I'll see what I can do. Now, tell me about the trial. How did you feel about that?"

"It was a bad thing."

"Why?"

"Because they said I killed my guardian. I didn't do anything. I was asleep."

The doctor leaned forward again. "At the trial, you refused to speak about that night, except to answer questions put to you by the judge. Why did you take that position?"

"Because I had already told them. I told the policemen I was asleep and didn't know anything. They didn't believe me. I knew if I told the judge the same thing, he wouldn't believe me either. It was better not to say anything."

"But when the judge asked you—you did answer his questions."

"I had to. He ordered it, and it was as I had expected. He didn't believe me. No one believes me. They all think I killed my guardian and I didn't. You don't believe me either, do you?"

Peter Vanais dodged the question by saying, "I don't know, Josephine. I wasn't there. I didn't see what happened. I don't know you very well yet. Besides, it really isn't important what I think. It's only important what you think. If you are saying that you had nothing to do with it, then I will take you at your word." He paused for a moment, then said, "However, if you did kill him, you may well have had good reason. Not all killing is wrong. There is such a thing as self-defense."

"I killed no one," she insisted.

"Very well. Tell me, how did you feel when you found out he was dead?"

"I was sorry when I found out."

"And why was that?"

"Because he was my guardian. He looked after me. He was a nice man and I was sorry I was never going to see him again."

"Do you miss him?"

"Of course."

Josephine kept her expression as blank as possible. The doctor stared at her for a few moments, made some notations on a writing pad, then asked, "Do you trust me, Josephine?"

She stared back at him for a moment and then said, "No. Not yet."

He smiled and closed the notebook. "Good for you. An honest answer. I don't blame you for thinking as you do, not one bit."

She smiled.

"I think that's enough for now," he said. "You're a very bright girl, Josephine. Did you know that?"

She shook her head.

Dr. Vanais rose from the chair and said, "Well, you are. I'll get to work on the diary you wanted and I'll see you again in a month. In the meantime, I want you to think about your relationship with your guardian. I want you to make two lists. On the first, write down all the things you liked about him. On the second, all the things you didn't like. The next time we meet, we'll discuss the lists you've made. All right?"

She nodded.

"And another thing. I want you to know I'm your friend. I really am. I won't do anything to break your trust and I won't do anything to hurt you. I know you don't believe that right now, but it's true. As time goes on, you'll start to feel better about talking to me. Remember what I said earlier. If I can help you, I help myself."

Josephine stood up and said, "I'll remember."

Dr. Vanais looked at those dark, cold eyes and wondered who was kidding whom.

He brought a diary on his next visit. It was a sturdy cloth-bound book, with a red cover and a clasp that locked securely. He handed it to her along with two keys on a chain that could be placed around her neck.

"I've talked to the head matron," he said. "She has promised me that none of the matrons or teachers will look at your diary. It is yours to keep in total privacy. You can write what you like without fear that they or I will ever look at it without your permission. As for your roommates, I'll leave that to you."

Josephine smiled and took the book from the doctor, ran her hand over it and placed the key chain around her neck. "Thank you," she said.

"You're entirely welcome." He opened his notebook. "Have you thought about those questions I asked you on my last visit? Did you make the lists?"

Josephine nodded and handed the doctor two sheets of paper. The first bore an innocuous list of complaints about her unnamed guardian, ranging from his strictness to his penchant for yelling at her. Nothing more serious than that. On the second sheet, she listed his attributes: hard-working, a good Catholic and a good provider. If the doctor was disappointed by such a description, he didn't show it.

"Good," he said, as he placed the lists in his pocket. "Now, I want to talk to you about something that many people find embarrassing. I don't want you to be embarrassed and I don't want you to be frightened, so if we get into something that bothers you, I want you to let me know. Will you do that?"

Josephine nodded.

"Good. What I want to talk to you about is the subject of sex. By that I mean the physical relationship between men and women. Have you taken biology in school?"

"No."

"Did your guardian ever talk to you about such things?"

The girl chewed on her lower lip, thought about it and finally said, "Yes."

"Can you tell me about those conversations?"

"There was only one I remember. One time, when the cattle were dropping, I asked him how that happened. He explained to me about how seeds were planted in the female, just like in people. He showed me a drawing of a woman and a man and explained the different things about them. He explained sex was for childbearing and that I must remain a virgin until I was married."

"Do you know what the word virgin means?"

"Yes," she answered. "It means a person who has never had sex."

"And do you know what a menstrual cycle is?"

"Yes. My guardian taught me about that. He explained how the human body works. Besides, I started to menstruate six months ago."

The doctor looked at her in surprise. "That's very young. You're only ten."

"I know."

Vanais seemed puzzled. He made some notes, then said, "So, you were told that sex is for childbearing and that you should remain a virgin until you are married. Do you agree with that?"

"Yes."

"I see. Now—I know this question is difficult, but don't be upset by it. You're very mature for a child of ten. I'm sure you can handle it."

"I hope so."

The doctor stroked his beard for a moment before posing the question. "Did your guardian ever have sex with you?"

Josephine looked shocked. "No," she exclaimed. "He would never do anything like that. It's a terrible, terrible sin!"

"Of course, but let us suppose that, just for the sake of discussion, you were forced to have sex with your guardian, or someone else for that matter. Let us suppose that they threatened you with harm if you didn't submit. Would you not agree that the sin was on their hands? That you could do nothing else but go along with it? That wouldn't be a sin for you, would it?"

Josephine's hands formed into fists. "It's a sin no matter what anyone says. It's better to be dead than to commit such a sin. My guardian knew that. He would never think of such a thing. Ever!"

Dr. Vanais looked at her carefully. "How could it be a sin if you had no say? If someone forced you to do something, it wouldn't be a sin."

She shook her head violently. "Yes, it would. What can they threaten you with? A beating? Death? It is better to be beaten or even die than to do such a thing. I would . . . I would never let anyone do that to me. I would spend an eternity in hell!"

Vanais leaned back in the chair again and looked at his notes. "According to the doctor who examined you at the time of your arrest," he said softly, "you are no longer a virgin. You've told me you understand what that means. How do you explain the fact that you're no longer a virgin?"

Her eyes glazed over. "The doctor was wrong. I don't know where he got the idea that I was no longer a virgin. I can't explain that, but I know I am. I don't know why they keep saying that my guardian did things to me when he didn't. Just like they keep saying that I killed him when I didn't. I don't know the answers. I just know what happened. He never touched me and I never killed him." Tears began to form at the corners of her eyes. "No one believes me. No one ever believes me...."

Dr. Vanais leaned forward, fixed his gaze on the eyes of the girl and said, "I want to, Josephine. I want to very much."

Again, he looked at his notes. "What was his name?"

"Who?"

"Your guardian. What was his name?"

She didn't answer immediately. She sat rigidly in the chair, her hands still formed into fists, her mouth moving soundlessly. Finally, agonizingly, she spoke the words. "Claude," she said. "Claude Beauport."

Dr. Vanais smiled and made another notation. For the remainder of the session, they talked about neutral subjects—schoolwork, her roommates, her favorite movies and books. Then it was over until next month.

Josephine went back to her room, removed the key chain from her neck, and opened the diary. She took a pen and sat on her bunk. Oblivious to the stares from the other girls, she began to write in the diary. On the first page, she wrote the date, and beneath it,

> I have just finished another meeting with Dr. Vanais. He is a very nice man, but for some reason, he seems to be confused. I don't know why, but he thinks like the others do. He thinks that my guardian was a bad person. He also thinks I sinned with my guardian. And worst of all, he thinks I killed him.
>
> I wish I could make him understand that none of this is true. My guardian was a kind man who took good care of me. He would never do anything to hurt me and I would never do anything to hurt him. I don't know why everyone keeps making up these lies about him and about me. I guess there is nothing I can do to change their mind. I wish I could.

She closed the diary and locked it. Then she leaned back on the bed and smiled to herself. Someday the diary would be read by the doctor. He would think he had been so very clever, getting her the diary and suggesting that she write her innermost thoughts in it. But she knew what he was up to. She knew that someday he'd take the diary from her and read it. He'd think that he was reading her real thoughts, but he'd be wrong. He'd be reading only what she wanted him to read. Someday she'd have a diary that she could protect from the prying eyes of others, a record of her true thoughts and experiences, but this was not the time.

She got up from the bed and shuffled the few meters between her bunk and that of Michelle's.

"How'd it go with the headshrinker?" Michelle asked.

Josephine turned the diary over in her hands and said, "Oh . . . well, I think. He let me have a diary. He says the matrons are not to look at it."

Michelle sneered. "And you believe that?"

Josephine smiled, "Yes, I do. And I want everyone in this room to know that this diary is not to be touched. If it is, I will slit the throat of the first one who lays a finger on it. Do you believe that?"

"Yes," Michelle said. "I believe it."

Dr. Vanais sat at his desk, reviewing, for the sixth time, the notes he'd taken during the interview with Josephine Cousteau. His mood darkened. It was clear his work was cut out for him, for the girl was as true a psychopathic personality as he'd ever seen. At the age of ten, she was simply toying with him, lying at will, totally at ease, like an adult who was fully aware of the techniques employed by psychiatrists to learn the inner workings of the subconscious mind.

He sighed and sank deeper into his chair. This one was a real challenge, a most difficult case. One of two things had happened. Either the girl had created a fantasy world, or she'd learned to cope within the real world in a way that was truly frightening. She trusted no one and revealed only what she wanted revealed. While understanding of the phenomenon, the doctor had never before encountered anyone, child or adult, with such total emotional control. He pondered his notes and wondered if it was already too late. Perhaps this child had slipped over the edge into true madness and could never be brought back.

Until she opened herself to him, he would never really know if her disorder was a result of repressed sexual feelings. He had many reasons to suspect that it was, but papers submitted for consideration by the Society required stronger evidence than the statements of a single doctor.

Another problem existed, the answer to the age-old question as to the causes for her condition. Was it something in the genes or a result of environment? In this case, the mother was known, and the father, according to official records, was dead. But the mother's diary, which had been provided by Marie Benoit, told a different tale. There was even a picture of the man, an American, once a pilot with the English during the war—and possibly still alive.

As the doctor continued wrestling with his thoughts, his secretary entered the office with some tea. To the doctor, she said, "You look very tired. Perhaps you would be wise to give it up for today. Is it a particularly vexing problem?"

He grunted and closed the file folder. "Vexing? Indeed, my young friend. I am dealing here with a child with the cunning of a fox, a pure psychopath, devoid of conscience, like no one I've ever encountered before. She'd make an interesting case study for the Society, but I'll have trouble substantiating my claims."

The woman's eyebrows shot up. "A true psychopath, you say. That's unusual."

"Yes. Most unusual. I think this one is beyond the help of anyone."

The young woman smiled and said, "You're just tired. You'll feel better in the morning."

"I'm sure I will, but that won't change the facts." He sighed. "The vagaries of life, Helga. They never cease to amaze me. Here we have a young child who is incredibly beautiful. Someday, she'll be a woman, and the young men chasing her will be jumping out of their skins with excitement. But she's terribly damaged, and any man who falls in love with this one will rue the day.

"And then," he continued, staring at the papers on his desk, "there is the case of Mam'selle Boule, a new patient in my care. A truly ugly woman, with the face of a horse and the body of a stick, but a woman possessed of a brilliant mind and a soul that practically radiates compassion. A lonely woman, because the young men steer clear of her."

He sighed. "If they only knew. Perhaps someday, she'll find a man, and when she does, he will think he's been blessed by God Himself, for this woman will shower him with affection like no other. If she weren't a patient, I would think of marrying her myself."

He laughed and said, "I'm being silly, yes?"

When there was no response, he looked up and realized he was talking to the walls. Helga had already left the room.

JOSEPH DIPAOLO: A STEP UP

Part Six

16

By January of 1956, Joseph DiPaolo was a respected member of the House, highly regarded by his peers in Washington and almost revered in his home district of Brooklyn. Like many politicians, he was gregarious, charming, and filled with righteous sincerity, but with Joseph, the sincerity was genuine. He was a good listener with colleagues and constituents alike, and they liked that. He was unfailing in his efforts to help constituents, even after an election, and those he helped remembered his consideration.

Unlike most of his contemporaries, Joseph had eschewed a house in Washington, instead keeping the small apartment and perpetually commuting to Brooklyn, to the point where the train conductors and porters knew him better than some of his friends. A quick study, he'd learned what it took to function

in the House and played ball with the best of them—
or so they thought. If he disagreed with a bill being
put forth, he would couch his arguments in quiet,
well-reasoned language, and his rejection of an idea
was never personal, but always based on some princi-
ple cloaked in a blanket of rationality. When he
wanted something or was presenting a bill of his own,
he was circumspect in his promises to return favors,
but once made, the promise was always kept. As a
result, he was trusted, even by the army of lobbyists
he usually turned away with a smile.

Now, with the political bit firmly in his teeth, he
sought higher office, feeling he could achieve even
more. But the doors seemed tightly closed. One of
the state's two incumbents, Senator Miles Taylor, a
member of Joseph's party, was seeking a fourth term
and was expected to receive the party's full support
in the fall election. The other New York senator, a
Republican reelected just over a year before, was
even more firmly entrenched than Taylor, and considered unbeatable. It meant another six years of
waiting, and Joseph, restless, impatient to move forward, chafed at the thought of waiting.

There was one possible shortcut, but it was a politi-
cally dangerous move. His eagerness quickly turning
to frustration, Joseph decided to discuss his future
with his closest political adviser—Sophia.

On a cold and snowy January night, with the children tucked in bed, he poured some brandy into two
large glasses and brought them into the front room of
their Brooklyn home. A fire crackled in the fireplace.
Sophia was curled up in a big chair in front of the
fire, reading a copy of Faulkner's *A Fable.*

"Have you read this?" she asked as she took the
glass from his hand.

"I'm afraid not."

She put the book down. "They gave him a Pulitzer
for this," she said, shaking her head. "I can't imagine

why. If you ask me, they were simply compensating for previous oversights. This is not the Faulkner I know."

Joseph had a serious expression on his face.

"What's the matter?" she asked.

Joseph, never one to mince words, got right to the point. "What would you think of my chances if I ran in the Senate primary?"

Sophia never blinked an eye. Slowly, she put the book down. "Do you want to?"

"Very much."

She smiled. "My impatient husband. What brought this on?"

"Two things. No, three, really."

"Tell me."

"Well, for one, I think Miles is doing a terrible job. His attendance record is fourth worst in the Senate. His voting record is equally abysmal. He's nothing but a rubber stamp for the party."

"And what's number two?"

"Even if he were there all the time, I think I can do a better job. He's just masquerading as a senator. He loves playing the role, mind you, but he does nothing. He's the stereotypical blowhard politician and represents everything I hate about this business. I don't like the idea of waiting until he's ready to retire. He'll never be ready. Why should he? He'll die in harness."

"That's it? You think you can do a better job than Miles Taylor? Joseph, almost anyone can do a better job than Miles Taylor. There has to be something more. This is your Sophie you're talking to."

He grinned sheepishly. "All right. The Senate is like the big leagues, Sophie. It's where the real action is, and I want a piece of it. I want to make my mark."

She chuckled. "That's more like it," she said. Then, her face as serious as his, she added, "Do you realize what will happen if you run in the primary?"

"Like?"

"The party will drop you. They'll think you're being disloyal, and you know how they feel about loyalty."

"There's a limit to everything. Even loyalty."

"I agree, but why not wait four years? If Macaroy runs again, which he probably will, you're sure to get the party's full support. They'd love to capture both New York seats, and with you and Taylor running in tandem, the chances are good that they can. But by going against Taylor now, you'll burn a lot of bridges."

"I realize that."

She raised her eyebrows. "What aren't you telling me?"

Joseph smiled ruefully. "If I run now, I serve notice that I'm my own man. I think it's time. That motivates me more than anything."

"Why?"

He stood by the fire and stared into the flames. "You know as well as I do there are wheels within wheels here in New York. The party's ties to the mob are getting stronger, not weaker. Carmine and his pals are doling out the patronage with little concern for the long-term damage resulting from it. They're pushing Harriman for the presidential nomination, and that's crazy. He just doesn't have national appeal, but De Sapio sees himself as a kingmaker. The whole organization has become arrogant and sloppy. I want to distance myself from them as soon as possible."

He turned and faced her. "They say power corrupts. It does. I've already been corrupted to a certain degree by paying political debts I owed. Sure, they were relatively small things, but I did what I did because I was asked to, not because I wanted to. That makes me a whore of sorts, and I don't like the feeling."

She laughed. "My love, if you're a whore, they're all whoremasters."

"Well, in fact, they are. It's how things get done. I know I can't fight it or change it. This is not the time to reinvent the wheel, but if I run in the primary and win, the party will have to support me, and that support will be on my terms, not theirs. I'd feel a lot better about myself."

She stood up and put her arms around him. "And if you lose?"

"I can run for the House in fifty-eight."

"You plan to resign your seat?"

"I do."

She let her arms fall to her side. "I can see you've given this a lot of thought."

"I have. But I'm not making a decision until we've talked it out. I value your judgment, Sophie."

For a moment, they stared into each other's eyes. Then Sophia said, "If you think things will be better in the Senate, think again. The wheeling and dealing is on a much higher plane, my love. A man coming in on a white horse will accomplish absolutely nothing. Others have tried and failed. Just ask Walter Rice."

"I'm not on a white horse," he said. "I know I'll have to make compromises. I don't have a problem with that. Making compromises is one thing, but being tied to Tammany Hall is something else again. That's how I'm perceived, you know. They all keep wondering when I'm going to really put the arm on them for something."

"You already did. Twice."

"Yes, but that was nothing. You show me a Democrat who's against a labor bill and I'll show you a man with no future, at least not in New York."

"But they know who was behind it."

"Of course. Still, the bills were good bills, and that's what counts."

"If the party isn't behind you, where would you get the money?"

"I've given that some thought as well. I'd go to the people. I'd make a general appeal. I've helped a lot of them over the years. I think they'd respond."

"I'm not so sure," she said. "Most of those you've helped are poor. They may want to help, but they can't. A primary race could cost half a million dollars, my love. Maybe more. The party hacks will be so outraged they'll pull out all the stops. They could spend a million, maybe two, in trying to beat you. And they'd be very upset with anyone who helped you financially. I don't have to tell you that money can make all the difference, Joey."

"I'm aware of that," he said, stiffly. "So, you think I'm wrong?"

Surprisingly, she beamed. "No. Not at all. I think you can win."

"Really?"

"Yes, really. Miles Taylor has about as much charisma as that chair over there. You, on the other hand, are the kind of man who makes a woman's toes curl."

"You're prejudiced."

"Maybe. That doesn't mean I don't worry every time you go to Washington. And don't tell me there haven't been a few dozen southern belles chomping at the bit to get my Joey between the sheets."

He blushed. "You can't possibly think—"

"Don't worry. I'm not saying you've been cheating on me. I'd know it the moment you did. That business about the wife being the last to know? Not this wife. I know you too well. Just the same, you have to admit they pursue you relentlessly."

"Well, there have been a couple. But I've never so much as—"

"Stop being defensive. Let's get back to the point. You can win, but you'll need money. Lots of it. You need to be on television, Joey. You look great on TV. Taylor doesn't. For some reason, he's terrified of television. He stammers and stutters and looks like the fool he is. That's the key, Joey. Television. But you need money, and those poor people aren't going to give it to you."

"What if they worked to get it?"

"How?"

"Suppose we formed an organization of ordinary folks and had them go door-to-door, encourage others to do bake sales, garage sales, whatever. If we could get ten thousand people in this state to support me, and each one was able to raise one hundred dollars, we'd have enough to win the primary."

"That would take a lot of organizing."

"I know. I have a person in mind who could pull it off."

"Who?"

"You."

She was stunned. "Me? Are you crazy?"

"Not at all. You're the best organizer I've ever known. Besides, you've always lived here in Brooklyn. You never became one of those Washington wives going to party after party. You stayed and mothered our children instead, though we both know how you love a good party."

"What has that got to do with anything?"

"Your image. You have one, you know, and it's a good one. The people around here know what you do. You may not wear black, but you're one of them. If you took this on, you'd make it work. I know it."

"What am I supposed to do with the children?"

"Mother can look after them for a while. She'd love it. So would the kids. She's only a few blocks away."

Sophia held up her hands in surrender. "All right. Let's say, just for the sake of discussion, that we did this. Let's even say you won the primary. And let's say the party gets behind you for the election. Have you considered the fact that Eisenhower is a cinch to win the presidency again? There's a very good chance that he'll pull a lot of Republicans in with him."

"I've considered that."

"And you still want to do this?"

"I do. I really do."

She kissed him lightly on the lips. "Well, we better get started. We have a lot of work to do."

The next morning, Joseph called a secret meeting of his closest advisers and fund-raisers, and he included the New York party chairman. The group met on the windswept Brooklyn Promenade on a bitterly cold day. Six men huddled together, their overcoat collars turned up to ward off a fierce wind sweeping unimpeded across the dockyards. Joseph looked down and picked out the very spot where he'd departed for England over sixteen years ago. Less than two decades, but it seemed like a century. Then, he'd been a kid, impatient for adventure. Now, at thirty-four, he was impatient for something else.

"What the hell's this all about?" John Milsome, the party chairman, complained.

"Yeah," Tuppio added. "Why can't we meet in your office?"

"What I have to say is confidential," Joseph told them. "For your ears alone. I don't want anybody overhearing anything."

"So? What's so important?" Milsome asked.

"I wanted you guys to know what's happening directly from me. You're the first to hear this."

"Hear what?" Tuppio asked.

"I've decided to enter the Senate primary."

Tuppio's jaw dropped. "What? Are you nuts?"

"I hope not."

"What's the big hurry? You got lots of time. You better think this over, boss."

"I have thought it over," Joseph said. "If I lose, I lose, but I have to find out where I stand. The only way I can do that is run in the primary."

"I don't understand," Tuppio said, shaking his head. "You never said nuthin' to us about this. Why the sudden urge to be a senator?"

"Simple," Joseph said. "I think Taylor's the wrong man for the party and the state, not to mention the country. He's been resting on his laurels too long. We're not getting what we need because he doesn't give a damn anymore. All he cares about is getting elected, then he sits on his ass until the party snaps its fingers. Then he votes. Big deal. He missed sixteen big votes last session, mostly because he was down in the Bahamas having a good time. Granted, the bills were never in danger, else he'd have been there. Still, the people deserve better than what they're getting."

"The people?" Milsome said, sneering. "What's all this sudden concern about the people, for Christ's sake?"

"That was the original idea," Joseph retorted. "You weren't there, but when I was asked to run for the House, I was told it was for the people's benefit. I happen to like that."

"Jesus. So now you want to turn on those who put you there? You called us out here for this?"

"Yes. I wanted you to hear it from me. I owe you that."

"You owe us a hell of a lot more than that, Joseph. We've busted our ass for you for six years. Now, you're stabbing us in the back. It stinks."

"I don't see it that way," Joseph said calmly. "I'll save the speech about democracy and all that. I'm not asking for your support or your enmity. I'm simply letting you know before anyone else."

"What's your beef with Taylor?"

"I already told you. Miles Taylor isn't doing the job he was elected to do."

"No? You don't hear us complaining."

"I'm aware of that."

Milsome threw his hands in the air. "Well, include me out, as they say. I want no part of this. I've never been here. I'm not getting involved. If you enter the primary, you're on your own."

"What if I win?"

"You won't."

"But what if I do?"

"We'll cross that bridge when we come to it."

"That's all I wanted to know."

Milsome shuffled off and Joseph turned to his advisers. "All right, what about the rest of you? Are you with me on this?"

Tuppio spoke for them all. "Joseph, you're a hell of a guy. We love you like a brother, but if you do this, you're goin' against Carmine. We can't help you, understand?"

"I do. No hard feelings, Frank."

The two men shook hands there in the freezing cold. Then, as if participating in a ceremony, Frank and the other three men—former close associates— turned and walked away, leaving Joseph alone in the wind and cold, wondering if he'd made the biggest mistake of his life.

Perhaps, but despite the cold, he felt as if he'd just stepped from a warm shower.

Within three weeks, he had the nucleus of his new organization in place, and Sophia had hers. His consisted of three men, disgruntled former party functionaries, all experienced hacks—but with a difference. Within their breasts burned a vehement hatred for Tammany Hall and its most important icon, Miles Taylor. As for Sophia, she'd marshaled a small army of women, housewives mostly, all of them thrilled at the prospect of raising money for the handsome and charming Joseph DiPaolo's political campaign. It was a beginning, though a modest one.

He announced formally on February 14, Valentine's Day, after having tendered his resignation as a member of the House because, as he said at a press conference, "I can't very well chastise Miles Taylor for failing to exercise his responsibilities and then spend all my time campaigning. That would make me a hypocrite. I have my faults, but I'm no hypocrite."

"Would you like to tell us what they are?" a reporter asked.

"What what are?"

"Your faults."

"Well," he said grinning, "for one, I'm impatient."

17

Using the Brooklyn storefront as his campaign headquarters, Joseph began his conspicuously impossible crusade. As the days passed, he drew from a pool of friends and family members (however remotely connected) to augment a small group of experienced pols that formed the nucleus of his fledgling political organization. The newcomers—naive, dewy-eyed supporters—were political outsiders, but their lack of expertise was offset by their slavish willingness to work long hours.

In addition to her duties as part of the inner circle, the brain trust, Sophia was the commander of a group dubbed "Sophia's Army," now sixty men and women strong. The army fanned out, covering much of Brooklyn, knocking on doors in an effort to raise precious resources.

At first, the campaign was confined to New York

City, but within weeks, Joseph was traveling to Albany, Syracuse, Rochester, and Buffalo, making speeches to Rotary clubs, Knights of Columbus, American Legion groups, and even Daughters of the American Revolution. His theme was always the same. He believed in free enterprise, but the working man was getting the short end, and every effort had to be made to stop Big Business from crushing the rights of labor. Miles Taylor was a part-time senator in the pocket of Big Business. The state needed a man who would give all of his time to the job and who wouldn't bend to the pernicious whims of those with power.

After three weeks of hard work, he read the results of his first poll. The numbers were shattering. If the primary were held on the day the poll was taken, Miles Taylor would have 67 percent of the vote, Joseph 23, with 10 percent undecided. And worse, Miles Taylor had yet to begin campaigning seriously. Clearly, the young man from Brooklyn had a long way to go.

By March, they had enough money for their first television commercial, a statewide, minute-long, face-to-the-camera appeal. In it, Joseph declared he was fighting for the little man and asked those who supported his views to send money. The receipts failed to pay for the cost of the ad.

In April, full-page newspaper advertisements appeared in every New York newspaper. Beneath a photograph of an unsmiling, grandfatherly looking Miles Taylor, was a single paragraph that read, "This is the man who has worked for the people of New York for almost eighteen years. A man who has dedicated his life to the people of this state. A man who deserves your support on election day." The ad was signed by one hundred of the most influential people in the state.

Sophia's Army, now six hundred strong, renewed its efforts to raise money. Each week, the level of receipts—an accumulation of coins, small bills, and checks—increased, but the targets set at the beginning of the campaign were far from being met. The early projections seemed, in retrospect, to have been flights of fancy.

Joseph, working twenty hours a day, expanded his efforts, hitting as many as fifteen cities and towns, his small entourage traveling by car. Sometimes they stayed in cheap motels. At other times, they slept in the car, using service station washrooms to wash, shave, and change clothes. Everywhere they went, they saw highway billboards, posters, and bumper stickers, all bearing the stern, patrician visage of Miles Taylor. The DiPaolo campaign had no money for such things, just a few thousand campaign buttons.

After two months of intense campaigning, another poll was taken. The wide gap had closed by seven percentage points. Movement, yes, but not nearly enough to make a significant difference. The battle seemed lost before it had really begun, and gloom settled over the campaign headquarters.

Alone, huddled together in a corner of the storefront, listening to the rain as it pelted down at one in the morning, Joseph and Sophia took stock.

"I can see why De Sapio fired those three turkeys," Joseph said. "They haven't a clue how to run a campaign."

"It's not their fault," Sophia said. "The party machinery is firmly in place, working against us. Our guys are used to working as part of a well-established and proven organization where their jobs are clearly defined. Here, they're expected to develop an effective campaign designed to counter their best previous effort. That's asking a lot. The failure is ours, not theirs."

"So, where did we go wrong?"

Sophia smiled. "You can't be serious."

"What do you mean?"

"You're the politician. And you're asking *me* where we went wrong? I think you know."

"I'm not sure I do," he said.

"Perhaps you just don't want to admit it."

He frowned. "Stop playing word games, Sophie. Spit it out."

"No. It has to come from you, Joey. If you don't understand what's happening here, we haven't got a chance."

He stood up, paced the floor for a moment, then turned and faced her. "The money, right?"

"What about the money?"

"We thought . . . I thought . . . we could get a few thousand people together, have them raise a hundred bucks apiece, and that would be that. It's not that easy. People don't like to give money to someone they think will lose. Oh sure, we've raised some from those who'd like to see me win, but the big bucks are controlled by the machine. That's what we're missing—and fighting."

"It's as much my fault as yours," she said. "I thought it could be done. I failed to account for apathy. Most people are pretty happy these days. They don't want to rock the boat. Politics is the last thing on their minds."

"So, where do we go from here?"

"Where do you think we should go?"

He never hesitated. "We fight to the end," he said. "Harder than ever. I'm not a quitter."

She stood up, walked toward him and placed her arms around his neck. "I know you're not. Neither am I."

"It won't be much fun," he said.

"I know. I don't care. We'll learn things. Lots of things. Next time, we'll do it better."

It wasn't much fun at all. It was hard work, with little good news to build enthusiasm. Still, Joseph looked and acted like a man who was going to win—

because he had to. But in his heart, he was convinced he would lose, and the thought of losing left a bitter taste in his mouth.

In the company of others, he was cheerful, and optimistic, but when alone he allowed his disappointment and dejection to emerge, like a black butterfly from a cocoon, an almost visible presence, laughing and taunting him. In those morose moments, he felt the anger building in his gut and fought hard to prevent it from overwhelming him. He was usually successful.

But when an old woman came to the storefront looking for help, Joseph soon felt his inner hostility consuming him. Hers was a common complaint. A pensioner with limited income, she lived in a hovel owned by one of New York's notorious slum landlords. With rent control, she was protected from sudden increases in her monthly cost, but not from the landlord's refusal to make needed repairs to a rapidly disintegrating building.

"It's the rats," she said, in heavily accented English. "My granddaughter killed in accident three month ago. There was no one to take the children except police. I could not let them do that. I tell judge I look after them. He say okay for little while. They send someone to check that my place okay."

She wiped a tear from her eye with a black handkerchief. "The children have bites from the rats. I set traps, I keep place clean, scrub all day, but they still come at night. I ask man from landlord to help me and he just laugh. Social worker say unless I get rid of rats I lose children. They go to orphanage. I die if that happen. You help me, please?"

Under normal circumstances, Joseph would have made a few phone calls to the proper authorities. This time, he felt the need to handle it personally. This time, he allowed his rage to surface.

"How many children are in the apartment?" he asked.

"Three. Two girls and boy. Oldest twelve, youngest seven."

Joseph grabbed a legal pad. "Where do you live?"

She gave him the address, a short street running off Flatbush Avenue.

"Do you know the name of the landlord?"

She glanced at a crumbled piece of paper clutched in her hand. "It's company called three-two-four development. Manhattan. I have address. Don't know landlord name. Man who work for him and comes for rent is name of Kravski. Big man. Polish, I think, like me. Won't speak Polish. Make no difference to him that I Polish. You talk to him?"

Joseph stood up and smiled at her. "I don't know how much I can do, but yes, I'll talk to him."

She grabbed his hand and kissed it. "God bless you. I have only one vote but I vote for you. I tell everyone. I also pray for you."

"I appreciate it, Mrs. Bulask. I really do."

Joseph, trembling with fury, made some phone calls and quickly found the name of the building's owner and the address of a Manhattan office. He left the storefront, hailed a cab, and headed there. Taking the elevator to the thirty-sixth floor, he gave his card to the receptionist and asked to see Vincent Battaglia.

The receptionist smiled at him. "Do you have an appointment?"

"I'm afraid not."

She looked at the card, then back at Joseph. "You're Representative DiPaolo!"

"I am indeed."

"Gee. It's nice to meet you, sir. I've never met a representative before. You're running for the Senate, right?"

"I am. Can I count on your vote?"

"Absolutely. You're my man."

"Well, thank you."

"I'll get Mr. Battaglia."

"Thanks."

In a moment, another woman escorted him into the slum landlord's plush offices. A big man with a florid complexion, Battaglia extended a hand and flashed a big smile. "Representative DiPaolo, how nice to see you."

"Thanks for seeing me."

Joseph shook the hand as he looked around at leather and thick carpet and good art and a large mahogany desk and a man dressed in expensive silk with a large diamond ring on his pinkie finger. And he thought of little children being bitten by rats while they slept.

"My pleasure," Battaglia said. "What brings you here? Let me guess. A campaign contribution?"

"If you like."

The man smiled and threw out his arms. "I'd like to help, really would, but I'm pretty well committed to Mr. De Sapio. I'm sure you understand."

"I do. Actually, I came to talk to you about one of your buildings."

For a moment Battaglia seemed confused. Then he grinned. "You want to buy it, perhaps?"

"No."

The grin faded. "Which building are we talking about?"

Joseph told him.

"Ah, yes. I know the one." He shook his head and clucked his tongue. "The people living there are pigs. Animals. What they don't steal, they break. What they don't break, they befoul. I've spent a fortune trying to keep that place up to code, but they wreck it in less than a day. Impossible! The Health Department understands we've made every effort."

"I'm sure they do," Joseph said.

"What's your interest?"

"Rats," Joseph said coldly. "I have a friend living

there. She has little children. The rats are eating the children while they sleep. She wants it to stop and so do I."

Battaglia frowned. Whatever he'd expected from this politician, it certainly wasn't a hard time about one of his buildings. The look in Joseph's eyes was odd, distant, unusual for someone seeking support in an upcoming election.

"You have a *friend* living there?"

"Yes. Some of my friends are poor. It happens."

"Well, I can assure you," Battaglia said, "everything that can be done has been done. As I said, these people are animals, and in saying that, I mean no disrespect for your friend, but if there are rats in the building it's because the other people living there encourage it. They're filthy slobs, pure and simple. I'm checked by the Health Department regularly. I'm well within my rights in not—"

"Cut the crap. I know all about the arrangements with the Health Department. You guys have your hands in each other's pockets and that's fine. I could go through channels on this, but I really don't have the time—or the inclination.

"I'm here because I want you to know the rats have to go. Right away. This minute. The only people I'm gonna talk to are some longshoremen, personal friends of mine. If there are rats in that building at the end of the week, my friends are going to find you and break an arm. If there are rats the week after, they'll break your other arm. In fact, every time they find a rat in the place, something very bad will happen to you, understand?"

Battaglia turned white. "You threaten me? Are you crazy? You can't get away with this."

Joseph threw him a malevolent smile. "Yes, I can."

"Like hell. I have friends, too. I'll have your ass in a sling."

"Really?"

"I'll report you to the authorities. I'll talk to De Sapio. You can't push me around."

"You do as you please," Joseph said. "I'll tell them you're lying. I'm here to raise money, that's all. Who are they gonna believe? You think a man like me would go around threatening people? That would be pretty crazy, don't you think?"

"You *are* crazy."

"Maybe. Meanwhile, while De Sapio sends his goons out to talk to me, you'll be in a lot of pain, and that pain will get worse every day. As long as the heat stays on me, you get hurt. No one will ever find out who's constantly breaking your arms and legs. Trust me."

Battaglia's eyes were now wide with fright. "I don't get it. You're nuts to do this. If this person is such a great friend, why the hell don't you move her into a decent place?"

"She likes it there. She doesn't want to move. She just wants the rats taken care of. Look, do yourself a favor. Don't try to figure it out. Just take the easy way out. Get rid of the rats and everything will be fine."

Battaglia shook his head in wonderment. "Look, maybe we can help you a little. Carmine doesn't have to know everything. Tell you what—"

"Just get rid of the rats," Joseph said. Then he turned on his heel and strode out of the office.

It was a stupid, mindless thing to do, but Joseph felt great. The confrontation had allowed him to exorcise some of his pent-up anger. The emotional high lasted for a few hours before the depression returned with a vengeance.

He'd not only wasted valuable campaign time, he'd antagonized a man who might have helped him. This one small act might well cost him the election. He worried about it through the night and into the morning, while he went about the business of campaigning. And just before noon, the old woman returned to the storefront and excitedly told him of an army of men in orange coveralls crawling all over the building, getting rid of the rats.

And he felt good again.

A few days later, on a rainy April Sunday, an escape from the increasingly depressing campaign trail, Joseph was alone at the storefront office, going over some new speeches prepared by his staff. In an hour, he was to meet Sophia and spend the rest of the day with the children.

There was a knock at the door. Joseph looked up and saw two men peering in the door window. He walked to the door and opened it. The older of the two introduced himself as Malcolm Cambridge. He was a tall man, about sixty, round-faced, with thinning hair and a pronounced potbelly made more noticeable by the tight-fitting three piece suit he wore. His clear blue eyes sparkled with intensity. He'd arrived in a chauffeur-driven Cadillac, accompanied by a younger, bearded man he introduced as Roger Callis. Callis held a large umbrella.

"What can I do for you gentlemen?" Joseph asked.

"You've never heard of me?" Cambridge asked.

"I'm sorry, Mr. Cambridge, I haven't."

"Well, I guess that's some sort of reflection on your campaign staff. I know a lot about you, though. My son flew with you in forty-four. His name was Fred. Do you remember him?"

Joseph's face lit up. "You're Fred's father?"

"Yes. I have a letter from you written when Fred was killed. You claimed he saved your life."

"It's true. He did indeed. Please, come in."

The men entered the storefront and followed Joseph to a corner of the room and a battered desk piled high with papers. The elder Cambridge removed his gray overcoat and flung it over a chair. "If you have some time," he said, "I'd like to hear about Fred."

"I'll be happy to tell you," Joseph said, offering both men a seat. Cambridge sat, but Callis, looking somewhat bemused, said he preferred to stand.

"Can I offer you some coffee? A soda?"

"Nothing, thanks."

Joseph took off his jacket, sat down and leaned forward. "Fred was a terrific pilot, Mr. Cambridge, and a wonderful fellow as well. And he damn well did save my life about three weeks before . . . he was shot down. I'll never forget it. We were escorting some nine hundred B-17s and Liberators on a raid over Munich to take out a major German fighter factory. On the way back, we were jumped by more Me-109's than I've ever seen in one place. It was chaos.

"I was running on about ten cylinders and three 109's jumped me. Fred fought them off, shooting down two of the bastards. That earned him a well-deserved Distinguished Service Cross."

"Which you recommended."

"As I said, he earned it. He was a very brave pilot."

For about fifteen minutes, Joseph regaled the older man with stories of his son, all of them true.

"And now," Cambridge said, "you're a politician, engaged in another battle. Less dangerous perhaps, but a battle nonetheless."

Joseph smiled. "I guess you could call it that."

"And you're doing poorly."

The smile left Joseph's face. "We've come up in the polls. There's still a long time to go."

"At the rate you're going, you'll need ten years. You've got but two months."

"Well, I—"

Cambridge held up a hand. "It's all right. I'm not trying to rub salt in the wounds. I'm on your side. That's why I'm here."

"Pardon me?"

"Let me tell you a little about myself. I'm no William Randolph Hearst, but in central and northern New York, I'm a pretty big fish in a small pond. I like it that way. I own six daily newspapers, three radio stations, and one TV station. Roger, here, is my general manager. He's as good as they get in marketing, whether it's products or people.

"I've decided to help you, Mr. DiPaolo. Not just because my late son thought you were Jesus Christ come again, but because I think you're the kind of man this country needs. I'd like to attach Roger to your campaign committee, let him help you with some ideas on campaign commercials. I'd also like to assign a reporter to your campaign full-time, cover your every word, and print it. It may not make much of an impression in Manhattan, but it sure as hell will north of the city."

Joseph was stunned. "Well . . . I don't know what to say."

"Nothing to say," Cambridge said. "The only thing that'll make a difference in New York City is lots of television exposure, and that takes money. Fortunately, I've got money, Mr. DiPaolo. Lots of it. And I'm prepared to part with a good portion of it to see you win the primary. With Roger, me, and lots of money on your side, I think you can win."

"I see," Joseph said slowly.

Cambridge grinned. "You want to know the quid pro quo, right?"

"Yes, I would."

"Well, I *am* a businessman, Mr. DiPaolo. And you're a politician. The two seem to go hand in hand. That's what makes democracy work."

"Go on."

"All I'll ask, should you manage to become a senator, is some help with the FCC in gaining some additional television station licenses. That's the future,

Mr. DiPaolo, television. In twenty years, nobody will read a newspaper or listen to the radio. They'll be as dead as the horse and buggy. Television will be everywhere, even in automobiles.

"Mind you, I'm not asking you to do anything illegal or unethical. I just want access to those who decide. I just want the chance to tell my story, that's all. If I get turned down, so be it. Right now, I'm losing out to people who are better connected and I don't like it. I figure to even the odds."

"By buying yourself a senator?"

"That's a crude way of putting it. Not true, either. Unfair to me and to yourself. As I said, all I want—"

"I heard what you said," Joseph snapped.

"There's no need to be offended, Mr. DiPaolo. You've been in the House long enough to know how these things work. The fact is, without me, or somebody like me, and I don't see anybody else beating down your door, you haven't got a prayer of beating Miles Taylor. Not a ghost of a chance. With me, you *do* have a shot. The man is vulnerable, but you can't reach enough people without money. I know what kind of man you are. That's one reason I want to see you back in Washington. But you can't do anything if you're defeated. First things first."

For a moment, Joseph sat back in his chair, just staring at Cambridge. Then he said, "Even if I were to agree to this, there's no guarantee I could do anything about those licenses. There are others with much more influence than I. You alluded to that yourself. I'd be the new kid on the block, at the back of the line, so to speak. And I can't do anything other than to introduce you to some people."

"I understand."

"I couldn't write a letter on your behalf, or make any other type of representation. That would be unethical and, in my view, reprehensible. I won't do it."

"I understand," Cambridge repeated.

"All I could do would be to assist you in making an appointment with some people. That's it. That's something I would do for any constituent, with or without money."

Cambridge leaned forward and stuck out his hand. "Then we have a deal?"

Joseph stood up. "Not yet. First, I want to check you out. Second, I want to talk to my advisers. I'll get back to you."

Cambridge rose slowly to his feet. "Check me out all you like, Mr. DiPaolo. I think you'll like what you see. And as you said, all I'm asking is something you'd do for any constituent, with money or not. I don't think we have a problem."

Callis reached into his pocket and pulled out a card. "We're staying at the Waldorf," he said. "Give us a call anytime during the next few days. If we don't hear from you by Wednesday, we'll assume you don't want help. If I were you, I wouldn't look a gift horse in the mouth."

Joseph didn't, and as Cambridge predicted, it made all the difference. Within ten days, the first of a new series of television commercials developed by Roger Callis aired. They started with a shot of Joseph, Sophia, and their three children walking along a Long Island beach, then quickly cut to scenes of Joseph making a variety of speeches. Then, another quick cut back to the beach, with the voice of Roger Callis saying, "The future is here. The future is Joseph DiPaolo."

Two weeks after the first commercial aired, another poll showed Taylor's lead shrinking slightly. Encouraging, but not nearly enough. Time was running out. It seemed as if the fresh approach and infusion of money wouldn't be enough.

And then, the bombshell. The Cambridge newspaper chain broke a story that changed everything. They printed an interview with a Bahamian native who claimed she'd been Miles Taylor's mistress for ten years and had borne him two children. An outraged Taylor flatly denied the claim and launched suit for libel, a suit that was dropped a week later when Taylor suddenly pulled out of the race. He announced he would serve out his term, then retire. He refused to address the issue of the Bahamian mistress.

At a party to celebrate Joseph's apparent victory, Joseph took Cambridge aside. "How long have you known about Taylor?" he asked.

Cambridge looked surprised. "What are you implying?"

"It seems too perfect. I think you knew about this before you talked to me."

"Not true."

"No?"

"No. I knew Taylor spent a lot of time down there, so I sent a reporter to check things out. No other newspaper bothered. Taylor's an old man in some ways, but it's no secret he's always been a womanizer. It was a natural assumption. All we had to do was find her."

"And you did."

"We did. Nothing wrong with that. The man is a hypocrite. He deserved to be exposed."

"If it's true."

"Oh, it's true all right. Why the hell do you think he dropped out? You think we would manufacture such a thing?"

"I don't know."

Cambridge shook his head. "You've got to learn to trust me, Joseph. You checked me out. Is there anything in my record that makes me dishonest?"

"Not that I could find."

"Then relax. Stop treating me as if I'm some criminal. I've done nothing to warrant your disrespect. Nothing. All I've done is help you."

Joseph hung his head. "I'm sorry. You're right. I have been unfair."

"I accept your apology," Cambridge said, in a voice surprisingly free of rancor. "You're not home free yet, you know. You still have to win the general election. That might not be as easy, but I like your chances. How do you like Roger?"

"I have to admit, he's very good at what he does."

"Then why not make him your campaign manager? I think he'd appreciate it."

It was time to make a change. Sophia was clearly exhausted and the children missed her terribly. They missed their father as well, but Joseph's presence on the campaign trail was vital. Not so Sophia. She would still be involved, of course, but others could do the heavy work.

Now, as sole representative of his party in the race for a Senate seat, Joseph could expect their complete support. The burned bridges had suddenly been rebuilt. Already, he was getting phones calls from some key movers and shakers wanting to meet with him. The New York race for the Senate was becoming a key race in the entire national political picture. With Eisenhower expected to win, a Republican majority in the Senate would spell disaster. Like him or not, the party would *have* to support him. He was the only game in town.

"I think that would be a good move," he said.

On Tuesday, November 6, 1956, Dwight D. Eisenhower was reelected President of the United States in a landslide. Joseph DiPaolo was elected to the Senate by a scant 2 percent plurality. Still, a major victory.

Five months later, Malcolm Cambridge received

licenses to operate four television stations in upstate New York. Joseph had done little to help him, simply brought certain members of the FCC to a private lunch in a downtown Manhattan hotel, where they broke bread with the friendly man from Rochester.

Once again, Joseph had kept a promise.

JOSEPHINE: THE BIRTH OF VENUS

Part Seven

18

$\mathcal{The}$ years Josephine Cousteau spent in supervised correctional school were the quietest, least turbulent years of her life. She studied hard, devouring everything on the required list plus a host of other voluntary subjects. She was particularly attracted to languages, and practiced English incessantly, to the unexpressed consternation of her roommates. She read books of all kinds, particularly those relating to history, science, and mathematics. Her marks were consistently excellent.

She caused no trouble and made no real friends, though she listened carefully to the talk of some of the girls who had lived a hard life in the cities. While volunteering none of the details of her own life, she continuously questioned the others about their experiences. Because of this intense interest, they looked upon her as someone who cared. She didn't care. All she wanted was the knowledge.

Her continuing interviews with Vanais were marked by a coolness and carefulness befitting a much older and more sophisticated person. Josephine discussed what she purported to be her feelings, expressing ideas that her instincts told her the doctor would want to hear. He wasn't fooled. He knew she'd never expose her true emotions.

Having made no progress, the doctor would have given it up but for the constant pleadings of Marie Benoit. The girl's welfare had become Marie's obsession, and Vanias's hints that Marie was wasting her time and money fell on deaf ears.

Then, three years into this most puzzling case, and to his utter astonishment, the doctor was handed a diary.

"I want you to read this," Josephine said. "It's my diary."

He was flabbergasted. "Do you really want me to read this?"

"Yes."

"Why?"

"Because I've grown to trust you, Doctor. You always ask me how I feel about things and I never express my feelings properly. I feel inhibited when speaking about them. With the diary, I am free to express myself. I thought this would be helpful to you."

"I'm very touched, Josephine. Very touched."

Once back in his office, the initial joy Vanais felt at her gesture disappeared. As he looked over the carefully written pages, he realized what it was, poppycock, a simple reiteration of what she'd said to him during their face-to-face sessions. To the untrained eye, it would appear she was putting her past behind her and looking to a future filled with worthwhile and useful living—but Vanais knew better.

She hadn't changed an iota. She was quite mad, but Vanais knew he'd have a hard time proving it. The courts were still not totally comfortable with this new experimental procedure and would be disinclined to believe such a diagnosis. Where was the proof? To the layman, her behavior was exemplary, devoid of violence or eccentric acts. Her marks were excellent, her study habits industrious.

Yes, she'd killed Claude Beauport, but that was in the past, an aberration, quite possibly due to reasons suppressed by a terrified and desperate child. To proclaim a diagnosis of psychosis could damage his career, perhaps irreparably. It wasn't worth the risk.

One year later, Josephine dropped another bombshell on the troubled doctor. He had long since given up hope of ever reaching the girl, but on her fourteenth birthday, Josephine told him, quite casually, that Claude had raped her when she was seven, which was true. She added that Claude had continued to involve her in sexual acts on an almost daily basis, which was also true.

Then, she revealed, "The night of his death, he dragged me into the barn. He tore off my clothes and threw me on the ground. He said he was tired of me and was going to kill me, but not before he raped me one last time.

"I managed to rise to my feet and grab the shovel. He was enraged, like an animal, actually foaming at the mouth. I was sure he would kill me, so I struck him with the shovel. He fell to the ground. I knew instantly he was dead.

"I was screaming hysterically, barely able to see. I knew only that I had to get out of there, and as I ran, I banged into the lamp, knocking it from the wall. A fire started and spread quickly, before I could even think. I ran outside and fell on the ground.

"As the barn burned, I thought about contacting the police, but I was afraid. I knew how it looked and what they would think. So, I said nothing. The rest you know."

Vanais was thunderstruck. "Why," he asked, "has

it taken you all this time to tell me this? It's been four years."

"I've been afraid. You're the only person in the world I completely trust, so I've decided to tell you my secret, but you must never tell anyone. You told me I could trust you, and I do. But no one else must ever know."

Vanais questioned her at length. As he did, he wondered whether this was just another manipulation on the part of this incredibly clever girl. He was ambivalent. Her story was utterly plausible in light of what he knew to be true. She had, after all, been sexually abused for several years, and had consistently exhibited evidence of severe mental trauma.

He decided it was impossible to determine the truth without the aid of some recently developed personality tests, tests very difficult to best, because the person being tested wasn't remotely aware of what the tester was really looking for. Several times in the past, Vanais had considered using them with Josephine, but had refrained, for many reasons. First, there was the fact that the child was lying to him on a regular basis, making it clear she didn't trust him. He had wanted to get past that barrier. Second, he was afraid that she would refuse to take the tests, making the barrier even thicker.

Now, the circumstances were contrary. Either his careful, patient work with her had led to this marvelous breakthrough, or she was continuing to act out an ingenious plan to deceive him. He simply had to know.

"I would like to try something new," he announced.

"New?"

"Yes. A series of tests. Not the kind of tests you are familiar with here at the school. These tests are different. They ask questions about likes and dislikes. They query choices, and the reasons for such choices. It would help me if you took them."

To his surprise, she readily agreed.

During their next meeting, he administered the tests, which took almost a full day to complete. When he finally finished reviewing them, the answer to the question that had been plaguing him for so long was clearly evident. While it was true that psychiatry was considered an inexact science, there were certain behavioral patterns that were predictable, standard. A liar was a liar. Such was the case of Josephine Cousteau.

The tests results revealed she was still trying to manipulate him. She didn't have an honest bone in her body. She was a true psychopath beyond his or anyone else's help.

He sighed and leaned back in the chair. The courts had yet to accept such tests as evidence. It would be foolish to attempt to persuade anyone of Josephine's madness. Again, his own career could be damaged. There was nothing he could do except declare this a case of a child being traumatized by the terrible events in her life. Certainly, he could claim she'd been helped immeasurably by psychoanalysis, and so he would. Such a view would support his own theories and those of Freud. It would be accepted by the court as reasonable and fair. It wasn't remotely true, but ...

At the age of fifteen, Josephine looked twenty. By regulation, her dark hair was clipped short, but the lack of framing failed to detract from her natural beauty. Thick eyebrows perched atop sensuous, dark eyes. Her chiseled nose and high cheekbones seemed crafted from marble, and her alabaster skin glowed with perfection. Her lips were full and lush, and her squarish chin merged softly with a long, taut neck. Her body was pure excellence, with long, trim legs leading to gently swelling buttocks, a narrow waist, and full, high breasts.

A month before the penultimate review of her case, the school supervisor was visited by a man named Michael Thorpe, an Englishman involved in volunteer social work through a private agency in Paris. The agency was well known to the correctional people as a provider of jobs for worthy young women released from school when their terms were up.

Thorpe expressed an interest in Josephine, saying he had heard about her from a recently released juvenile, and so he had. But when he was introduced to her, her beauty took his very breath away. Under the watchful eye of the supervisor, he presented a proposal to Josephine.

"You realize," he said, "that one of the conditions of your release concerns employment. If you don't have a job waiting, you could be sent to an adult facility when you turn sixteen."

Josephine nodded. "I am well aware of that, Mr. Thorpe. I have a benefactor, Marie Benoit, who has been working here in Paris in a clothing factory. She has assured me that I can have a job there as soon as my time comes up. In fact, she intends to bring the manager to see me in another month or so."

Thorpe cleared his throat and said, "Well, that's fine. Perhaps you might consider something that is considerably more interesting than working in a factory, not to mention the fact that the money is much better."

"And what would that be?"

Thorpe looked at the supervisor and then back at Josephine. "I work for a company always seeking beautiful girls to be models for various magazines. I realize that there are those in this business who are unscrupulous, but these people come with the highest recommendations, I assure you. Otherwise, I would not be allowed to present such a proposal."

"Go on," Josephine said.

"These people," Thorpe said, "are very legitimate and highly regarded in the field. The girls they employ do photographic work as well as actual salon showings. The agency has a tutorial program that allows you to continue your education as you build your career. It's the best of all possible worlds, available only to a few fortunate girls who have the looks and bodies that appeal to the public."

Josephine's eyes instantly brightened. "I would be very interested in such a career, Monsieur. Very interested."

The man seemed to be bursting at the seams. "Well then, that's fine. Just fine. I'll start the paperwork rolling. Since you have no guardians and are not of legal age, the court will have to make the determination, but I don't think there'll be a problem. I understand your marks here have been excellent and you've piled up a lot of merit points."

Josephine nodded.

"Good," Thorpe said. "I'll get on it, then."

Josephine's last interview with Dr. Vanais was a very cordial one. The doctor was in the process of writing a paper about her case in which she would be discussed anonymously. He was beaming with pride as he talked to her about it.

"You probably don't remember, Josephine, but the very first time we met, I told you that if I was somehow able to help you, I would be helping myself."

"I do remember."

"Well," the doctor continued, "this paper will be a great step forward for the entire justice system. It will show what can be done with children who have been terribly affected by physical and mental abuse. You are to be congratulated on your efforts. It wouldn't have been possible without your cooperation."

Josephine leaned forward and kissed the doctor on the cheek. "Thank you," she said. "I owe you a great debt. Without your caring I don't know what would have become of me."

They said their goodbyes and Josephine went back to her room. As she lay on the bed she couldn't help but smile. The poor man was such a fool.

In the midst of a raging rainstorm, Helga Linstrom, Dr. Vanais's longtime assistant, made her way through the lobby of the Majestic Hotel in Paris, removed her dripping raincoat, and took a booth in the bar. She ordered a brandy and waited patiently for the person she was to meet.

Ten minutes passed before the lanky frame of a blond man slipped quietly into the seat across from the woman. His name was Sven Kohnor, resident of Paris, a member of the French Communist Party, and one of Moscow's top foreign agents. Kohnor, a Swedish misfit as a teenager, had worked as an undercover agent for the Americans and British during the war, but had been turned by a KGB agent just as the war ended. The Americans and British considered the war over, and they had no further need for his services. But to the Russians, a new battle was just beginning, and they made Kohnor feel needed. His allegiance was to adventure, not a country, so he wholeheartedly welcomed his new employers—on his terms. He would work for them, yes, but as a nonexclusive independent. They'd reluctantly agreed.

"It's a hell of a day, Helga," he said. "What's on your mind?"

The woman raised her brandy glass and swished the amber liquid. "A few years ago, you suggested you might be interested if I ever came across certain individuals that met the exact specifications you required."

"I remember."

The woman smiled and sipped the brandy. "What would it be worth to you to be introduced to child soon to be sixteen, who looks twenty, and an incredibly gorgeous twenty at that—a woman who is a completely controlled psychopath, devoid of any real feelings whatsoever, capable, in the right hands, of course, of being used for . . . some of your activities?"

"Tell me more."

Helga leaned forward and said, "She's been trying to con Vanais for six years. When she talks with him, it's as if the words and thoughts were coming from someone who'd spent years studying mental disorders, but she does it instinctively. She's the coldest human being he's ever encountered, yet, she functions beautifully. She can be charming, gregarious, and warm. But it's all an act. She's a machine. A woman without a soul."

"Really?"

"Yes."

"Could she kill?"

Helga smiled. "She already has. The doctor thinks she really enjoyed it. In fact, he's sure of it. It may well have been the most enjoyable thing she's ever done in her life. She's unique, Sven. Most of these people are driven by devils that are uncontrollable, but not this one. She's in total control at all times. Vanais has never seen anything like it. I think she'd be ideal for your purposes."

The man ordered a brandy and sipped it in silence.

"How much do you want?" he asked finally.

"Fifty thousand francs."

He winced. "That's a lot of money. I thought you joined our organization because you wanted to save France."

"I did. I still do. But it was you who suggested that there was money to be paid if I kept my wits about me. I don't expect it all at once. Let's say twenty-five thousand now and the rest when she proves out."

"Why don't we say five thousand francs now, and another ten when I've had a chance to talk to her. If she's everything you say, we can negotiate the rest."

Helga Linstrom shook her head. "That's not enough. I've had my eye on this one for years."

The Swede grinned. "Helga, don't be greedy. We can break into the doctor's office and grab his files. We don't even need you."

"You bastard! You wouldn't!"

Sven Kohnor looked at her disdainfully. "Please don't insult my intelligence. Five thousand francs. More later. Are you interested or not?"

Helga Linstrom hesitated, but only for a moment.

An hour later, Kohnor was seated at a table in another Paris hotel, enjoying a meal with a young man most people would shy away from, for his grotesque countenance gave him aura of sinister malevolence.

"So, what did he want this time?" the man asked, as he brought another forkful of food to his mouth.

"The same as before," Kohnor answered.

"Can you do it?"

"Perhaps. I told him it would take some time, but he's impatient. He's always been that way."

"Like all Americans. They have an attention span measured in seconds."

Kohner smiled. "As you say. In some ways, Bower is quite cunning. In others, he's so incredibly naive, it's almost embarrassing. A paradox."

"Aren't they all?"

"Perhaps. Incidently, I may have found someone who will be of great help to us in the future."

"Really? Who is he?"

"I'd rather not say right now. In a few months, perhaps. And he's a she. A beautiful young woman."

"How young?"

"Fifteen."

Pierre Charrette smiled and said, "Ahhh. I like beautiful young women. I like them very much."

"I know you do," Sven said.

19

On her sixteenth birthday, Josephine was released from the correctional school that had been her home for six years. Marie Benoit, who had conspicuously surrendered her life to help the girl, met her assumed charge at the gate with a bouquet of flowers and a hug.

"Oh, Josephine," she said effusively, "I'm so proud of you. You've done remarkably well in school, but that's not the best part. Dr. Vanais says you're well-adjusted and level-headed. I'm so happy. Your days of suffering are finally over."

Josephine kissed her supporter and solitary friend. For a moment, she rested her head on Marie's shoulder. Softly, she said, "Without your help, I probably would be headed to another jail or worse—the asylum. I can never repay you for everything you've done, the sacrifices you've made. You paid for the doctor, came to see me every month, gave me such encouragement. I'm forever grateful."

Marie beamed. "The look of happiness I see in your eyes is my reward. Come. I've been preparing a feast for us. I was allowed the day off just for this occasion. I can't tell you how wonderful it is to have you free, and on Monday, you start at Madame Bouvard's. It's so exciting! My, you're going to be famous. I just know it."

She ran a hand over Josephine's dark hair as she gazed deeply into the girl's eyes. "You're so beautiful."

They hugged again. Then, Marie said, "We have four days before you have to report in, so let's make the best of it. Sunday, we'll go to Mass and then I'll show you Paris. At least some of it."

Arm in arm, they walked to the bus stop. Less than an hour later, they were feasting on a variety of delicacies in Marie's small flat. Josephine was sure the food had cost Marie a week's salary. Well, if it made her happy . . .

Friday and Saturday, Marie had to work. Josephine lazed about the flat, reading fashion magazines and staring out the window from time to time. It felt marvelous to be free. No more stupid discussions with that idiot doctor, no more rules. Well, that wasn't completely true. For two more years, she'd still have to follow rules, less stringent than before, but rules just the same. After that, her life would be unrestricted.

During her period of probation, she'd have to live with Marie or in a dormitory at the modeling agency. She'd have to stay out of trouble, but that was easy. She knew how to avoid trouble. Staying with Marie—a doting, easy-to-fool woman without a brain in her head—would be more difficult. If the woman wanted to waste her life, that was up to her, but staying with her was out of the question. Josephine would quickly be bored to death.

She decided to stay at the dorm, where she'd be surrounded by peers who could teach her the valued tricks of the trade. Marie would be disappointed, but that was just too bad. Josephine would make her understand.

The idea of becoming a model appealed to Josephine. She opened a fashion magazine and compared pictures of the women to her image reflected in the mirror. After skipping though the entire magazine, she concluded she was much more beautiful than any of them. She sighed. Soon, it would be her face staring out from those glossy pages.

Sunday, Marie and Josephine attended Mass at a church not far from the flat. Then, it was on to the bus for a tour of Paris. They took in a few of the major tourist attractions. For five hours, Josephine, who had never before seen a big city, was entranced by the sights, sounds, and smells of Paris.

Marie never seemed to stop smiling the whole time as she watched the wide-eyed enthusiasm of the beautiful girl. She felt that Denise Dijon, somewhere up in heaven, must be smiling, too.

That night, the last before Josephine was to report to the agency, Marie found it difficult to sleep. Restless, she pushed the bedcovers aside, rose out of bed and padded quietly into the front room. Carefully, she placed a chair beside the bed of the sleeping Josephine and sat down, gazing at the face of the girl, now pale from the light cast by the moon. The girl looked so peaceful, almost angelic.

For Marie, it all seemed worthwhile—the uprooting, the long, hard hours at the factory. She'd eschewed any opportunity for a life of her own, feeling that she had no time for romance. At times she had despaired, but now the evidence was clear. What she had done was right. The girl sleeping so soundly on the small bed in the living room was healthy and free of the mental anguish that had plagued her over the years. Without Marie's help, it would not have happened.

"I've decided to live at the dorm," Josephine announced in the morning.

"The dorm? But, I thought you'd stay with me."

"I know, but I've been thinking. It's too much of a burden for you. Besides, by staying at the dorm, I can spend my evenings talking with the other models. They can teach me what they know. That way, I'll learn faster. You want me to succeed, don't you?"

"Of course, but—"

"It'll be better for both of us. You'll have your privacy and I'll have my career to worry about. I'll come see you at least once a month, and I'll write."

Marie held a hand to her mouth. "Josephine, I've waited so long to be with you."

"Please. I've made my decision. I have to start making my own decisions now that I'm working, don't you agree?"

"Yes, but—"

"Come, now. Let's not argue."

Josephine hugged Marie, kissed her on the cheek, then grabbed her battered suitcase and skipped down the stairs without another word. Marie stared after her in stunned silence.

Josephine reported to Madame Bouvard's Modeling and Talent School, arriving by bus. Thorpe, the Englishman, met her outside and rushed her in to meet the woman he worked for, one of the top providers of modeling talent in Paris.

Madame Bouvard, founder and sole owner of the respected firm, was a woman of fifty who looked much younger, a living testament to the art of makeup and careful attention to one's health. Like most of her models, she was tall and thin. Some would say skinny. She was dressed in a long, flowing red dress, the color of her long fingernails. Her neck, wrists, and fingers sparkled with diamonds. Even at this hour of the morning, she wore long false eyelashes that made her eyes appear much larger. Her hair had been carefully coiffed and piled atop her head. She was so exquisitely turned out that Josephine assumed she was on her way to some important function. It wasn't so. Madame Bouvard dressed to the hilt at all hours of the day.

As Josephine stood there, the older woman walked around her, looking at her from every angle, as one might look at a new dress, while she took short puffs from a cigarette stuck in a long, diamond-studded holder.

"Well," she said, finally. "You certainly are a natural beauty. My Mr. Thorpe does have an eye. Come, my dear, take off your clothes."

Josephine stared at her in astonishment. "What?"

The woman laughed. "It's all right, my dear. I want to see what you look like so we can determine exactly what your regimen will be. Diet, clothes, hair, training, all of it. If you think you're beautiful now, wait, I'll make you an angel."

As Josephine hesitated, Madame reached for a glass of wine and took a small sip from it. She drank wine constantly, but never allowed herself to become intoxicated. "My child," she said, "you must understand something right at the beginning of this venture. Your face and body are your stock in trade. You must not be self-conscious about either. Think of your body as a flawless diamond. Your energies must be devoted to keeping it that way at long as possible.

"Your body is simply the envelope of your being, the wrapping on the package. There is nothing to be ashamed of. Remember, you are sixteen. You have seven, eight, perhaps nine years to make it pay, and then, unfortunately, your career will be all but over. The world cares little about older women—unless they're rich. Remember that. Now, take off your clothes."

Josephine did as she was asked. She stood nude and motionless as, again, the woman walked around her, examining every detail. Then, with a wave of her hand, Madame said, "All right, get dressed."

As Josephine began to dress, the woman barked orders to Thorpe, who made notes in a small steno pad. "Her breasts are too large. She'll never do for salon work. We'll have to confine her to photographic. She needs some attention to the feet and the hands. They look terrible. Her waist needs to lose an inch and the calves need muscle tone. Other than that, the skin is dark enough, forget the tanning room."

Madame stared at Josephine for a moment and then turned her attention back to Thorpe. "Work on the makeup, the walk, the voice—especially the voice. She sounds like a crow in distress. As for the hair, I want it long. No styling for at least six months, and even then, I want minimum cutting. She is no gamine, you understand?"

"Oui, Madame."

"This morning, start by giving her the full treatment, and include a mudpack on the back. There are some pimples there. I want her kept out of sight for at least three months. No photos. None. I want her perfect before we do her comp."

Josephine listened in silence. They were talking about her as if she were a piece of meat, but it didn't bother her. She was well aware of her beauty, and had read enough to know that beautiful women stayed that way by working hard, not by accident. This was her chance for the riches she so desperately wanted. She would do what she must.

Madame Bouvard continued to prattle away, like a bird clucking over a newly hatched chick. "We'll let the photographers in on our little doll, but not until she's ready. The name has to go. We need something that sounds pretty and seductive. I'll work on that."

Then she turned to Josephine and said, "There are

stains on your fingers from smoking. If you want to smoke, fine, it helps keep the weight off. But always use a holder like I do. That way, you'll avoid stains on your fingers. Understand?"

"Yes."

Madame beamed. "Good. You're very beautiful, my dear. After we get you cleaned up, Thorpe will take you shopping and help you pick a wardrobe. Let him do the picking because he knows his stuff, believe me. Right now, he'll show you your quarters. A room all to yourself. I'm aware you're on probation. We have rules here as well. Thorpe will tell you what they are. We'll teach you everything you need to know to be a model. I have a feeling you'll make a lot of money. A *lot* of money. Do you like that idea?"

Josephine smiled. "Very much."

"Good."

Thorpe showed her to her room. Part of the agency building had been turned into a small hotel. Josephine's room was small but adequate, equipped with a single bed, a large dresser with a makeup mirror, a chair, and a radio. The largest feature was the mirror that covered an entire wall, floor to ceiling. A small Persian rug graced the floor.

There were two other parts to her quarters, a walk-in closet and a fully equipped bathroom complete with bidet. Obviously, Madame liked her models to enjoy a certain level of privacy.

There was something else that the long-imprisoned Josephine especially appreciated, a single window that looked out over the narrow street behind the building. The view wasn't much, but it reminded her that she was free. There was no heavy wire screen. There were no fences, no gates, and no matrons.

Thorpe placed her suitcase on the bed and said, "Make yourself comfortable. I'll come back shortly and take you to the spa, where you'll indulge yourself for a few hours. Then we'll go shopping. Only the best stores are good enough for Madame. You'll love it."

"I have very little money. I can't afford such things."

"Don't you worry about that. Madame gets the clothes at a special price, a professional courtesy from the stores, as many of their models are supplied from this place. Madame is paying for everything now. Later, when you start to earn money of your own, you'll share your earnings with her to pay her back. It won't be a burden for you. Now, relax. I'll be back in a bit."

He left, closing the door quietly behind him. Josephine opened her suitcase and started to put away her things. Her body quivered with excitement as rivers of adrenaline sped through her veins.

The next three months were a whirlwind of activity for Josephine. A faculty of teachers taught her how to walk, talk, apply makeup, do her hair, sit, stand, and above all, smile. The smiling was very important, they said. Josephine, who'd rarely smiled in sixteen years, found it the most difficult to learn.

Three visits to the dentist took care of some dental imperfections, then her teeth were cleaned and polished to a high gleam. There were sessions devoted to personal hygiene, crash courses on current events within France and elsewhere, as Madame Bouvard liked to have her girls conversant with a variety of subjects for idle conversation. Trips to the Louvre were combined with trips to other centers of culture. Culture was important, according to Madame.

Of course, there were the exercises designed to heighten muscle tone and accentuate the best features while eliminating the smallest imperfections. The food at the school had been starchy and fattening, but Josephine's particular metabolism had burned off the offending calories. Nevertheless, she was placed on a strict diet, her weight monitored daily, so a determination could be made for future diets.

When the initial training ended, Madame examined her with even more intensity than that displayed the first time. Done, she smiled, clapped her hands, then shooed everyone out of the room.

"Put on your clothes."

Josephine dressed in clothes much different from those she'd worn three months ago.

"I have this talk with all my girls before I turn them loose," Madame said.

"Yes?"

"Sex. It's forbidden to have sex with clients at any time. The photographers as well. They're all studs, you know, especially the homosexuals. They're always calling here for male models, trying to set up speculative shooting sessions in the hope they can take the models to bed. As for the others, they're almost as bad. I know you all do it. If you do, I don't want to hear about it, you understand?"

"You needn't worry," Josephine said firmly.

Madame sighed. "You all say that. I'm going to give you the name of a doctor. You'll see him and be fitted with a diaphragm. He'll tell you everything you need to know to protect yourself, and believe me, you need to protect yourself. The diseases can be very debilitating, and pregnancy will end your career. You listen to what he says and remember it."

"I will."

"Good."

It was almost time to expose Josephine to the Paris photographers' community. First, her portfolio of photographs, the series of photos that would be her calling card, known as a composite, were taken in the agency's in-house studio, under the watchful eye of

Madame herself. The session took almost the entire day, with two hairdressers fussing over her and changing her hairstyle hourly. Makeup was changed with each style, giving her a range of "looks" from dark and sultry to innocent and childlike. Through the lens of the camera, her age ranged from fourteen to twenty-five. Throughout the session, wigs and falls were used to give her an even broader range of expressions.

When the session finally ended, Madame put an arm around the girl and hugged her. "I was right about you," she said. "You're a natural. A born winner. I can't wait to see the pictures tomorrow. Welcome to the world of fashion, my dear Venus."

Josephine looked at her in surprise. "Pardon me?"

Madame Bouvard pushed another cigarette into the jeweled holder and lit it. "Yes," she said. "I have chosen your new name. Henceforth, Josephine Cousteau will be known as Venus. No second name—just Venus. It suits you."

Josephine wanted to laugh out loud. She'd seen the statue of the armless women at the Louvre, and the choosing of such a name seemed outrageous. But the more she listened to the impassioned reasoning of her mentor, the more she liked it. As Madame explained it, a single name had an aura of mystery to it, and it did, after all, relate to a timeless beauty. "It's a bit pretentious, but this is a business of pretention, is it not?"

Madame Bouvard smiled. "You have a firm grasp on the realities of this life, my dear."

Once the comp was distributed, the clamor for her services began immediately. It seemed as though every photographer in Paris wanted to use this new girl with the fresh look. There hadn't been this much excitement since Brigitte Bardot first burst upon the scene. Madame, building for the future, was very selective, picking jobs with the precision of a neurosurgeon.

On her third job, Josephine was driven to the studios of a small but very important advertising agency.

She was told they wanted to use her for a series of print toothpaste ads, and wished to discuss it first. When she arrived, she was ushered into an office, a short discussion was held, and a shooting schedule worked out. Everyone was pleased. Then she was escorted to an underground garage, where the same corporate Citroën that had brought her to this place would take her back to Madame Bouvard's.

Halfway back, the driver turned down a small side street and brought the car to a halt at the curb. Josephine, concerned, placed her hand on the door handle, preparing to bolt from the car. The driver, a dark-haired man in his fifties, turned in his seat and said, "Please don't be alarmed. I want to talk to you for a minute privately."

"What about?"

"About a project that will make you more money in two months than you can make modeling in ten years. Something I'm sure you would enjoy to the fullest."

"Whatever are you talking about?"

"I have a friend who wants to meet you. I won't beat about the bush. The man's a spy. He's prepared to discuss something with you that will make you rich. He asked me to set up an appointment."

Josephine laughed. "A spy? You can't be serious. Take me back to the agency."

"I'll do so immediately. Let me say this. If you go to the Majestic Hotel tonight at nine, he'll be there. Wear something old and try to look as unattractive as possible so as not to draw attention to yourself. He'll meet you in the lobby and discuss the project. If you're not interested, so be it, but you should hear him out. He will pay you a great deal of money."

With that, the driver turned around, put the car in gear and drove off. He never uttered another word until he opened the door for her at the agency and said, "It's worth looking into, you know."

Josephine grabbed her handbag and strode into the agency building without saying a word.

Later, back in her room, she stared out the window, smoked a cigarette, and thought about what the driver had said. She was just beginning this new life of a photographic model. Already, she was making good money, even after the split with Madame Bouvard, an arrangement that would change once her training had been fully paid for. It was an exciting life. She reveled in the looks from the men who hovered around her, desire clearly evident in their eyes. There was comfort in the knowledge that none of them would ever know the pleasures of her body. She could tease them at will, watch their eyes light up, and when they would make their clumsy advances, exult as she turned them down. Each time their precious egos were crushed, Josephine experienced a narcotic power surge within her.

The driver had talked of a great deal of money, money that would not have to be split with Madame. He'd said the man was a spy. For whom? What did he want with her? Her body began to tingle as her imagination conjured images. A spy? Dangerous, yes, but exciting.

She stubbed out the cigarette and put the holder in her handbag. If she was to meet with this man, it would have to be through a ruse of some sort. Because of her age and the conditions of her release, she was not allowed to travel outside the agency alone at night. Madame Bouvard would have to give permission, and even then, she would have to be accompanied by one of the other girls.

Suddenly, her curiosity intensified. She realized she wanted very much to meet this person, if only to hear what he had to say. She left her room and walked down the hallway until she came to the door of Giselle, a model who'd been with Madame

Bouvard for some time. Josephine knocked and heard a small voice say, "Enter."

Giselle threw down a magazine and smiled as Josephine entered the room. "Ah, Venus. So, how do you like the business? They say you're going to be big."

"Perhaps."

"How do you like it so far?"

"It's fun. I've only had two shoots, but they went well."

"And today?"

"I was over at LeBerche. They may use me in a toothpaste ad."

"You have the face for it. Who's the photographer?"

"I don't know."

"If it's Vila, the Italian, better watch yourself. He likes to screw all his models."

Josephine's face hardened. "He won't screw me, I guarantee it."

Giselle grinned. "Maybe. He's very charming. So, what brings you to me?"

"I need your help."

"My help?"

"Yes. I . . . I've met a man. I want to meet with him for an hour, but you know how Madame is. I thought perhaps you would help me. We could say we were going to the cinema."

Gizelle shook her head. "Venus, you're only sixteen. My God! They'll be plenty of time for that. If you get involved with a man at this point, you could spoil everything for yourself."

"You don't understand. I was in a prison for six years. This isn't something that's going to last. It's just a little fling. He's a nice man and it's all very innocent."

"Innocent?"

"You know what I mean. He's married. He just wants to make love to me for a little while. I want it too. Nothing more serious than that."

Giselle sighed. "Do you have a diaphragm?"

"Yes."

"You do move fast. They don't always work, you know. Make him wear a rubber if you know what's good for you. You get pregnant and Madame will have a fit."

"I'll be careful."

"When do you have to meet him?"

"Tonight at nine. Near the Eiffel Tower. A little hotel. It should take no more than an hour at most."

"Okay, but just this once. Understand?"

Josephine planted a kiss on her cheek and said, "I understand."

Precisely at nine o'clock, Josephine entered the lobby of the Majestic Hotel and headed for one of the upholstered chairs in the lobby. Before she reached it, a man was at her side, a tall, blond, bearded man who said quietly, "Thank you for coming, Josephine. Say nothing and walk with me to the elevator. I'm going to take you to my room."

"No."

"There's no need to be alarmed. I only want to talk to you."

She hesitated, then, throwing caution to the winds, walked with him to the elevator and quietly accompanied him to his room. Once inside, he removed a briefcase from beneath the bed, placed it on the mattress and opened it. It was filled with bundles of hundred-franc notes. He took out a single bundle and handed it to her. "There's two thousand francs there. It's yours. You need do nothing further. I simply want to impress you with the resources that are at my disposal. Thank you for coming."

Josephine looked at the stack of bills in awe. It was more money than she'd ever seen before. She looked into his clear blue eyes and asked, "Who *are* you? What do you want of me?"

He smiled and gestured to a chair. "Have a seat. I will explain."

Josephine sat on the chair, placed the money in her handbag, and waited. The man went to the dresser and removed a bottle of wine. He held it up and asked, "Some wine?"

Josephine shook her head.

The man started talking as he uncorked the bottle and poured some wine into a tall glass. "I am a spy, just as the driver explained to you. In my business, I need the help of certain people from time to time. People who realize the benefits of money and want to get their hands on as much of it as possible. People who have no allegiances, except to themselves. People who realize the world is comprised of sick bastards like Claude Beauport."

She was stunned. "How do you know about that?"

"I told you. I'm a spy. It's my business to know things, especially things concerning the people I do business with, like you. I know everything about you."

"That's not possible."

Again, the man smiled as he sipped his wine. "Try this. You killed your guardian with a shovel, and for good reason. You spent six years in correctional school where you were seen on a monthly basis by a shrink. You played him along like a fish on a string, letting him think that he was seeing inside your head, when the opposite was true. You told him only those things you wanted him to know and nothing more.

"For example, you never once told him that you enjoyed killing your guardian, that it gave you the only pleasure you've ever known in your life."

The words struck her like hammer blows. It was as if she'd been stripped of all defenses, allowing him to look into her very soul. For a moment, she thought she was in a room with the devil himself. How could he know?

The color drained from her face. She felt slightly lightheaded. Beads of perspiration popped up on her forehead. Immediately, the man took her arms and guided her gently to the bed. Though dizzy, she still prepared for battle. He stepped away.

"Take it easy. Nothing bad is going to happen to you. You'd had a shock, that's all. It will pass."

She stared at him. "How do you know such things?"

"I know what goes on in your head because I'm cut from similar cloth. Someday, I will tell you of my own experiences, but for now, all you need to know is this—I understand you and will never betray you. I want to help you become very rich. By doing so, I will become richer myself.

"We live in a terrible world, a world we can't change. Money is all that counts. Those who have it do as they please, those who don't, do what they must. Sometimes, we are presented with incredible opportunities. If you decide to work for me, you will be able to do as you please for the rest of your life."

The room was swimming. The man left her side for a moment, then returned, a cold, wet towel in his hand, which he placed on her forehead. He said nothing as he pressed the towel to her forehead with one hand, while the other stroked her hair, as a parent might do with a child. In a few moments, the faintness left her and she sat up and leaned against the headboard.

"Who *are* you?" she asked, for the second time.

"As I told you. A spy. Names are not important at this point."

He looked about thirty-five, with hair that was long and unkempt. Bushy eyebrows topped large, blue eyes, almost hypnotic in nature. The face was rectangular until it disappeared into a forest of hair below his rather thick lips. His good looks rivaled those of some male models she had met at the agency, except for the beard, of course.

He was tall and muscular, with strong hands, the nails clean and trimmed. His voice was resonant and full, as though he had spent time as an actor. He was dressed in an old tweed sports jacket and corduroy pants that gave him the look of an overage college student.

Josephine reached in her handbag, removing a cigarette and the holder. He lit it for her and said, "I know what you've been through. I can help you in ways that nobody else can, besides the money."

Josephine took a deep drag from the cigarette and exhaled the smoke toward the ceiling. Now firmly in control of her emotions, she asked, "What do you mean?"

He took another sip of the wine and said, "I know how you feel about men. All men. You hate them. You also hate sex. The thought of having sex with a man makes you vomit. You never discussed this with the doctor because you didn't want him to know your true feelings. You were afraid it would hinder your release from the school. You were afraid if you told him this, the authorities might change their minds and put you in the asylum.

"I understand all that. I don't blame you a bit for feeling the way you do. I'm sure you realize your attitudes are shaped by what happened to you. That's only natural. What you may not know is that those feelings can be successfully treated. In a few months, I can help you change those attitudes."

She glared at him with an expression of shock and disgust. He really knew her. It was frightening. "If you know me so well," she said, "you must know that no man will ever touch me again. Never in a million years."

"That's how you feel now, and rightly so. Still, suppose I could train you to derive a different kind of enjoyment from the sex act? Not the thrill of having sex itself, but the thrill of watching a man become your slave because of the desire you create. Add to that the thrill of watching that man be destroyed by his desire. The same thrill you felt when you killed your guardian could be repeated over and over again."

Her eyes widened. "You mean—"

"No. You don't have to kill, but the pleasures would be just as great."

"You want me to be a whore!"

"Not at all. I want you to be a spy. A master spy, like myself. Naturally, sex is involved, but I can train you. You'll never enjoy the sex, just the result it brings. Can you understand what I mean?"

"No! I'll never let a man touch me. Not for any amount of money. I'd puke first!"

"No, you wouldn't. You're a strong person, Josephine. A survivor. You're here today because you have a brilliant mind and know how to use it. You've got everyone fooled. Your doctor, your friend Marie, the people at the agency, no one knows the real Josephine because you are in control of your life. That control is power. But if you don't use your power, what's the point?

"You can easily handle any man you want. You can derive immense enjoyment from seducing him and turning him into a stupid, slobbering fool who'd do anything you asked. A slave. You can make him give you information. You can watch him squirm as he tries to force himself to turn away from you and finds that he can't, that he's hopelessly and forever in your control. That control—that power—gives you money, and the satisfaction that you so desperately need to live your life.

"Let's be honest with each other. Few things give you satisfaction. This is something you'll enjoy more than you can possibly imagine."

He paused, drained the wineglass and then sat on the edge of the bed again. "Right now," he said, "I want you to go back to the dorm. Think about what I've said. In a week's time, I will again be in the lobby of this hotel. Same time, same day. Meet with me again if you decide to discuss this further. If you decide not, that will be the end of it. But if you decide to join me, I can guarantee you'll be a millionaire before you're twenty-one. I think you'd like that."

Her gaze went to the briefcase at the foot of the bed. It was full of money. There were probably a million francs in that case alone. Then she looked into the eyes of this strange man and tried to fathom what lay beyond. His eyes told her nothing.

"Are you really a spy?" she asked, "or an agent of the devil?"

"Just a spy, my beautiful friend, a man who holds the key to your future happiness. I know how hard it is for you to trust anyone, so I won't ask you to trust me. I'll simply say that every step of the way, I'll pay you in cash. You can walk away any time you wish.

"Imagine if I'm right. Imagine if it's true what I say. Suppose I can show you how to experience intense pleasure unlike anything you've ever known. You owe it to yourself to at least look into the possibilities, don't you agree?"

"If I come next week, will you give me another two thousand francs?"

He reached for the briefcase, opened it and pulled out another bundle, which he handed to her. "You have it now," he said. "I'll look forward to seeing you next week."

20

Josephine, after reflecting for a week on her conversation with the mysterious blond spy, ultimately found his proposal irresistible. Money was itself a potent incentive, and the promise of excitement and adventure was just as powerful, but the clincher was her awareness of his perception of her.

With him, there was no need to pretend. She could be herself, speak the truth, smile when she wanted to instead of on command. He knew the truth about her, saw into her soul, and made no judgment. She found a perverse freedom in that.

Using a reluctant Giselle as her foil for the second time, Josephine arrived at the Majestic Hotel promptly at nine o'clock, a week after the first meeting with the enigmatic stranger who knew so much. She found him waiting for her in the lobby. Quickly, without uttering a word, he took her by the arm and ushered her to a cab outside the hotel. He whispered a name to the driver, and almost pushed Josephine into the cab.

"I thought it best we get used to staying out of sight," he explained, as the cab pulled away.

"Fine."

"I've already rented a room at a small hotel some fifteen blocks away. Room thirty-five B, on the second floor. I'll go first, you follow in three minutes. Understand?"

"Yes."

He grinned. "I'm glad you came."

Josephine looked into his clear blue eyes. "So am I," she said.

Once inside the dingy room, Josephine lit a cigarette and sat on the edge of the bed. "I'm not sure I can do what you want," she said, "and there are certain conditions. First, I want to know who you are and how you know about me."

"My name is Sven Kohnor," he said. "I was born in Sweden thirty-nine years ago. That's all you need to know about me. As for my knowing about you, I can't tell you that right now. Perhaps later. It's enough for you to know that I am very good at what I do. I have to be. In this business, mistakes can cost a life. I try very hard not to make any.

"In choosing people to work with, I am very careful. I do extensive research to make sure the people I choose are not likely to fail. I have chosen you because you're very, very bright and very, very beautiful."

"And you want me to be a whore."

As he had the first time they met, Kohnor reached into the dresser drawer and pulled out a bottle of Medoc. He raised it in the air and asked, "Wine?"

This time, Josephine nodded. As they drank the wine, Kohnor reiterated what he'd said during their first meeting. When he finished, he smiled knowingly. "So, how does it sound so far?" he asked.

Josephine turned away from him and stared out the window. It had begun to rain and the sound of the drops as they gently brushed the glass was the only sound in the room. She'd felt freedom when contemplating working with a man who knew her soul. Now she realized his knowledge of her included her anticipated response to his demands. She found it unsettling.

Sensing her discomfort, Sven said, "Here's what I propose for the moment. I will arrange for your employment, ostensibly a catalogue shoot for one of the department stores. The photographer is well known to Madame Bouvard, so there'll be no problem with her. The shoot will take three or four days.

"There'll be no shoot. What we will actually do is begin your training. I have another . . . contact . . . a young man, who is well-versed in the business of sex. He is someone a lot like yourself. At first, he was as repulsed as you, but now makes a great deal of money.

"He will work with you and teach you what you need to know. I realize it won't be easy, but I know you can do it. All I ask is that you try. If, after all, you just can't do it, then that will be that. We'll part company, you keep the money I gave you, and there'll be no hard feelings.

"However, if you try hard enough, I'm sure you can learn what you need to know. Once you've passed that hurdle, I will arrange for other modeling sessions where I will train you on other matters. Within weeks, you'll go to work."

He reached into the dresser drawer and pulled out another bundle of hundred-franc notes. "I told you that I would pay you every step of the way. There's another two thousand here, and you haven't done a thing yet. Imagine how much money you can make when you actually begin."

Josephine looked at the money and then at Kohnor.

He was smiling. "Well then, will you give it a try?"

She put the money in her handbag. "Yes," she said softly. "I'll try, at least. No guarantees, but I'll try."

A week later, Josephine was sent to a photographer's studio for a purported catalogue shoot. She shook off her apprehension. She'd already placed six thousand francs in a new bank account and the thought of more spurred her on.

She was ushered into the photographer's rear studio and introduced to another man, a young, handsome man with gentle eyes and black, curly hair. "Venus, this is Tony," the photographer said. "Tony Cecchi."

"Hi," Tony said. "I'm real happy to meet you." He spoke French with an American accent.

"As am I, you."

Tony was six feet tall with a muscular body. His lips were full, his teeth straight and white. Like Cary Grant, he had a cleft in his chin that only enhanced his good looks. His body language reflected a relaxed attitude that carried over into his mannerisms and voice.

The photographer interrupted their eye lock. "You two are to disappear for now and be back by five. My car will take you wherever you want to go."

"What are we going to do about the shoot?" Josephine asked. "Madame Bouvard will be very suspicious if there are no pictures."

The photographer waved his hand in the air. "Don't worry about it. I'll tell her that today's session was ruined by bad soup. It happens from time to time. Tomorrow, we'll take some shots, but we'll do it fast. What happens after that depends on you two."

Tony seemed to sense her trepidation. He placed a hand on her arm. "Take it easy, Venus. This isn't going to be as bad as you think."

"We'll see," she said.

They were driven to a hotel near the center of the city, where Tony had taken a suite. Once inside, Tony reached in his pocket, extracted a gold case and offered her a hand-rolled cigarette. Josephine knew instantly what it was, having learned about drugs in the correctional school. She shook her head.

Tony grinned at her and said, in English, "Look, this will help you relax. It's no big deal. We're here to do a job, that's all. I'm not gonna hurt you. Christ! If I screw this up, Sven will cut off my balls. So give me a break, will ya? Take one. It'll make this much easier for both of us."

"How did you know I spoke English?"

"Sven told me. How else?"

"You're an American."

"You noticed. Yeah. I'm American."

"What are you doing here in France?"

For a moment, a hardness entered his eyes but quickly disappeared. "I'm here for the bucks, just like you."

"I see."

"Now, Sven says you've got some hang-ups about sex. That true?"

Josephine looked at him coldly. "I don't have any hang-ups."

Tony grinned and handed her a cigarette. "That's what this is all about, right? Come on. Take a few deep drags and we'll get down to business."

Reluctantly, Josephine took the cigarette from his hand, lit it and inhaled deeply. It was the first time she had ever tried marijuana, and she wasn't quite sure what to expect. After three deep drags, Tony took the cigarette away from her, removed the burning ember, then placed the remaining part of the smoke back in the gold case. "That's enough," he said. "We don't want you getting sick."

He removed his suit jacket and hung it up in the closet. Then he moved to the radio that sat on a mahogany dresser and turned it on, flipping the dial until the room was filled with the sound of violins. It was classical music, unfamiliar to Josephine. Then, he turned, faced her and gestured toward the bed. "Well, time's a-wastin'. Take off your clothes and we'll begin."

To Josephine, everything seemed to be moving in slow motion. The anxiety she'd felt when she first entered the photographer's studio disappeared. Mechanically, she started to disrobe. By the time she was done, Tony was already naked and lying against the headboard of the bed, one arm behind his head, the other patting the mattress beside him.

The first time she had stood naked in front of a man had been at the modeling agency. The man had been Thorpe. Even as he made furious notes, she could see the look in his eyes, gleaming with wetness as he stole glances at her body. But this man, this American, looked at her with bored eyes. Like Madame Bouvard, he saw her body as a piece of meat, a tool of the trade.

She padded over to the bed and lay down beside him. Immediately, he sat up and leaned over her. "Okay," he said. "The first thing we need to understand is that this is strictly a job for both of us. I'm here to teach you how to use your body, how to make a man feel like you're crazy about him. So remember, there's nothing personal. Got that?"

Josephine nodded. She could feel the revulsion easing in her.

"Good," he said. "First, we're gonna spend some time just touching each other. I'll show you what to expect when you touch a man, where and how to touch him. And I'll show you how a man expects a woman to react when he touches her. Some of these guys will make you wanna puke, but you gotta tough it out, dig? You gotta be an actress."

"Dig?"

"That's American jive talk. Dig means understand."

"Oh. Okay, I dig."

He laughed.

They began. Tony taught, and Josephine learned. He was careful and gentle and explained everything in great detail. To her surprise, it quickly became an exercise in pure knowledge, as opposed to anything emotional. She discovered how the human body acted and reacted sexually. Some of it was familiar, thanks to her experience with Claude, but most was not. It was a study, nothing more, except that this was practical study leading to knowledge. Knowledge meant power. Power meant money.

After an hour, they took a break. Tony let her take a few drags from the marijuana cigarette, then it was on to more detailed activities, all done coldly and dispassionately. Josephine's fascination increased.

They took a lunch break, dressed, had room service, then went back to work. Tony taught her how to fake an orgasm and how to bring a man to orgasm with her mouth, her hands, even her breasts. At no time did she feel involved. It was simply knowledge.

He explained exercises that would assist her in controlling the various muscles that simulated the sex act. He taught her tricks that would make it appear as if she were lost in some wild feeling of joy, and finally, he discussed with her the various aberrations that some men liked, explaining which were allowable and which were not.

He taught her how to handle a man almost out of control with lust without crushing his tender ego, by begging him to do it her way, then bringing the man to a quick orgasm, reducing his sex drive.

When it was over, he complimented her on being a quick study and said, "I think we can wrap this up tomorrow. About three hours should do it. The rest you can learn on your own. I'll give you some books to read and you can practice with a device I'll give you. No problem."

Josephine finished buttoning up her blouse and asked, "Do you really think I can do it?"

"Absolutely. You got over your . . . resistance . . . the first hour. You'll do just fine. You'll have those idiots going crazy. Sven's gonna be really pleased. Now come on. We gotta get back."

It hadn't been nearly as bad as she'd thought it would be. Of course, there'd been those cigarettes. Tomorrow she'd do it without the cigarettes. That would be the real test.

The next day, they acted out a seduction, with Josephine pretending that Tony was simply a dupe. Without the aid of the cigarettes, Josephine expertly undressed him, covering his body with kisses and little bites, then removed her own clothes and began to make love to him right up to the point of her own simulated orgasm.

Tony critiqued her effort, offered suggestions, and they began anew. Five times she went through what was, by now, a ritual, and each time Tony would react differently, keeping her off guard. He would explain to her what she had done wrong and show her how to correct it. Finally, he called a halt and said, "Okay. You need to hit the books. Take a week and study hard. Then we'll have one more session."

Busy with an increased schedule of modeling sessions, Josephine had to study late at night. To avoid detection, she used a flashlight and read under a blanket.

A week later, after many hours of practice, Tony pronounced her ready. "Don't get dressed yet," he said, picking up the phone. "I have to let Sven know. He wants to be here for your final exam."

"What?"

"No big deal," he said. "Remember, this is like acting. Once Sven sees you work in front of him, he'll know you can do it."

"He can't take your word for it?"

"Sven takes nobody's word for anything."

"God! How repulsive."

Tony grinned. "You'll be fine. Just forget he's there."

Sven arrived in less than a half hour. "Tony tells me you're just about ready to graduate," he said.

Josephine held the sheets to her neck. "I know what to do, if that's what you mean."

"Show me."

"Is this really necessary?" she asked.

Sven nodded. "How else will I know if you can really handle any situation? Remember what I told you. The body is simply an extension of your being, a weapon, you might say. You have to be able to drive everything from your mind except the job at hand. If you can perform with Tony while I sit here and watch, I'll know you've got what it takes."

Josephine hesitated for a moment, then let the sheet fall away. She turned to Tony and began what had now become a ritual. She made it appear as though she was consumed with a passion that knew no bounds. When it was over, even Tony had a strange look in his eye, as if he believed what had happened was real.

Sven applauded the performance. "Wonderful! Just wonderful! Josephine, you're even more fantastic than I imagined. Next week, I'll teach you some other things you need to know. Leave Madame Bouvard to me. I'll arrange everything."

"Very well."

"Now, both of you get dressed. We'll all go out for dinner. It's time to celebrate. You did very well."

Tony beamed with pride. "Thanks, Sven."

The following week, Sven taught Josephine how to

use a small Minox camera, how to develop film, how to code and decode documents, how to pick locks, and a score of other interesting skills. Throughout the training, he was supportive, attentive, and effusive. At the end of the week, he announced, "You're ready for your first job."

She felt her heart stop. "So soon?"

"Why not? You learn by doing. This one is easy. If you fail, it won't be fatal."

"I'm glad to hear it."

His face turned hard. "You won't fail. I refuse to tolerate failure."

Two weeks later, Josephine was seated alone at a small outdoor café in Brussels, sipping a glass of red wine and casually reading a newspaper. She was dressed in a blue silk dress cut low in front, allowing a good measure of cleavage to show. Her legs were sheathed in dark blue stockings and her red-tipped fingers were adorned with a variety of rings. The diamond necklace around her neck glittered in the bright sunlight. Her face was carefully made up with blue eye shadow that matched the dress and lipstick that matched the nail polish. Topping off the image was a broad-brimmed straw hat, also in blue. She projected the image that had been intended, that of a beautiful but bored wife of some diplomat attached to NATO headquarters, whiling away the afternoon while her husband attended an endless series of meetings.

The jewels were as false as the papers she was carrying, which identified her as Madame Beatrice Boudreau, wife of a minor functionary of the French government attached to NATO headquarters.

Her quarry sat with two other uniformed men at a table less than five meters away. His name was General Roger Paxton, a senior British Army officer attending a week-long NATO conference. Already, the gray-haired, mustachioed general had found it necessary to glance in her direction several times, receiving faint smiles in return. As he began to partake of his third martini, he was seized by impulse, excused himself, and made his way to Josephine's table. He bowed slightly and introduced himself.

"Madame, I don't wish to impose, but my name is Major General Roger Paxton, Third Light Brigade, Her Majesty's Army. Do you speak English?"

Josephine glanced up from her newspaper and smiled sweetly. "Yes," she said.

"Splendid! I wonder if I might have the very great honor of buying you a drink."

"General, you are most kind, but I must tell you that I'm expecting my husband to arrive at any moment. If you wish to sit down, please do so, but you will excuse me if I am forced to leave when he arrives."

The general looked disappointed, but having gone this far, thought it ungallant to retreat immediately. He took a seat and signaled the waiter.

"I must seem like an old fool," he said. "Perhaps I am, but I found myself sitting there, looking at you and saying to myself that I simply must speak to you. I've never seen anyone so incredibly beautiful in my life."

Josephine blushed. "Thank you, General." To the hovering waiter, she said, "Another glass of the red, thank you."

As the general practically drooled into his martini, Josephine's face took on a sad expression. "Such words are music to my soul," she said. "I'm afraid my husband takes me completely for granted. I thank you for your kindness."

Paxton grunted something, then said, "Your English is excellent. You're so young. You can't have been married long."

"Two years," she said, pouting. "I'm at my wit's end already. As you can see, I've been sitting here alone, something I despise doing, for some time now. He promised me he'd be here on time this once and look at the hour!" She lifted her head and glanced around as though her husband might, at this very minute, be arriving by cab or private car.

"What does your husband do?"

"He's with the French government. He begged me to accompany him to this dreary conference, knowing how I hate to be left alone. No matter, he still leaves me alone most of the time, and when he finally staggers into our suite at a late hour, he's too tired to talk, or anything else. It was a mistake coming here."

If the general seemed nervous about being drawn into a potentially messy domestic argument, he didn't let on. Instead, emboldened by the liquor, he moved his chair closer to that of Josephine's, patted her hand with his beefy paw, clucked his tongue and shook his head. "I can tell you, my dear—"

Josephine rose to the bait. "Beatrice," she said. "Madame Beatrice Boudreau. My husband is Pierre Boudreau. Perhaps you've met him. No, that would be impossible. You're military and he's a bureaucrat." She laughed. "You usually don't mix too well, do you?"

"Not if we can help it. I was about to say that if you were my wife, I would probably never let you out of my sight."

"You're too kind, General."

"Not at all."

"Are you married?"

He blushed, glancing quickly at the band on his finger. "Yes. It's been a long time. Three children, all grown up now, living their own lives. It's some consolation."

"Consolation?"

He looked away for a moment, then fixed his gaze

on the table. He turned the glass in his hand, making an ever-larger series of circles from the moisture that had condensed on the outside. "Yes," he said, sadly. "It's a terrible thing. The doctors just can't seem to find out what it is. First they say it's a virus of some sort, then they say no, it's something else. In the meantime, she simply lies around doing nothing, getting worse every day. It's been almost two years now."

Josephine let his hand rest on hers. "I'm so sorry," she said. She could hardly keep from laughing. They were all such fools, thinking that some tale of woe was about to gain sympathy when in fact it was clear that they all lied through their teeth. They were all the same, thinking women were stupid, not deserving of enough respect even to tell the truth about the simplest of things.

She looked around again, sighed and slowly drew her hand away from the general's. "Well," she said, "enough is enough. I've been humiliated once too often by Pierre. This time, I'm going to teach him a lesson. When he finally arrives, I won't be here."

She stood up and prepared to leave. The general rose to his feet. "Where are you going?"

Feigning outrage, Josephine practically spit out the words. "I don't know. Not back to the suite. He might show up there and I want him to worry for a few hours at least. I'll go to a restaurant and have some dinner, then perhaps to the cinema. I don't know."

She smiled and patted the general's arm. "Thank you for the drink. You've been very kind. I hope your wife gets better soon."

"Wait!"

His eyes were like saucers. This beautiful creature was angry with her husband and about to disappear from his life forever. It had taken a considerable amount of courage to even speak to her, and now—

"Perhaps you would do me the very great honor of

joining me for dinner," he blurted. "I'm quite familiar with Brussels. I'm here all the time, actually. The restaurants are the finest in all of Europe, even better than Paris, if you can believe it. I'd be deeply appreciative."

"What about your companions?"

"Oh, they have appointments of their own to attend, I assure you. The thought of you wandering about this city by yourself terrifies me. At least allow me to offer some protection. If you'd rather not have dinner with me, that's quite understandable, but the thought of you being all alone . . . well, quite frankly, it disturbs me."

Josephine looked angry. For a moment, she looked around at the streams of people and cars passing by. Then her face broke into a smile. "General Paxton, you are most gallant. I accept your kind offer."

"Wizard!" he exclaimed, his face bright with joy. "Absolutely wizard! I'll get my things and we'll be off. Won't be a moment."

She watched as he spoke briefly with the two other men at his table, and grabbed his cap, walking stick and briefcase. Then, he was at her side, breathing hard, his hand on her arm as he guided her to the taxi stand.

Three hours later, they were in bed in his hotel, their clothes strewn about the floor as if both had been overcome with uncontrollable passion. It was true of the general. Josephine worked carefully and relatively slowly, but he was so excited, there was no holding him back. He exploded quickly and lay back on the pillow, exhausted.

Josephine rose from the bed, mumbling something about the bathroom. Upon her return, she picked up the bottle of champagne still resting in the silver bucket, and refilled their glasses. He never saw the small vial in her hand, a vial containing exactly six drops of chloral hydrate.

"To us," she said, raising her glass.

"To us," he parroted.

They drank. A few minutes later, Paxton felt even more exhausted.

"General," she said, "please don't go to sleep on me yet. I want to talk to you some more. I've been so lonely. You must have sensed that."

Paxton opened his eyes. The vision of this impossibly beautiful creature, completely nude, her large, high breasts inches away from his mouth, inspired him. With some effort, he pushed himself up, leaned against the headboard and smiled at her. "My dear," he said, "I'll be happy to talk with you. I can't tell you how much I've enjoyed the evening. You're the most exquisite woman I've ever encountered."

He smiled as Josephine touched the rim of her glass to his own. They toasted the evening, Brussels, the Queen, and love. Then he passed out.

Josephine went into the bathroom, took a towel from the rack, and wiped up the spilled champagne from the bed. Then she opened her handbag and removed a rubber cap. She placed it over her head while she took a long bath. She wanted to get the smell of this man out of her nostrils as soon as possible.

The bath completed, she dressed, put on a pair of rubber gloves, then slapped Paxton across the face. Satisfied that he was totally unconscious, she searched through his clothes until she found the key to the briefcase. She opened it, removed the papers it contained, and placed them under the lamp on the dresser. She took a small Minox camera from her handbag and photographed each and every paper. There were so many, it took five rolls of film.

That done, she put the papers back in the case, locked it, and placed the key back in his trousers. Then she wrote out a note on the hotel stationary, signed it "Beatrice," planted a lipstick impression just below her signature and placed the note beside his head.

Finally, she took the towel she'd used earlier and wiped all the furniture, the glasses and the champagne bottle, anything she might have touched. Satisfied, she removed the rubber gloves, put them in her handbag, and left the room.

The next morning, the general awoke with a slight headache. He sat up in bed, noticed the note, and reached for his glasses. He read the note and smiled. "It is I who should thank you, my dear," he said aloud.

Once the pictures were developed, Sven was ecstatic. He gave Josephine a bonus of ten thousand francs and told her she'd better consider doing her banking in Switzerland. She was earning so much money that there might be problems if she continued to deposit the funds in Parisian banks.

Josephine beamed with pride. The encounter with the general had been exciting and fulfilling. Sven had been right. Seducing the stupid general had been almost as thrilling as killing Claude. For the first time since that remarkable day, her heart was bursting with joy. She felt alive and free. This was a life that could fill her needs.

21

$\mathcal{P}i\varepsilon\imath\imath\varepsilon$ Charrette held the thin strips to the light, one after another, carefully examining each negative with a small magnifier the size of a jeweler's loupe. "Excellent," he exclaimed excitedly. "Just excellent." He put the magnifier in his pocket and placed the negatives back in a small caviar tin. He beamed at Sven. "The British are amazing," he said. "Even more stupid than the Americans. To allow these papers to be handled in such a way. Such idiocy!"

"A common mistake," Sven said. "We thrive on the mistakes of others, but you'd be just as much a fool to consider all of your adversaries as stupid as this one. We got lucky."

"Lucky? I don't think so. The man was thoroughly investigated, was he not?"

Sven nodded.

"So, how can you call it luck? It's a tribute to

American ingenuity—and the competitive requirements of capitalism. These American companies
devour one another in their constant craving for what
they call increased market share." He laughed. "They
don't want a share. They want it all, and to get it,
they'll steal, kill—whatever it takes. Do you realize
what these documents are?"

"I don't care what they are."

"No? Well, you should, my friend. These documents detail NATO weapons requirement estimates
for the next ten years, right down to the caliber of the
standard-issue rifle. With this information, your
friend Bower will be months ahead in research and
development."

"He's not my friend. He's a client, as you are."

Charrette bristled. "I stand corrected," he said.

The Swede smiled. "Nothing personal," he said
softly. "This is a business, Pierre. I make it a point
never to mix business with pleasure."

"Is that why you refuse to introduce me to your
newest find, the vexatious child who produced
these?"

Sven laughed. "No, that's not the reason. You
know my policy. You deal with me, not my people.
Besides, you'd be wasting your time."

"Am I that unattractive?" Charrette snapped.

He was understandably sensitive about his appearance. Not yet thirty, his face was badly scarred from
burns suffered in a botched Allied air attack on a
Luftwaffe airfield in 1944. Flying at night and bombing through partial cloud cover, the Americans had
dropped their bombs five miles short of the airfield,
blasting a small French town into oblivion.
Charrette's entire family had been killed outright,
but he'd survived after enduring months of agonizing
pain. Now he endured another kind of pain, as people either turned away or gawked at the hideous
mass of tissue that covered the front of his skull.

"That's not what I meant," Sven said quickly. "You could be the handsomest man in the world, and it wouldn't matter. The 'child' is a woman who fucks for reasons that have little to do with sexuality. The only way you'd ever be able to sleep with her is to become a target, and I doubt your associates would approve."

"So, you have little control over your people?"

Sven stood up quickly. "Put your needle away, Pierre. If you're dissatisfied with my services, say the word and I'll strike you from my list."

The Frenchman's anger softened. "You're a bit sensitive today, my friend. Oh, yes, I forgot. You don't like to be called a friend. Excuse the error."

Kohnor grabbed his coat.

"I'm sorry," Charrette said. "I'm somewhat testy today. Please, don't go just yet."

"Why not?"

"I have some things to discuss."

"Make it quick."

"I will. Have you given the copies to Bower?"

"Yes."

Charrette shook his head. "It's incredible. Without Bower, you never would have known these documents existed. Without his insatiable greed—" He stopped talking and wiped his face with a towel. "My associates have hundreds of agents in the field, but give them a few more T. J. Bowers and they could cut that in half. The man is so consumed with greed that he must have his own network of spies to gather information for him."

Sven let him ramble. It happened often, usually at times like these, when a successful mission was being celebrated. Whenever Charrette felt secure, he pontificated, spouting the party line, railing against the corrupt and stupid Americans, oblivious to the defects inherent in Communism. Charrette's enmity toward the Americans and British was explainable, considering what had happened to him, but his love affair with Communism was less so. He was convinced that

France would eventually become a Communist state, but while he waited—and perhaps hedging his bets—he engaged in industrial espionage in an effort to provide certain French industrialists with the latest Western technology. At the same time, he made sure his KGB contacts received copies of all intelligence.

Officially, he was a registered member of a political party, a lawyer by profession, though he'd never practiced law. His ever-widening circle of contacts gave him a reflected patina of legitimacy, and even those in the bureaucracy fervently opposed to socialism treated him with deference, unsure of the depths of his true conviction. For a Communist, he seemed very much immersed in capitalism and could, at times, be extremely generous. Of course, they knew nothing of his KGB contacts.

Kohnor—apolitical though he had joined the party for the sake of convenience—let Charrette's long-winded discourses go in one ear and out the other. With all his shortcomings, he was a good client, careful about meetings and prompt with payments—the two key elements in any Kohnor relationship.

Charrette continued his tirade. "Bower amazes me," he said. "A very wealthy defense contractor who, to further protect his interests, pours money into the coffers of a variety of politicians. Imagine! Some day, he may buy himself a president. Can you imagine what we could do with him if that happened?"

Sven laughed out loud. "You know, Pierre, sometimes you are prone to fantasy. I wouldn't count on anything."

Charrette frowned. "Why are you always so negative?" he asked.

"I am disappointed less often. Besides, I'm not being negative. I just don't want you thinking that it will always be this easy. Sometimes, when people are disappointed, they cast blame on those who are blameless. I don't want that to happen to you. Or to me."

Charrette snorted. "You're a worrier, Sven. That's not good."

"Pierre, if you've got something for me, get to it."

"You're always so impatient."

"And you take forever to get to the point."

"Yes, yes. All right. It's a very important task."

"I'm listening," Sven said wearily, "but not for long."

Josephine Cousteau worked hard during the next two years, becoming, at the age of eighteen, one of Paris's most sought-after photographic models. Madame Bouvard had long since been paid back for the training and the clothes; and just as Josephine had fantasized that day in Marie's Paris flat, her face and form now peered out from the pages of most of France's top fashion magazines. Her popularity spread throughout western Europe and America, where she graced the cover of several immensely popular periodicals.

Her American exposure, coupled with her fluency in English, led to three Hollywood screen test offers. She turned them down immediately. She reasoned she couldn't live in the United States and work for Sven, and she very much liked working for Sven, despite the severe time constraints imposed by her modeling success.

Her schedule drove Sven to distraction, forcing him to set up assignments with little advance notice or planning, much against his better judgment. Nevertheless, he continued to use her, for her competence and efficiency were well beyond that of any of his other operatives. When he did so, she performed flawlessly on missions of both industrial and military espionage.

As a result of her bifurcated efforts, the balance in her secret, numbered Swiss bank account was ten times larger than her account in a Paris bank. But the Paris bank held more than money; it held the diary she'd been keeping ever since her sixteenth birthday, a diary in which every detail of her life was noted weekly, a diary too incriminating to be left unprotected.

Once a week, she'd visit the bank, remove the diary, trek to a nearby library, spend two hours making her entries, then return to the bank and lock the diary away. Like her mother, she was obsessed with the need to record the events of her life.

After her eighteenth birthday, when all restrictions were removed from her life, Josephine had her own flat in one of the posher residential sections of Paris.

She had almost instant recognition when she appeared in public and was shown to the best table in a restaurant or the best seat in one of the new discos flooding Paris. Perhaps most important, she had fulfillment in her life. Modeling, while it provided a measure of self-esteem, failed to give her the depth of satisfaction found in working for Sven. Aside from the money, there was the validation she felt every time she made a fool of another idiot military man or politician, as they helplessly succumbed to her charms.

But it was getting tougher. Her face was so recognizable that to carry out missions for Sven, she had to resort to drastic changes in makeup and hair styling, sometimes even resorting to elaborate disguises to avoid being identified as Venus, the famous model. Yet, to seduce the targets successfully, she still had to look beautiful, and it was becoming increasingly difficult to disguise her appearance so that she wouldn't be recognized.

Madame Bouvard was making more and more demands on her time, realizing that the lifetime of a popular model was a short one, and wanting to make the most of it. Since the vast majority of Sven's missions took place outside Paris, he worked feverishly to set up sessions, but Madame was beginning to refuse the jobs, regardless of the money offered, fearful they were taking Venus away from Madame's regular clientele.

And then there was Marie. For two years, Josephine's visits to the small flat were infrequent, but necessary. She was, after all, still under the court's supervision, and failure to make regular visits to her longtime benefactor would have looked suspicious as best, callous at worst. Now, freed of the need to pretend, Josephine set out to rid herself of a woman she considered tiresome.

Marie still hadn't found a man for herself, and at her age, probably never would. She seemed to think that because she had disrupted her life to help the young Josephine, she was owed something. How nonsensical. She had made the decision to do that on her own. Nobody had asked her to do it, least of all Josephine, who felt she owed Marie nothing.

So it was that on this Sunday evening, after a dinner of pot roast and potatoes, Josephine decided to tell her so.

"I'm afraid I won't be able to see much of you anymore," she said flatly.

Marie looked at her in shock. "Whatever are you talking about?"

Josephine stared vacantly at a long, red fingernail that needed some repair. "It shouldn't be that hard for you to understand. I'm a very busy woman these days and you . . . you seem to have this attitude that I should spend all of my free time with you. It's quite impossible. It's difficult enough to arrange the time, and when I do, you carry on about how long it's been since I was last here. You don't realize the sacrifices I have to make to see you at all."

"Sacrifices?"

"Yes. I hardly have any time for myself. Madame

works me night and day. It's a rare occasion when I can just sit in the tub and soak."

Stunned and hurt, Marie lashed out. "You amaze me, Josephine. You've become an astonishingly selfish woman. Are you aware of that?"

Josephine continued to pick at the errant nail. "I don't think so. I'm here when I could be doing something for myself. I'm not saying I'm never going to see you again. I'm just saying that it will be a few months before I can find the time."

"I see. Coming here is doing me a favor. Is that it?"

"To be truthful, yes. Let's be honest with each other. We have nothing in common. You work in a factory. You have no friends, no lovers, and your life is quite uninteresting. Every time I come here, you tell me the same old tired stories about how you and my mother fought in the resistance and how you helped me when I was in correctional school.

"Well, I'm tired of those stories. I never asked you for help and I resent the fact that you constantly bring it up. That was another time. I have a life of my own now, an exciting life. I don't want to hear about the past. I don't want to hear how beholden I should be to you."

She opened her handbag and removed a check, which she placed on the table. "This should cover whatever expenses you incurred on my behalf. I want to be free of this debt forever. If it isn't enough, let me know and I'll send you more."

She stood up, picked up the handbag and said, "I have to go now. I'll call you when I have the chance."

Without another word, Josephine turned, opened the door of the flat, and was gone. Marie stood there for a moment, stunned, then picked up the check. Without looking at the amount of money written on the face, she slowly tore it into little pieces and dropped the pieces on one of the plates. Then she sat down on the chair and stared at the door to her tiny flat.

Her eyes were dry. Even if she'd wanted to cry, it would have been impossible. Her soul was a vacuum, her emotions dead, her mind numbed by the pain, uncomprehending of the cruelty that had been visited upon her.

Back in her flat, Josephine sat on the sofa, sipped a brandy, and contemplated her future. She was at a crossroads in her life. She couldn't be both a model and a spy any longer. One of the careers would have to go. But which?

Sven's missions were more exciting than modeling, more rewarding both emotionally and financially, but their timing was erratic. There were times when a month would pass between jobs, whereas modeling kept her busy daily. Sven seemed anxious for her to drop the modeling and work exclusively for him, but she resisted. She hated having nothing to do.

She was still pondering the problem a week later, while performing yet another mission for Sven, this time in London. She had successfully taken an American Air Force general to bed in his hotel room, had administered the drug and waited as he passed out. Then, as was her custom, she bathed, dressed, slapped his face, and began to take photographs of the papers in his briefcase. This time, however, it all came apart, and the problem she'd contemplated became redundant.

She was in the process of photographing the documents in his briefcase when, inexplicably, the general awoke. To Josephine's astonishment, he moaned, sat up in bed, then opened his eyes, staring at her as she bent over the table, the small camera in her hands. He lurched from the bed with a shout and stumbled toward her. "You scheming bitch!" he screamed, as he staggered groggily toward her, his face twitching with anger, his hands formed into fists.

For a moment, Josephine stood frozen, the papers spread out on the table, but only for a moment. She leaped to the sofa, grabbed her handbag and removed a switchblade knife. With a push of a button, the six-inch blade snapped into position. Without hesitation, she rammed the blade into the lower chest of the bewildered, semiconscious general and pushed it upward, under the rib cage, into the heart. At the same time, she kept her other hand over his mouth, muffling the scream that erupted from his lips. His shocked eyes rolled back into his head, and he fell to the floor.

Josephine calmly removed the knife and checked his pulse. He was dead. She felt an involuntary shudder go through her body, not the normal shudder of fear or apprehension, but a strange quiver that surprised and pleased her. She moved quickly to the bathroom, using a wet towel to clean the small streaks of blood that had splattered on the rubber gloves. She checked for blood on her clothes. There was none. She cleaned the knife, closed it, then finished photographing the papers, put them back in the briefcase, locked it, and tidied up the room.

She went through the general's clothes and removed his billfold. From his wrist, she took his watch. From his finger, she removed his wedding ring. Finally, she used a towel to wipe off any fingerprints from the furniture, then quietly slipped out of the room.

As she left the hotel, she gave no thought to the man in the lobby staring at her, a rumpled-looking man in a dark blue suit, sitting on a sofa, looking slightly out of sorts. Men often stared at her. It was expected.

His name was Roland Lockwood and he was an inspector with Scotland Yard. He was investigating the theft of weapons from an American Air Force base just outside London. General James Brill was

visiting from Washington and had asked for an
update on the investigation. He had asked the inspector to meet him in his hotel, rather than at the base,
to avoid the appearance of superseding the commanding officer of the base.

Lockwood had gone to the hotel for the meeting
and had been surprised when the general was not in
his room. He'd gone to the bar and observed General
Brill engaged in serious and animated conversation
with a stunning woman he recognized immediately,
despite the blonde wig.

Quickly realizing what was going on, and none too
happy about it, he nevertheless waited patiently in
the lobby as the twosome made their way upstairs.
Scotland Yard inspectors were expected to treat
high-ranking Americans, be they military or civilian,
with utmost respect. Lockwood, the epitome of dis-
cretion, waited for almost an hour, cogitating the sexual proclivity of Americans as he did so.

Finally, after seeing the woman leave the hotel,
Lockwood made his way to General Brill's room.
When there was no answer to his knock on the door,
he summoned the maid, displayed his credentials and
gained access to the room.

Within ten minutes, a bulletin was issued for the
arrest of the famous model Venus, wanted for ques-
tioning in the murder of the American general,
James Brill.

Once back in her own hotel room, Josephine
Cousteau packed her things and reapplied the elaborate makeup, including the rubber appliances, that
she'd used when she'd left Paris. The rubber appliances
gave her skin a rather mottled appearance. They took
over an hour to apply, but the effect was worth it. Once
again, she was a dark-haired woman in her late twenties, with a rather unattractive face and a body that was
hidden by ill-fitting and badly styled clothes.

From the dresser, she removed a small package

that contained a complete negative developing kit. She arranged the bottles and little black canister on the table, then measured the temperatures of the three chemicals, developer, stop, and fix. They measured twenty-two degrees Celsius, a bit too high, but within tolerances if she cut down the developing time.

Using the kit, she developed all four rolls of film. When she was finished, she washed the negatives in the bathroom sink and put them up to the light. They were fine. She dried the negatives off with a towel and secreted them in her suitcase, behind the liner. The bottles of chemicals and the canister were placed in a small plastic bag along with the blonde wig she'd used for her rendezvous with the general, his now-empty billfold, the watch, and the ring. The switchblade knife was placed inside a rather large tin of talc.

The room smelled of vinegar, just like any other darkroom. She took out a package of cigarettes, removed the entire contents, and one after another lit them all. While they burned in three separate ashtrays, she took the plastic bag and left the room. A block away from the hotel, she found a garbage can and stuffed the plastic bag into it, then went back to the hotel.

Her room now smelled like a poker parlor. She took a towel and wiped the entire room clean, then called the bellman. It was time to return to Paris.

At Orly Airport, she retrieved her bags from the claim area, breezed through customs without a hitch, and started walking out of the building. A man walked along beside her and said quietly, "Don't look at me. Just follow me. I'm from Sven."

Something was very wrong. "Sven?" she asked. "What are you talking about?"

The man never looked at her. "Don't be stupid," he said. "They know about you. You can't return to your flat."

Impossible! No one had seen her. The general was dead. How could it be?

She fell in step with the stranger and followed him outside. Instead of heading for the taxi stand, they walked to the parking lot and got into an old Peugeot. Once inside the car, the man said, "You screwed it up, Josephine. Sven is really upset."

He was a man in his forties, a small man with beady little eyes and scruffy, thin hair. He looked dirty and classless, not the kind of man that Sven usually employed.

Josephine's face reflected her concern. "I can imagine," she said. "Where are we going?"

"Sven told me to take you to a house outside the city. He'll meet you there."

"Who are you?" she asked.

"Just another one of Sven's people. Now be quiet. Sven will explain everything to you when we get there."

He never spoke again the entire trip. Fighting traffic, the drive took over an hour. Finally, they stopped in front of a small nondescript house in the suburbs. They both got out and went inside, where Sven was waiting.

He was indeed upset. Without a word, he took the suitcase from the startled Josephine, unlocked it and opened it. He ripped away the lining, took out the negatives and held them up to the light. "Well," he said, his voice dripping with sarcasm, "at least you did something right."

Josephine sat on a chair and pouted. "Sven, I had to kill the man. He woke up and saw me taking pictures. I had no choice!"

He whirled to face her. "He woke up? You gave him the drug?"

"Of course!"

"Well, sometimes it happens. There are those who seem to have a tolerance to it. Very rare. And most unfortunate. Did you wear a disguise?"

"Yes."

"Well, you screwed up somewhere. They know it was you. Someone recognized you with the general. You're being sought throughout Europe."

She was beside herself. "Look! I did everything I usually do. If you remember, it was I who warned you that this might happen. My face is so well known now. God! What am I to do?"

For the first time since she arrived, he smiled. "Don't worry."

"Don't worry? What does that mean?"

"I guess I pushed you too far. You were right to kill him. You had no choice. However, I have a solution."

"What would that be?" she asked.

"Later," he said. "Right now, we have other things to be concerned about. You can never go back to your flat again, nor can you go to the agency. Josephine Cousteau is dead, as of now."

Her jaw dropped.

"I mean that figuratively," he said. "Not literally. I won't kill you."

Sven put the film in his jacket and said, "We'll have to get you out of the country. Switzerland. We'll have to change your face. I know a plastic surgeon in Zurich who can do the job. Nothing major, just some work around the eyes and the nose, perhaps the chin. You'll look different enough that they'll have a hard time making the connection. We'll have to do some work on your hands. Your fingerprints are on file and that's no good. You won't look like Venus anymore, but you'll still be pretty, so don't worry."

He rubbed his hand across his face and said, "You'll need to stay out of sight for a year or two. You've got lots of money, so that's not a problem."

She stared at him in shock. "Is all this really necessary?"

"What do you think?" he said harshly.

She thought about it for a moment, then nodded.

"How did it feel?" he asked.

"Pardon?"

He looked at her intently, one eyebrow slightly raised. "It's been some time since you killed a man. How did it feel?"

He knew her well. She had no compunction about revealing her true feelings to this man. Without hesitation, she said, "It felt very, very good. Much like you said it would years ago, Sven. In fact, when I realized he was dead, I had an orgasm. A real one. Can you imagine?"

"Yes, I can," he said.

The next day, Sven entered the Ritz Hotel in Zurich and took the stairs to the third floor. He walked down the hall, stopped in front of a room, looked both ways to make sure he was alone, then rapped his knuckles lightly on the door. It was opened almost immediately.

Thomas J. Bower, an American industrialist, known to his friends as T.J., grabbed Sven's hand and shook it warmly. "Come in," he said.

Sven entered the expensive suite, removed his overcoat, threw it over the back of a chair, and sat down in one of the long, soft sofas.

"Well, well," T. J. Bower said, as he smiled at his visitor. "Too bad about Scotland Yard."

Kohnor waved a hand. "No matter. She got out, and that's all that's important. The plan called for her face to be altered in any case. The fact that she was discovered only made it easier to convince her. In fact, I suspect she would have refused had it not been for the discovery of her identity."

"Where is she now?"

"At the clinic. It will take some time."

Bower walked over to the bar and motioned with his arm. "Drink?"

"Yes. I'll have some gin."

"Gin it is."

Bower prepared the drinks, walked back to the sofa, and handed one to Sven. Holding his glass in the air, he said, "Here's to crime. They say it doesn't pay. How wrong they are."

Sven smiled as the glasses touched. "You've come a long way, Major. I read about you now in the European papers. The American OSS hero who took over his father's small company after the war, now becoming an industrial giant."

Bower smiled. "I have several people to thank for that. There was a greedy German general hoarding gold bullion. Then, there was a young Swedish assassin with the connections to convert it into American money." He raised his glass again. "That was a most fortunate day, my friend. How easily we could have missed it. Had the general hidden it somewhere else in the house, we never would have suspected."

Sven ran a hand through his thick hair and said, "Life can sometimes hand one opportunities."

Bower leaned forward and stared at his glass. "Tell me, Sven. We both received over three million dollars from the sale of that gold. I used mine to build a business. You, on the other hand, continue to engage in dangerous adventures. You have enough money to live a life of luxury for the rest of your days. Why do you continue?"

"What about you?" Sven countered, laughing. "Your business is booming. You have much more money than I, yet you take risks. You're a fine one to talk."

Bower looked up. "True. I guess we both feel the same way. It is never enough, is it, Sven?"

Instead of answering, Sven reached into his jacket pocket and removed an envelope. "Here are the negatives," he said.

Bower grabbed the envelope, removed the negatives and held them up to the light. Then he put them back in the envelope and placed it inside his brief-case. "Excellent," he said, as he handed Sven a large manila envelope. "One hundred thousand American dollars. You did well, my friend."

"Thanks."

"Do you think she suspects?"

"Josephine?"

"Yes."

"No. I let her read the newspaper accounts. She thinks it all happened naturally. There's no problem there."

"What did you tell her?"

"Just that some people respond less to chloral hydrate than others. She accepted that. She's no fool, you know. She reads all the time. Fortunately, what I told her was the truth. I didn't, however, tell her that the drug I provided was a sixth the strength."

"You're amazing. She reacted exactly as you sus-pected she would."

"Exactly. I knew she could kill. Faced with discov-ery, she reacted instinctively, knowing precisely what to do. There was not a moment's panic. She enjoyed it, as I thought she would. It gave her the chance to relive the killing of her hated guardian. She said she had an orgasm, in fact."

"Really?"

"So she says, and I have no reason to doubt her."

"An unusual reaction."

"Not for her."

"So we have our assassin."

"Yes."

T. J. Bower raised his glass in the air and said, "To Josephine."

"No longer. We've changed her name. She'll now be known as Annette LeClair. She picked the name herself."

22

$\mathcal{M}uch$ to Josephine's relief, the operation that took place three weeks after the death of the American general was an unqualified success. The surgeon at the Swiss clinic picked by Sven, Dr. Hans DeVol, was a magician. Though the wounds had not yet healed and the cut lines were still red and angry looking, Josephine could tell that the transformation would be easy to live with.

She *did* look different. There was a new shape to the eyes that would remain after the bruises waned. Now, they were almost sloe eyes, giving her a hint of the oriental, with thin eyebrows that arched higher than before. Her nose was slightly thicker, the nostrils smaller. That was fine. She'd always thought of her nose as too thin. Her lips were thinner and less pouty, giving her a more mature look. All the changes were subtly done, but the effect was completely natural. Despite the puffiness in her face caused by the operation, soon to disappear, she knew she still looked beautiful. Different, but beautiful, just as Sven had promised.

A month later, with most traces of the operation gone—what thin scars remained were easily masked by subtle makeup—Josephine met with Sven in a small Paris café three blocks from her newly acquired apartment to talk about the future.

"You look marvelous," he said.

"Thank you. I feel marvelous, if a little odd."

"The new face will take some getting used to."

"That's not what I mean. For two days, I've walked about the city, passing within inches of gendarmes, all of whom are looking for me, without getting so much as a curious glance. Oh, there've been the usual slavering stares, but not a hint of recognition. The change is remarkable. It's like being reborn."

"I knew you'd be pleased."

"I am."

"You'll be even more pleased when I tell you what's in store for you."

"Really? What?"

"You're going to become an assassin, *ma chérie.*"

She knew immediately that he was serious. Sven rarely joked. Another might have been shocked, but she wasn't. It was a natural progression, an acceptable development. And with Sven, the man who could see into her soul, there was little point in pretending she wasn't pleased.

"That alone?" she asked.

He looked surprised. "I don't understand."

"It's simple," she said. "The modeling kept me busy. Obviously, I can't model anymore."

"You're still quite beautiful, Annette."

"I agree, but that's not the point. All we need is to have a photograph of me lying around for some curious policeman to study. To be sure, my face has been altered, but not enough to thwart the careful examination of a clever detective."

"You're right, of course."

She smiled. "Surely, there can't be that many people you want terminated."

He smiled.

"So, what am I to do with the rest of my time?"

"Hmmm. Good question. He rubbed his chin for a moment. "You're a voracious reader, are you not?"

"What's that got to do with anything?"

"Have you ever considered becoming a writer?"

"A writer?"

"Yes. A novelist, perhaps. You could write spy stories. They say those who know what they are writing about make the best authors. It would occupy your time and keep you from the public eye. An ideal occupation for you, I'd think."

She laughed, thinking of her diary. "That's not a bad idea. You're extremely inventive, Sven."

"Well?"

She took a moment to answer. "I might give it a try."

"Good. So, we have a deal?"

"Not yet."

"What's the problem?"

"Killing of necessity is one thing. Killing by contract is another matter entirely."

"You love to kill. I don't see the distinction."

"It's a matter of trust, Sven. You know all about me, always have. I know little of you. When we first started working together, I asked you how you knew. You put me off. 'Later,' you said. Well, later is now. I want to know everything."

"I can't do that."

"No? You don't trust me?"

"Of course I trust you."

"Then?"

"It's a matter of policy."

"Ahhh. A need-to-know basis, as they say."

"Exactly."

"Well, I need to know."

He looked into her eyes and realized she spoke the truth. It was no game for her. As she had said, she was reborn, embarking on a new life. In the past, she'd never made demands unless she felt them absolutely necessary. Usually, they were. Now, she perceived this as equally important. He knew what would happen should he refuse.

"It started during the war," he said softly. "Sweden was neutral, surrounded by Germans and Russians, a precarious situation. I was young, hot-blooded, and resentful, anxious to do something, but prevented from doing so by law. Then, in early 1944, providence. I was recruited by the American OSS to assist in an assassination, purely by chance.

"A German general had stashed his mistress in a house in Unfors, out of harm's way. The general visited her regularly, and the Americans eventually found out. They decided to parachute in a small team of commandos to kill him prior to D day, but needed someone local to meet them at the mountain drop zone and guide them to the house. They picked me because I lived close to the house. I was more than eager.

"I was supposed to be a guide, nothing more, but on the night of the drop, things changed. Three men left the plane, but only one survived, a Major named Thomas Bower. The other two got blown off course and landed in deep snow, miles away from anything. We were never able to find them. To this day, their bodies have never been found.

"Bower and I proceeded alone. He gave me a gun and asked if I knew how to use it. I did. We made our way to the house and shot the general and his mistress while they were in bed, using handguns equipped with silencers. Some of the slugs chipped away the plaster behind the bed, and something caught our eye.

"It was gold bullion, stolen by the Germans from a Norwegian bank. I guess the general and his troops decided to split it instead of turning it over to the Reich. Whatever, there was a lot of it, and Bower and I took it. Together, we buried it under a cabin my parents owned in the mountains.

"After the war, Bower came back to Sweden, and together, we arranged for the sale of the gold. Bower took his share of the proceeds and poured it into his father's small industrial company, with excellent results. I put mine in a Swiss bank, and started an industrial espionage ring. Bower started using my services. Then, I was recruited by the KGB to work for them as well. So, there you are."

"So you're rich?"

"Very."

"Why do you continue?"

"I like the life. I told you we're both cut from the same cloth."

"How did you find out about me?"

He smiled. "You remember the doctor who worked with you while you were in the correctional school?"

"Of course."

"He kept voluminous notes. His secretary was a friend of mine. When she transcribed the doctor's notes after every session, she absorbed the contents. She spotted you as someone who would work well with me."

Her jaw dropped. "The doctor knew my true feelings?"

"You thought you had him fooled, eh? Not at all. He saw you for what you are, and said so in his notes. He didn't report his feelings to the court because he was afraid they wouldn't believe him."

She leaned back in her chair. "I had no idea."

"I know."

"So, this assassination business. Who are you working for?"

"I have several clients. Bower, of course, and a couple of Englishmen, and there's a Frenchman named Pierre Charrette. I'll introduce you to them one of these days. Interesting people. Survivors, like us."

"I thought you had a policy that precluded my ever meeting your clients."

"I do. But things are changing. I regard you more as a partner than an employee. You should be treated as such."

"You're beginning to trust me?"

"Perhaps. Am I making a mistake?"

"No."

"Good."

"I knew about Bower," she said, "but not Charrette. What's he do?"

"He's got his finger in several pies. A very wealthy man. He sells information to many parties, including the Russians."

"So, everything you do for the others is reported to the Russians?"

"Not everything, but most of it. They pay well. So, do we have a deal?"

"It depends on the money," she said.

"Let me put it this way. You'll be a millionaire within two years."

Josephine underwent a rigorous, week-long training period in the north of France, under Sven's careful tutelage. He taught her how to use a variety of weapons, from pistols to garrotes. At week's end, he handed her a manila envelope.

"Everything you need for your first job," he said. "And ten thousand English pounds. The name of the target and the names of two men who may be of assistance to you if need be. Another ten thousand will be placed in your Swiss account when the job is complete. Unless, of course, you want it in cash."

She fingered the envelope, then placed it in her handbag. "No. Placing the rest of the money in my account will be fine."

Kohnor smiled and said, "Good. They want it done within a fortnight. When you get home, look over the material. If you have any questions, you'll see a note inside where you can call me tomorrow at noon. If I don't hear from you, I'll assume you're on your way. All right?"

"Fine."

"Good luck, *chérie*."

She took a train back to Paris, then hailed a taxi and headed for home. She could hardly wait to open the envelope and see what the job was. Once safely inside her new apartment, she rushed to the bedroom and tore the envelope open, allowing the contents to spill out onto the bedspread.

There was a picture of a man in his fifties, with photos of his home, his car, and his business. There was a list of clubs that he frequented, marked maps pinpointing locations, and a sheet of paper that listed the names of two men and their addresses. And a bound bundle of crisp, new English pounds.

The target's name was Bruno Kowalski, sole owner of a company in London that manufactured aircraft parts. He was to be killed within two weeks by whatever means necessary, as long as it looked like a gangland-style job. The more bodies the better. She was to use three different weapons, for subsequent ballistics identification purposes, and leave no witnesses. There were no restrictions.

Kowalski was a man who liked to gamble. He belonged to two private London gambling clubs and took frequent trips to Monte Carlo. Obviously, the idea was to make it look as if he'd been killed by someone to whom he owed money.

She showered, dressed, then took a taxi to her new bank. There, she retrieved her safe deposit box, went into a small room, and closed the door. She opened the box, removed her diary, and started to place the English pounds in the box, but stopped. Her mother's diary beckoned her.

She removed it as well, put in the money, then closed the box.

At the library, she sat at a long walnut table and made her entries. An hour later, she closed her diary and picked up her mother's. She held it in her hands and closed her eyes. It was the only thing in the world that really meant anything to her, the only connecting thread to someone in the past who cared about her.

Her father didn't know she existed, and that fact had numbed any curiosity she might have had about the man—until now. For some unknown reason, she began to wonder about him. She knew he was an American, and that he'd been alive when her mother'd been killed. Still, a war was raging, and he might have been killed. No. He was badly wounded, having lost a foot. Neither the Americans nor British were in the habit of forcing the wounded to fight.

He was probably alive, middle-aged and fat, oblivious to the legacy he'd left behind in the form of a daughter. She fingered the photograph, and smiled as she envisioned an imaginary meeting. "Hello, Monsieur DiPaolo. I am your daughter. Yes. What do I do? I kill people for money. Do you have someone you'd like to see disappear?"

Bruno Kowalski lived in a large stone house in Islington, north of London, with a wife, three children, a cook, two maids, and a butler. The servants lived in a separate, much smaller house near the rear of the grounds. An eight-foot-high wrought-iron fence surrounded the two-acre estate.

Josephine drove through the neighborhood in a rented car and surveyed the situation. She stopped on a street running behind the estate and placed binoculars to her eyes. From her position, she could see the rear of the house clearly. She made notes.

She sat in the car for a moment, smoking a cigarette and thinking it through. Then she headed back to downtown London to one of the addresses that Sven had given her. She parked the car, entered a jewelry store and asked for Robert Grimes. The female clerk excused herself, went to the rear of the store, and rapped on a glass partition. Josephine could see a man examining a piece of jewelry, a loupe in his eye. He listened to the clerk, removed the loupe, wiped his hands, and came out front.

"I'm Robert Grimes," he said.

"We have a mutual friend. Sven Kohnor."

He never even blinked, just smiled slightly and said, "Yes, of course. I'd suggest we meet somewhere else. Say in about an hour. There's a library three blocks from here. I often go there after I close the shop. Why don't we meet there?"

"That'll be fine."

Grimes smiled again, bent forward slightly in a small bow, and returned to the back of the store.

An hour later, they met at the library. In whispered tones, she told him what she needed. "I want three semiautomatic pistols equipped with silencers, extra clips for all three, a set of coveralls, black, and a balaclava, also black. Oh, and some leather gloves, thin, supple."

Grimes seemed amused. "That's all?"

"Yes."

"And when would you like it?"

"The sooner the better."

"Would tomorrow be all right?"

"Yes."

"Do you want large- or small-caliber weapons?"

"Large."

"All the same?"

"No."

"How about a forty-five and two nine millimeters?"

"That would be fine."

Grimes made some notes on a piece of paper. "I'll meet you outside the library tomorrow at the same hour. I'll need two thousand pounds in cash."

"I'll have it."

Grimes blinked and said, "No. You don't understand. I'll need the money now."

"Of course," she said. She reached into her handbag and withdrew an envelope. Looking inside, she counted off two thousand pounds, placed it inside a book, which she handed to him.

"You're rather new at this, I suspect."

She looked offended. "Why do you say that?"

"Because you're quite young."

"I see. Well, I'm not as new as you might think."

He smiled at her as one might smile at a small child. "Might I ask a question?"

She was wary, but said, "Go ahead."

Grimes touched his index finger to his lips and leaned forward. "Are you alone in this, or are you working with others?"

She looked at him suspiciously. "What difference does it make to you?"

"Only this," he said. "If you are working alone, I would suggest that you use three versions of the same weapon. In the heat of . . . battle . . . one might be inclined to attempt to place the wrong clip in the wrong weapon. You see my point?"

She did indeed, and inwardly cursed herself for not thinking of it.

"Yes," she said. "A good idea."

"Fine."

The next evening, they met outside the library as planned. Grimes handed her a heavy package wrapped in brown paper and string. "I think you'll find everything in order," he said.

She put the package in the car and drove off, back to Islington. Finding a suitably out-of-the-way place to park, she took the package out of the trunk, put it in the car, and opened it. Everything was there. The guns were identical Llama Omni semiautomatics with extended barrels to accept the screw-on silencers, big .45 caliber guns with a heavy kick. She'd asked for large-caliber weapons and that's what Grimes had given her.

She loaded the clips and screwed in the silencers. She pulled back the slide of each gun and let it spring forward, placing a round in the chamber. Then, in turn, she held the hammer of each gun as she pulled the trigger, uncocking them. Satisfied, she placed everything under the two front seats.

She looked at her watch. Hours yet. She put the car seat in the recline position and decided to sleep until the early morning. When she awoke at one, it was time.

She struggled into the coveralls, then drove to the street behind the house and parked the car. Quietly, she got out of the car, placed the extra guns and clips in various pockets of the coveralls, put on the balaclava and walked through an open field until she reached the fence at the rear of the Kowalski estate.

Most of the lights in the main house were out, but the servants' quarters were still alight. She climbed the fence, dropped quietly inside the grounds, and was halfway to the house when she heard the sound of barking dogs. Dogs! There'd been no mention of dogs!

Cursing under her breath, she pulled out one of the Llamas and cocked the hammer. She saw them as they bounded around the corner of the house, two German shepherds, their eyes gleaming in the moonlight, their powerful legs pushing them ever closer to her.

The Llama bucked in her hands four times and the dogs fell to the ground, emitting horrible wails of pain. Almost instantly, the lights inside the house went on, and the door to the servants' quarters opened.

Josephine stood her ground, calmly switched weapons, and waited. A man dressed in a dark blue robe stepped from the servants' quarters and peered out into the semidarkness. She whirled and let off another shot. Without a word, the man fell to the ground. Then she turned and ran toward the house. Using the butt of the gun, she smashed the stained-glass windows in the door, reached in, and unlocked it. Racing through the house, she headed for the stairs leading up to the main bedroom. To her surprise, her prey was coming down, dressed in a silk robe, a pistol in his own hand.

Kowalski yelled and started to point the gun at her. Before he could aim, she fired her gun twice, and two bullets found their mark. Kowalski screamed and fell down the remaining stairs to the floor.

Quickly, she switched to the third gun, and ran over to the prone body. She took careful aim and emptied the clip into the man's head. Seven bullets reduced his head to a bloody mess.

She shoved new clips into all three weapons as she ran to the door and out. As her feet skipped across carefully clipped grass, she noticed two women standing over the still body of the man lying on the ground, one screaming at the top of her lungs. Josephine fired four more times and the screaming stopped.

By the time she reached the car, lights were flicking on all over the neighborhood. Almost out of breath, she started the car and, leaving the lights off, drove as fast as she dared through the streets, one hand on the wheel and the other unzipping the overalls.

Her heart was pounding with excitement but she wasn't afraid. It was something else. For the third time in her life, she'd experienced an incredible joyfulness that made her quiver. She had the power of life and death. It made her a goddess. It thrilled her. As each body had hit the ground, she'd felt renewed again. There was nothing like it. And when she heard the singsong sound of the police cars in the distance, the excitement grew.

Just before reaching the Holloway expressway, she flicked on the car's headlights. When she entered the flow of traffic, heavy even at this late hour, she felt safe for the first time. Still, the adrenaline sped through her veins, the fight-or-flight chemical competing with a flood of newly released endorphins for attention. She'd never before experienced such a remarkable high.

Two days later, Josephine met with Sven at the Paris bar they so often frequented. "You did a good job," he said. "The money has already been deposited."

"Excellent. Next time, tell me about the dogs. It could have ruined everything."

"Yes, but you handled it. It was exactly what they wanted."

He threw a copy of the *London Daily News* on the table. The Kowalski killing was front page news. Josephine read avidly and relived her exploits. As planned, the police assumed there were at least three assassins, and rumors were flying, though Scotland Yard had yet to make an official statement.

Sven raised his glass. "To you, Annette. You've found your place in the world."

And so she had.

JOSEPH AND JOSEPHINE: A FATEFUL MEETING

Part Eight

23

"Senator?"

Joseph DiPaolo looked up from the stack of documents on his desk into the clear green eyes of his secretary. "Yes?"

"You asked me to let you know."

He looked at his watch. "Is it that time already?"

"I'm afraid so."

"Thanks, Tracy."

He stood up, stretched, rebuttoned the top button on his shirt, straightened his tie, put on his jacket, then strode out of his office.

At fifty-three years of age, DiPaolo looked extremely fit. His salt-and-pepper hair was full and thick, topping a ruggedly handsome face that exuded warmth and humor. The wrinkles at the corners of his eyes and mouth gave added character, especially when he smiled, which was often. His practiced stride gave no hint of the loss of a foot.

An animated and forceful speaker, he was much in demand, the honorariums received augmenting his income nicely, allowing him to put three children through college. Vincent was in law school, while Joe junior and Mary were undergraduates. All were eventually headed for a career in law, then politics, for politics was a newborn tradition in the DiPaolo family.

Joseph entered a room in the senate office building, took his seat in a high-backed leather chair, one identical to eleven others, all occupied by members of a subcommittee investigating charges of waste in Pentagon procurement procedures. DiPaolo was the second ranking member.

He looked at the agenda placed in front of him by one of his aides. Beneath it, a stack of documents, copies of those he'd been studying in his office, all relating to the next witness,

T. J. Bower, CEO of Bower Industries, one of the country's smaller defense contractors.

Once, Bower Industries had been a family business, engaged in the production of small parts used in the manufacture of aircraft, both civilian and military. Ten years ago, the company had gone public, raised large amounts of money, and expanded. They'd dropped most of their civilian business, concentrating their marketing efforts on military hardware, with considerable success. While the company still produced small parts, their biggest project was the manufacturing of fuselages for two Air Force supersonic fighters, the F-3 and F-5. Like almost every company engaged in the production of these two aircraft, Bower Industries had been dragged, kicking and screaming, to Washington to answer charges of cost overruns, false invoicing, and a variety of other complaints, part of an ever-expanding scandal.

Bower, flanked by two attorneys, took his place at the table, adjusted his microphone, and sat back, waiting for the chairman's gavel. He looked cocky, DiPaolo thought. A hint of a smile on his lips, a slight twinkle in his eyes, a certain air of relaxation in the way he held his body.

Well, he had reason. To this point, the evidence against Bower was slim at best, most of it coming from the statements of two ex-employees, neither of whom was able to substantiate his claims with solid evidence. There'd been talk of letting Bower off the hook, since he was known to be a major financial contributor to the party, both overtly and covertly, but in the end, it had been that connection that had forced his presence here. The appearance of favoritism was something to be avoided, what with the media jackals tightening their circle around an apparently paranoid president in very hot water himself.

DiPaolo suppressed a smile as Chairman Clark banged his gavel, bringing the hearing to order. Soon, that smug smile would be wiped from Bower's face.

"I'd like to make an opening statement," Bower said, his voice as smooth as velvet.

"Do you want to read it, Mr. Bower, or could we just have it on the record?"

"I'd like to read it, Mr. Chairman."

Clark, a rotund, respected, good old boy from North Carolina, almost groaned. "Mr. Bower, I've been given a copy of your statement. It appears to me it'll take an hour to read. Since we are a little pressed for time today, I wonder—"

Bower cut him off. "With all due respect, Mr. Chairman, I'm sure you'll agree our company has cooperated fully with this committee in every respect. Nevertheless, we've been falsely depicted in the press as greedy and unpatriotic, unmindful of the needs of the country we try so hard to serve. As you well know, it is our right to make an opening statement, and we feel it is in the best interests of not only the—"

Clark could take no more. "You may read your statement, Mr. Bower."

"Thank you, Mr. Chairman."

Bower launched into a stupefyingly boring speech in which he invoked the Constitution, the flag, Robert Frost, the Bible, Christopher Columbus, Neil Armstrong, John F. Kennedy, Captain America, apple pie, motherhood—even Mother Goose. When he finally wound it up, an hour and fifteen minutes later, three senators were sound asleep in full view of the phalanx of reporters covering the hearings. Mercifully, no television cameras were present, though the hearing was being filmed by a crew from the Office of Information. It was August 8, 1974, a time when the nation's interests were focused elsewhere in Washington.

Chairman Clark thanked Bower for his statement as the sleeping senators were jarred awake by nearby colleagues. Then Clark turned to DiPaolo. "You have some questions, Senator?" He resisted the impulse to wink, for he knew Joseph had plenty.

"I do, Mr. Chairman."

"Please proceed."

"Thank you." Joseph leveled his gaze at Bower. "Mr. Bower, according to document number thirty-four sixty-two, on May twenty-third, 1973, you billed the Pentagon—"

One of Bower's lawyers was holding up a hand. "Could you give us a minute to locate that document?"

"Certainly."

It took a full minute.

"You have it now?"

"I think so. Number thirty-four sixty-two?"

"Correct."

"We have it."

"According to the document," DiPaolo continued,

"your company billed the Pentagon for three hundred sixteen thousand items listed as 'hexagon magnesium alloy pressure application fasteners—item two-seven-seven-seven-four-nine-three-F—two point five four centimeters.' Is that a true copy of the invoice?"

"It appears to be."

"Fine. Can you tell me what that item is, in plain English?"

"Yes. It's a hex nut, but a very special kind of hex nut."

"How special?"

"Well, the specs are determined by the Pentagon. All we do is provide what they want."

"I realize that, but how special is this particular hex nut?"

"This nut was used on both the F-three and F-five, and in large quantities. It must withstand pressures of one ton per square inch, be noncorrosive, and last for a minimum of twenty years without cracking. There are additional specifications, and those are just some I can remember offhand."

DiPaolo picked up a nut from in front of him and held it up. "Is this one of the items in question? I'll have a clerk pass it to you."

The clerk took the nut and gave it to Bower, who examined it for a moment. "Yes, it is," he said. "It has our code stamped on the rim."

"I see. Now, you didn't manufacture these yourself, did you?"

"No, but we weren't required to. The nuts were incorporated into fuselages that were then shipped to the main contractor handling the F-three and F-five projects."

"But you billed the main contractor item by item?"

"Yes. Again, all of what we did was according to Pentagon requirements."

"Do you remember where you bought these hex nuts?"

There was a hurried consultation with the lawyers before Bower replied, "I can't recall."

DiPaolo held up a document. "This document is not in your files. I'll have the clerk give you a copy." Again, a young clerk scurried from the dias to the table, giving copies to the three men. At the same time, another clerk handed copies to the other members of the subcommittee.

Immediately, Senator Frank Irving, one of the Pentagon's staunchest supporters, leaned forward. "Mr. Chairman, I think this is uncalled for. It was my understanding that the members of the subcommittee were to receive copies of all data relative to these hearings before each witness appeared."

Before the chairman could respond, DiPaolo said, "You're quite right, Senator. This information just came into my possession, and I thought it pertinent. Rather than further trouble the witness by having to call him back at a later date, I thought it best to proceed at this time. My apologies for any inconvenience."

Bower, having examined the document, had his own complaint. "I think this circumvents the doctrine of fair play, Mr. Chairman. Neither my attorneys nor I have had the opportunity to examine this document. We've been denied the opportunity to discuss it. I add my protest to that of Senator Irving."

Chairman Clark grunted, then said, in his folksy drawl, "Well, all we're trying to do here is sort this thing out. I don't think it's a problem."

"I do," Bower snapped.

"Well, would you rather come back and testify again after you've had the chance to look over everything?"

Another consultation, then, "If necessary, yes, but I submit that this document should not be allowed in evidence."

Clark shook his head. "This isn't a court, gentlemen,

just a hearing. If it turns out that Senator DiPaolo's information is unverifiable, we can reflect that on the record, and remove any references. I assure you, Mr. Bower, your rights will be protected. Just try and be patient. Please proceed, Senator DiPaolo."

"Thank you, Mr. Chairman. The document referred to is a purchase order signed by an executive of Bower Industries, containing the exact specifications for the hex nut we've been discussing. Do you agree, Mr. Bower?"

Red-faced, Bower said, "It appears so. I've had no time to examine the document."

"But it appears so?"

"I said that, yes."

"Thank you. The purchase order was issued to a company called Genesis Engineering Inc., right?"

"Yes."

"And you've noted the price per unit Bower paid?"

"Yes."

"Twenty-six dollars and eleven cents each. Is that right?"

"As far as I can tell."

"And, according to document thirty-three forty-five, you charged the prime contractor sixty-three dollars even per nut. Is that not so?"

This time, Bower didn't need to search for document 3345. he responded instantly. "Yes, but you don't understand. Each and every one of those nuts had to be extensively tested, a labor-intensive task, not to mention the cost of the equipment used to do the testing."

"Isn't it true that the supplier tested each and every nut before shipping them to you?"

"Yes."

"Why the need for additional testing?"

"Often, things happen in transit. We want to be sure that we're providing a top-quality product."

"I'm sure, but the fact remains, the testing by your supplier is reflected in the price you paid, is it not?"

"I'm sure it is."

"And you, in turn, retest, and the cost of that is reflected in the price you charged the Pentagon, true?"

"You can never stint on testing when the lives of our young fighting men are on the line."

"So you feel your charges are perfectly reasonable?"

"Absolutely."

DiPaolo pulled out another document. "Again, I have a document I'd like distributed."

Before anyone could protest, Chairman Clark said, "This is the same as the other. You'll all have a chance to remove this testimony should it prove unverifiable."

"Thank you, Mr. Chairman," DiPaolo said. "The document in question is a quotation from a company called Allied Engineering Services, in Houston, Texas. It states the specifications as supplied by the Pentagon, and offers to provide three hundred sixteen thousand 'hexagon magnesium alloy pressure application fasteners—item two-seven-seven-seven-four-nine-three-F—two point five four centimeters,' at a price of two dollars and eleven cents each.

"Attached to the quotation is a report from an independent testing laboratory attesting to the fact that this item meets all Pentagon specifications. Further, Allied asserts that each item will be tested by this same lab before shipment to Bower Industries.

"I'm very curious, Mr. Bower. There seems to be a very big difference in prices for the same item. Both appear to meet Pentagon specifications, and both companies test before shipping to you. Yet, one charges twenty-six dollars and eleven cents, the other two dollars and eleven cents—a difference of twenty-four dollars per item, for a total of seven million, five hundred and eighty-four thousand dollars.

"Tell me, Mr. Bower, why didn't you give the business to Allied?"

Bower's face was almost purple. He consulted with his attorneys for a moment, then said, "I cannot give you a definitive answer until I've had the opportunity to investigate the matter thoroughly."

DiPaolo smiled, then dropped his bomb. "Would it have anything to do with the fact that the company that did supply this item is sixty percent owned by a company that's sixty percent owned by another company that's sixty percent owned by Bower Industries?"

The room almost exploded with sound, both from the floor and the dais.

"This is an outrage," cried Bower. His words were echoed by Senator Irving, who added, "This subcommittee has been investigating this matter for months. None of the investigators reported any such evidence. What right has the senator from New York to do his own, independent investigation? How are we to know that these documents are genuine?"

Chairman Clark banged his gavel. Gradually, order was restored. Clark was about to say something, when one of the clerks handed him a piece of paper. He looked at it, blanched, then leaned toward the microphone. "This hearing is adjourned. We'll reconvene at such time as the chair announces." Again, he banged his gavel.

DiPaolo stared at Clark, a question in his eyes. Clark whispered, "The president is resigning tomorrow. He's making a speech to the nation tonight."

It was not unexpected, for the Watergate investigation had reached its predictable nadir. All that remained was the final disgrace. This was, after all, politics, and the workings of a subcommittee would receive no media attention for some time. Besides,

Clark had correctly presumed that no one on the committee would have the heart to continue for the rest of this dark day.

Back in his office, DiPaolo was unsurprised when Senator Irving came storming in, still enraged, his arms flapping the air like eagle's wings. "You sandbagged him," he yelled. "You had no goddamn right to put your own investigators on this. No right at all."

DiPaolo stood his ground. "I didn't put anyone on this. The information came to me this morning."

"Really? This morning? You expect me to believe that?"

"I don't give a shit what you believe. Right now, the president is poised to throw in the towel. The whole goddamn country is in disgrace. Bower's problems mean very little."

Irving was unmoved. "You made Bower look like a fool out there. He's no fool, and as soon as he has the chance, he'll be able to justify everything he's done. All that crap about the companies is just that—crap. You know there's nothing illegal about what he'd done. Nothing! It's all aboveboard. You sabotaged a reliable and honest defense contractor for no good reason. I want to know why."

"I didn't sabotage anyone. I just allowed the facts to be revealed to the American people. Unfortunately, not many of them give a damn. With the flap over the president's resignation grabbing the headlines, even less will care."

"You didn't answer my question."

"Come off it, Frank. Seven and a half million dollars is a lot of money, and that's just for a simple hex nut. If you look over the billings item by item, you'll find there are billions being wasted on every program. How long do we sit back and let it happen?"

"Save me the sanctimonious bullshit," Irving thundered. "Billions are *not* being wasted. The money goes into the pockets of hardworking craftsmen. We're providing jobs for thousands of skilled workers."

"Yeah, right. And most of them are in your state."

Irving turned on his heel and stormed out.

DiPaolo's secretary glided into the office. "I just heard the news."

"Yeah. Well, it saves an impeachment trial, thank God."

"I feel awful," she said.

"So do I. First time in history. Makes us all feel bad."

"Shall I cancel tomorrow's appointments?"

DiPaolo nodded.

Joseph was right about the American public's reaction to the revelations. The hearing received a small three-inch column in the *Post,* and even less attention in the *Times,* but in Paris, the machinations of Bower Industries was given a bigger play, thanks to a lengthy article in *La Presse.*

The reason was simple: Over the years, the French government had purchased millions of dollars worth of small parts from Bower Industries, much to the chagrin of nationalists who viewed anything American as absolute evil. Now, some enterprising reporters had estimated that Bower had cheated the French out of tens of millions of dollars, and a scandal was brewing. The newspaper reports caught the attention of Josephine Cousteau.

She read the newspaper over coffee and toast, enjoying the embarrassment caused one of her employers. Thomas Bower was a man she disliked intensely, and the thought of him squirming gave her profound pleasure. But the laugh died in her throat when she saw the name Joseph DiPaolo. Reading further, she knew at once that this was her father, for a short sidebar to the story gave a profile of the man, including his war record.

Until now, she'd had not the slightest curiosity about her father. Throughout her life, Josephine had spent little time being introspective. She reacted more than acted, and cared little about her motivations. But now, she was seized by a sudden, intense, irrational desire to see this man, to speak to him, and to have him see her, without knowing who she really was.

For days, she fought the urge, reasoned with herself, using every rationale she could think of. But, after all of it, she was left not just with a simple need, but with a fresh, overwhelming obsession. She had to see him, and that was all there was to it. The fixation frightened her, for she'd never felt so compelled before. It made no sense.

She was thirty-two, rich, beautiful, and—she thought—fulfilled. Sven, her mentor, had died of cancer years ago, leaving her two legacies. The first was the business, which she took over without missing a heartbeat. The second was his suggestion that she become a writer.

She'd taken the suggestion seriously, studied, and had published three spy novels under a pen name. The last had become a major best-seller in Europe. The book had even been sold to an American publisher, who'd offered twice the advance if she'd consent to come to America and help promote the book. She'd refused, just as she'd refused to make public appearances in Europe. Still, the book had done well, and the next novel by the mysterious and reclusive author was eagerly awaited on both sides of the Atlantic.

Now, for the first time, she'd go to America, not for publicity, but to answer a craving that mystified and terrified her.

24

Joseph and Sophia DiPaolo sat in the book-lined den of their Brooklyn home, staring at the television set, almost mesmerized by the events unfolding in front of their eyes. The former president of the United States stood on the helicopter's steps, turned, spread his arms and gave the victory sign to the assemblage positioned on the White House lawn.

Just as the green helicopter slowly lifted off, the phone rang. "I'll take it in the kitchen," Sophia said.

When she returned to the room, her face was pale and her eyes rimmed with tears. "It's Yale," she said.

"Yale?"

"It's Joe Junior. He's been arrested."

Joseph was on his feet. "Arrested! For what?"

She shook her head. "You talk to them. They'll explain."

Joseph grabbed the telephone in the den. "Joe?"

A deep voice answered. "This is Dean Wallace, Senator DiPaolo. I'm sorry to be the bearer of bad news."

"What's this about Joe?"

The dean took a deep breath, then said, "Your son and two of his friends were arrested by our security people. They were using LSD in their dorm. Your son apparently suffered a psychotic experience and destroyed everything in his room. It took four men to hold him down."

"My god! I'll be there as soon as possible."

"There's no need, Senator. Joseph is on his way home. He spent some time at the clinic, but he seems fine now, so they released him. However, he's all through here."

"You've expelled him?"

"I'm afraid I have no choice. I would have liked to have limited the expulsion to summer school, but I can't in good conscience. I've managed to settle the matter without involving the New Haven authorities. We'll have to be reimbursed for the damages, of course, but there will be no formal charges."

"I appreciate that, at least. What about the press? Have they gotten wind of this?"

"I've taken the appropriate steps, Senator. Our security people have filed an internal report, which I've had sealed. I can't promise this won't eventually become public knowledge, but I've done what I can to prevent it."

Joseph sighed. "Well, again, I appreciate your consideration. More than I can say."

Five hours later, a thoroughly chagrined Joseph DiPaolo, Jr., sat stiffly on a chair, steeling himself for the verbal onslaught he was sure to come. A handsome kid, tall and well-muscled, his large, expressive eyes were filled with sadness. His father paced the floor anxiously, his hands stuffed in his pockets, his eyes glowing with fury.

"So, tell me about it."

"I'm real sorry, Dad. Real sorry."

"Where'd you get the stuff?"

"Tommy had it. It was just a lark, honest. You know I don't mess with drugs."

"I thought I knew. Now I'm not so sure."

"One time, Dad. That's all. I swear. I've never done it before and I'll never do it again."

Joseph stopped pacing and sat in a chair facing his son. "How do you feel?"

"Feel?"

"Yeah. About yourself. About this."

"Not good."

"What's that mean?"

"It means I'm sorry."

"Besides being sorry, how do you feel?"

"Stupid. Very, very stupid?"

"Sorry and stupid? That's it?"

He looked like he wanted to cry. "I know I let you and Mom down, and I let myself down by getting kicked out of college. I guess I messed up pretty good."

"You sure as hell did."

"I don't know what else to say, Dad. It was a crazy thing to do. I thought all that stuff about acid causing bad trips was bull. It isn't. It was the worst experience of my life."

"Are you aware you could have flashbacks the rest of your life?"

He nodded. "I've heard that too. I never believed it before, but I do now. Is there some way I can stop it from happening?"

"I don't know. You'll have to talk to a doctor experienced in this kind of thing. Do you want to graduate?"

"Of course."

"Do you want to be a lawyer?"

"Sure."

"Really?"

"Really."

"I didn't."

"Excuse me?"

Joseph took a deep breath, then said, "When I was your age, my father wanted me to be a lawyer more than anything else in the world. He was on my back constantly, but to me, the idea of being a lawyer was anathema. It seemed boring, a lot of shuffling of papers, sitting behind a desk all day pushing a pencil. I wanted action, so when war broke out, I ran off to England to join the RAF. Actually, what I was really doing was running away from college and my father's dream. I thought college was stupid, a waste of time.

"After the war, I still wasn't interested in being a lawyer, but I'd had enough action to last me a lifetime, so I caved in, went back to college, graduated, and then went on to law school. I'm not that sorry I did, but I would certainly understand your antipathy, if it exists. Does it?"

"Dad, I really want to be a lawyer. I swear. Dropping acid was stupid, sure, and I never would have done it except Tommy was being the wise guy and I just wanted to be cool, you know? I mean, what could I say?"

"What could you say? Do you really need me to answer that?"

The boy hung his head. "I guess not."

Joseph leaned back in the chair, more relaxed now, the anger gone from his eyes. "We all screw up, Joe. Some pay a price and others don't. Take President Nixon. Now there's a guy who really screwed up. That's major league, don't you think?"

"Yes, sir."

"Time will tell as far as you're concerned. Maybe you've screwed up your life for good. Maybe not.

One thing for certain. You'll have to be the captain of your own ship."

"What do you mean?"

Joseph stood up. "Aside from seeing a doctor, I'm not going to tell you what else to do. If you want to continue in college, you'll have to make your own arrangements. Yale's out, but there are other schools. Being expelled from Yale will make it tough, but not impossible. You'll have to be persistent and a little creative, and *very* humble. It's up to you, Joe. I'm not going to get involved."

The boy seemed relieved. "I appreciate that, Dad. I won't let you down again."

Joseph placed a hand on his son's shoulder. "Do me one favor," he said.

"What?"

"Never make a promise you can't keep. Don't tell me you'll never let me down again. Tell me you'll *try* not to let me down again. That I can accept. Okay?"

"Okay."

"One other thing."

"Yes?"

"Don't sell yourself short. I love you very much, Joe. You've done some things that have made me very proud. This isn't one of them, but it doesn't wipe everything else out."

"Thanks, Dad. You know I love you, too."

"I know that. Don't bullshit me now. If you have any doubts about this lawyer thing, tell me now. I'm not demanding that you become a lawyer. Not at all. I want you to make your own footprints, not follow in mine."

"I understand. I know what I want."

Joseph smiled. "Better get a move on. Most colleges are set for the fall. You've got your work cut out for you."

"I know. I'll make it right, Dad. I swear."

Joseph watched as his son headed upstairs, then strode into the living room and Sophia.

"Well?" she asked, wringing her hands.

Joseph laughed. "My mother does that when she's upset."

"Does what?"

He pointed at her hands, "That."

"Never mind. How did it go with Joe?"

"It went fine," he said. "He learned a valuable lesson today, one that will hold him in good stead in the future. He sees it himself, and that's a real plus."

"What are you going to do about college?"

"Nothing. I told Joe it's up to him. The whole thing."

"You're not going to help him?"

He shook his head.

"But why?"

"Because he's a man, Sophie. It's time he learned to handle his own problems. And he will. You watch."

Josephine Cousteau took a Pan Am flight directly to New York. She slept through most of it, arriving refreshed and alert. The customs officer took the proffered passport from her hand, compared the photograph with the beautiful woman standing in front of him, smiled, and asked, "What is the purpose of your trip, Miss LeClair?"

"A holiday," she said.

"May I see your ticket, please?"

She handed him her airline ticket, which he examined carefully. "You plan on being with us for two weeks, is that right?"

"Yes," she said, "although it seems hardly enough. America is so vast, so multifaceted, I'll never be able to see it all in that time."

The customs man smiled as he reviewed the stamps in her passport. "You've been everywhere except America, it seems. What's the nature of your business back home?"

She removed a press card from her handbag and

handed it to him. "I'm a freelance journalist," she said. "I work for a news magazine in Paris, as you can see."

The man looked at the card. "And you're sure that you're not here on assignment?"

She shook her head. "This is strictly for fun."

"Would you open your suitcase, please?"

She opened the large bag and waited as the man sifted through it. It was the first time in years that she had gone through customs with absolutely nothing hidden in her bags. Most countries had inspection systems that were easy to beat, except Israel, of course. In Israel, they were paranoid, and visitors— all visitors—were viewed with suspicion. Even so, she'd managed to beat them.

But this was America, decidedly unparanoid, and she was almost telling the truth. Other than seeing her father for the first time, and a hastily arranged meeting with an astounded T. J. Bower, she was here on a vacation.

The customs man closed the bag, handed her documents back to her and said, "Thank you, Ms. LeClair. Have a nice vacation."

"*Merci.*"

She took a cab to the Hilton in downtown Manhattan and checked in. Then, she showered and changed and walked the streets for several hours. New York City was a bustling, busy, noisy place, like Paris, but with a much more concentrated heart. She could almost feel the sense of power emanating from the tall buildings.

She became a tourist for three days, wandering all over the city, taking in the sights, snapping pictures with her newly purchased Nikon, sampling the food, the theater, the shops, and fending off a never-ending stream of amorous, brash American men who assumed that a woman alone was seeking sex. Idiots.

Gathering all her courage, Josephine flew to Washington early the morning of her fourth day, taking a room at an expensive, newly remodeled hotel.

Its interior design and furnishings reminded her of those in Paris, making her feel somewhat at home.

After checking in, she bathed, then sat in front of the mirror and carefully applied her makeup, a specially prepared concoction that made her skin appear much lighter. She used a dye to change the color of her eyebrows and inserted colored contact lenses that changed her eyes to blue. The contact lenses were custom made and reduced her vision slightly, but were detectable only upon careful inspection. A blond wig completed the transformation.

She selected a white silk blouse and a tailored blue suit that showed off her magnificent figure. Dark stockings and blue pumps with a matching handbag completed the outfit. She stood in front of the mirror, examined herself, and nodded approvingly. She seemed a professional, perhaps a doctor or a lawyer, more than a journalist, exactly the image she wanted to project.

She left the hotel and took a cab to the senate office building on the corner of Constitution and Delaware Avenues. She looked in the directory for the office of Joseph DiPaolo, found it, and after submitting to a search, walked down the hall and entered the anteroom to his office. The woman sitting behind the desk looked up and said, "May I help you?"

Josephine smiled sweetly. "I certainly hope so." She presented her press credentials. "I'm doing an article on some of the American airmen who were helped during World War Two by the French resistance organization. My information is that Senator DiPaolo was one of those. Is that true?"

The secretary gave her a strange look. "That's rather old news, Miss . . ."

"LeClair. Annette LeClair."

"Miss LeClair."

"Would the senator be available for an interview?"

The woman looked at the credentials and handed them back. Countering her earlier thoughtless rudeness, she smiled and said, "Well, the senator is extremely busy just now. I'm afraid it would take some time to arrange an interview, but I'm sure he'd want to help you. His affection for those in the resistance is well known. How long will you be in town?"

Josephine grimaced. "Not long. My editor says no more than five thousand words. Perhaps two days, maybe three. Three at the most. Do you have a bio of the senator available?"

"Of course." The secretary reached inside a drawer, pulled out a folder, laid it on the desk and opened it. "This should be helpful. It contains some photographs of the senator during his service years and every year thereafter, including his family, right up to the present. There's also a concise but complete biographical summary that makes reference to his experiences with the resistance, along with his record as a senator. I think you'll find it quite useful."

Josephine took the folder and thanked the woman profusely. "So you think an interview would be impossible?"

The woman frowned and said, "I'm afraid so if you're only going to be here that short a time. The senator usually likes to arrange these things at least a week in advance, and—"

Her words were cut short as Joseph DiPaolo came out of his office, a clutch of papers in his hand. "Where the heck is Nancy?"

"She went to see Paula. The Bickell amendment, if you remember."

"Of course. Well, these need to get over to Jim as soon as—" He noticed Josephine and broke into a grin, extending his hand. "Hello. I'm Joseph DiPaolo. I certainly hope you're one of my constituents."

The secretary blushed, made the introductions and explained the purpose of Josephine's visit.

"I'm sorry," he said. "You're only here for a couple of days?"

"Yes."

He looked at his watch. "I'll tell you what. If you can keep it to under fifteen minutes, we could do it right now."

"That would be wonderful," said Josephine.

She followed him into his small office and took a seat across from his desk. Instead of getting behind the desk, the senator sat down in a chair facing her, so close she could smell the muskiness of his cologne.

Suddenly, she felt weak. She took a stenographer's pad from her handbag and opened it. Pencil poised, she said, "I haven't had the opportunity to review the bio your secretary was kind enough to provide, so if I ask you anything that's included, just let me know."

The senator nodded. "I'll do that. By the way, I must compliment you on your excellent English."

"Thank you."

The realization that she was sitting inches away from her father affected her more than she'd feared. She felt a bit light-headed, almost giddy, and her heart was pounding so loudly, she was sure he could hear. For an instant, she felt the urge to bolt, to run, to get away from this man. What was happening here?

She struggled for control. Her strong survival instinct and training finally conquered the fear. Gradually, she could feel her body responding to the orders of her conscious mind, as she continued with this ridiculous charade that had been such a mistake.

In a voice that seemed strangely divorced from her body, she said, "You were shot down over France in 1940, I believe, and were one of the very first pilots to be rescued and returned to Britain, even before the resistance was fully organized. Do I have that right?"

DiPaolo smiled. "You certainly do," he said. "I'll never forget it as long as I live. I'd been shot up pretty bad. The Germans captured me and placed me in a hospital in a town called Abbeville. I was there about a week. They were about to move me to a prisoner of war camp when those wonderful, crazy guys in the resistance blocked the road, killed all the Germans and hid me out in the basement of a farmhouse."

She could feel the pounding of her heart ease, her breathing return to normal, the dizziness recede, the sense of pure panic dim—a triumph of conscious mind over subconscious mind. "Do you remember any names?" she asked.

"Oh, yes," he said, firmly. "There was Jean-Luc Dijon. He was the leader of the group. A real hard case, that one. Tough as nails. He took me to the farm of his cousin, a woman named Denise Dijon. Wonderful woman. She hid me in what amounted to a makeshift grave in the basement for three days and nights."

He laughed. "I was told it was three days, but it seemed like three years. I was buried alive, so to speak, with some food and candles, my leg hurting like hell, and—"

"Your leg?" Josephine interrupted.

"Yes. My right foot had been amputated in the hospital. Anyway, I thought for sure that the Germans would find me. They searched the place twice, but they never did. Finally, Jean-Luc and Denise arranged for me to be taken through the Demarcation Line, which was the line that separated occupied France from Vichy France—" He stopped and grinned sheepishly. "I'm sorry. You'd know that, wouldn't you?"

"I did know that, but I'm sure there are many who do not."

"Well, in any case, they got me through, then onto a train to Marseilles and from there to Gibraltar. They had it all set up. After I got back, I had British Intelligence contact them. I know that several other pilots owe their lives to those two and their group."

"And you returned to the war as a pilot, even with your wounds?"

"Yes. It was no big deal. I was inspired by Group

Captain Douglas Bader of the RAF. Bader lost both legs before the war, but that never stopped him. He was one hell of a pilot until he was captured."

Josephine was making furious notes. "Did you ever look them up after the war? I mean the people who helped you in France?"

The senator's expression changed, a look of sadness darkening his eyes. "I inquired about them long before the war was over. I went back to England in 1942, and transferred to the American Army Air Corps, as it was called in those days. The British had a special section, as you know, that dealt with the resistance groups. I did inquire, and discovered that the ones I'd been associated with had all been killed. The entire group."

"You must have been very sad."

"I was indeed. They were wonderful, brave people. I can tell you that the French resistance saved the lives of many, many Americans during that awful time. We'll all be forever grateful, though I know de Gaulle never saw it that way."

Josephine smiled. "So you never went back to France after the war?"

"Oh, I've been there several times. I love your country. As a matter of fact, I was in Paris three months ago."

The room was beginning to close in. "Well," she said, "I know you're busy."

He looked at his watch and sighed. "You're right. I'm really sorry, Miss LeClair, but I have a meeting I'm already late for." He stood up and extended his hand. "I hope I've helped you. If there's anything else you need, don't hesitate to ask my secretary, or leave some questions with her and I'll try my best to answer them. As a journalist, you must know that things are pretty hectic around Washington these days."

"I can imagine. Is he as bad as they say?"

He smiled. "I'd rather not comment. If you're ever

in Washington again, please let me know in advance. I'll give you as much time as you need."

Josephine put away the steno pad, shook the senator's hand firmly and said, "I will, and thank you for seeing me today."

"You're entirely welcome. By the way, you might want to see Senator Bill Timms. He was a B-17 pilot, rescued by the resistance in forty-four, I think it was. Talks about it a lot. He'd be very interested in helping you, I'm sure."

"I will, and thank you again."

DiPaolo escorted her out of the office, shook her hand again, and smiled as she disappeared down the hall.

Once outside the building, now that the dreaded encounter was over, Josephine expected to feel relieved. She felt the opposite. A wave of dizziness washed over her like a tidal wave. The sense of panic returned in full force. Beads of cold sweat appeared on her upper lip and her forehead. She had trouble focusing her eyes. Her legs seemed suddenly weak, as though the muscles had atrophied. Her heart began to pound unmercifully and she feared she would faint.

With some effort, she made it to a concrete bench near the entrance of the building. She sat on it heavily and placed her head down low, between her legs, trying to will her body to respond as before. Desperately, she fought to pull herself together. She was vaguely aware of a man in a blue uniform asking her if she needed help. She waved him away.

"I'll be fine," she said shakily. "I'm sorry. Morning sickness. Happens all the time. Terribly embarrassing."

"Are you sure you're all right?" he asked.

She looked up. The man was coming into focus and the spinning world seemed to be slowing down. "Yes, I'll be fine. Just give me a minute." She felt very cold.

The policeman stared at her. "I think I should call for an ambulance. You look terrible."

"No! Please. My husband will kill me. I've been having these attacks for over a week. He told me to stay in bed. If I end up in the hospital, he'll be so angry. Just give me a minute."

Gradually, her senses returned. She smiled bravely at the policeman. "I'm so very sorry for the inconvenience," she said. "I'm much better now. Thank you for your kindness."

He watched carefully as she stood up, now almost fully restored, and walked purposefully toward the cab stand.

When Josephine got back to her hotel room, she opened a bottle of Scotch, poured a full three-ounce shot into a glass and drank it straight. She lay on the bed and cursed her stupidity. She'd thought she could handle the emotional impact of seeing her father, but it had almost destroyed her. She'd been assailed by feelings that had frightened and astonished her. A sign of weakness. Terrible weakness. She vowed never to see him again. It was imperative that she put him out of her mind forever.

But, after a few moments of rest, she removed the press kit from her handbag and studied it carefully. She had just seen this man for the first time. She wanted one last look before she excluded him from her thoughts.

It seemed so very strange to be reading about a man who was her father. She looked at a picture of the senator taken fifteen years ago, smiling at the camera, his arm around his wife, the three children seated on the ground, one of them with his small hand on the neck of a cocker spaniel. The perfect American family.

As she stared at the picture, she could feel the tears trickling down her cheeks. She cursed in French and threw the brochure against the wall. Then she threw herself onto the bed, her body shaking with deep, gut-wrenching sobs.

In the morning, she left Washington for Atlanta. The meeting with the Bowers was not for another four days. Too bad. The Bowers would have to change the schedule. She wanted to see them as soon as possible and get back to Paris.

But when she arrived in Atlanta, she felt somewhat better. She was, she told herself, a professional. She had to act like one.

They met at a small motel near the airport. T.J., wearing a confused look on his face, introduced his son. "I was amazed when you told me you were coming to the States," he said. "I'd planned on coming over there."

"I saved you a trip."

"What on earth brings you here?"

"A holiday," she said. "I've never been to America. I thought it was time."

Bower shrugged. "Funny."

"Funny?"

"I just never thought of you as someone who took vacations."

"Why not?"

"I don't know. It never occurred to me."

"Because you see me as a nonperson? A killing machine?"

"I didn't mean that."

"Of course you didn't. Why did you want to see me?"

"Two reasons," he said brusquely. "For one, I'm retiring. My son Donald will be handling the business—all of it."

She grinned. "The heat getting a bit intense?"

He stiffened. "Lady, I've been facing heat all my life. Those assholes in Washington don't scare me. This is all for the press's benefit. I own enough of those assholes to know nothing much will happen."

"So, why retire?"

"Why do you take a vacation?"

"Touché."

Josephine shook hands with the younger Bower. The handshake alone was an insight into his character. His hands were cold and clammy, the handshake almost feeble. All in all, he seemed as weak as the father was strong. She disliked him instantly.

"And the second reason?" she asked.

"I . . . well, Donald has a job for you."

"Ahhh. Who's the lucky person?"

"A Parisian. A man named Devers."

She nodded. "I know of him. Minister of Munitions."

"Exactly," Donald said, taking over the conversation. "It must look like an accident."

"Of course. When?"

"As soon as possible."

"All right. You have the money?"

Donald opened an attaché case stuffed with hundred-dollar bills.

"Put it away," she said. "This time, I want you to wire the money to a numbered Swiss account. I might have trouble carrying cash through customs."

"As you wish," he said.

She turned her attention to T.J. "Well, the changing of the guard, as they say. Like Sven and me. I imagine I'll never see you again, Thomas."

"You've been great, Annette."

"I know. I'll continue to be great."

"I'm sure you will."

She handed Donald a piece of paper with a name and number on it. "As soon as I hear the money is in my account, your man is history."

On the flight back to Paris, she only thought about her father once. It sent chills up and down her spine.

THE CAPRICIOUS HAND OF DESTINY

Part Nine

25

In the summer of 1992, almost eighteen years after Joseph DiPaolo met his daughter Josephine for the first time, he received a telephone call. It came two weeks before his political party's national convention, and the call was from William Caldwell, a young, personable firebrand who'd come from political obscurity to be the front-runner for the party's nomination for president of the United States.

"Joseph, how are you?" Caldwell boomed. As always, the man never announced who he was, assuming the person he'd called would immediately recognize the affected, clipped speech. He was usually right.

"I'm fine, Bill. And you?"

"Great. Have you seen the latest polls?"

"I did. You've gone up another two points. You must be very proud."

"I am. Of course, the pundits give us no chance at

all in the fall, but a lot can happen in a short time. All one has to do is look at history for proof of that."

"I agree."

"Though the convention has yet to begin, my advisers tell me I'm assured of the nomination."

"Again, I agree. You've earned it, Bill. Your performance in the primaries was outstanding. I can't think of any reason you won't get the nomination. In my view, you're the strongest candidate we could possibly offer."

"I appreciate that very much. I want to go to that convention with my running mate firmly in place. I realize there are some who view this as negating the very purpose of the convention, but I'm sure I can assuage them. My feeling is that setting the team as early as possible will allow the momentum to build much sooner. I want us coming out of there with all systems go."

"I can see your point. Have you talked to any of the others about this?"

"This very morning. While they're not ready to concede, and who can blame them, they see the wisdom in presenting a united party. The convention needs to focus on our strengths, not our intraparty differences."

"I can't fault your thinking."

"That's why I want you as my running mate."

DiPaolo almost dropped the phone. "Me? Bill, I'm extremely flattered, but my God! I'm seventy-one years old, a little long in the tooth, don't you think?"

"You look sixty," Caldwell said. "What's more important is how you're perceived by the public. You have the highest Q rating of any man we've tested, nationwide. You're the absolute best man for the job. The only reason you've never succeeded in your national campaigns is you lack the killer instinct. We all see it and recognize it."

"I see."

"Don't take offense, Joseph. You know by now

that I'm brutally frank when discussing important matters with those whose opinions I respect and value. No time for bullshit among friends. As I say, I don't think you're presidential material. If I were an older man, I wouldn't consider you, but I feel confident I'll be around for two terms should we manage to capture the White House. You'd make an excellent vice president, and that's what I'm after."

"I'm not offended," he said. And he wasn't. Joseph had reached the point in his life where he no longer took offense at the truth. "I've always been a realist," he added.

"Good. Well, what do you say?"

"I'd like a few days to think about it."

"You have an hour, Joseph. I want your answer then."

Joseph hesitated, then said, "You'll have it."

He hung up the phone and turned to face Sophia. She was aghast, having heard his side of the conversation. "You're not seriously considering accepting, are you?"

"Why not?"

She threw her hands in the air. "You're a senior senator. You chair the most powerful committee in the Senate. You have the respect of people in both parties. You want to give that up to be Caldwell's lackey?"

"I'm not anyone's lackey, ever."

"Not now perhaps, but what do vice presidents do except run errands for the president? And Caldwell, that arrogant, pious prole, a man born in Kansas sporting a Boston accent—does he really think he's kidding anyone? How can you consider even supporting that man?"

Joseph glared at her. "Back off, Sophie. In the first place, the man has a first-rate mind, a good grasp of both domestic and international concerns, and he's probably going to lose."

"Then why—"

He waved a hand to cut her off. "Because I'm tired, Sophie, physically and mentally. I've been at this too long and seen too much. Nothing changes. The same old tired song gets sung every day, the same old bull-shit gets dished out to the press, and the same old gang line their pockets. The faces change, but that's about it. It's been that way forever and that's the way it'll stay until someone comes up with a better system.

"It's all I know. I can't quit. Oh, I guess I could, but I don't like the idea much. So, this gives me the opportunity to take a hike with some dignity. I accept the second slot and after the election, drift off to a world filled with speeches and long philosophical think pieces in some of the nation's better magazines. I get to relax a little and pontificate on demand. That appeals to me."

"That's what you want?"

"Yes. I've been working my tail off since I was seventeen years old. That's enough. I'd like to sit a little, see a movie once in a while, read a book from start to finish in one sitting, maybe lie in bed until ten. God, it would be great."

She stared at the ceiling. "What if he wins?"

"He won't, and even if he does, better still. I get to do all of the above and keep the perks. Vice presidents travel all over the world, and they get to take their wives along. Air Force Two is a pretty fancy rig. You should know, you've been on it twice. Wouldn't it be nice to travel without the pressure of developing some little-read fact-finding report? Vice presidents are little more than PR people. No pressure. I like that."

"That's just it. You'd have no power. None at all."

He smiled. "So you like the power, huh?"

"Don't you?"

"Sure I like it, but the flip side of power is responsibility, and I'm good and tired of being responsible. I like the idea of relaxing more than you can possibly imagine."

"I guess you do at that."

He laughed. "I'm going to do this, Sophie. You can bitch and moan if you want, but I'm going to do this."

She lay back in the bed and threw the covers over her face.

Thirty minutes later, Joseph picked up the telephone and punched some numbers.

"Good evening, Mayflower Hotel."

"Room twelve forty-six, please."

"One moment, please."

The phone was answered on the second ring by a man who said, "Yes?"

"This is Joseph DiPaolo. I'd like to speak to Bill Caldwell."

"Oh, yeah. Just a sec', Joe."

DiPaolo winced at the informality of one of Caldwell's youthful insiders. They all seemed to be young, irreverent, nontraditional. To Joseph, they represented the new politics, a profession devoid of charm. In a moment, Caldwell was on the line.

"Joseph?"

"Yes. I've decided to accept your offer."

"Terrific! Come on over here and we'll start getting things set up. I'll schedule the announcement for the morning. We'll have . . ."

As he listened to the young man ramble on, Joseph DiPaolo felt a chill run down his spine. There was no rational reason for it, and the chill left quickly. Still, he was puzzled by such a strange subconscious reaction.

It was a long, arduous campaign, filled with acrimony, false charges, red herrings, and the other assorted non sequiturs that have marked every presidential campaign since Jefferson's. In the end, Caldwell won by a margin even slimmer than John Kennedy's, to the astonishment of the poll-takers, who had predicted a five-point edge for the incumbent.

Caldwell and DiPaolo were sworn in on a freezing

January day. As expected, Joseph's duties as vice president gave him more free time than he'd had in over forty years. He reveled in time spent with his children and grandchildren, a luxury long denied. He relished his time with Sophia and his lighter work load. As for Sophia, she seemed to be getting used to her husband's new role.

In contrast with most vice presidents, who resent the lack of respect paid the office, Joseph cherished the sudden retreat from the limelight. He found the constant presence of the Secret Service amusing. He did miss the repartee with his former colleagues in the Senate, but that was partially compensated by his inclusion in the regular Thursday night poker game. He was only the third vice president in history to be so honored.

For five months, Joseph withdrew slowly from the adrenaline high he'd experienced most of his life. With good humor and anticipation, he prepared for the next four years, and then retirement. He never thought he would welcome retirement, or accept it, but he was doing just that, much to his surprise. On a warm spring Washington night, he walked with Sophia along the banks of the Potomac, the scent of a million cherry blossoms filling his nostrils.

"It's lovely, isn't it?"

Sophia smiled up at him. "You're becoming positively revolting, you know?"

"Why?"

"You're really enjoying this, aren't you?"

"I shouldn't?"

"Of course you should."

"Aren't you?"

"I guess I am at that."

"Ahah! The best is yet to come. Caldwell wants me to go to Japan in three weeks. Another trade conference. And then, two weeks later, we're to go to Berlin."

She shuddered. "I hate that place."

"I know, but we'll also hit Paris and London."

"What's going on?"

"The forerunner of an economic conference. The Europeans are a little upset with Caldwell's aggressiveness. For years, other governments have been subsidizing their industries, but now that we're starting to do it, they're screaming foul. I have to lay some groundwork for a future conference. Mostly dinners and parties and some sucking up. Nothing serious. You can shop till you drop."

She smiled at him. "You know, you look five years younger already."

"I do?"

"You do."

"You wanna fool around later?"

"How 'bout now?"

He laughed. "What would they say if they knew the vice president of the United States makes love to his wife twice a week at the age of seventy-one?"

"They'd probably give you a medal."

Late that night, Joseph received a telephone call from White House Chief of Staff John Gruber.

"Mr. Vice President," Gruber intoned, his voice filled with sadness.

"Yes."

"This is John Gruber."

"Yes, I know." DiPaolo looked at the clock on the bedside table and winced. It was three-sixteen in the morning.

"Yes, John. What is it?"

For a moment, Gruber said nothing. Then, in a voice that was almost incoherent, he said, "The . . . president . . . is dead. Heart attack. We need you here, Mr. President."

Joseph felt his heart stop. "What?"

"No mistake, sir. The president is dead. You . . . are the president."

"Impossible! He's forty-eight years old. It just can't be!"

"I'm sorry, sir. It's true. They say his aorta burst. Totally unexpected. Not a hint of—"

"I'll be right there, John."

Stunned, Joseph hung up the phone, reached over and gripped Sophia's arm.

"What is it?" she mumbled, still half asleep.

With shaking hands, he reached up and switched on the lamp beside the bed. "What *is* it, Joey? What's happened?"

Joseph's eyes were closed tightly, his breath coming in short, shallow bursts. "Caldwell just died," he said, shaking his head from side to side. "I am now the president. God help me! God help us all."

26

$\mathcal{P}ierre$ Charrette looked out the dirt-streaked window of his sumptuous office while absently tapping a stubby finger on the cover of the thick file on his desk. Outside, the rain continued to fall, as it had since early this morning.

He stood up and moved closer to the window. As he watched the cars splashing through the wet, horns blaring as usual, he felt a tremor shake his body. It was strange, this new unfamiliar emotion, for in all his life—a life sated with death and duplicity—he'd felt not the slightest whisper of trepidation. This, however, was a major step, a historical decision, destined to affect entire nations for decades, and he perceived the tremors as being caused by excited anticipation.

He smiled. The Americans—those fat-cat purveyors of everything material, sanctimonious evangelists for free markets and democracy, saviors of humankind with their relentless godliness—had become economic tigers in the face of the now-realized European Community. Free markets indeed! The Americans perceived a united Europe as a threat more sinister than the Japanese, and were pulling out all stops in order to stifle the fledgling alliance.

Government subsidies once confined to foodstuffs had been broadened to embrace all manner of goods. Autos, airplanes, computers—anything that would compete with European-made products—were being offered at bargain-basement prices. American salesmen, an army without guns but dangerous none the less, were everywhere, offering sweetheart deals and money under the table in a mad effort to stave off the inevitable collapse of a decayed American system. It was a war, and something had to be done.

The president of France, cowering in the face of German bluster, was doing nothing, nor were any of those in the government, the cowards. Their strategy, if you could call it that, was to let the Americans burn themselves out in an orgy of deals, deals they could ill afford. The world's largest debtor nation was bound to go broke, they claimed. Perhaps, but *when* was the question. If something wasn't done soon, Europe's new economic muscle would soon atrophy like a withered arm.

It was left to men with courage and guile to tip the scales, and two such men—businessmen with an eye to the future and longtime clients—had listened to Pierre Charrette as he proposed a possible solution. At first, they'd been repelled by the thought of such a drastic act and the possible consequences should something go wrong, but in the end, they'd agreed to finance the entire operation. They had faith in his abilities and so did he. He felt it was his destiny.

His right hand went to his throat, loosened his tie, and unfastened the top button of his shirt, finally easing the personal suffering he'd attempted to ignore the entire day. How many times had he told Colette not to put starch in his collar? A hundred? A thousand? And still, she would use it, blandly insisting it was an unfortunate oversight. Each time she would apologize, and for a time, there would be no starch. Then, in a few days, it would be back. He would notice it early in the day, and by evening, his neck would be red and sore. He would be forced to loosen his collar, as he had today. Invariably, he would be seen this way. Did Colette think it was better for him to look slovenly? Did she care?

He sighed. More important things concerned him now. He returned to his desk and picked up the phone.

Two days later, a former KGB agent now living in Paris arrived in the United States. After leaving Atlanta's Hartsfield Airport, he checked into a Days Inn less than four miles away. He seemed to know his way around, and for good reason; the former KGB man had spent nine years living in America before the collapse of the Soviet empire. Now he worked for Pierre Charrette.

In the morning, the man placed a telephone call to Donald Bower, president and CEO of Bower Industries, Inc. He was told Mr. Bower was busy. The man demanded to be connected with Bower's personal secretary.

"This is Alice Bowman. How may I help you?"

"My name is Fred Brown," the man said heatedly, in perfect New York English. "I must speak to Mr. Bower immediately."

"I'm sorry, but he's in a meeting."

"I must talk to him now! It's most urgent."

"I'm sure it is, but in order to interrupt the meeting, I have to tell Mr. Bower the nature of the urgency."

"I'm afraid this is rather embarrassing," Brown said, lowering his voice's decibel level about thirty percent. "You see, it's a personal matter."

"Oh. Well, I appreciate the problem, Mr. Brown. However, Mr. Bower is a very busy man, and I'm unable to connect you unless I can explain the nature of your call."

"I see. Well, it concerns a woman, a mutual friend."

A pause. "Sir, I'm afraid—"

"The woman's name is Annette LeClair. You just tell him that. I know he'll want to talk to me about Annette."

The secretary, a proper lady always, was appalled by what she was hearing. It sounded sordid, disgusting. She wanted no part of it. Still, she had a job to do.

"I see," she said. "I'm terribly sorry, but I expect Mr. Bower will be tied up most of the day. May I take your number and have him return your call when he's free?"

"No. I must talk to him now."

"I'm afraid that would be quite impossible."

The man was insistent. In a voice now deceptively calm, he said, "Look, what I have to tell Mr. Bower is of the utmost importance. It can't wait. You must tell him I am on the phone. Let him make the decision whether or not to talk to me—not you. What I have to say is of more importance to him than any meeting he'll ever have."

Ms. Bowman responded in kind. "I'm sorry, Mr. Brown, but my instructions are quite explicit. Mr. Bower cannot be disturbed."

Brown took a deep breath. "Tell Mr. Bower the FBI will be all over his ass unless I talk to him within the next ten seconds. You tell him that!"

There was a hesitation. Then, Brown heard the woman say, "One moment, please."

With much anxiety, the secretary walked down the hall to the conference room, tapped lightly on the door, then entered. Eight men were seated around a massive oak table. All of them stared at her with unconcealed hostility as she entered the room. Bower, sitting at the head of the table, snapped, "I told you we were not to be disturbed."

Donald Bower, a member of the third generation of a family that epitomized the American dream, had always been an arrogant man, like his father before him. He now ran the business, yet it was under T. J. Bower that it had blossomed into a monster conglomerate whose stock was traded on the New York Stock Exchange. Its far-flung international divisions engaged in everything from the packaging of tea to the manufacturing of supersecret guidance systems for nuclear-tipped missiles.

Donald Bower treated his secretary as he treated everyone, from mailroom attendants to vice presidents—with total disdain. He perceived himself as strong, like his father, but Alice knew he was weak and vain. His arrogance was a defensive response to imagined slights, all stemming from Donald's belated realization that he'd never measure up to his father, whose own high-handedness was at least earned.

"I'm very sorry, Mr. Bower," she said, refusing to cringe under the harsh stare of those in the room, "but I have a man on the telephone who insists on speaking to you. His name is Fred Brown."

"Brown? I don't know any man named Brown. Besides, it doesn't matter who is on the phone. When I say no interruptions, I mean just that."

The secretary walked up to Bower and whispered in his ear. "He mentioned a woman, and something about the FBI. It's most confusing."

"The FBI? What woman?"

She looked down at the pink slip in her hand. "Annette LeClair. I have no idea what it means, but I was sure you didn't want the FBI coming up here. I don't know if it's an idle threat or not, but I felt it wasn't my place to make the decision."

For a moment, the industrialist looked as though he'd seen a ghost. Then, recovering quickly, he smiled, looked at those gathered around the table and said, "Excuse me, gentlemen. We have a problem in Nigeria. Mr. Brown is an attorney, whose name had momentarily escaped me. I better speak to him. I'll return shortly."

With that, he strode briskly out of the room.

Once inside his office, he picked up the telephone. "Who are you?" he demanded.

"Donald Bower?"

"Yes, yes."

"My name is Fred Brown, Mr. Bower. I want to talk to you about Annette LeClair."

"I don't know any Annette LeClair."

"Sure you do. She's knocked off thirty people for you and your father over the years. We have lots to talk about."

Bower felt the blood drain from his face. His heart was pounding unmercifully. His hands were turning to blocks of ice and perspiration was beginning to form a thin coating on his face. He felt faint.

"Don't say such things, you fool."

"Well, I wanted to get your attention."

"What do you want?"

"I want to talk to you."

"Why?"

"Why do you think?"

"I'm very busy right now."

"Look, asshole, I don't care about your problems. You get yourself down to the Days Inn by the airport within an hour, room three thirty-four, or everything I have goes to the FBI."

"No! You mustn't."

"Then move your ass."

"All right. What was that address again?"

Bower, his hands shaking, left his office and stopped by his secretary's desk. He had difficulty speaking coherently. "I have to go out for a moment," he mumbled. "Apologize to the others for me. Ask them . . . no . . . tell them that I asked that they keep at it until I get back. I shouldn't be long."

"Are you all right, sir?"

"I'm fine. Not a word of this to anyone, you understand? Tell them nothing. I'll be back as soon as possible."

"Yes, of course. But—"

"Just do it!"

Forty minutes later, Donald Bower, wearing a trenchcoat, a fedora, and dark sunglasses, exited a cab in front of the motel. He went directly to room 334.

The door opened before he could knock on it. He stepped in quickly, closed the door behind him, and stared at a man he didn't recognize. "Who the hell *are* you?" he asked, a note of feigned defiance in his voice.

"My name is Fred Brown, Mr. Bower. I'm here to give you some instructions."

"Instructions?"

"Yes. You thought blackmail, eh?"

Bower shook his head. "I don't know what to think. How do you know about Annette?"

"It's not important. What's important is that you understand we know it all. We know your father's relationship with Sven Kohnor, we know about the killings, who, when, and where. We have the evidence and will release it to the press and the authorities if we have to."

Bower, white-faced, his hands shaking uncontrollably, asked, "Why? Why are you doing this?"

Fred Brown folded his arms in front of his barrel chest and said, "Because we want something from you."

"We? Who's *we?*"

"You ask too many fucking questions, you know?"

"All right. What do you want? Money?"

"No, Mr. Bower, not money. We want you to contact Annette LeClair and hire her for one last job."

It was coming too fast. Much too fast. Donald Bower was having difficulty breathing, let alone comprehending what was being said to him. Never in his life had he been seized with such a sense of panic.

"A job? Annette?" His mouth was barely able to utter the words. "She's been retired for years. I don't even know if she's alive."

Brown fished a small piece of paper from his jacket pocket and threw it on the bed. "She's alive," he said. "Her address is on that paper. You are to contact her, give her the job and pay her whatever she asks. The job must be done within three weeks. Do you understand? Three weeks."

"What if she refuses? I told you she's retired."

"She's an assassin. Always has been, always will be. Give her enough money and she'll do it. It's up to you to convince her."

Bower nodded numbly.

"Once it's done, you'll never hear from us again."

Bower, his face reflecting his agony, said, "I wish I could believe that."

"You don't need to. You only need to carry out the assignment. If you fail, the information will be released. You will be destroyed. I'm sure you can understand that."

Bower picked up the small piece of paper and

looked at it. Then he turned to Brown and asked, "The target. Who is the target?"

Brown's face broke into a smile. "President Joseph DiPaolo," he said.

Half an hour later, Donald Bower was sitting in the family room of his father's rambling estate, located just outside Atlanta's city limits. The younger man was breathless as he recounted his meeting with the mysterious Fred Brown.

In contrast to the business suit worn by his son, Thomas Jefferson Bower wore Western attire. Slightly smaller than his son, he was nevertheless muscular and strong, a fine specimen of a man, especially considering his advanced age. His face was deeply creased and permanently tanned, the result of a retirement that had allowed him to spend much of the past few years out of doors. The darkness of his skin served to highlight the pure-white thatch of hair atop his head and the equally white bushy eyebrows. His clear blue eyes stared at Donald as he told his story.

When the younger Bower was finished talking, T.J. walked unsteadily over to the long oak bar and poured some brandy into a large snifter. He motioned to his son and said, "Want some?"

Donald shook his head. "I never drink during the day. You know that."

Ignoring the comment, T.J. poured some brandy into a second glass, then walked back to stand beside his son. "You better drink this," he said, gravely. "You're going to need it."

Donald Bower took the glass and placed it on the coffee table.

T.J. went back to his chair and sat down. Leaning back, he sipped the brandy, then let out a deep sigh. For a moment, he looked around the room, his eyes taking in the paintings, the mementos, and the varied bric-a-brac accumulated during a lifetime. Then, he sighed again and fixed his gaze on his son.

"So," he said, "They—whoever they are—want you to hire Annette to kill DiPaolo. Do you have any idea who these people are?"

The younger man shook his head. "I haven't had time to think about it."

The elder Bower rubbed his forehead with both hands as he tried to think. "This guy was an American, you say?"

Donald Bower nodded.

"And he said he knew all about Annette and us? He specifically referred to thirty killings?"

"Yes. He also mentioned Sven Kohnor by name. And he had Annette's address in Paris."

T.J. gritted his teeth. "Damn! In all the years, I never knew where she lived. We did everything with personal ads in the newspaper. If this guy . . ." He let the thought drift off as he rubbed his temples. "Why Annette? And why involve us? It doesn't make sense."

Donald Bower sat in total confusion and frustration.

T.J. stood up and paced the floor as he tried to sort it out. Annette, Kohnor, a man named Brown who seemed to know everything. The assassination of the president. Why? Who would gain?

Charles Rutman would gain, becoming the new president, but what of it? To be sure, Bower money had helped give Charles Rutman the exposure he needed to become a prominent politician, but Rutman couldn't possibly know about Annette. Even on nights spent drinking and whoring, Bower had never revealed anything about her or her activities. Of that, he was sure.

For six months leading up to the national convention, they'd spent a fortune trying to buy the nomination for Rutman, but had failed. Caldwell had won. Rutman had remained a senator until DiPaolo tapped him for the vice presidency, an act not caused by any influence by the Bower family, but because the party had pressed DiPaolo to do so.

So it wasn't Rutman. Then who?

His thoughts drifted back to another time. It seemed a thousand years ago. He thought about his initial meeting with Sven Kohnor. He thought about how easy it had been to persuade Sven to keep the gold they'd found in Sweden. He remembered how sure he'd been that Sven would keep the gold for himself and how astonished he'd been when Sven hadn't. He could have melted into the background, and Bower would never have found him.

At the time, T.J. had been so relieved, he'd never taken the time to analyze the Swede's motives, for he was convinced that magnanimity was nothing but a ploy. Now, he took the time.

Why had Sven shared the gold? Was the Swede laying the groundwork for the future? Did the Swede see, in his relationship with T.J., a future source of income?

Sven had not only shared the gold but had eagerly agreed to perform industrial espionage. Then later, it had been Sven who'd suggested the first assassination, that of a Belgian munitions expert who'd been competing with Bower for years. Sven had assured T.J. it would look like an accident, and so it had. One of Bower's major competitors was never able to compete effectively again.

The others came almost naturally. Some were bureaucrats who, for whatever reason, were standing in the way of international commerce. Others were competitors who were receiving unfair aid from their governments and blocking Americans from penetrating their protected markets. Then, there'd been two killed for purely political reasons, men who were enemies of America, but the gutless wonders in Washington were too chickenshit to do anything. Annette had killed them all.

He stopped pacing the floor and stood stock still. His mind was working well now, analyzing, calculating, remembering. The initial shock had worn off. Now, it was a question of survival—his, not DiPaolo's. Screw DiPaolo.

What if, he wondered, Sven had had two masters all along? The information gathered—and the killings—had been most helpful to Bower's company. The information was the kind that could be helpful to America's enemies as well. What if Sven had made two copies of all the stolen documents? What if he'd told others about the assassinations? Clearly, he had.

He started thinking about Annette, Sven's beautiful, efficient protégé. Sven, knowing he was dying, had been so insistent that Bower continue to use her. Why? What did Sven care? He was dying. What difference did it make to him? Unless there was a reason, a family to protect, not from the Bowers, but from someone else.

His head was beginning to pound. He could make no sense of it. His thoughts returned to the original question. Who would gain most from the death of Joseph DiPaolo? Rutman, yes, but Rutman hadn't the stomach for this—or the contacts. Who else? The Russians? Impossible. DiPaolo was in the forefront of those trying to ease their agony. Who, then?

T.J. buried his head in his hands. After a moment,

he looked up, stared at the ceiling and said, "It's over, Donald."

Donald Bower looked at him sharply. "What are you talking about?"

T.J. Bower began pacing again, talking as he walked. "I said it's over. Everything we've built, everything we've accomplished. It's all gone, you hear me?"

Donald was on his feet. "Don't be ridiculous," he said. "It isn't over by a long shot."

"Yes, it is," T.J. insisted. "They have us by the nuts. No matter what we do now, we're finished. We'll have to do what they say, but once it's done, they're going to destroy us anyway."

"Why?"

"Because it all fits into their little plan. I can see it clear as a bell."

"What plan?"

"I don't know exactly. All I know is they aren't about to let us be after we set this up. Kohnor must have been playing both sides of the street from the first day. I should have seen it, but I didn't. God! How stupid! How incredibly stupid!"

Donald Bower looked ill. "I don't understand."

"There's nothing *to* understand. Whoever's behind this wants the president dead, and you can bet the moment he is, we'll be next. They'll want to cover their tracks. Damn!" He threw an arm around his son. "Don't feel bad, son. It isn't your fault. It's mine. I made the mistake almost fifty years ago when I got hooked up with that fucking Swede. I compounded it when I allowed myself to work directly with Annette. Jesus!"

T.J. drained the last of the brandy and ran a hand across his lips. Then he said, "The man said three weeks?"

"Yes."

T.J. ran a hand through his hair. "There is one

possible way out of this mess. Only one." He slapped his son on the shoulder. "Buck up! We're not dead yet!"

Donald Bower looked at his father with eyes that held faint hope.

27

At the age of ten, Josephine Cousteau could easily have passed for thirteen. Now, at the age of fifty-two, she looked forty-five. The bizarre urge to kill, fueled by concupiscent rage, had finally waned, and she'd long since retired from a life of spying and killing, devoting herself entirely to her writing. Much to her surprise and satisfaction, the name Denise Dijon was often found near the top of best-seller lists on both sides of the Atlantic.

She was unique. She wrote of death and deceit; dark tales with few heros and many villains, filled with characters who displayed the worst of human instincts. Hard-hitting and bleak, her novels gave food for thought, and often controversy. One had been banned in America as pornographic. After two years of legal action by her American publisher, the ban had been lifted, and the book had risen quickly to the number-one spot on the best-seller lists.

Her critics were almost equally divided in their appraisals of her work. Some called it pure trash, while others hailed it as the new reality in fiction. But her critics, pro and con, had two things in common; none were neutral, and none had ever clapped eyes on Denise Dijon, the profoundly introverted author who resolutely refused all pleas for interviews or personal appearances. Not a single person owned a signed copy of any of her works.

Sensing a trend in the making, some established authors attempted to emulate Denise Dijon's style and substance, but, lacking her intimate association with her fictional characters, they failed miserably.

Her spacious home, nestled behind a stand of tall, leafless trees in a suburb of Paris, looked more like an American-style bungalow than a typical Parisian house. The dead-looking trees added gloom to this gray, bleak February.

Inside the house, Josephine sat at her word processor, hard at work on the third draft of yet another novel. She heard her maid tap lightly on the door to her library/workroom, call out, then enter.

"What is it, Ellie?" she said, not looking up.

"There are two men to see you."

"So? Send them away. You know I see no one."

"They refuse to leave. They say they know you."

Josephine stopped typing. "They know me? What are their names?"

"A man named Thomas Bower—and his son."

Josephine felt a sudden, sharp pain in her chest, just behind the sternum. In all the years she'd worked with them, not once had she given either of the Bowers her address. How had they found her? There was only one way to find out.

"Take them to the *salon*," she said. "Make them comfortable, and tell them I'll be there momentarily."

"Yes, Madame."

Josephine went to her bedroom, changed into blue jeans and a white sweater, tied back her hair, applied some makeup, then opened a dresser drawer and removed a small Beretta, which she slipped in her back pocket.

She walked quickly down a hall and into the austere room where T.J. and Donald Bower waited.

"How did you get this address?" she asked.

T.J. answered with a groan. "Annette, we have problems."

"Answer me," she said in a snarling voice, the Beretta now pointed at T.J.'s head. "How did you get this address?"

"A man gave it to us," Bower answered.

She was mystified. "A man?"

"If you'll give me a chance, I'll explain everything."

She sat in a chair across from the sofa, trained the gun on the older of the two and said, "All right. Start talking."

T.J. talked as Josephine Cousteau, still known to the Bowers as Annette LeClair, listened. He summed up by saying, "So you see, we have one chance and one chance only. Once the job is done, the bastards will kill us anyway. Don't you agree?"

Josephine stood up, walked to the large mahogany serving table, put down the gun, and poured some liquor into three glasses. Without asking, she handed a glass to both men, then looked out the window. "This man knew you'd be coming here?"

"Of course. He demanded it."

Her mind was working feverishly. As a precaution, she swept the house for listening devices weekly. She'd never found one. That didn't mean they weren't there.

"The man—did he have a name?" she asked.

"He was an American," Bower answered. "He said

his name was Fred Brown, but that's a phony for sure."

"What did he look like?"

Bower described the man.

"I don't know him."

"There's no reason you should," Bower said. "He's probably working for the people you used to work for."

"What do you mean?"

"Come on, Annette. We weren't your only clients, were we? If we had been, this never would have happened."

Josephine gave him a hard glance. "You're saying that our only hope is to go to South America and hide? What makes you think these people won't follow us there? What make you think they aren't listening to this very conversation?"

Bower turned pale. "We better pray they aren't. Look, you're the professional. You know how to get from place to place without being spotted. You know where to get false passports and stuff like that. You can figure out a way to get us from here to there.

"We came directly to you because we were expected to. I thought we better make it look good. If these people are listening, we're dead, but if they aren't, they're probably figuring we're working this thing out. We're safe for the moment, but not for long. We'll have to continue to make it look good, Annette. If it's money you're worried about, I have access to lots of it in the Bahamas. Enough to let the three of us live out our lives in comfort."

"Once we disappear," she said, "they'll send someone else to do the job and claim it was me, directed by you. Is that how you see it?"

"Exactly," he said.

"And you think the Americans will stop looking for us after a while?"

Bower nodded. "Look, we can get lost in several

places down there. With enough money, we can have our own security force. Nobody will be able to get near us. It's our only chance, Annette."

"And your family?" she asked, turning her gaze to Donald Bower.

"We'll have to leave them," he said. "There's nothing I can do about that. They'll be all right."

"I see."

T.J. Bower's eyes were clouding over as he sought to convince this woman of the merit of his plan. "Annette," he said, "you must understand. These people aren't playing around. We've got ourselves into a situation here. It wouldn't have happened if you and Sven had been straight with me from the beginning. Your duplicity is what's brought us to this end."

Again, she ignored his complaint. "Where are you staying?" she asked.

"We're both at the Moderne," T.J. said.

"Let me think about this for a few hours," she said. "Both of you stay in your room. It may be bugged by now, so in your conversations, make it appear I've agreed to do the job."

"We will."

"I'll contact you. When I do, you may have to move fast, so be prepared. Don't worry. I won't leave you in—what is it you Americans say?—oh, yes, the lurch."

They didn't seem convinced, but Josephine was the one holding the cards. She showed them to the door, reassured them that she would be in contact, then walked back to the library.

For a moment, she circled the room, her fingers caressing the spines of thousands of books she'd collected over the years. She stopped in front of twelve framed dust jackets, all for novels by Denise Dijon.

She'd taken her mother's name as her pen name for reasons she couldn't explain. A slight risk, since the name was a common one in France. By never appearing in public or allowing a photograph of her face to be taken, she'd avoided a possible chance identification. Until now, everything had worked to perfection.

For the second time in her life, she was fulfilled, but this time, the fulfillment was not due to explosive moments of violent release. This time, she was at peace with herself. By pouring her residual pain into her novels, she'd successfully exorcised it, and now, she looked to the future with secure anticipation, the desire to kill entirely subdued. At least, until now.

She sat in her chair, smoked a cigarette, and tried to make sense of it. Like Bower, she had it figured out in a very short time. Should she refuse to kill her father, they'd simply send another, but kill him or not, her life was over. That much was clear. For political reasons, she was now a pawn of those behind this insidious plot.

Bower wanted to run away, a most reasonable solution, since he was wise enough to know what trouble he was in. That was her best bet as well, if one were rational. She could run and hide in any of several countries, leaving the Bowers to face their fates, along with her father.

She cared little for the political ramifications of what these people were planning. Communism, democracy, socialism, they were all the same to her. Money ruled the world, not politics. Those with money lived well under any system, while those without lived poorly. She had more than enough.

That was the most logical move—running. Still, she felt an odd pang at the thought of her father being killed. She remembered meeting him, and the irrational terror their meeting had ignited. In her mind's eye, she saw him being gunned down and the vision troubled her. Why? What did she care?

She'd been powerless to prevent the death of her

mother and defenseless against the abuses of the animal Claude Beauport. She'd been unable to act until the day she'd picked up the shovel and killed her tormentor. She was a child no longer. Now, she was a woman of experience and considerable knowledge. She had the power to act, to stop these cowards. To what end? What was in it for her? Nothing but satisfaction. They planned to kill her anyway. Perhaps, she could outwit them at their own game, turn the tables, and not be forced to run. Perhaps, if she was clever enough, she could live her life the way she wanted to, here, in Paris, surrounded by her books and her work, and the birds and the squirrels, and the sounds of the night that no longer frightened her. Not in this house, of course, but one just like it, one protected by a grateful nation. Was it possible?

She stared at the dust jackets, then took a seat at her work station. She squared her shoulders, switched on her computer, inserted a disk and let her fingers fly along the keys.

She'd started transposing her memoirs a year before, taking the written words in her diary and entering them into a new document. She'd never really considered what she would do with the memoirs once they were completed—until now. Today, she had a purpose. The memoirs would be her ticket to freedom. But first she had to complete the final chapter.

Thomas Bower hung up the phone, turned to his son and smiled. "She says she's got it set."

"She does? Thank God! It took her long enough."

"I told you! The woman is a pro."

"So what's the plan?"

"We're to leave the hotel, make sure we're not followed, and take the eleven o'clock train to a town called Sens. About a two-hour ride, she says. She'll meet us there, at the station."

"And then what?"

"She'll tell us when we get there."

"Are you sure we can trust her?"

T.J. poured himself a stiff drink, gulped half of it down, and stared out the window of the hotel room. "Do we have a choice?"

It was just before one in the morning when the train stopped at the small town of Sens. The two men disembarked, both carrying heavy suitcases. As promised, Josephine was waiting.

"Quickly," she whispered. She motioned them to follow her.

They placed their bags in the trunk of an older model Mercedes and clambered into the back seat.

"Where are we going?" Donald asked, as the car lurched out of the parking lot and headed south on a road that ran parallel to the Yonne river.

"I have arranged for us to meet with a man who can fly us out of the country," Josephine said, talking over her shoulder. "First, we go to Spain, then we board a freighter that will take us to Brazil. Another associate will meet us there. He'll help us make the final arrangements."

Thomas Bower slapped his son on the shoulder and said, "I told you! The woman is a pro!" Then he leaned forward and said, "Annette, you won't regret this. I'll pay you well for what you've done."

She continued to give them details of the plan as the car raced along the narrow roadway. Then, suddenly, in the middle of nowhere, she applied the brakes and brought the car to a stop by the side of the road.

"Why are we stopping?" T.J. asked.

"My associate said he would meet us here," she said, pointing ahead. "He must have been delayed. We'll wait. I'm sure he'll be along soon."

As she said it, she turned and faced the two men sitting in the back seat. In the darkness, they failed to notice the gun in her hand. It fired twice, making a sound like a muffled firecracker. Both slugs found their marks, making small, round holes in the center of two foreheads. Both men slumped back in the seat.

Josephine got out of the car. She looked to see if there were any other cars on the road. There weren't. First, she opened the trunk and removed the suitcases, then opened the back door. Working quickly, she removed all clothing and jewelry from the bodies and placed everything in a burlap sack. She wanted identification to take as long as possible. Leaving the naked bodies in the back seat of the car, she removed the license plates, got back behind the wheel and put the car in gear. She turned the wheel to the left and drove slowly to the river's edge, where she stopped again.

She got out of the car and looked around. Satisfied, she reached inside the car and put it in gear, watching as the Mercedes moved slowly forward, finally slipping into the fast-moving river. In moments, it disappeared from view. As it did, another car appeared on the roadway, its lights out, stopping beside her. She threw the suitcases and the sack in the back seat, then got in the passenger's side.

"Right on time," she said.

"Where to?" asked the young driver.

"Back to Paris, you fool."

When Pierre Charrette arrived at his office on another rainy winter morning, he placed his briefcase on a chair, removed the newspaper, spread it out on his desk, then walked over to the Krups coffee maker positioned in the small bar built into the wall. Set to begin brewing at eight in the morning, the machine had done its job, and a full pot of fresh coffee awaited him.

He poured a cup, added sugar and milk, then took his place at his desk and began reading the newspaper.

"Pierre."

Startled, he whirled around to see Josephine, a long-barrelled gun in her hand. "What?"

"Open your mouth," she commanded.

"What are you—"

"*Silence!* Open your mouth."

He opened his mouth. Josephine placed the end of the barrel inside. "This is one of the newer silencers," she said. "Hardly a sound."

He grunted.

"I am going to tell you a story," she said. "You will listen, and then you will answer whatever questions I have. If you don't, you'll be dead. Blink your eyes if you understand."

Pierre blinked.

"Good. I was visited by two men yesterday. Do you know who they were? Blink if the answer is yes."

Pierre blinked.

"I thought so." She removed the barrel from his mouth but kept the weapon pointed at his forehead. "Why didn't you come to me directly?"

Pierre removed a handkerchief from his pocket and wiped his badly scarred face. "I wanted you to think it was their idea."

"Why?"

"In case something went wrong. I didn't want anything getting back to me."

"You didn't think I would figure it out?"

He shrugged.

"You think I'm a fool?"

He held up a hand. "Of course not. It's just . . . you've worked for them for many years. I thought you wouldn't care."

She sneered at him. "A few businessmen, some minor military men, some nonentities, yes, but the president of the United States? That's asking a lot, Pierre."

"They are to pay you well."

"And so they have."

"Then you'll do it?"

She smiled. "Of course."

"Then why are you acting like this? Why do you frighten me unnecessarily."

"Because I'm insulted, Pierre. You should have come to me directly. You should have told me things."

"What things?"

"Like who is behind this?"

"Me."

She moved the gun closer.

"All right," he said quickly. "Why do you care?"

"I told you. The assassination of such a major figure is not to be taken lightly. He's well protected. I want to know why this is so important. If I'm to risk my life, I want to know the reason. Money isn't enough."

"Please put the gun down."

"I will. When you tell me everything, Pierre."

28

In his twenty-five years as a law enforcement officer, FBI Assistant Director Leland Cole had interviewed or interrogated thousands of people, but he'd never met anyone quite like the middle-aged woman who sat calmly in front of him now. Her slightly accented voice was even and controlled, her mannerisms few, her entire demeanor cold and remote. Vestiges of outstanding beauty were still evident in the high cheekbones, the almost sloe eyes, the full lips, even—astonishingly, considering her age—the near-flawless skin. Plastic surgery, Cole thought. A masterful job, with not a hint of a scar to be seen. Magnificent, and very expensive, but nothing new. It was the commanding authority beneath the skin that was.

As she fixed her clear, dark eyes on his—unwaver-

ing, unblinking, emitting an aura of mystery that was
extremely unsettling—he could almost feel the coldness penetrating his very being, as if she possessed
some telekinetic energy capable of scrambling his
brain cells. It was beyond anything in his experience.

"Tell me again," he said, his eyes filling with undis-
guised hostility, his jaw becoming more firmly set, his
face beginning to flush with the first hint of genuine
anger.

It was only one of several interrogations being conducted inside the Washington headquarters of the
FBI. Cole, a large man, sat behind a marred walnut
desk in a starkly furnished room with green walls and
matching ceiling. Josephine sat across from him, staring at him.

"I have said what I have to say," she said. "I have
proof I will present only to him. Should you choose
to dismiss me, you do so at his peril, not yours. I suggest you let him make the decision."

"That's impossible," Cole replied quickly, his voice
betraying his increasing sense of frustration.

He leaned back in his chair and drummed his fingers on the desk. "I don't understand you," he said.
"You walk in here off the street of your own free
will, tell us that you have information deemed vital to
this nation's security, yet you're unwilling to take it
one additional step. Why?"

"Because," she answered, "only he can give me
what I must have."

"Which is?"

"I can't tell you that."

"Why not?"

"Because I can't trust you."

"Then why are you here?"

"Because I have to go through you to get to him.
He is a man I trust. He will keep a promise made."

"How do you know?"

"I know. It is enough."

"How do you know I won't keep a promise?"

"I cannot take the chance."

"You'll simply have to provide me with more. You say you have proof? Then present it to me. I'll decide if it warrants a private audience."

The dark eyes continued to stare at him. He heard his stomach rumbling, which only served to make him angrier. She was just a woman, yet her presence seemed to fill the room, shrinking it somehow, her lungs sucking up all the available oxygen, leaving none for anyone else. He could almost feel his mind influenced by an irrational, unworldly anxiety created by this invisible force she emitted.

"I cannot do what you ask," she said, in that flat, unemotional voice that seemed to scratch at his very bones. "There are reasons that cannot be explained. Only he can see the proof and only he can hear the rest of what I have to say."

She paused, took a deep breath, the first sign of any emotion whatsoever, and went on. "I will, however, tell you this much. If you fail to arrange an audience, I will not pursue the matter further."

"You think not? Lady, you have no idea what you're into here. We make the rules."

"Your rules mean nothing to me. I am presenting you with the opportunity to prevent a terrible tragedy. If you choose to ignore it, so be it."

He wanted to throw her out on her ear. "Look," he said, his patience almost at an end, "you walk in here with a French passport in the name of Annette LeClair and documents identifying you as novelist Denise Dijon. I've read several of Denise Dijon's books. She seems to know a lot about FBI and CIA operations and procedures. Someone doing that kind of research should know how we operate. You appear not to."

There was a knock at the door. A man dressed almost identically to Leland Cole entered the room and handed Cole a note. He turned to leave.

"Tom," Cole said, "stay here for a moment."

"Yes, sir."

Cole looked at the note, laid it on the desk upside down and turned his attention back to the woman, whose face now held the smallest of Mona Lisa smiles. "My publisher has verified the documents, *oui?*"

He ignored the remark. "Do you realize," he said, "that I can have you arrested right this minute? I can charge you with any number of offenses, including conspiracy, malicious mischief, and obstruction of justice. I can also hold you as a material witness. You could spend months, maybe years, in jail. Is that what you want?"

"Do what you wish," she said. "What I have told you is the truth. You may arrest me, but you will learn no more. You will have succeeded only in assuring his death."

The smile was gone. The mask was back.

Cole leaned back in his chair and frowned. "Very well. I've wasted enough time. The answer is no. As I said before, if you have information, you can present it to me. If you refuse, you'll be held as a material witness until you change your mind."

He threw her a look of disgust, stood up and headed for the door. With his hand on the knob, he turned and said, "Lock her up, Tom. I'll get the paperwork started." Then he stormed out of the room.

Back in his office, he picked up the phone and punched some numbers. To the person who answered, he said, "This is Leland Cole, FBI. I'd like to speak to Deputy Director Hanes immediately."

In a moment, CIA Deputy Director Cecil Hanes was on the line. "Leland?"

"Cecil. I need your help."

"Concerning?"

"I want everything you've got—or can find out—

regarding a French national named Annette LeClair. Address . . ."

Six hours later, three men gathered in the White House Oval Office. Besides President Joseph DiPaolo, the group included CIA Director Jack Gallagher, FBI Director Horace Clark, and Secret Service White House Detail Chief Bill White. All had gathered for an emergency meeting requested by Gallagher.

After some brief pleasantries, Gallagher opened a manila file folder festooned with a red stripe on one corner and the legend, "Level One—Eyes Only." In a deep, booming voice, he said, "Mr. President, the FBI has been contacted by a French national, a woman named Annette LeClair. She claims to have information regarding an assassination attempt on your life."

DiPaolo sat upright in his chair. "My God! Does she have details?"

"That's just it, sir. She won't tell us anything other than the fact that she has the information. She won't tell us what the information is. She insists on talking only to you."

"I don't understand."

Gallagher sat stiffly in his chair as his fingers played with the folder. Then, he leaned forward and said, "We've done a preliminary check on the woman. There seems to be some confusion about her. In some ways, she checks out. In others, she doesn't."

DiPaolo shook his head. "Jack, you're not making any sense."

Gallagher took a deep breath and tried to calm down. "Okay. She claims to be author Denise Dijon. You've heard of her, I'm sure. One of her books was the subject of a CIA paper. They wondered where she got her information."

The name triggered a response in DiPaolo. He'd read one book written by Denise Dijon, drawn to it more by the author's name than anything else. After the first hundred pages, he'd set it aside. It was distasteful at best. Now he found it odd that a woman by the same name would insist on seeing him. It was as if the ghost of the Denise Dijon he'd once known was haunting him.

"She was in possession of contracts between a New York publisher and Denise Dijon," Gallagher continued. "They appear to be genuine, and the publisher is sure she's the genuine article. However, as I said, her passport carries the name Annette LeClair, and there we have a problem. We can trace her back to 1960, but before that, she never existed."

"When was she born?" Clark asked.

"Nineteen forty-one. July fourth, she says."

"Really? Where?"

"Paris. Then she moved to a place called Saint-Quentin."

"Well, many original birth records were destroyed during the war. It's possible hers were among them."

"True, but there are no school records or anything."

Clark smiled. "We've only been on this a few hours. The French can take months to come up with documentation. That you've traced her back to 1960 in such a short time is a major miracle."

Joseph DiPaolo was almost as disturbed by Gallagher's obvious discomfort as he was by the news. In the short time he'd known the man, Gallagher had always appeared unflappable. If Gallagher was as upset as he appeared now, the woman was more than a crank. "What is it you're trying to tell me, Jack?"

Gallagher winced. "She says she'll reveal the details of the assassination plot to you and you alone. Leland Cole told her it was impossible, but she insisted. Right now she's being held as a material witness."

President DiPaolo ran a hand through his still-thick hair and said, "If she'll talk to me, then why don't we do it? Perhaps we can get to the bottom of this quickly."

Horace Clark cleared his throat and said, "It sets a bad precedent, sir. It's possible she's just doing this as some wacko publicity stunt."

President DiPaolo stood up. "Horace, it has to be more than that. This kind of stunt could see her spend a few years in jail. Let's go and talk to her." He smiled. "With all of you around, I'll be well protected."

Clark was insistent. "If she's a nut case, sir, the ramifications of her actions wouldn't mean squat to her. We have an established policy on this kind of thing."

"Which is?"

"No contact with the president. None."

Joseph DiPaolo looked at Clark for a moment, then said, "Your main concern is she's crazy? That's not enough. She may be nuts, but she may also have heard something."

Clark started to protest. DiPaolo held up a hand. "No more arguments. I want to talk to her. I want this out of the way as soon as possible."

"Yes, sir."

Less than an hour later, Joseph DiPaolo was ushered into a small, green, windowless room inside the J. Edgar Hoover Building. The tiled floor was adorned with a table and four plastic chairs, nothing else. Josephine was seated at the table, dressed in a blue, shapeless smock. Standing against the walls were four FBI men, three CIA men, two Secret Service men, and one female matron. Already, the temperature inside the room had risen some ten degrees from the body heat generated by so many people.

Josephine's face lit up as she saw the president. "Thank you for coming," she said.

"What's on your mind, Miss LeClair?"

She turned to one of the FBI men. "In my belongings, you'll find a locker key. The key fits box number twenty-three forty-three at Dulles Airport. If you'll bring me the contents of that locker, we can proceed."

The FBI man looked at the president, who nodded, sending the agent scurrying out of the room. Josephine turned to the president and asked, "Could we have some privacy? What I have to tell you is quite astounding. It could also be embarrassing for you."

DiPaolo looked at her closely. Somewhere, he'd seen this woman before. As though reading his mind, she said, "I interviewed you years ago when you were a senator. We talked about the resistance and how they rescued you during the war. We also talked about a woman named Denise Dijon."

DiPaolo's eyebrows rose. "Yes," he said. "I remember. I understand you use that name as a pseudonym for your writing."

"For good reason. She was my mother."

He felt his heart skip a beat. "What?"

"It's true. You knew her, *n'est-ce pas?*"

"Yes." He was stunned, and suddenly desperate to know more. His mind reeling, he talked with Clark. After some discussion, it was resolved that Clark and Gallagher would remain inside the room. The others would wait just outside. It left three men and one woman seated at a small table in a windowless room— the most powerful man on earth, a woman who had information that could create havoc for America, and two witnesses. The three men waited, and then Josephine began to tell them what they'd come to hear.

"My real name is Josephine Cousteau," she said.

"For a time, I was a photographer's model in Paris. I was known as 'Venus.'"

At the mention of the name Venus, Jack Gallagher's face turned crimson. The voluminous CIA files contained one marked "Venus." For years, the agency had searched, without success, for the killer of an American Army general. Now, the woman was apparently inches away from him. There was much he wanted to ask her, but he held his tongue.

"Denise Dijon was my mother," she continued. "And you, Mr. President, are my father."

Joseph DiPaolo stared at her in dazed silence. Gallagher looked like he wanted to punch her in the face. Clark's mouth fell open.

"She *is* crazy," Gallagher snapped. "I'm sorry, sir. I'll have her charged. I'm sorry I wasted your time."

DiPaolo held up a hand.

"A DNA test will prove it," Josephine said calmly. "But I know that takes a few days. While we're waiting for the results, I will show you some things, such as my mother's diary, which makes mention of you. It places exactly the time of my conception."

DiPaolo could barely breathe.

"That is not why I'm here," she went on. "Though, in some respects, I guess it is. If you were not my father, perhaps I would view this differently."

DiPaolo had partially recovered from the shock. "You told the FBI you knew details of an assassination attempt on my life," he said.

"It's true, but, before I continue, I want to strike a bargain."

"What sort of bargain?"

"I will tell you everything I know, holding back nothing. If what I tell you proves true, you will arrange for my safe harbor in Paris. You will work with the French government to give me a new identity and allow me to live out my life as an author, untouched. That is all I ask."

Immediately, Clark and Gallagher started to caution the president. DiPaolo, spurred by unrestrained, demanding curiosity, waved a hand to silence them. He was the president. He had the power.

"You have a deal," he said quickly. "Now, let's hear the rest."

Josephine allowed a small smile to grace her lips. The gamble had been worth it. She'd beaten the bastards at their own game. Then, the stoniness took over again. "I know the details of the assassination," she said, "because I am the one sent to kill you."

Shock upon shock. "You?"

"Yes."

"You . . . you're an assassin?"

"Yes."

He fought to keep his voice level and still the pounding of his heart. "Who sent you to kill me?" he asked.

"A man named Pierre Charrette."

DiPaolo looked at Gallagher, who said, "I know who he is."

DiPaolo turned back to Josephine. "Please go on. There's no hurry. I want to hear everything you have to say."

The three men listened attentively as Josephine told them everything; how she had worked for Sven Kohnor, first as a spy, then as an assassin; how she'd discovered, after becoming a partner and eventually taking over the business from Sven, that her mentor had been working for Thomas J. Bower, Charrette, and through him, the Russians; how Thomas and Donald Bower had come to her in Paris and told her that they must try to escape to South America; how she'd killed them both, for fear Charrette would send someone else in her stead. And she told them about Charles Bonnet and André Lecour, the two French industrialists who'd commissioned Charrette.

"Bonnet and Lecour. Why do they want me killed?" DiPaolo asked.

"It's business," she said. "They feel that your death will create a leadership vacuum, especially when they release the information they have about the vice president being a pawn of the Bowers. He'll be disgraced, forced to resign, and your country will be in chaos. While America regroups, the members of the European Community will stake out their markets, telling their customers that the United States will soon be as bankrupt as the Russians."

She told them everything Charrette had told her, and later, when what had been in the airport locker was brought into the room, she showed them the picture of a young Joey DiPaolo and Denise Dijon.

DiPaolo looked at the picture for a moment, then handed it to Gallagher.

Gallagher glanced at it and said, "It could be a fake, sir."

DiPaolo shook his head. "It's no fake. I remember the moment it was taken. That photograph is real."

Clark looked at the photo, then at DiPaolo. For a moment, his head drooped.

Like hungry animals fighting over a scrap of food, the three men tore into the material, reading various entries from Josephine's memoirs, now compiled in a Denise Dijon manuscript titled *The Venus Diaries: Memoirs of an Assassin,* and her mother's diary. They bombarded her with questions, some falling on top of others. Decorum and posturing were discarded in the thirst for information.

Josephine answered every question put to her without reservation, including one about the American general. She provided details only the killer would know, and at that moment, Gallagher finally believed her.

"How many copies of this manuscript exist?" DiPaolo asked.

"You have the only one," she answered. "I prepared it on a computer, printed one copy, then erased the document from the hard disk memory. No one will ever know, unless you choose to tell them."

DiPaolo held the manuscript in his hand for a moment, and then put it back on the table. "What were you planning to do with this? Publish it as a book?"

"Originally, I simply wanted to have a record, for no reason. When I was approached by the Bowers and asked to assassinate you, I thought it might serve a useful purpose, so I brought it with me."

The questions and answers continued. Finally, after they'd been closeted in the small room for almost two hours, Joseph DiPaolo stood up, stared at the woman for a few moments, and asked, "What is it that caused you to take this action, Josephine? Why didn't you just carry out your mission?"

"I knew they would kill me afterward. So did the Bowers. My only chance at survival is to place myself under your protection. I was sure you were an honorable man and would honor an agreement made between us."

"You said earlier that the fact I was your father had something to do with this."

"Yes, but only in one respect. These men know nothing of my true heritage. Had they known, it would have changed everything. By being able to prove to you that I am your daughter, I give credibility to the rest of it."

"That's all?"

"Yes."

"Very well. I must leave now, but I'll be back. If your story turns out to be true, you will have done this nation a great service. You will have your safe harbor in France."

Josephine nodded. "Thank you."

DiPaolo motioned to Clark. "You can take her out

now, but come back. I want to talk to you and Jack for a moment."

Clark escorted Josephine out, then returned and closed the door. The three men sat at the table and stared at one another for a few moments. Then, DiPaolo said, "As incredible as it sounds, her entire story may be true. The part about her being my daughter is very possible. As she says, a DNA test will determine that. I want it done immediately. Is there some way we can verify the rest?"

"Absolutely," Gallagher said. "We'll get started right away. I'll send out priority locate orders, based on the contents of the manuscript. We should have some answers in a matter of hours."

"Good. Do it, but be careful. I don't want the vice president or anyone else to get a whiff of this. I want you to talk to everyone who was in this room and impress that upon them. Any leaks, and people will be in serious trouble. Understand?"

"Yes, sir."

"As this investigation proceeds, I want you all to keep some things in mind."

The two men waited.

"One," the President said, "it's vital that we keep a very tight lid on this, not for my sake but for the country's. During this investigation, you must keep in mind the consequences should this become public knowledge. If the press should ever get their hands on this, there'll be turmoil."

Both men nodded.

"Two, I want her held incognito until we have this settled. Other than you two, no one is to speak to her under any circumstances."

"Yes, sir."

DiPaolo turned to Gallagher. "You know who this Charrette is?"

"Yes, sir. In the old days, he was a KGB agent. Actually, he worked both sides of the street, industrial espionage, arranging arms deals with Arabs, selling stolen information to the Russians, whatever would make a buck. He's even supplied us with intelligence on occasion."

DiPaolo shook his head. "How the hell do you justify working with such people?"

"Sir, it's a lousy business, but we get what we can get from wherever."

"Do you think," the President asked, "that this scheme, if it really is that, could have been concocted by someone in the French government? Some sort of power play?"

"It's possible," Gallagher answered. "If you were assassinated and Rutman was disgraced by his association with the Bowers, and if what she says about the Bowers is true, we'd be in a hell of a fix. It would certainly make us look bad. It's entirely possible that we'd be in a less than competitive position, since we could be perceived as unable to deliver on future contracts. Our customers throughout the world would look upon the Europeans as more stable."

DiPaolo ran a hand over his lips. "How do we find out if the French government is involved?"

"Leave that to us, sir."

"No way. Talk to me."

"Well, we'll start by having our people interrogate Charrette, Bonnet, and Lecour. For one thing, we need to make sure she's the only weapon in their arsenal. We'll know a lot more after we talk to those three."

"Can you do this without the French government getting wind of it?"

"Absolutely."

DiPaolo scowled. "What a goddamn mess. I don't care what it takes," he said firmly, "I want answers, and I want them as quickly as humanly possible. Do you understand?

Both men nodded.

DiPaolo, suddenly looking very old, shook their hands and left the room.

Josephine Cousteau sat on her bunk in the holding pen and stared at the wall. She felt calm and relaxed, which surprised her. The last time she'd seen her father, the experience had almost torn her apart. This time, she'd felt no emotion, save for the sense of relief when he'd agreed to provide her with security. Was it age? she wondered. More important, was it truly her own skin that concerned her? Or was there something she didn't want to admit, even to herself?

She shrugged and pushed the unfamiliar introspection from her mind. What did it matter?

29

$\mathcal{D}r.$ Hans DeVol drove his black BMW up the winding driveway of his Zurich estate and parked at the front door of his house. He got out and looked around for Rolph, the servant who took care of this and his other cars. He was nowhere to be seen.

DeVol slapped a leather glove against his thigh in irritation, then walked to the door of the house. The conference he'd been attending had lasted longer than anticipated. Now it was quite dark and well past the normal dinner hour. Slightly obsessive-compulsive, DeVol never enjoyed anything done at other than the appointed hour.

The front door was open, which was usual, but unattended, which was most unusual. What was going on? First Rolph, then Gibson. Was no one at his post this night?

He would deal with both soon enough. Right now,

his main concern was getting something to eat, unless, of course, the cook has deserted him as well.

The house was quiet and empty. DeVol sensed something amiss and started to tense. When he heard a voice behind him, he jumped.

"Dr. DeVol?"

The doctor whirled and saw a man in a business suit standing in the doorway to the library. The man had spoken in English, and the gun in his hand was pointed at the middle of the doctor's chest. DeVol froze.

"What do you want?" he stammered in English.

The man motioned to the library and said, "I want to talk to you. Come in here."

DeVol walked toward the room on unsteady legs. "Where is my wife? Where are the servants? What have you done with them?"

The man waited until they were in the den. Then, he said, "They're all dead, Doctor. We've killed them all. We'll kill you too if you don't tell us what we want to know."

DeVol almost fell into a nearby leather chair. His face paled and his breathing became difficult. For a moment, his eyes jerked in their sockets as he looked around the room. Then, he jumped again as he noticed another man, also dressed in a business suit, standing in the corner of the dimly lit room. Now, two pistols were pointing at him.

They were killers. Killers and robbers. His mind reeled as his imagination envisioned them firing bullets into the bodies of his wife and servants.

The man who had spoken moved closer. He removed a photograph from his pocket and handed it to the doctor, whose hand trembled as he held it.

"You worked on this woman's face in 1959. Her name is Josephine Cousteau, but she was better known as a French model named Venus. Do you recognize the photo?"

For a moment the doctor didn't recognize either the face or the name, his brain numbed by the incredible fear that immobilized him. He looked at the photograph and then at the man who had given it to him. "Why . . . why did you kill my wife? What kind of people are you?"

The man was becoming impatient. "Look at the picture," he commanded.

The frightened doctor looked at the picture. Nothing registered. Then, like a bolt of lightning, his memory returned. "Yes," he said. "Yes, I remember. What do you want to know?"

"Two things, Doctor. We want to know what she looks like today, and we want to know where we can find Sven Kohnor."

The terrified doctor stammered, "I haven't seen Kohnor in years. As for the woman, I have no pictures . . . I don't know. . . ." His voice trailed off.

The first man motioned to the second man who put his gun away and came over to sit in a chair beside the doctor. His hands now held a sketch pad and pencil. Quietly, he said, "Doctor, you will use the photo in your hand and describe all changes that have occurred, both from the surgery you performed and the natural aging process. I will sketch and you will describe, and together, we will create an accurate portrait of this woman as she looks today. Do you understand?"

The doctor shook his head. Tears began to stream down his face. "No," he said, "I will do nothing. You have already killed my wife. You will kill me, too. Do it now."

The first man sighed, reached down, and pulled the doctor to his feet. He dragged the shaking plastic surgeon into the kitchen and pointed to the corner.

Madame DeVol and three servants were bound and gagged and seated on the floor. Aside from the fear evident in their eyes, they were in perfect health.

"We just wanted to get your attention, Doctor. Nobody's been hurt. We'd like to keep it that way, but it all depends on you." He pushed the doctor into a chair at the kitchen table and said, "Now, are you ready to show us what she looks like?"

Imbued with a sense of relief that defied description, the doctor nodded.

In Paris, the young man from the U.S. embassy looked at a dust-covered carton containing documents once belonging to Dr. Peter Vanais. He blew the dust from the top of the carton and looked inside. "Wonderful," he exclaimed. "You've found them!"

The man from the *Société de Préservation des Dossiers Médicals* shrugged. "I can't imagine what you would want with the old records of a minor talent long since dead, but there you are. You realize that no records may be removed and no copies may be made. You may examine, but that is all."

"I understand," the young man said. "And thank you."

"As you wish," the man said huffily as he left the American to peruse the documents under the careful supervision of the security guard.

Marie Benoit, now old and frail, greeted the visitor and offered him some tea. It was a strange offer, coming from a woman lying in a hospital bed, incontinent, hardly able to move, her brain addled by the ravages of Alzheimer's disease. For a few minutes, the agent talked with her quietly, then took his leave. He talked to one of the nurses, made some notes and finally left the hospital.

Later, Marie Benoit asked the nurse, for the thousandth time, when Josephine was coming to visit.

■ ■ ■

Robert Grimes sat in his wheelchair and stared out the window of his small room in a retirement home just outside London. It was getting dark, and most of the cars had their lights on as they wound their way down the expressway after another day at the office.

He sighed and turned away from the window. Once, he had been able to drive a car. Once he had driven every day to and from his jewelry store and ...

There was someone in the room. A man in a business suit, standing there quietly, a gun in his hand. Grimes hadn't heard the man even enter the room.

"Good evening, Mr. Grimes," the man said. He was American.

"God's teeth! What's going on?"

"Mr. Grimes, I'm going to ask you some very important questions. Before I do, I think you should know that I am in contact with a man who has your daughter under surveillance. If you fail to answer my questions properly, she will suffer terribly. Do you want that to happen?"

For a moment, Grimes felt fear surge through his body. Then, as quickly as it had come, it receded. For years, he'd been expecting something just like this. Someone would want to know what secrets were stored within his mind. It had been so long ago. "What do you want to know?" he asked.

"Everything," the man said.

"Who are you? American CIA?"

"We don't have much time, Mr. Grimes."

"All right, but I have to know what you want!"

The man leaned forward and said, "A woman named Venus. In 1958, you provided her with three weapons that she used to kill an industrialist. I want to know who your contact was and why the man was killed."

Grimes sagged down into the chair. "Venus? I don't know any Venus."

He heard the sound of the hammer being cocked. "I remember a woman," he exclaimed. "Nineteen fifty-eight, you say?"

"Yes."

"I didn't know her by that name. I remember the deal. Three guns, all the same. I don't know why the man was killed."

"Think!"

"I am thinking. I was involved in the business of purchasing stolen gems. It was a long time ago. I only did a little, you understand. Things were a bit tight and I needed the money."

He took a deep breath. "I was visited by a man. He set it up. He looked Scandinavian, but he never gave me his name. He spoke excellent English. He told me he knew all about me and said he'd turn the information over to the authorities unless I did something for him."

"Which was?"

"He said a young woman would be visiting me. He never gave me a name. All he said was that she'd be asking for weapons and I was to provide them. Of course, I told him that I didn't know where to get such items, but he wouldn't hear of it. He said the people I did business with would know and I was to make arrangements. He made it quite clear I would be arrested if I didn't comply with his wishes.

"Fortunately, one of the people I'd bought some gems from was able to get what I needed. The woman came to the store about three days later, I gave her the weapons and that was the last of it. I never saw her or the man again. And that's the truth."

The American looked unhappy. He put a cigarette in his mouth and lit it.

"You can't smoke in here," Grimes said.

The American blew the smoke directly into Grimes's face. Then he drew closer, his eyes hardly six inches away from those of Grimes. "I'll worry about that. You just worry about the details. So far, I'm not impressed. Let's hear it again."

Grimes coughed for a few minutes. Then, his eyes wet from the exertion and the smoke-caused irritation, he repeated the story. This time, he filled in the details.

At the U.S. embassy in Stockholm, George Nichols opened a large envelope that had been delivered by special messenger. It read:

CONFIDENTIAL

To: The Honorable George Nichols
    United States Ambassador to the Kingdom of Sweden
    United States Embassy
    Stockholm

From: Colonel Orst Ungmann
      Director General
      Swedish National Police
      Stockholm

Reference: Your request on information regarding one Sven Kohnor.

Please refer to file #1666388 in any correspondence. Eyes Only, the Director General.

Subject: Sven Kohnor, Swedish National, born February 22, 1911, Östersund, Sweden. Died August 11, 1962.

Kohnor was arrested several times during the 1930s and was judged to be incorrigible in 1938. He was placed in prison for an indeterminate sentence. At the outbreak of World War II, he wrote a letter to British Intelligence asking to work for them in return for his release. (see app. 4)

After being interviewed, he was released into the custody of British Intelligence on March 25, 1940. Some of the information contained within the balance of the report is based on information provided by officials at British Intelligence.

The report went on to describe Kohnor's training in England, his work for British Intelligence, including the successful assassination of a German general in 1944, in concert with the American OSS, and Kohnor's subsequent disappearance. He had remained at large until his death.

According to the report, Kohnor had a sister living in Argentina, who was totally supported by a large trust set up by Kohnor until her death three years ago. There were no living relatives. Upon her death, the Argentine government liquidated her estate and put the money, equivalent to fourteen million American dollars, in its own coffers.

Photographs of Kohnor were attached, some taken when he was in his twenties, others when he was in his thirties. There was also a request for more information from the Americans. According to the Swedish report, some Danish gold was involved. Files that had lain dormant for almost half a century were being dusted off and re-examined.

The ambassador punched a button on his desk and said, "I want a military jet ordered to stand by. I'm leaving for Washington as soon as the plane is ready. There is to be no announcement. Clear?"

"Yes, sir."

. . .

In Atlanta, an FBI agent entered the main admin-
istration building of the Centers for Disease Control,
presented his credentials, and asked for a senior
administrator. He was taken to the office of Dr.
Philip Linder.

"What can I do for you, sir?" the doctor asked,
after offering the agent a seat, which was declined.

"Doctor, I realize the confidentiality of your work,
but in the interests of national security, I wish to con-
firm certain information that has been gathered elsewhere."

"Go on."

"I have information that one Anthony Cecchi, a
resident of Hollywood Hills, California, died of
AIDS last November sixteenth. Can you verify that
for me?"

The doctor shook his head. "Not without a court
order, I can't."

"I understand. Can you tell me this much? Did he
die on that date? Death records are public, as you
know."

The doctor nodded, tapped a few keys on his computer terminal and then looked up. "Yes, I can con-
firm that he died on that date."

"We have his age as fifty. Is that correct?"

"Yes."

"That's all I need, doctor. Thank you very much."

In Paris, officials of the *Sûreté,* acting on an anony-
mous tip, drove to a location near the town of Sens
and began dragging a section of the river. Within an
hour, they winched up a car, and when it was finally
ashore, found it contained the bodies of two naked
men, both shot in the head. They were unaware that

their actions had been observed by a man hiding in the bushes some two hundred yards away.

Ten miles east of Paris, behind an abandoned filling station, three very frightened men met for the second time within a few days. Pierre Charrette had been accosted at his office, a gun stuck in his chest, and ordered to accompany two young Americans. He'd been driven to this lonely place and taken behind the ramshackle building. His fear took a quantum leap when he saw Bonnet and Lecour had preceded him. Both men were strapped to wooden chairs.

"Are these the men who hired you?" Charrette was asked.

"I never saw them before in my life," he said.

Turning away from Charrette, one of the Americans leaned toward Bonnet. "Is this the man you hired?"

Bonnet shook his head. "I don't know the man. I told you before, I don't know what you're talking about. What's this all about? Why have you kidnapped us? If it's money you want, name your price."

The American shoved a rag in Bonnet's mouth, then doused him with gasoline from a large plastic can. Without another word, he removed a packet of matches from his pocket, lit one, and threw it. Bonnet instantly burst into flames, his tortured screams muffled by the gag. Charrette immediately vomited. Lecour squeezed his eyes shut.

The other American turned to Lecour. "You're next, unless you tell us the truth. We know what we're looking for, so lies will get you killed. Speak the truth and you live."

Lecour, his breathing rapid and shallow, had difficulty speaking. Immobilized by fear, he shook his head from one side to the other, trying to get air into his lungs, trying to escape the terrible stench of blackened human flesh.

"Speak to me, asshole," the American ordered.

Charrette, his eyes spinning, his heart pounding so hard it seemed about to explode, screamed, "Yes, yes! They were the ones. I had to do it. They said they'd kill me! God help me. I'm telling you the truth."

"Now we're getting somewhere," one of the Americans said. For almost an hour, he fired questions at the two men. Each poured out his story, each blaming the other for the plan. Eventually, under fear of death, the truth emerged.

Lecour told them Charrette had approached Bonnet and him together with the idea, looking for someone to pay for the job. Lecour and Bonnet had agreed for the sake of the European Community in general and France in particular, and had provided five million American dollars. Neither man had ever heard of Annette LeClair. No one else was involved, to Lecour's knowledge.

Charrette confirmed the story, explained his long association with Sven Kohnor and Annette, and confirmed that no one in the French government was involved. "The idea," he said, tears streaming down his face, "would never have occurred to me had your president not chosen Charles Rutman as his vice president. Don't you see? Rutman and Bower? The connection? I'm a businessman. How could I let such an opportunity pass?"

"Beats me, pal."

Lecour started to weep. "What happens to us now? We've told you the truth. You said you'd let us live if we told the truth."

"I lied," the American said.

30

Jack Gallagher and Horace Clark, now working as a team for one of the few times in recent memory, sat slumped in chairs fronting the large desk in the Oval Office. Both men were clearly exhausted, their faces reflecting bone-deep weariness caused by lack of sleep and hours of intense concentration. On the other side of the desk, President DiPaolo appeared even more drained than his two visitors, having slept not at all the past twenty-four hours.

Gallagher held a thick file folder in his hands, while Clark's held a yellow legal pad filled with handwritten notes. All three men waited patiently as coffee was served by the president's butler, a ceremonial effort to project a modicum of normality. Finally, they were alone.

"Well," DiPaolo said, his voice barely audible, "how much have you substantiated?"

Clark reported first. "We've just received word from the New Jersey firm. The DNA test is under way. They've given it top priority, but we won't have the results for another twenty-four hours."

"You're sure security has been preserved?"

"I'm sure."

DiPaolo nodded. "Let's proceed on the assumption that the test will be positive. What else?"

Gallagher opened his file and shuffled some papers. "We have confirmation that the bodies of both Bowers have been found about a hundred yards from where she said the car went in. Our people eye-balled their faces and are positive on the ID, though the French have no idea who these people are."

"You don't intend to tell them?"

"No, sir."

DiPaolo thought for a moment, then said, "Go on."

"We have confirmation that Thomas Bower and Sven Kohnor were involved in a joint British-American exercise during World War Two. Kohnor died in 1962. We have a full report from both British Intelligence and the Swedish National Police. There's a real hornet's nest of stuff there that we'll have to deal with later."

"Such as?"

"You really don't want to know, sir."

DiPaolo grinned. "If you say so."

"We have confirmed that another Swede, working in Zurich, prepared false papers for the Cousteau woman several times. The dates match her narrative. We have confirmation from various other foreign offices, some in London, some in other parts of Europe, and some in South America, with respect to several of the assassinations. All check out. She . . . she really was an assassin, sir."

DiPaolo detected the note of sensitivity. "Don't worry about my feelings," he said. "Just lay it out."

"Yes, sir. We found the doctor who performed the cosmetic surgery on Cousteau. He helped us produce a rendering of what she might look like today. We had him do it that way to ensure accuracy. The rendering is conclusive. There's no question she's Josephine Cousteau, and no question she's also the author. At this point, I'm willing to bet that everything she's told us is the absolute truth, despite her background and record."

"You're convinced?"

"Yes. I have a checklist of sixty-seven items to this point. Not one has been proven false."

"Go on."

"With reference to the planned assassination, we're sure it's exactly as she stated. We've talked to the three men involved in the plot, and we're convinced they acted alone. There's no evidence the French government was part of this, either as a group or any member individually."

DiPaolo nodded. "Good work."

Gallagher turned to Clark, who said, "We've got confirmation that a man named Anthony Cecchi did exist. He's now deceased, but it appears he worked for Kohnor for years as a gigolo, seducing homosexuals, then blackmailing them for information.

"We've checked with the passport office, customs, and immigration. Either T.J. or Donald Bower—sometimes both—were out of the country at times coinciding with the entries in the Cousteau manuscript. We've also reexamined the transcripts of the investigation into the vice president's campaign finances. There's no question that fund-raising laws were badly bent, probably broken. The investigation was sloppy, perhaps intentionally. However, aside from common knowledge that the vice president and the Bowers are very, very close, there's nothing to indicate that either the Bowers or the vice president is behind this."

"That's good to hear," DiPaolo said, his voice thick with sarcasm.

Gallagher leaned forward and said, "It looks like this was all precipitated by you picking Charles Rutman to be vice president, sir. Charrette knew what the Bowers were up to, both internationally and domestically. He saw this as a golden opportunity to really screw things up."

DiPaolo sighed, leaned back in his chair, and closed his eyes for a moment.

"It's almost providential," he said, opening his eyes and staring at the ceiling. "If Charrette had had the slightest idea that the woman was my daughter, he wouldn't have used her in a million years. He wouldn't have used Bower either. He would have brought in someone else to do the job."

He brought his gaze back to the two men. "Do you realize how incongruous this is? I'm cursed in that I unintentionally produced a daughter who became an inhuman monstrosity, and yet the actuality of that paternity becomes a blessing. It's incredible."

"I don't think she did this out of any love for you, sir, with all due respect," Clark said.

"The fact remains, Charrette wouldn't have used her had he known, and that's what counts. Someone else, whatever their motivation, might not have done what she has. They might have succeeded, too. After my death, the results would have been the same, once the data were released. Can you imagine what would happen to this country?"

Gallagher rubbed his chin and said, "Yes, I can, sir. Charrette would have made sure that the information on the woman's contract killings for the Bowers was made public. Once that was out in the open, the relationship between the Bowers and Rutman would make it appear that the vice president had you killed. The perfect frame. There's no way the vice president could have functioned as president of the United

States. The ensuing chaos would have made us look like a country being ripped apart. Economically, it would have been nothing short of catastrophic. No question."

DiPaolo sighed. "Well, we owe this woman a great debt. I want you to get started on the arrangements for her safe harbor in France. You'll have to cook up some story, but you're good at that."

Both men stared at him.

"All right. What is it?" asked DiPaolo.

Gallagher looked at Clark. Clark looked at the thick carpet. Gallagher turned to the President and said, "Sir, we've been giving this a lot of thought. There are some serious risks in allowing Miss . . . LeClair to go free."

Instantly, DiPaolo was alert and aware. "Such as?"

"Well, according to the medical records of the doctor who treated her as a child, she's a psychopath, sir. Our own shrink hasn't spent enough time with her to make a full evaluation, but based on the old records and her admitted activities, he's prepared to concur at this point."

"So, she's a psychopath. So what?"

"Let's be realistic, sir. She's responsible for the deaths of at least thirty people, the latest being Thomas and Donald Bower. I realize she may be your daughter and by coming forward, she's done this country a great service. Still, she is what she is. Nothing can change that. It's entirely possible that she could, at some time in the future, decide to publish those memoirs."

"Why would she do that?" DiPaolo snapped. "She came to us with them. She prevented a disaster!"

"She did that to save her own skin, sir."

"All right, I'll give you that, but there's no logical reason for her to publish that manuscript, now or ever."

"That's just it, sir. There *is* no logic to this woman. She's a loose cannon out there, a walking time bomb, loaded with information that could destroy you."

Gallagher was warming to his task now, his eyes flashing, his hands moving as he talked, the concern clear in his voice. "With all due respect, sir," he continued, "should all of this come to light, it would create even worse havoc than before."

"My assassination isn't havoc enough?"

"Of course, but—"

"Sorry. Go ahead."

"Can you imagine what would happen if the press found out that the president of the United States has an illegitimate daughter who's assassinated thirty people? Who's worked for people who in turn have worked for the Russians and given them precious secrets? A spy and a killer? A woman he personally pardoned?"

"They'll never find out," Joseph said. "Besides, I made a bargain."

"You can't be sure they'll never find out, not as long as she's free. As for the bargain, you agreed to that under duress. It has no legal validity. If she goes back to France, there's a very good chance she'll be arrested by French authorities and forced to tell them of her connection to you."

DiPaolo's eyes became thin slits. "You're leaving something out. Just what kind of interrogation did you conduct on those three bastards?"

"You gave us carte blanche," Gallagher said. "You're the commander-in-chief. You ordered us to get to the bottom of this—at any cost."

They were right. He had done exactly that. For a moment, the room was silent save for the gentle ticking of the old Regulator clock on the wall.

"Touché," DiPaolo said, finally, "If she can't go back to France, I want her placed in a witness protection program. We've placed other killers in that program in return for information. What's so unusual about another one?"

"This one is more dangerous to the United States than all the rest together. That's what's unusual. She has to be . . . kept secluded, sir,"

"A prisoner?"

"Yes."

Joseph laughed. "You amaze me. You say you're worried about what might happen if her revelations became public. What in the world would happen if it became known that I allowed her to be kept a prisoner without a trial, without so much as a hearing? What's the matter with you people?"

Gallagher pressed on. "Sir, that's just it. No one must ever know about any of this. Our people will keep quiet, just as they've kept quiet over the years on other important matters. But, she's not one of us. She must be—"

Joseph jumped to his feet. "I won't hear any more of this," he said angrily.

Gallagher's eyes flashed. "Sir, you must listen. You are the president of the United States. You have a *responsibility* to the people of this country! You cannot allow your personal feelings to interfere in matters of such importance."

"My personal feelings? How dare you!"

Gallagher's face reddened. "Sir! I am an expert in these matters. I know what I'm talking about. You're a fine man, but you are, after all, a politician. You don't realize . . . you can't possibly realize the danger you're placing yourself and this country in. You simply must listen!"

Clark, fearing Gallagher was becoming hysterical, grabbed his arm. Gallagher ripped it away and continued to glare at Joseph. Joseph, shocked by such an outburst, slowly resumed his seat, then stared at the two men. "Are you both in agreement on this?"

"Yes, we are," they chorused.

"Let me get this straight. You're saying we lock this woman away for the rest of her life?"

It was Clark who answered. "Yes, sir. I can appreciate your feelings, but you must consider the damage to this country if this woman is ever allowed to talk freely. There are risks there, as we've already outlined. To allow her to go free is unacceptable. I'm sure you realize how utterly devastating her revelations would be. You cannot allow this country to be imperiled by one individual to that extent. It isn't right."

Joseph's lungs seemed empty of air. It was finally dawning on him what they were saying, what they were *really* saying. He looked down and noticed his right hand was trembling slightly. He wanted nothing more than to be left alone, but he had to know. With great effort, he said, "You're not really talking about incarceration, are you?"

No one answered. He repeated the question. Finally, Clark said, "There are times, Mr. President, when, as distasteful as it is, we are required to . . ."

Again, Joseph stood up. "Leave me now," he said, his voice filled with sadness. "You've presented your case. I'll think it over and let you know."

Two hours later, Joseph was seated in the same small room as before, staring into the dark eyes of the bizarre woman he now knew to be his daughter. This time, at his request, they were alone, except for a single Secret Service man who pressed himself against the wall in a futile effort to be unimposing.

Josephine Cousteau sat rigidly in the plastic chair, a cigarette in one hand, an almost bored expression on her face.

"I wanted to see you before this went much further," DiPaolo said, trying to explain his own unusual behavior, more to himself than to her.

She looked at him vacantly. "You've changed your mind about our agreement?"

"No," he said. "I just wanted to ask you a few questions."

"Such as?"

He ran a hand through his hair and said, "Your reasons for bringing all this out in the open. Was it strictly for survival, or was there another reason?"

Josephine laughed. "Ahhh, you are a romantic, my dear father. You think, despite that fact that I never knew you, there beats in my heart some affection for you? Well, I hesitate to disappoint you, but you mean nothing to me, other than a vehicle for my freedom.

"We made a deal, you and I. I agreed to tell you what I know in return for my freedom. I have kept my end of the bargain. Now you must keep yours."

"And if I don't?"

"Then you will not be an honorable man. I will have made a mistake. What will you do? Kill me?"

"Don't be ridiculous. Sending you back to France has become a problem since certain . . . steps . . . were taken during the investigation of your story. I'm proposing that you be placed in our witness protection program. Are you familiar with that?"

"Some. You hide people who have testified against criminals, usually the Mafia."

"Partly. It would mean you'd have to live in America under an assumed name. You could still write, and we'd guarantee your safety."

"Guarantee? That's a strong word."

"As best we can."

"Ahhh. That's more what I would expect."

He just stared at her. "Tell me a little about your life. The early part. As much as you can remember."

Josephine shook her head and stood up. "I see it in your eyes, this terrible guilt you feel. Well, I refuse to assuage it. If you want to know of my life, you have only to read the manuscript. It will tell you everything you want to know."

"I didn't—"

She cut him off. "I would like to go back to my cell now. I don't have much time."

"Time? What's the rush?"

"I know what's happening. You are going to have me killed. I can see it in your eyes. I want to be alone before you do."

He felt a chill run down his spine. "I'm not going to kill you, damn it! Put that idea out of your head!"

That small Mona Lisa smile came to her lips. "As you wish, my dear father."

Later, alone in the Oval Office, the crushing weight of "responsibility" pushing him down in his chair, Joseph considered the harsh words of Gallagher and the others. He was in agony. This time, there'd be no discussion with Sophie. This was his decision, and he knew it.

On one hand, there was the reality of extreme danger should this woman—his daughter, by God—be allowed to go free. He could see that now. Still, was it possible that such a secret could be kept? Perhaps. Since he'd become president, he'd been given information that had astonished him, details of other actions taken, some clearly illegal, for the sake of expedience, or, as they liked to euphemistically call it, responsibility. Secrets had been kept, some for over fifty years, secrets known to a very few, secrets that would revolt and disgust an American public not yet inured to deceit. What happened to a single individual was hardly important when weighed against the potential damage she could inflict.

The woman was a psychotic. Had to be. Who but a psychotic could do what she'd done? He wasn't responsible for her actions. In truth, though part of his being had created her, that was the limit of his involvement. She'd told him herself he meant nothing to her, that her reason for coming forward was simply the desperate act of a person bent on survival. Not a scintilla of affection, emotion, or attachment to him. She'd said it, not he. She'd set the limits, not he. She was cold, inhuman, almost an animal.

No, not an animal, a human being. His daughter. Sick, yes, but still a human being, a trained, experienced assassin hired to kill him. She hadn't, and he probably owed her his life. Could he now turn around and allow hers to be taken? What kind of humanity was that? What did that make him? A monster? Yes. Nothing less. He'd made a promise, and throughout his life, he'd prided himself on his ability to keep promises.

Still, as Gallagher and the others—no matter their intemperance—had said, there was danger to the country as a whole. A real danger. There were things that could never be satisfactorily explained. If Josephine, suddenly demented, decided to tell the world her story, it would, as Gallagher had stated, be a disaster.

To whom did he owe his allegiance?

He considered the problem for an hour, until the once-niggling headache had the makings of a migraine, threatening to bring him to his knees. It was a horror. They were right, and that was the terrible, cruel reality.

He made his decision.

Back in her cell, Josephine Cousteau lay on her bunk, staring at the ceiling. She wondered what her life would have been had Joseph DiPaolo and Denise Dijon met under different circumstances. What if there had been no war? What if he had known that Denise Dijon was pregnant? What if they had married? What if there had never been a Claude, or a diary, or an argument, or a killing?

She pushed the thoughts away. Stupid woman. For a time, she'd thought she'd won the gamble. Now, she knew she'd lost. The Bowers had had the right idea. She should have gone to South America, as they'd suggested. She might have made it. Instead, she'd told her father everything, and now he was going to have her killed. She knew it. She wondered what death would be like.

31

They came for her at two in the morning, two pleasant-faced, neatly dressed young men with short hair and gleaming white teeth.

"Where are you taking me?" she asked.

"To Nevada," they told her. "We've set you up in a small town with a new identity. You'll be protected around the clock. You can write, watch TV, do whatever you like, as long as you stay on the grounds. We'll provide whatever you need."

"So I'm to remain a prisoner?"

"Not at all. You're a guest, and only for a few weeks. Right now, things are a bit screwed up. Once we get them straightened out, a decision will be made about your future."

She didn't resist. Not when they took her by elevator to the subbasement and placed her in the back seat of a black car. Not when they drove her to

Andrews Air Force Base and placed her on a small jet military aircraft, and not when the plane took off and headed west.

She wasn't sure.

And when they landed in Nevada four hours later at a small dirt strip in the middle of nowhere, she wasn't surprised. Nor was she surprised when they put handcuffs on her before removing her from the airplane.

She remained quiet in the back seat of another car as it moved quickly through the predawn darkness, traveling a dirt road a million miles from civilization. But when it came to a stop, she knew.

They walked with her into the desert to where a hole had been dug, these same men who had taken her from Washington. And she turned to them and smiled. "You're making a mistake," she said softly.

"Can't be helped," one of them said. "Nothing personal."

"There's another copy of the manuscript," she told them. "If I'm not somewhere I should be in two days, it will be released. It will spell disaster for your president."

One of the men had a gun in his hand. "I don't think so, lady. We searched your place pretty good."

Her eyes widened. "Listen to me," she pleaded. "Tell him there is another copy of the manuscript. I swear it. If you—"

A muffled shot from a silenced gun stopped her in midsentence. She fell to the ground, the sand stinging her open eyes. Strangely, she felt no pain, but she knew she was dying. As a strange numbness overwhelmed her, she mumbled, "A man of dishonor. Why am I surprised?"

And in Paris, a tall, courtly man from Switzerland entered the offices of André Coutard, executive director of *Livres Hectar,* one of France's major publishers. Coutard extended his hand in welcome.

"Gunter, my good friend. How nice to see you again."

"And you, André."

"I'm delighted to receive your call. I was wondering when Denise would have something new for us. It's been some time."

Gunter Steicher was a Swiss lawyer who'd acted as author Denise Dijon's attorney and literary representative throughout her career. Always, when a new manuscript was completed, Gunter was the one to deliver it and discuss the terms of any agreement. Usually, such discussions were held over a period of days, with much give-and-take. Today, however, judging from the expression on Steicher's face, something was wrong. He looked pale and upset.

He placed a package wrapped in brown paper on André's desk. "This is Denise's last book," he said. "And I mean that quite literally. I'm not sure, but I think she's dead."

André's jaw dropped. "Dead? I don't understand."

"The answer to your questions will be found in the manuscript. Denise left it with me before she went to America. She also left me a sworn statement attesting to the veracity of everything she's written in this new work, which is not a novel, by the way. It's her personal memoir. In addition, I have material . . . documentation . . . that authenticates much of what she's written.

André fell back in his chair. "I don't understand," he said. "What are you talking about?"

Steicher tapped the package. "You'll understand when you read this. I spent yesterday with it. I must say, it's astonishing. I'd suggest you keep it to yourself until you're ready to publish."

André picked up the package and looked at it. "If she's dead, how do we—"

"The contracts?"

"Yes."

"She left instructions. The rights have been assigned to a woman here in Paris. A Marie Benoit. I've never met the woman, nor do I have her current address, but I'll find her. I just hope she's still alive. If not, I'll make other arrangements. I have Denise's power of attorney, should she be alive, and I'm the trustee of the estate, should the fact of her death be established."

André tore away the brown wrapping and examined the manuscript. "Six hundred pages," he said.

"Yes."

"You've read this. What does it say?"

Steicher stood up. "You'll have to read it, André. I can tell you it's shocking, the most shocking document I've ever read. I can also tell you there's danger in possessing such a manuscript. I cannot emphasize that too much. Be careful."

"I will."

"One more thing."

"Yes?"

"This will be Denise's most successful work. Of that, you can be sure."

HARRISON ARNSTON is the author of eight novels. He lives in Florida with his attorney wife, Theresa.

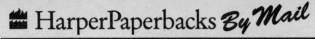

MORE THAN FRIENDS
Barbara Delinsky
The Maxwells and the Popes are two families whose lives are interwoven like the threads of a beautiful, yet ultimately delicate, tapestry. When their idyllic lives are unexpectedly shattered by one event, their faith in each other — and in themselves — is put to the supreme test.

> "Intriguing women's fiction." — *Publishers Weekly*

CITY OF GOLD
Len Deighton
Amid the turmoil of World War II, Rommel's forces in Egypt relentlessly advance across the Sahara aided by ready access to Allied intelligence. Sent to Cairo on special assignment, Captain Bert Cutler's mission is formidable: whatever the risk, whatever the cost, he must catch Rommel's spy.

> "Wonderful." — *Seattle Times/Post-Intelligencer*

DEATH PENALTY
William J. Coughlin
Former hot-shot attorney Charley Sloan gets a chance to resurrect his career with the case of a lifetime — an extortion scam that implicates his life-long mentor, a respected judge. Battling against inner demons and corrupt associates, Sloan's quest for the truth climaxes in one dramatic showdown of justice.

"Superb!"

— *The Detroit News*

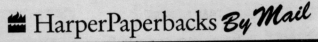

HarperPaperbacks *By Mail*

LEN DEIGHTON

Spy Sinker

British agent Bernard Samson, the hero of *Spy Hook* and *Spy Line*, returns for a final bow in this thrilling novel. Through terrible treachery, Samson is betrayed by the one person he least suspects—his lovely wife, Fiona.

Spy Story

Pat Armstrong is an expert at computer generated tactical war games. But when he returns to his old apartment to find that someone who looks just like him has taken over his identity, he is thrust into an international conspiracy that is all too real.

Catch a Falling Spy

On the parched sands of the Sahara desert, Andrei Bekuv, a leading Russian scientist, defects, setting off a shadow war between the KGB and the CIA. Yet, nothing is what it seems—least of all, Bekuv's defection.

BERNARD CORNWELL

Crackdown

Drug pirates stalk their victims in the treacherous waters of the Bahamas, then return to their fortress island of Murder Cay. Then comes skipper Nicholas Breakspear with the son and daughter of a U.S. Senator. What should have been a simple de-tox cruise soon lurches into a voyage of terror and death as Breakspear is lured into a horrifying plot of cocaine, cash, and killings.

Killer's Wake

Suspected of sailing off with a valuable family treasure, sea gypsy John Rossendale must return to England to face his accusing relatives. But in the fog-shrouded waters of the Channel Islands, Rossendale, alone and unarmed, is plunged into someone's violent game of cat-and-mouse where a lot more is at stake than family relations.

CAMPBELL ARMSTRONG

Agents of Darkness

Suspended from the LAPD, Charlie Galloway decides his
life has no meaning. But when his Filipino housekeeper is
murdered, Charlie finds a new purpose in tracking the
killer. He never expects, though, to be drawn into a
conspiracy that reaches from the Filipino jungles to the
White House.

Mazurka

For Frank Pagan of Scotland Yard, it begins with the
murder of a Russian at crowded Waverly Station, Edinburgh. From that moment
on, Pagan's life becomes an ever-darkening nightmare as he finds himself
trapped in a complex web of intrigue, treachery, and murder.

Mambo

Super-terrorist Gunther Ruhr has been captured. Scotland Yard's Frank Pagan
must escort him to a maximum security prison, but with blinding swiftness and
brutality, Ruhr escapes. Once again, Pagan must stalk Ruhr, this time into an
earth-shattering secret conspiracy.

Brainfire

American John Rayner is a man on fire with grief and anger over the death of his
powerful brother. Some
say it was suicide, but
Rayner suspects
something more
sinister. His suspicions
prove correct as he
becomes trapped in a
Soviet-made maze of
betrayal and terror.

Asterisk Destiny

Asterisk is America's
most fragile and chilling
secret. It waits some-
where in the Arizona
desert to pave the way
to world domination...or
damnation. Two men,
White House aide John
Thorne and CIA agent
Ted Hollander, race
to crack the wall of
silence surrounding
Asterisk and tell
the world of their
terrifying discovery.